CIRCUMVENTION

CIRCUMVENTION

Dwayne Morrow Mystery #2

Darin Miller

ISBN: 978-1-7368666-3-4 (Paperback)

Library of Congress Control Number: 2021921908

Any references to historical events, real people, or real places are used fictitiously. Names, characters, and places are products of the author's imagination.

Front cover photography by Nicki Miller.
Front cover deceased foot provided by R.M. Scarberry.

Printed by Kindle Direct Publishing, in the United States of America.

First printing edition 2021.

www.darin-miller.com

This one is dedicated to Traci and Nicki.
You are my everything.

Table of Contents

CHAPTER ONE

A green-yellow wad of phlegm splattered across the windshield, completely disrupting my concentration. I involuntarily jumped and nearly sent my 35mm camera (complete with long-range lens) flying out the open window of my red Optima.

"*Hey!*" I yelled, turning on my windshield wipers and giving the glass a healthy dose of washer fluid.

"I wash window," said a toothless, stubble-faced vagrant who persisted in trying to shine the glass with what appeared to be soiled underpants.

"No," I insisted, shaking my head and waving him away. He promptly cursed my existence and kicked the side of my car before weaving through stopped traffic at the intersection to approach a fresh victim.

The wiper fluid had mixed uneasily with the phlegm, and now my entire windshield looked as if it had been coated with a film of mucus. I expected flies to descend next, a swarm of biblical proportions.

I checked my camera to make sure I hadn't damaged it in my awkward fumble to keep it in the car with me. It seemed fine. As I raised its viewfinder to my eye, I realized Alan Carter had disappeared from sight during my momentary distraction.

Dammit!

My name is Richard Dwayne Morrow, but everyone calls me Dwayne. I am a thirty-four-year-old freelance systems analyst and private detective-in-training. I am a little over six feet, average build with dark hair and blue eyes. At my day job, I set up new computer systems and resolve configuration issues for various small businesses in the area. When I say 'area,' I would be referring to Columbus, Ohio, although I actually reside

1

near one of its suburbs, Grove City. My expertise was gleaned through rigorous self-study, and while I cannot command as high a price as a tech who has the paperwork to back up his know-how, my reputation has begun to spread via word of mouth. I stay busy enough to live comfortably. Within the last year, I had been bitten by the PI bug, involuntarily drawn into the murder investigation of my high school best friend, Ryan McGregor. Afterward, I had been unable to simply return to my mundane existence. There is something about the very real threat of danger that appeals to me on a perverse level. My parents have decided I've lost my mind, but they worry far too much. From what I can ascertain from practicing PIs, most assignments are hazard-free and somewhat tedious.

Take my current assignment: It was horrifically hot for March, and I had been stewing in my own juices for hours behind the wheel of my car, parked curbside in downtown Columbus. I was trailing one Alan Carter on behalf of one Geneva Carter, his wife of twenty-plus years. I had witnessed every menial task which comprised his morning, and it was a repeat of the last two mornings. He ate breakfast at Destination Donuts on Spruce followed by a couple of hours at the Columbus Metropolitan Library's main branch on South Grant, where he poured over back issues of *Field & Stream*, occasionally intermingled with chosen selections from Sir Arthur Conan Doyle's bibliography. Alan Carter was retired, wealthier than I doubt I'll ever be, and basically just killing time. This particular morning, his routine had varied only in that he had checked the books out and then driven to Franklin Park Conservatory where he had spent the last several hours reading while basking in the sun on a park bench. In the time it had taken me to shuttle my window washer away, Alan had abandoned the bench and was nowhere in sight. It didn't really matter. By this point, I thought Geneva was being needlessly concerned, and I was merely wasting my time. I maneuvered through the downtown traffic until I was able to merge with I-70 west. I was going home.

2

The whole thing had come about innocently enough; I don't take paying customers because I'm not yet a licensed detective. I was in the middle of a painstaking project for Thomas Baldwin, a crotchety old man who hired me on the referral of one of my long-standing clients, Marti Timberlake. If she had warned me about the man's temperament, I probably would have refused the assignment. He was loud, vulgar, cheap, and his expectations for a one-man team were far too high. I had never been fired from an assignment nor had I abandoned one of my own free will, but I teetered on the line every day I spent at Dial-Tech Labs. I was hoping to regain my mental stability during the week-long leave which had been imposed upon me by a major waterline break on the third floor. It had rendered several workspaces unusable, and repairing that damage took precedence over the individual hardware upgrades I was performing on the many workstations in the lab.

I had only been on the job for about two weeks when Geneva Carter had approached me. She was a sturdy woman in her late fifties with a kind, grandmotherly face and short, salt-and-pepper hair. She had read the human-interest article *The Columbus Dispatch* had run on me some months back detailing my hometown adventure in which I had helped to discover my best friend's killer. When she had heard my name around the building in connection with their system upgrade, she eventually worked up the nerve to approach me with a proposition.

"I believe my husband is cheating on me," she said simply over lunch one day. "I would like you to find out for sure. Of course, I'll pay you for your time." I have to give the woman credit; I didn't see it coming. We had been eating lunch together in Dial-Tech's cafeteria for the past several days—always small talk, nothing important. Her sense of humor was at times surprisingly bawdy, and I'm always a sucker for that. When she finally stated her intended purpose, I sat across from her with my mouth hanging open, partially chewed sandwich threatening to spill out.

I swallowed and shook my head. "I can't take your money. I'm not licensed. Why don't you hire a real PI? I'm sure the Yellow Pages are loaded with them."

The disappointment on her face was evident. "It is," she said. "But I wouldn't know a good one from a bad one."

"What makes you think I'd be any good?"

"I read the article in *The Dispatch*. More importantly, I've worked with you for several weeks now. I can see that you are conscientious, honest and hard-working. I make most of my decisions in life based on my gut instinct. It tells me you're the right man for the job. Besides, going to a complete stranger and spilling out my sordid suppositions about my personal life—I just don't know if I could bring myself to do it."

I sat back in the hard plastic chair and sighed. The only thing that kept me from snapping the case up was my lack of licensure. I had been itching for something more engrossing than wiring new components into CPU cases.

"I'll tell you what," I said, after mulling it over. "I'll do it for you, but only with the understanding that I'm not a professional. I don't expect to be compensated."

"You can't just do it for nothing!" protested Geneva.

"It's not for nothing," I replied. "I'm considering it an educational assignment. And you can cover my gasoline," I added. I'd been slowly forming a plan to legitimize my sleuthing credentials, and there was nothing like the thrill of field work, or so I thought.

And so, I had collected what little information Geneva had about her husband's daily activities and had begun my surveillance. The water break at Dial-Tech provided a much-needed reprieve from the tedium of being there, but now I was forced to admit I had only traded one boring activity for another. Alan Carter was about as exciting as a drawer full of socks. It was difficult to picture him as a Casanova; he was a few years older than his wife, had a belly that nearly tickled his kneecaps and the disgusting habit of sniffling instead of blowing when his nose was full. He kept his wispy gray hair (or what remained of it) combed over the top of his head from an ill-positioned part just above his right ear. At least it wasn't a toupee.

It was obvious even from my limited exposure to the Carters that the biggest enemy to their relationship was lack of communication. It had been so long since the two of them had talked—really *talked*—they had forgotten how. The couple had two adult children, a son and daughter, both of whom now lived out-of-state. After the child-rearing years, the Carters had been returned to each other's company, realizing belatedly they had each changed dramatically in the time since they had shared the house with each other exclusively. Geneva's imagination had now filled in blanks for her with paranoid suspicions that had grown slowly over the years. It was a shame to see what could become of a marriage when partners gradually forgot about each other's needs.

I had made up my mind I was going to cut the assignment short if something didn't happen soon. Of course, I would prepare what I hoped would be an official-looking report, detailing my activities and my findings. I didn't see any purpose in prolonging it. I wasn't having fun with the case anymore.

I laughed when I thought about that. I had begun referring to this as a case, which somehow made me feel a little more legitimate while I snapped countless photos of Alan doing nothing interesting whatsoever.

Traffic crawled through the center of town, where I-70, I-71, I-670 and State Route 315 come together in a snarling tangle of cars before branching off in their respective directions again. After several miles of stop-and-go, I finally managed to hit highway speed on I-70 and continued west toward the outer-belt on the far side of town.

It was past one on Thursday, and I had the rest of the afternoon free. My older brother, Matthew, and his girlfriend, Sheila, had invited me to dinner that evening with the promise of big news. I suspected they would be announcing their engagement which, after more than a year of living together, would thrill our mother to no end. Mom tries very valiantly to maintain a modern perspective, but deep inside, she's very old-fashioned.

My own love life is uncertain at best. I developed a rather strong attachment to my best friend's widow, Melanie, during my hometown stay in Lymont the previous fall. She's a beautiful, intelligent blonde with a figure most models would kill for. Her eleven-year-old daughter, Jasmine, has been my pen pal since I had begun coaching her in darts, an activity she enjoyed with her father before his untimely demise. Melanie and I both felt things were heating up a little too quickly, so when I returned to Columbus, she stayed behind, determined to get her life in order. In the time since, she had enrolled in college in the neighboring city of Portsmouth and was working toward a degree in English. We have maintained contact, seeing each other a couple times each month as well as spending most of the Christmas holiday together. I have to admit, the busier her schedule gets, the more jealous I become. It seems as though she has less and less time to offer, and I don't know if it's because of school or if her feelings toward me have changed. I'm chicken-shit to find out. I want to send her a note that says, "Do you like me? Circle one: Yes, No, Maybe." Pathetic.

Twenty minutes later, I was pulling into the driveway of my white colonial farmhouse tucked away in a relatively unpopulated area just outside of Grove City. I am a big fan of solitude, enjoying quiet evenings on the wide covered porch which runs the entire length of the front of the house. Occasionally, I've been known to inadvertently sleep through the night on the swing.

I emptied my mailbox (junk and bills) and let myself into the house. The phone was ringing, and I almost stepped on my longtime feline companion, Dexter, in my quest to retrieve the receiver. He growled his disapproval and darted down the hallway.

"Hello?"

"Dwayne? Hey, it's Melanie."

I smiled. I hadn't spoken to her in a couple of weeks because of all the time I was spending at Dial-Tech. "Hi. I just walked in the door."

"I knew it would be a real crapshoot trying to catch you in, but I didn't want to disrupt your work by calling your cell phone, and I figured if you were out, I'd just leave a message on your answering machine. Guess what?"

"What?"

"I'm coming to Columbus," she said. "Maybe we'll actually get a chance to see each other."

"That'd be nice," I said. "What brings you up?"

"It's sort of school related," said Melanie. "Besides, I've got some things I want to discuss with you."

I paused. That didn't sound good. "Is everything all right?"

"Oh, yes," she said. "Everything's wonderful! Look, I have to go pick up Jaz at school. She made the softball team."

"Yeah, she told me in her last email," I said.

"Practice let out about two minutes ago," she said. "Gotta fly. I'll see you Saturday."

The phone clicked in my ear, and she was gone. It was only Thursday. Shit. That meant I had to ponder the meaning behind her cryptic words for two days. For her to say that 'everything's wonderful!' could easily mean she's met someone new and needs to see me so she can rip my heart to shreds in person. Not that I suspect she would take any great joy there, but she would consider it cowardly to break things off in a note or a message on an answering machine. If there's one thing Melanie McGregor is not, it's cowardly. Really, it isn't as if we were actually even *together*. We both sensed strong feelings a while ago, but it had been months. We lived one hundred miles apart. Long distance relationships generally tank.

Realizing I could only handle so much dread at one time, I decided to call Geneva Carter and put an end to our pointless arrangement. In some ways, it seemed worse that Alan *wasn't* having an affair. Geneva would

7

interpret that to mean having no one at all was more appealing to her husband than being with her. I didn't know Geneva well, but I suspected how she would react. If Alan was having an affair, she would at least have someone to *fight*.

I entered Geneva's number.

"Hello?" Her voice was timid and unsure, as if it were the very first telephone call she had received in her entire life.

"Geneva? It's Dwayne," I said.

There was a long sigh at the other end, as if she were bracing herself for my next words. "So, what did you find?"

"Absolutely nothing. Alan's in a very big rut," I winced as the last of the words slipped through my mouth, realizing she would interpret 'rut' as meaning Alan's life with her.

"You've come to this conclusion after only three days?" asked Geneva in a tone which made me aware I was about to get dressed down.

"Three days of absolutely *nothing*, Geneva," I said. "He reads, he eats, he wanders around town. None of it is illegal, none of it is immoral. I actually thought you might find some relief in that."

Thick silence loomed between us. I could feel the woman's temper scorching the lines which separated us. I wished I had waited until we were face-to-face to do this. The telephone inspires a certain amount of bravado in most individuals, allowing them to say things they would never normally consider. Geneva Carter was utilizing it to its maximum potential.

"If you didn't want to help me out, that's all you needed to say in the first place," she finally said.

"That's not fair," I said, straining to keep my voice cool and professional. "If there's nothing to uncover, there's nothing to uncover. Your husband is in a routine, that's all. He—"

"I knew I should have hired a real detective," she muttered, verbally kicking me squarely in the crotch. "I suppose I get what I pay for."

"Hey, you were the one with a 'gut instinct' about me—" The phone went dead in my ear.

I couldn't believe the unmitigated nerve. I paced long strides until I had my own temper back in check. I had approached the case with a completely open mind. Hell, I *wanted* there to be some action! I *wanted* to catch Mr. Alan Carter up to his elbows in mischief! Field experience was only worthwhile if there was something to *experience*.

My rational mind eventually kicked in, reminding me Geneva Carter was very distraught with her current situation. She needed someone to blame for the things that were wrong in her marriage, and I was currently the bad guy. I figured she would settle down before I spoke to her next.

By the clock on my mantel, it was only three. Although I badly needed a haircut, I didn't have the proper motivation to crawl back to the car. Instead, I swept my dark bangs from my forehead and held them back with a Cincinnati Reds cap, grabbed the newspaper and a frosty glass of lemonade and settled on the swing on my porch. I wasn't due at my brother's until eight, and I hadn't read the paper in weeks. The headline from *The Columbus Dispatch* immediately caught my attention:

EVISCERATOR CLAIMS THIRD?

A family trip turned into an evening of horror as six-year-old Macy White discovered a mutilated corpse in the bathroom of a rest area just east of Columbus on I-70. The body was found Wednesday evening, shortly after 11:00PM. The victim's identity is being withheld until the family has been notified.

Early information suggests this may be the third slaying by the person dubbed by the media as the Eviscerator. In January, Gigi Garson, 43, of Scranton, PA, was found in a wooded area near Bennett's Diner, a truck stop along the northern outer-belt of Columbus. Her body had been mutilated in what police have deemed a ritualistic fashion. Her family stated that she was on a cross-country trip to see the Grand Canyon.

The second victim, Paul Nicholas, 32, of Albany, NY, was discovered in late February near Scioto Downs on Route 23, just south of Columbus. Nicholas was collecting geographical data of the United States for a book he was authoring. He was last seen alive at a Speedway on South High, where he reportedly purchased gasoline and cigarettes. Nicholas's body was found in a similar condition to that of the first victim. The police continue to follow up on leads from eyewitnesses but have issued no statements to date. STORY CONTINUED ON A-5.

I bristled as I read the article. Serial killers belong in movies, not real life. Certainly not in Columbus, Ohio. Both victims had disappeared while on road trips, and there was speculation the killer might have posed as a hitchhiker. It amazes me in this day and age, people are still naive enough to pick up strangers from the side of the road. Not that all these people have mutilation on their minds, but as with any other bad apple, the bunch has long since spoiled. As a child, I was taught to never accept candy or rides from strangers. After I received my driver's license at sixteen, I was forbidden to even *consider* picking up a hitchhiker. I thought *everyone* knew this.

Despite my awakening desire for adventure and excitement, even *I* knew capturing a serial killer was police work. It was a line I drew without hesitation. Someone who kills randomly and without obvious motivation has a mindset I'd just as soon not explore. The difference between someone who has been driven to do something horrific and someone who does something horrific because the little voices in his head tell him to—it makes my blood run cold just to think about it. The serial killer could be the man you just passed on the sidewalk or the woman who just loaded her trunk with groceries. He or she could be driving the car to which you just flipped the bird because they cut you off in traffic. The possibilities are endlessly plausible and equally frightening. Entire cities have been known to develop a sort of mass hysteria as known serial killers operated within their corporation limits. Innocent citizens inevitably ended up dead as a result of the itchy trigger fingers of ever-vigilant neighbors, protecting with force that which did not need protection in the first place.

I flipped to the funny pages to try and shake the paranoia I had managed to stoke, but I was finding it difficult to chuckle over Beetle Bailey. My nearest neighbor was well over the horizon, and stories like this one sometimes made quiet evenings at home almost unbearable. My house stands on several acres of flat land. A large expanse of it is maintained as my yard, although much of my acreage is comprised of tall grass bordering the property. A dilapidated barn stands in the far corner, a testament to the fact this was once, in fact, an actual tobacco farm. The barn had been used at harvest time to dry out the long, flat tobacco leaves suspended from the rafters. For my purposes, I store a riding lawn mower and a few gardening implements in there, things which would easily fit in a smaller, more modern outbuilding; I could house a small plane in the wasted space. Under a full moon and light fog, my property was transformed into the creepy estate in every horror movie ever made.

Of course, the modus operandi of this particular serial killer appeared to involve some type of random contact with his victims. None of them had been killed in their homes. I figured by the time the moon rose and the fog descended, I would have the heebie-jeebies fully in check.

Reflecting on that innocent hope seems ironic now. I had no way of knowing then the serial killer and I were already intertwined in a single, collective fate.

11

CHAPTER TWO

With nothing to do for five hours, I decided to run—well, I prefer to think of it as running. And really, it almost is. I made myself a promise last fall I was going to work off those soft and rubbery love handles I had developed from years of inadequate exercise, and I always do my best to keep promises. I had started by walking three miles a day, every day. While many might scoff—walking doesn't seem grueling enough to be actual exercise—I was amazed at the difference I saw after only a couple of months. Regardless of the weather, I plodded down my drive like a trooper, turning west on Orin Way, the hard dirt road which stretches in a straight line toward both horizons. I had marked the distance of one-and-a-half miles with my car odometer, and for eight weeks, I took this same path. While the initial results were encouraging, I began to get impatient and soon started working a sad sort of jogging into the routine. My endurance was still not high, and I felt foolish running, so I would drop back to a brisk walk any time I got winded or a car passed. I figured, what the hell? Every little bit helped.

On this particular afternoon, I noticed I was doing more jogging than usual. It was understandable; I was still agitated from the phone conversation with Geneva Carter. It irritated the hell out of me that she was blaming me for failing to dig up dirt on her husband. I mean, if the man was *that* inattentive, divorce him. Right?

I knew I should have hired a real detective.

I may have actually growled a little. Those nine words burned. The more I tried to push them out of my mind, the louder they replayed through my head. Why was it bothering me so much? I knew I was right; any more effort on my part would just be a waste of time. Right?

I was still running, and a thin sheen of perspiration had broken out over my skin. I realized a car had just passed, and I had continued jogging unimpeded, modesty out the window. Maybe it was a good sign. I hadn't heard any hysterical laughter floating back from the receding vehicle.

Why would Geneva suddenly decide her husband was having an affair? He had exhibited habits that were as regular as clockwork. A person doesn't build those kinds of routines overnight. What was it that had made Geneva suddenly think, 'By God, he's cheating on me!'? I honestly felt badly for her. Although I didn't know her well, she seemed like a pleasant enough woman, certainly entitled to her fair share of happiness at the end of the day. It was a pretty pathetic straw she was grasping at, trying to find a 'why' where there was none. Or maybe there were a thousand of them, each so small and insubstantial that by itself, it meant nothing. Collectively and over time, they coalesced into something more substantive, something which acted like a fire extinguisher on the flames of their passion. Granted, seeing them now, it was difficult and perhaps a little unsettling to picture them in the throes of white-hot passion.

I knew I should have hired a real detective.

Dammit, now my ears were burning. The embarrassment couldn't have been any worse had I actually done something wrong and been chastised in front of an entire arena of my closest friends and colleagues. The burning muscles of my legs were not punishment enough, so I increased my pace. My heart was thumping away, and my lungs were raggedly pulling at the humid air. My t-shirt was completely saturated and drops of perspiration were raining freely from my armpits. My hair was glued to my head, its dark color pulling heat from the sun and making me feel a little woozy. I

13

had reached the halfway point and cut a wide arc, reversing my direction without ever breaking my stride. *Whew*, it was hot.

All of this physical abuse, and for nothing. It wasn't helping me release that great internal pressure which was hammering away at me. What if Geneva was right? I had only been on the case for three days. How in the world could I make a proper evaluation of the situation in such a short time? Although I consider myself a private eye in training, I have to admit the training has consisted mainly of a steady diet of crime dramas and mystery novels. Now, let me assure you I have every intention of doing more than just *that*. I began by diligently improving my physical condition. I bought a gun and have gone to the firing range fairly frequently. For God's sake, I helped solve a murder! It's just that I had to earn a living in the meantime, and I can only accomplish so much in a single day.

What if I was wrong? What if I had bailed too soon? My ears were absolutely ablaze now, my temples throbbing, my teeth grinding together. If I were to ever become a full-fledged PI, the last thing I wanted was the reputation of a quitter.

I glanced at my wristwatch through sweat shrouded eyes. It was only four o'clock. I knew Alan Carter's routine like the back of my hand. At four-thirty, he would be in the brewery district at one of his three favorite pubs, tossing back a couple of cold ones before heading home to Muirfield. I could easily intercept him. I could call Geneva in the morning and at least establish some sort of mutually agreeable time frame in which I would continue to watch Alan until something happened—or something didn't. It seemed like a reasonable idea to me, provided Geneva was still speaking to me, and there was no guarantee of that.

I had already made up my mind by the time I reached my house. I wasn't due at my brother's for hours yet. After a quick shower and wardrobe change, I could see Alan Carter safely home and still make my own dinner plans.

Or so I thought.

*****

Traffic was surprisingly mild. Although rush hour was building, I was driving into town, unlike most of the other cars, whose occupants were heading home after a long day's work. I spent $10 to park in a pay-and-park and began searching for Alan Carter. He shouldn't be hard to find. I went to Drago's Tavern first, scanning the light crowd only to come up empty. I went back out on the sidewalk and searched the throngs of pedestrians, searching for the loping gait with which I had become so familiar in the last few days. I decided it would be next to impossible to spot him on the sidewalk; there were far too many people. As five o'clock approached, the crowd continued to thicken. I turned left and headed to Champions, another of Mr. Carter's favorite pubs.

The first day I had spent in surveillance, my ears and eyes had pricked up when Alan had gone to a succession of bars. I was thinking, 'Pay dirt!' while busily reloading film into my camera. I was disappointed to discover he was up to nothing more sordid than an afternoon cocktail, pulled up elbow-to-elbow with others at the bar. Belonging. He didn't have a young, big-breasted cocktail waitress who paid too much attention to him. He wasn't meeting anyone specific at all. He conversed with strangers easily and seemed to enjoy it enthusiastically. His forward manner seemed to put some people off, but there were plenty of takers, participating in an hour's worth of easy conversation which covered topics as diverse as alchemy and extraterrestrials to politics and conspiracy theories. He reminded me quite a bit of Cliff from the classic sitcom, *Cheers*, an opinion on every topic under the sun and the proper determination to inject it into a roomful of strangers.

The crowd was thicker, but I still had no luck. I glanced at my watch. It was five o'clock now. Soon, the bars would take on another layer of customers, making it even more difficult to spot Alan, although not impossible. He always gravitated toward the bar itself, never hiding at the gloomy tables set around the periphery. I turned and headed back into the street. The traffic had increased substantially, but clusters of pedestrians flowed forth at the crosswalks nonetheless, trusting the flashing neon indicator to guide them safely to the opposite curb. It usually did. It was the careless driver who wasn't paying attention to *his* neon indicator who sometimes caused trouble. I still prefer to look both ways before crossing the street, regardless of what the flashing neon says.

Murphy's was my next stop, and if he wasn't there, I would be forced to loop around and start again. He invariably ended up at one of the three establishments every night. Murphy's was a narrow little hallway sandwiched between two larger clubs. Its clientele was primarily older, the average customer probably in his or her fifties. The walls were paneled in rich oak below the chair rail, and the carpeting was a rose and wine jacquard print. The tops of the walls were painted deep burgundy, and carriage lights were interspersed with golden wall sconces. Somehow, the combination of deep, rich hues sucked the very light out of the air, as if the room were being seen through nonexistent sunglasses. I stood out like a sore thumb; I definitely was on the lower end of the demographic.

And there he was, leaning his ample frame against the counter while gesticulating wildly to a somewhat captive audience. A heavyset woman who leaned close laughed throatily, her eyes already a bit glazed from her afternoon libations. I settled into a booth near the entrance, taking advantage of the added darkness found there. I reached into my pocket for a cigarette and cursed. Although I had quit smoking some time ago, I couldn't seem to break the old habit of reaching for the damned things, especially in a bar. The two were somewhat synonymous. Instead, I ordered a club soda and tried to remain inconspicuous.

Alan Carter's floppy jowls danced merrily as he continued to chatter animatedly with his fellow patrons at the bar. As I watched him command his part of the room, I tried to picture him with Geneva and found it difficult to do. She was her own lively sort, and I couldn't see her fading into the woodwork every time Alan opened his mouth—which was quite often.

Abruptly, he turned and looked directly at me.

I froze, then looked away too quickly. I was mentally kicking myself for being so careless, and I refused to look back up. I knew he would still be looking at me. I was keeping a list of lessons learned as I went along, and this was the latest: It is not only impolite to stare, but people seem to have a sixth sense about it when they're the target.

I had no choice but to look at him when he stood beside my table and cleared his throat. I tried to look blank, but I didn't think it worked.

He smiled politely, indicating the chair across from me. "May I sit?" he asked.

I shrugged. "Sure. Is there something I can help you with?"

He chortled. "Now you've taken the words right out of my mouth."

I raised an eyebrow. "I don't follow."

Again, with the polite laugh. "Now, that's an amusing choice of words, don't you think?"

I shook my head vaguely and said nothing. My mouth was working against me, and I thought silence was the best option at this point.

He leaned in close across the table, and the smile fell from his face. "I don't know what you're doing," he hissed. "But you better stay the hell away from me."

And he was gone. For such a portly man, he bobbed and weaved through the crowd with amazing stealth, finding the door and then the sidewalk beyond. I was still sitting at the table, my mouth hanging open a bit, trying to absorb exactly what had gone wrong. This was very, very bad form on my part. How long had he known I had been following him? Had I been *that* obvious? Apparently so.

I threw down enough bills to cover my drink and followed Alan out into the street. I scanned the sidewalk in both directions, trying to pick him out of the thick crowd. I don't know why I continued following him. It seemed like the most illogical thing to do, in fact. I had clearly blown my cover and could hardly blame him for being irate. I wouldn't be too fond of someone who followed me wherever I went. But still, I had to prove to both myself and Geneva that I was no quitter; I would see this through until she felt it was appropriate to call it off. By my best guess, that should be about two minutes after she heard he'd spotted me. Sometimes, I really do suck at this.

I was about to give up when I saw him round the far northwest corner. As his eyes met mine, he actually began to run. This was no small feat for the overweight man, jostling pedestrians as he fled. This was ridiculous! Why in the world was he running away from me? Was I really worth risking a heart attack over? And yet, I followed, being a little less aggressive with my fellow citizens. Alan's size prevented him from gaining too much of a lead, but he was still several blocks ahead by the time I rounded the corner. He paused at the mouth of an alley, leaning against the building to rest. I could see his belly rise and fall with each labored breath. When he saw me, he ducked into the alley and disappeared.

I stopped and put my hands on my hips, grinning at how ridiculous this was. He had no idea who I was or why I was following him. It occurred to me I was probably scaring the hell out of him, chasing him down like a bloodhound. With all of the talk in the *Dispatch* about a serial killer, he was undoubtedly looking for a policeman right now.

Or did he know what I was doing and decide it was time to lose me? I only hesitated a moment, because I knew if I waited any longer than that, he would be gone. I cursed under my breath and entered the alleyway.

On the sidewalk, the waning sunlight was still strong in the western sky. The alley ran north and south, tall brick buildings on both sides obscuring the daylight and bathing the lane in deep shadows. This place only saw the light of day at high noon. Stepping into the alley was like leaving a crowded party; the thrum of civilization stayed at my periphery, but the stillness of the alley was so complete I could hear droplets falling from a waterspout onto the pavement below. My own footsteps were thunderous, and I dropped my pace, advancing slowly through. I appeared to be alone. The alley continued for a full city block, and Alan Carter couldn't have possibly bridged the distance that quickly, especially in the shape he was in.

I suddenly felt foolish. If the man had a heart attack and dropped dead from fright, I would be responsible. Everything I had seen in the past few days contradicted Geneva's fears. Why was I stubbornly refusing to let this go? Did I have no better judgment? Later, I would replay that moment in my mind, realizing how very different things might have unfolded had I turned around and walked back to my car, an urge so strong I still don't know why I didn't.

The alley was just as you might expect an alley to be. There were junk food wrappers ground into a layer of mucky sludge that trailed along the bases of the buildings. Scattered shards of broken glass were the aftermath of a beer party apparently held behind a dumpster. Cars continued to roll by each end of the alley, engines thrumming by in a Doppler effect.

I still saw no sign of Alan Carter. It was as if he had vanished into thin air. I examined the buildings on each side of the alley. These buildings housed businesses, and service doors blended into the brick facades at fairly regular intervals. Rusty dumpsters sat beside each door, some open and overflowing. Most of the businesses were bars and restaurants. I could imagine the size of the rats that lived off of the waste.

Surely, that was the answer. Alan must have found a door that wasn't locked and disappeared into one of the businesses. That did take some balls, though. Alan would have no way of knowing what type of reception he might receive on the other side of the door.

I scanned the alley again. It was possible he was hiding behind one of the dumpsters, squatted low to the ground. If he was, I would feel like a total shit. The thought of the man hunched down in fear, his heart drumming in his ears and panic seizing his throat—

"Mr. Carter?" I called. My voice reverberated off the surfaces of the buildings, bounding down the alley before disappearing into the street. I took a few more steps forward. "Mr. Carter? I'm a friend of your wife's, Mr. Carter. I'm feeling a little stupid here. I'm afraid I've scared you."

The silence which followed put goosebumps on my arms. I am a creature of instinct, and all of my instincts were telling me something was not right with what I was seeing. A slight breeze wafted through the alley, shuffling newspapers and sending some loose pages scuttling across the pitted pavement. What was I missing? I moved forward slowly and cautiously. After all, I was in a dark alley in downtown Columbus. There might be someone a lot more threatening than Alan Carter waiting for me somewhere along the passageway.

"Alan?"

As the wind again picked up and the newspapers resumed their lazy paths, I saw what it was that had bothered me. A clump of newspapers had collected behind one of the dumpsters near the end of the alley. Pages fluttered in the breeze, but they remained anchored in place, as if caught on something.

I continued forward, the sounds of my heartbeat and footsteps competing for dominance. When I had nearly reached the dumpster, I heard a loud clatter behind me and whirled around, ducking against the building to my left.

The back door of the building closest to the entrance of the alley stood open, and a short, fat man dressed in black Dickies and a grease-smeared apron stared at me while he smoked a cigarette and casually tossed garbage into his dumpster. I grinned inwardly, feeling completely idiotic. It wasn't even dark yet.

I turned back around and continued toward the clump of newspaper, quickening my pace. I stopped cold when I saw what held them in place.

It was a foot.

CHAPTER THREE

"So why were you in the alley?"

"I've already told three different officers," I groused. "Don't you all share notes?"

"Humor me." There wasn't a trace of humor in her voice. She had identified herself earlier as Special Agent Nina Crockett with the FBI. After making my gruesome discovery, it didn't surprise me in the least the FBI was on the scene so quickly.

"I was following someone through the alley—"

"Are you an investigator of some sort?" she asked, her steel blue eyes studying me from beneath thick eyebrows. She had jet-black hair pulled into a knot at the nape of her neck and wore a dark, pinstriped blazer and matching slacks. She was nearly my height, but much more powerfully built. I suspected steroids.

"Sort of," I hedged.

"What kind of answer is that?" she asked, her eyes boring holes through me.

"I mean yes, I was following someone and yes, I'm in the process of becoming a private investigator. A friend of mine had asked me to follow her husband—"

"Practicing without a license?"

"No! Not at all," I said. "I didn't accept any cash for the assignment, and I didn't misrepresent myself to her. She knew I was doing it as a sort of training exercise."

"Her name?"

I considered the proper etiquette involved. Was I allowed to mention a client's name or was that a violation of privilege? Or did that only apply to attorneys? And priests? Special Agent Crockett was waiting for my response rather impatiently, a vein pulsing along her right jaw line.

"Geneva Carter," I said.

She nodded and made a note of it. "So, this Carter woman asks you to tail her husband. Why?"

"What does all of this have to do with anything?" I asked.

"Just answer the question."

I was getting grumpy. I had been in the alleyway for hours, watching patrol cars arrive with wailing sirens and blue and red strobing bubble lights. The ambulance had followed shortly thereafter, but their services would be limited to strictly transport; the girl was far beyond resuscitation.

The foot I had seen was attached to the mutilated remains of a woman crumpled behind the dumpster. Actually, I'm assuming it was a woman based on the clothing and the toenail polish on the foot; there wasn't much else identifiable about the corpse. Multiple lacerations and stab wounds perforated the torso, and the face had been shredded in a series of horizontal and vertical slashes. I had lost more than I had eaten for lunch and was now seated far, far away from where the body still lay. I assume the body was being left in place until the FBI had a chance to comb the scene.

"You think this is the work of the Eviscerator, don't you?" I asked.

She looked at me coolly. "I'm not prepared to say that, no. Now, how about answering my question?"

I sighed. "Geneva Carter suspected her husband was having an affair."

"Was he?"

"Not that I could tell."

"So why was he slinking around in alleys?"

"Trying to lose me," I grudgingly admitted. "He had spotted me inside Murphy's."

"Nice work," she said, gallons of sarcasm loaded into those two little words. "What's the husband's name?"

"Alan," I said.

"How long was he out of your field of vision?" she asked. I wondered if her voice ever changed pitch.

"Oh, just a few minutes—certainly not enough time to do *that*," I said, indicating the other end of the alley where the corpse lay.

"And where did he go then?"

"You know, I wasn't really thinking too much about Alan Carter at that point," I said. "I wasn't thinking about much of anything at all except calling the cops. Now I've done my part—as a matter of fact, by my count, you're the fourth officer I've spoken to, so I've done my part four times. Is there anyone else who needs to hear the story straight from me or can I go, because I'd *really* like to go."

Special Agent Crockett narrowed her eyes and said nothing, and I could feel her summing me up.

"*Well?*" I said.

She sighed. "Let me know how to get in contact with you if we have any more questions. I'd also like an address and phone number for this Geneva Carter."

I gave her my address and phone number, just as I had done for the three other officers who had interrogated me. I told her she'd have to get Geneva's address from Dial-Tech, but I supplied her telephone number, again wondering if I were violating some sort of privilege.

"We would appreciate it if you don't leave town without giving us a call first," said Special Agent Crockett as she closed her notebook and tucked it into a pocket.

"Am I a *suspect?*" I was outraged. I felt as though I had been run through a wringer for doing what was my civic duty.

23

"Actually, not at this time," she said, and I was immediately somewhat relieved. I had been a prime suspect in the murder of my best friend, and it ain't a great feeling, let me tell you. Not only do you have to deal with the grief of losing one so close, you also have to deal with the unwavering scrutiny of the police. "We would also appreciate it if you would refrain from speaking with the media," she added.

"I can go?" I asked.

She tossed me a curt nod and went about her business. I wasted no time in getting the hell out of that alley. It might have been my imagination, but the smell of death seemed to hang in midair, making each breath bitter and nauseating. At the end of the alley, I was accosted by several aggressive reporters demanding my attention with their cameras flashing, but I was too intent on getting away to even distinguish the individual features of their faces. I could already see myself plastered across the front page of the next edition of the *Columbus Dispatch*, but it couldn't be helped.

The sidewalk was thick with curious gawkers, people on their way to the various bars and clubs in the area who had gotten distracted by all the pretty flashing lights in the alley. I merged with them and finally shook the last of the most aggressive reporters. I passed a small drugstore that was sandwiched between two bars and made a quick detour inside, buying a pack of cigarettes and a lighter. I promised myself I would smoke exactly one cigarette then toss the pack.

The lot in which I had parked was now packed, and it took me a minute to find my Optima. Once I had finally located it and let myself in, I started the engine and put the air conditioner on full blast, drawing noxious hit after hit from my cigarette. My hands were shaking, uncontrollably. I have read that people who work with dead bodies on a regular basis build a type of detachment from their natural revulsion, but I'm certainly not so acclimated. If there had been anything left in my stomach, I would have heaved right then. Slowly the nicotine calmed me, and my hands stopped twitching. I put the car in reverse and backed out of the parking spot.

Regardless of what Special Agent Crockett said, I knew this had to be the work of the Eviscerator. I found the scenario a little out of profile from his or her reported past work, but the thought of two mutilating killers walking the streets of Columbus was more than I was willing to accept. There was nothing that said the girl had even been killed in the alley. In fact, from what I had seen, I would guess that she had been dropped there after the fact. There was plenty of blood, but it was mostly on her body, very little on the ground around it.

My cell phone suddenly chirped from where it was sandwiched between the armrests. As I pulled out into traffic, I snapped it up and barked, "What?"

There was a long silence on the other end before the receiver was slammed down. I looked at the display to confirm the call had been disconnected. It had. I shrugged and tossed the phone into the passenger seat. I didn't want to talk to anyone anyway.

WNCI was playing Top 40 on the radio, and I stabbed at the power button to squelch the newest boy band's latest number one. I wasn't in the mood for empty-headed pop. I wasn't in the mood for any music at all.

Geneva Carter was going to have my balls for breakfast. Alan was bound to discover she had "hired" me to follow him. Whatever problems Geneva had with their relationship was going to be brought out into the open, whether she liked it or not. Maybe it was a good thing. Still, I sensed whatever happened as a result would be blamed squarely on me.

I merged onto I-70 west, gliding up to highway speed. The sun had gone down some time ago, and the oncoming headlights stabbed at my tired eyes. I had gotten a full-blown headache about an hour ago, exacerbating my roiling stomach. I just wanted to go home and sit in a dark room.

The phone rang again, and I cursed the person who invented the damn thing. What once seemed like such a marvelous invention had entirely lost its novelty with me. I'm not sure I want to be able to be reached at any given moment of the day or night. I'm not wild about using the damn thing while I'm driving either.

I snapped it open and said, "Hello?"

"Hey." It was my brother, Matt.

"Oh, shit," I said, looking at the digital display on the dashboard. It was nine-thirty. I was supposed to have been at my brother's for dinner at eight. "Oh, God, Matt. I'm sorry. I got tied up with something."

"It's okay," he said, but his tone of voice told me differently. "I was just wondering what happened to you."

"It's been a bad night," I said. "I'm sorry I didn't call. I didn't realize the time."

"We can do it some other time," he said.

"Dinner was shit anyhow." The comment was hurled from somewhere in the room behind Matt, Sheila's voice crystal clear through the digital network.

"Sheila's pissed," I said.

"Um, yeah," said Matt. "It'll pass."

I felt like shit. Sheila always went all-out whenever she planned a dinner for guests. I could bet she had spent hours in the kitchen, preparing something heavenly I couldn't even begin to pronounce. I wondered how long they had waited before they had finally eaten their dinners.

"You said there was something important you wanted to tell me tonight," I said.

"It'll keep," said Matt.

"No," I said. "Look, I can be there in twenty minutes—"

"It's late. We're just going to go on to bed."

"Tell him to fuck off." Sheila really *was* pissed.

I sighed. I wanted nothing more than to be back in my own house, locked in safely for the night, but sometimes familial obligations took precedence over personal comfort. "I'm on my way," I said. "Take all of the sharp knives out of the drawers before I get there, okay?"

Matt paused a second before answering. "You really might want to wait until tomorrow."

I tuned my car radio between stations and cranked the volume, filling the cabin with static. "You're breaking up," I said. "I can't hear you. I'll see you in a few." I disconnected the call before he had a chance to protest and turned the phone off. It may have been selfish motivation on my part, but I don't sleep well when a bad situation is left unresolved.

As I merged onto I-270 north, I tried to assemble a palatable excuse. I was reluctant to tell Matt and Sheila what had transpired over the course of the evening. Matt thought I had a mental defect which was forcing me to romanticize the notion of detective work. I make decent money doing freelance consulting, but at times, the job is as bland as a carton of whole milk. Another curious phenomenon of the profession is the dismantling of social skills. I'm sure it depends on the individual, but when I was teaching myself network protocols and hardware configurations, I found myself spending many lonely nights hovering over a keyboard or a dismantled CPU. I have a few friends in the Columbus area, but not really that many. The piece of property that I purchased virtually guaranteed no neighborly neighbors. For the last eight years, my best friend had been my black cat, Dexter. Sad, huh? Sweet cat, though.

I had reached the Sawmill Road exit before realizing it and still had no idea what I was going to say. I suddenly felt very hungry, having lost my lunch to the pavement in the alley. Judging from Sheila's mood, it would probably be ill-advised to ask for a sandwich once I arrived, equally ill-advised to show up with a bag of take-out from McDonald's. I would just have to go hungry for the time being. I took the exit and turned left at the light, passing a Wendy's, Taco Bell and McDonald's while my stomach hurled gurgling insults at me.

Matt and Sheila lived in an apartment community off of Hard Road. A dozen or so brick-faced buildings contained six townhouses each, positioned like an inverted "C" around a blacktop lake of parking spaces.

Signs promising the prompt removal of your vehicle (at your own expense) deterred me from parking amongst the residents. Instead, I found a slot near the small clubhouse which was designated visitor parking and began the journey across the lot toward the building at the far left end. At least it wasn't raining.

The lot was fairly well lit, orange illumination spilling across the pavement at regular intervals. The night air had cooled considerably, but it was still unseasonably warm for March. The grass hadn't emerged from its winter state, looking like yellow straw under the evergreen shrubs which dotted the property.

A maroon Saturn suddenly glided to a stop at my side, startling me. I hadn't even heard it enter the parking lot. The driver was a man about my age with dark, curly hair and a smile from a magazine, pearly white teeth glinting in the afterglow of orthodontia. He rolled down the passenger window and leaned across the seat. "Hi," he said. "Are you Dwayne Morrow?"

I was too tired to hide my perplexity. "Yes," I said cautiously. "Do I know you?"

He shook his head and switched the ignition off. "Brady Garrett, *Columbus Dispatch*. Can I have a minute of your time?" He was out of the car before I could respond, moving around the hood and offering his hand earnestly. Involuntarily I reached out, and he pumped my arm up and down with vigor.

"I already subscribe, and I don't live here," I said.

He laughed robustly. It was the kind of insincere guffaw that businessmen toss each other in the boardroom before getting down to the nitty-gritty. "I don't work in subscriptions. I'm on the crime beat."

"Oh."

"I understand that you're the one who found the Eviscerator's latest victim," he said, his eyebrows raised expectantly. When I didn't respond, he added an earnest, "Right?"

28

I smiled wearily and shook my head. "I really can't talk about that."

"Oh, come on, Mr. Morrow. Don't you think it's in the public's best interest to stay apprised of any new developments?" He was all teeth.

"Maybe you should talk to Special Agent Crockett," I suggested.

His face lit up like a Christmas tree. "The FBI was called in already? The body must fit the same profile as the others."

"What an opportunity for you," I said, disgusted with his apparent elation. "How many more will he have to kill before you have enough bylines to get promoted out of this cow town?"

Again with the canned laugh. "It's a tragedy, of course. I didn't mean it *that* way."

"Sure," I said, turning to resume my path.

"Oh, Mr. Morrow? One more question—"

I pivoted and stared at him. "No, let me ask *you* a question. How did you know where to find me?"

He looked sheepish. "I followed you."

Well, duh. I had been doing the same thing to Alan Carter for days, and even *he* had noticed he was being tailed. Apparently, I had been so wrapped up in my own thoughts I hadn't noticed Garrett behind me on the highway. I turned and started to walk away.

He called out, "I'll be at the *Dispatch* for the next few hours, putting the finishing touches on my article for the morning edition. If you change your mind and would like to add some helpful details, I'll leave my card. It really *is* your civic duty, you know."

I snapped. I was in his face before he knew what was coming.

"Don't even *begin* to talk to me about civic duty. All you're interested in is advancing your career, and please spare me the bullshit. You're seeing dollar signs at the expense of some poor girl whose parents haven't even been notified that she's dead yet! I could go on and on about what a soulless asshole you are, but it would go right through your empty head, so just do me a favor and fuck off, all right?"

29

He had taken several defensive steps backward as I ranted, his arm still outstretched with a business card I wasn't about to take, and his pearly whites arranged in what I now felt was a satisfactory grimace. I was so pissed I could feel veins I didn't even know I had throbbing in my temples, and my hands were drawn into tight fists. Garrett cleared his throat and tucked the card back into his pocket as he tried to regain dignity and get into his car. I didn't move until he had started the engine, tossed me a 'Oh hell, I had to try' shrug, and pulled out of the parking lot.

I turned and continued toward Matt's building. I couldn't believe the gall of the guy. His motivation was nauseatingly transparent. I suspected if he had known the identity of the girl, he would have dearly loved to be the one to break it to her family so he could record their devastation for the morning edition as well.

I stepped up to Matt's door and pressed the buzzer.

"*I'm not talking to him!*" screamed Sheila from somewhere deep inside the apartment. I could hear Matt's voice modulating soothing noises in her direction, punctuated with unintelligible single-syllable retorts from Sheila. What in the hell was up with her? I mean, for heaven's sake, it was only dinner. Sure, I could appreciate her being upset, but she had now crossed into irrational. It wasn't at all like her. I wouldn't go so far as to say she's bubbly or even easily approachable, but our rapport had always been fine before.

I waited patiently, allowing the conversation to continue on the other side of the door. It sounded as if Sheila was losing momentum. Maybe she had gone to the basement. I didn't know. In any case, I soon heard my brother's footsteps approaching.

As the deadbolt clicked and released, something occurred to me, and I turned to stare out into the parking lot.

"Dwayne?" Matt stepped out onto the small concrete stoop and squinted over my shoulder. "What are you looking for?"

I shook my head absently and turned around. "Nothing. Never mind."

30

Matt looked at me questioningly, but stepped back into the apartment, holding the screen door open for me. I was so deep in thought that I nearly walked right into it.

How had Brady Garrett known my name?

CHAPTER FOUR

The door of the apartment opened to a stairway leading up, and I could see Sheila standing at the top of the stairs, her arms folded across her chest. Even in relative darkness, she couldn't hide her angry eyes regarding me with contempt. She stayed just long enough for them to make contact, then turned and went into hers and my brother's bedroom, slamming the door behind her.

"Well, geez," I said. "I'd hate to be on her *bad* side."

Matt smiled weakly and said, "She's a little off her game lately."

We went into the living room and sat on the sofa. The apartment was pretty much a straight shot through. The living room was to the left of the staircase, beyond which lay a small dining area on the right, a half bath and kitchen further down on the left. As is traditional with rental properties, all of the walls were white, and the carpets were the color of dirt.

Matt is two-and-a-half years older than me. It's a little difficult to describe him. In many ways, we look alike. We are approximately the same height. Our hair color is close, although I think his is a little lighter. Physically, we were definitely not constructed from the same mold. Matt favors my father's side of the family; angular face, skinny legs, narrow hips and a tendency for a pot belly if not careful. I favor my mother's side; oval face, muscular legs and a tendency for 'pot belly of the ass' if not careful. Some say we look alike, some don't see it at all. Take your pick.

"I really *am* sorry," I said. "I got held up downtown with something."

"Downtown? I thought you were working in Dublin."

"I am, but I've got this week off while they repair some water damage," I said.

"You could have called."

I sighed. I figured, what the hell, it would be in tomorrow's papers anyway. "No, actually, I couldn't have. I was with the police."

"*What?*"

"You've read about the Eviscerator, right? I had the great misfortune to stumble across his latest handiwork."

The color drained from Matt's face. "You're still piddling around with the notion of becoming some great detective, aren't you?"

I grinned and shrugged my shoulders. "I wasn't specifically looking into it. As a matter of fact, I was doing routine surveillance—"

"Routine surveillance," Matt mimicked.

I shot him a look and continued, "—and I discovered the body in an alley down in the brewery district. I don't expect to have any more to do with the case."

"Which one?"

"Well, either one, I guess. Geneva Carter is a lady I've been working with at Dial-Tech. She thinks her husband is cheating on her and asked if I could confirm her suspicions. I'm embarrassed to admit her husband spotted me watching him and took off. I doubt she'll want any more of my services after he comes home with the story. As far as the other goes, I can't imagine the police could have any more questions than they've already asked. I was down there forever."

Matt shook his head. "You're a lunatic, you know that?"

"I want to be a PI," I said. "Do you tell Gina that she's a lunatic every time she flies out to some third-world country to document the horrible living conditions? I didn't think so." Our older sister Gina had been a freelance journalist for several years, traveling the globe, experiencing life from every possible cultural perspective. Depending upon where she was, she might find herself in the middle of warring countries or amidst citizens who didn't think too highly of Americans. She was strong and courageous, and no one ever questioned *her* better judgment.

Suddenly, the bedroom door slammed open upstairs, and Sheila came roaring down the stairs, her short brown curls dancing with each step. She stopped in front of me and put her hands on her hips, murdering me with her eyes. "Well? So, what's the big excuse *this* time?" she demanded.

I had had enough. "You know, Sheila, I don't deserve this shit. I've had a really bad evening. I *am* sorry that I missed dinner. I would've much rather been here than answering a bunch of questions about the dead body I found."

She looked as if I had struck her. Her expression shifted drastically into confusion. "What?" she asked, looking at Matt to see if she had heard me correctly. He nodded, and she promptly burst into tears. "Oh, God, Dwayne. I'm so sorry—"

I stepped over and awkwardly put an arm around her, and she folded into me like she was grieving for someone close to her. Her whole body shook as she sobbed, and I looked at Matt questioningly. They had told me that they wanted to tell me something tonight. Maybe it was that Sheila had gone clinically insane and was being put into a home? He simply shrugged and smiled, crossing to us and deftly transferring Sheila from my arms to his own.

"I think I'll leave you two alone," I said, edging toward the door. I really should've listened to Matt when he had suggested I wait to come over—at least long enough for Sheila's Prozac to kick in.

"No, no, no," said Sheila, pushing away from Matt and wiping her moist face along her arm. She had been wearing mascara which now spread outward to underline her eyes. She sniffled a nose full of snot into her throat and smiled. "I just wanted tonight to be perfect, and you're kind of like our test run, and—"

I waved my hands to slow her down. "Back up a little. Your test run? I don't get it."

Matt stepped up behind Sheila and put his arm around her waist. "How does 'Uncle Dwayne' sound to you?"

I have to say, for someone interested in becoming a detective, I was awfully slow to absorb that one. I stood vacantly for a second, waiting for the story to continue, then realized what had just been said. A big, dopey grin spread across my face, and I said, "*Really?*"

Sheila nodded, and we all hugged and babbled happy things at one another. "Are you okay with this?" asked Sheila.

"Okay with this? I think it's fantastic!" I said. Our mother would be ecstatic. She had started the subtle pressure for one of the three of us to produce grandchildren post haste. I was glad it wasn't me. Don't get me wrong, I love children, but despite my attachment to Melanie's daughter, I just haven't developed that particular yearning.

"Don't say anything to Mom or Dad," said Matt. "We're waiting for the right time to tell them."

"Of course not," I said. "That's your surprise. I wouldn't dream of spoiling it. Are you going to—"

"We don't really know if we want to know the sex of the baby yet," Matt interrupted, incorrectly anticipating my next question. I wondered if they were planning to tie the knot, a query our mother would almost certainly entertain.

"No," I said. "I just wondered when—"

"The baby's due in October," interrupted Matt. "Sheila's just nearing the two-month mark." His forced grin and the pleading look in his eyes told me that he knew full well what my question was and to drop it.

I decided to oblige him. "This is just great, you guys. I can't tell you how happy I am for you. But it's late, and I don't want to keep you from getting your rest, Sheila. Let me take you out to dinner next week to celebrate. Sound okay?"

"Sure," said Sheila. "But what was that about a body?"

I grimaced and shook my head. "Matt can tell you all about it if you insist. I'm pooped and would really rather not inflict the story on you right before bedtime. Hey Matt, you wanna walk me out to my car?"

Sheila's eyes became guarded. She was no dummy; she knew I was pulling Matt aside to talk beyond her range of hearing. "Call me about next week," she said. "*Don't forget.*" It was with this last barb that I realized her mood had shifted again, and I should beat a hasty retreat.

Matt and I went out into the parking lot and walked slowly toward the clubhouse where my car was parked. "So, are you guys getting married or what?" I asked.

"I want to," said Matt. "But right now, Sheila thinks I'm only asking because she's pregnant. She's really sensitive about the whole issue."

"She's really sensitive about a lot of things," I said.

"It's the hormones. Pregnancy is wreaking havoc with hers. If I survive the next seven months, it'll be a miracle."

"It already is a miracle," I said, smiling. "'Uncle Dwayne.' I really like the sound of that."

"It sounds like some fat goober from *Hee-Haw*," said Matt. "Listen, about the Eviscerator. From what I've read, you don't need to be getting all messed up in this."

"Matt, I told you I have no intention of getting involved. This one is strictly for the police. I can't help it if I happened to be the one to find the body."

"But I know you," said Matt. "If you let this get under your skin, you won't be able to let it go."

"Trust me," I said. "It's not getting under my skin. I'm not *that* much of a glutton for punishment."

Matt waved and headed back to his apartment. I started to unlock the door to my car when I noticed the small card tucked under the windshield wiper blades. Brady Garrett, Investigative Journalist - *The Columbus Dispatch*. There was a direct extension listed in the lower right-hand corner, and on the back, he had scrawled, "If you change your mind, call anytime." This was followed by a cell number.

The weasel had circled around to come back and leave this on my car. I involuntarily scanned the parking lot, half expecting him to pop up out of a bush and rush me with a micro-cassette recorder and an onslaught of questions. I wadded the card into a ball and tossed it to the curb before getting into my car and driving home.

*****

I slept erratically, waking up from dreams which starred the mutilated corpse of the evening. It seemed so ironic. My brother and his girlfriend were having their first child, and the possibilities were endless. The mutilated girl had once been someone's baby, full of hope and promise. Her life had been wrenched from her by a madman with a penchant for butchery. I wondered if it was quick or if she had known she was going to die. I wondered if she suffered. The images yanked me from sleep almost as soon as I went under. A dead body is quite a bit different in real life than in the movies.

I woke the next morning around ten and pulled on a pair of shorts and a muscle shirt. I decided to do my running early to get it over with. I knew that at some point I would have my ass chewed by Geneva Carter, and I figured I wouldn't feel like doing much of anything else after being informed of my extreme incompetence.

It remained unseasonably warm, the temperature already in the upper 70s. A cold front was supposed to move in later in the day, bringing the possibility of snow by the end of the weekend. Springtime in Ohio is volatile and unpredictable. Within another month, tornado season would be underway, targeting trailer parks all over the Midwest. Southern Ohio is somewhat protected from tornadoes by its naturally hilly geography. North of Chillicothe, Ohio flattens out like a pancake, affording tornadoes a veritable stage upon which to dance. I haven't had the firsthand pleasure, but every season, I await the inevitable.

I fed Dexter on the way out and started jogging toward the western horizon. Branches of trees which had been stripped bare by winter were beginning to show signs of premature buds. When the weather turned cold, these optimistic little growths would die off, returning the trees to their post-winter apocalyptic states.

By the time I had made the three-mile round trip, I was soaked with perspiration. I can thank my father for my overactive sweat glands. I was mentally patting myself on the back for running the entire distance instead of walking half of it when I noticed a car parked in my driveway. It was a shiny white Lexus, spotless and waxed to a blinding finish. I didn't know anyone who drove such a car, so my curiosity was instantly piqued. The license plate was from Ohio, but I wasn't close enough to determine the county. There were two people waiting in the front seat; judging from the hair, a man and a woman. I approached the car cautiously, wondering if this was another set of reporters.

I had nearly reached the rear bumper when the passenger door flew open and Melanie McGregor emerged, her honey-blond hair fastened in a ponytail at the nape of her neck. She wore form-fitting jeans and a pale blue sleeveless blouse. Her big, warm smile faltered as she took in my sweat-soaked appearance.

"Dwayne!" she said, the smile turning into one of amusement. "Been swimming?"

"Melanie," I said, ignoring her remark. I smiled nonetheless; she had already turned my insides to goo. "You're a day early. I thought you said you were coming up on Saturday."

"Did I?" she asked. "School has been so busy lately, I just don't know where my head's at half the time. I probably said Saturday because the first conference is tomorrow."

"Well, come in, come in," I said, crossing the lawn and climbing the steps of the porch. "I need to grab a shower. I just finished running."

"So, I see," she said, following behind me. I had nearly forgotten about the other occupant of the vehicle when she said, "I want you to meet Jordan McCleary. He's the professor of my English Lit class."

"Nice to meet you," Jordan said, offering a thousand-watt smile. He was around my height, but obviously spent a lot more time working out than I did. I swear his individual fingers had muscle tone. He wore beige dress slacks with crisp pleats and a matching jacket, doubtlessly of Italian origin, probably carrying a price tag equal to one of my mortgage payments. His sandy hair had been shaved close to his head around the sides and back, the top allowed to grow just long enough to suggest its natural wave. He offered a hand, then retracted it before I could muck him up with my plebian perspiration.

My smile was more grimace, and I nodded, "Sure."

I tried to inconspicuously retrieve my hand from where it was left dangling in the air. I noticed Jordan had one of his immaculately manicured hands positioned at the small of Melanie's back.

"Jordan has absolutely been an inspiration for me," gushed Melanie, giving him a quick squeeze. "He has helped me *so* much with his objectivity in my written work."

"That's great," I said, managing another smile. I was pissed. *I* could be an inspiration. *I* could provide objective feedback.

I unlocked the front door, and we went inside. I was mortified to see Dexter had lost his breakfast on the floor of the foyer, a fact not overlooked by Jordan. He wrinkled his nose distastefully and cut a wide path around the mess. "I'm gonna kill that cat," I said, running to the kitchen to retrieve a paper towel.

"You have an indoor *cat?*" he asked, his eyes wide.

"Um, yeah," I said, feeling as though I had created a social faux pas I was too ill-bred to realize. I stooped to wipe the mess off of the hardwood floor.

"I'm sorry, Melanie," he said, turning his back to me while he gathered both of her hands into his own. "I'm allergic to cats. I'll have to wait on the porch."

"Oh, Jordan," said Melanie, disappointed. "I'm sorry. I didn't realize. Well, look, we have to check into the hotel anyway, so if Dwayne doesn't mind, I'll just make quick use of his facilities, and we'll be off. You can go on out. I won't be but a minute."

Melanie dashed back into the hallway, and I walked Jordan back out to the porch where we stood in uncomfortable silence.

"Nice farm," he finally said, although his expression conveyed he was seeing and smelling *Green Acres*.

"Thanks," I said. "So, Melanie's your student?"

He nodded his head and smiled, and I wanted to poke out every one of his glistening white teeth. "She's a real ball of fire," he said. "I'm looking forward to having some time together outside of the academic arena."

Through gritted teeth, I said, "I thought Melanie said this was school-related."

Jordan shook his head. "It's a creative writing workshop, but it's not officially sanctioned by the University. It runs through next weekend. I figure that we'll have plenty of time in the evenings to spend together."

I could feel the heat rising in my cheeks. I'm not particularly good at hiding my feelings, and I wanted to beat this guy with a ball bat. I couldn't manage any more small talk, so I figured the next best thing would be to keep my mouth shut.

Melanie came through the front door and took her place beside Jordan. "I'll call you when we get settled into the hotel. Maybe we can get together for lunch."

"Sure," I said. "Sounds fun."

Melanie looked at me crookedly, as if she knew something was amiss but didn't quite know what it was. "Are you feeling okay?"

"Yeah, why?"

"You look like you're running a fever. Your cheeks are all splotchy."

I forced a laugh and said, "I always get this way after I run. I'll be fine after I cool down."

"You might want to try a shower," suggested Jordan, ever-so-helpfully. His crinkled nose suggested I might be odiferous, and I involuntarily wiped my chin against my right shoulder, taking a subtle whiff of my armpit in the process. *Whew!* I *did* need a shower.

"I'll try to call later this evening," said Melanie as she and Jordan headed back to the Lexus. My red Optima looked like a junk heap in front of it, with its unwashed exterior and the jagged gouges which had been carved into its paint the previous fall. I noted with disdain that the front tire on the driver's side had gone flat overnight, and the car was leaning sadly in that direction.

Melanie said, "I could hardly wait to see you. I want to sit down and talk about all that's happened in the last few months."

"I can hardly wait," I said. I waved as they got back into the car and pulled out of my drive. The car's engine was so quiet it was lost in the gravel crunching underneath the tires. My car needs a muffler and can be heard from two blocks away. I sat down on the porch and stewed for a minute. I didn't want to have lunch with Melanie. I didn't want to hear about all that had 'happened' to her in the past few months. I didn't want her to explain to me how Jordan McCleary had entered her life and captivated her heart. I sensed the guy was a materialistic phony, and Melanie could do much better—namely me. The thought of them sharing a hotel room—and bed—turned my stomach.

I stood and left a wet butt print on the porch. I caught sight of myself in the reflection of my storm door and realized how much I truly looked like hell. My hair was glued to my head in places and sticking up in others, and my temper had prompted hives across my cheeks and forehead. My shirt was stuck to my chest, and my shorts looked as though I had lost control of my bladder.

I went inside and immediately began peeling off my wet clothes. Dexter emerged from underneath the sofa and jumped up on its back, watching me with interest. "I have nothing to say to you, cat," I said, still bitter about the mess in the foyer. He chirped and began to purr at high volume. "Not gonna work," I added, although I scratched his black hindquarters as I passed.

I had nearly made it upstairs when the phone rang. I turned mid-step and trotted back to the first floor. I snatched up the receiver and said, "'Lo?"

"We've got to talk."

It was Geneva Carter, and she sounded pissed. "Oh, hey, Geneva," I said. "What's up?"

"Don't give me any of that innocent bullshit. My husband and I have spent the whole morning with the FBI," she said. "And thanks to you, Alan knows I hired you to follow him. He's packed a bag and gone."

"Gone? Where?" I asked, scratching my rear end.

"How the hell should *I* know? What did you do? Walk up and introduce yourself to him? I don't understand how any of this happened," she said.

"Last night was a mess," I said. "I don't know how he spotted me, but he did—"

"I don't even know why you were still following him! Didn't you tell me just yesterday afternoon that you were done?"

"Well, um, yes, but you seemed so upset with me I figured I should keep on until you and I had a chance to discuss the duration of the surveillance more completely."

Geneva sighed. "Well, I guess it's true what they say: You get what you pay for. Thanks a lot, Mr. Morrow. My marriage is probably over. Why don't you do me a favor and just stay the hell away from me and my husband? Are you competent enough to handle that one simple instruction?"

"Fine," I said. "I'm sorry you feel this way."

"One piece of advice," she said. "Don't quit your day job." Then she slammed the phone down in my ear.

As I lowered the receiver into place, someone pounded firmly on my screen door. Special Agent Nina Crockett was standing there with a copy of *The Dispatch* pressed to the glass. "EYEWITNESS CONFIRMS FOURTH VICTIM OF THE EVISCERATOR" screamed from the headline. Crockett looked pissed as hell but refused to look directly at me, and it was only then I realized I was standing there completely naked.

CHAPTER FIVE

After a speedy retreat to retrieve a bathrobe, I let Special Agent Crockett in. I was still a little embarrassed by my indiscretion, and Crockett's wandering eyes didn't ease the feeling.

"Sorry about that," I said. "I was headed to the shower."

"What's the meaning of this?" she asked, holding the paper in front of me. "I asked you not to talk to the press."

"I didn't," I protested. "I mean, not exactly."

I scanned the article by Brady Garrett and found he had manipulated our little exchange to put the proper spin on his material. It sounded as though I had readily provided him with all the confirmation he needed: "A key eyewitness confirmed the latest victim of the Eviscerator, found in an alley in Columbus's brewery district, was an unidentified female. Federal investigators were immediately called to the scene after striking similarities to the previous murders were noted."

"What do you mean by 'not exactly'?" asked Crockett. "You think it's okay just because he didn't use your name?"

"No!" I said. "He followed me out of that mess last night and cornered me in a parking lot. He was hammering away for information, but I told him to talk to you."

"Well then how did he get this information? He certainly didn't call me."

I reflected over the brief conversation I had with the reporter. "When I referred him to you, he knew you were FBI from your title. I may have slipped and mentioned that the body was female, but I'm not sure. I was really pissed off, you know?"

She sighed and set the paper down. "I thought you were training to become a private detective."

"Exactly what do you mean by that?" I was defensive. I was sick and tired of hearing about my shortcomings in this field.

"Discretion 101: Never, and I mean *never*, volunteer information. It'll come back on you every time." She perched on the arm of my sofa and massaged her temples. Although immaculately dressed, she looked tired. "*Especially* to a reporter. This goddamn Brady Garrett is whipping Columbus into a panic."

"Well, the public should certainly be *aware* of what's going on, don't you think?" I asked.

"To a certain degree, yes," she said. "But Garrett's making the whole investigation seem insufficient, despite the hefty manpower allocated by the Bureau. Pretty soon, we'll have every nut job with a handgun shooting at shadows. A lot of innocent people could get hurt." Her eyes kept flitting over my robe, and I realized with amusement I was pushing several of her buttons. She was very attractive, despite the matronly bun at the nape of her neck.

"I assure you," I said. "I didn't expect to see this in the paper. I understand your point. From now on, I won't say even one word to Brady Garrett. Hell, I won't even brake if I see him crossing the street."

She smiled, which instantly softened the hard edges of her countenance. "Thanks. The Director's been all over my ass for this."

"Why? It's not like you can control what people say."

"He thinks I should be able to. He feels that I failed to properly assert the importance of discretion."

"That's pretty unrealistic, isn't it?" I asked. "I mean, aren't most people money motivated? Highest tabloid bidder and all? I would think the FBI encounters this type of information leak all the time."

She shrugged. "He's new. Feels he has something to prove. He thinks he should be able to control everything and everyone. He's a real pain in the ass."

"So have you gotten any more leads?" I asked.

She looked at me dumbly, then said, "Discretion 101."

"Ah," I said and surprised myself by smiling. "If you don't tell me anything, there's nothing I can leak. Got it."

She smiled. "I also thought it might be appropriate to give you fair warning. The Carters weren't amused with the intrusion into their lives. They both probably have a few choice words for you."

"Thanks for the warning, but it's a little late," I said. "I spoke to Geneva just a little bit ago."

"I really think she might've tried to nail you for practicing without a license if she had caught onto the idea sooner."

"I *told* you I didn't accept any payment for my services," I said.

She waved her hands to stave off my protest. "I know, I know. And she confirmed that, but I think if she had the interview to do over, she would've said anything to cause you some trouble. Even if it wasn't a confidential interview, I couldn't repeat half of what she said."

"Geneva told me her husband packed up and moved out as soon as you guys left," I said.

Crockett raised a thick eyebrow. "Really? He didn't seem that upset when we were there. The wife—she's a different story."

We sat in uncomfortable silence for a moment longer. "I really need to get into the shower," I said. "Is there anything else?"

"I guess not," she said, giving me another once over. "I would appreciate it if you could stay out of the news."

"Will do," I said, walking her to the front door.

"Would you like to maybe catch a drink some time?"

"Sure," I said, startled by the abruptness of her question. It wasn't every day I was asked out. As businesslike as Crockett had been up until now, I certainly hadn't expected it from her.

"I'll give you a call," she said with a smile. She went back to her vehicle, a nondescript navy blue Chevy, and I finally made it into the shower.

Feeling much better afterward, I padded down to the kitchen in my bare feet—although fully clothed this time—and began fixing lunch. I was eating salads these days. I was determined to get my body in shape at least once before I died, and I was getting so much closer. My cat was a little disappointed in me because the table scraps weren't nearly as interesting. He needed to lose a few pounds, anyway.

Just as I was sitting down, the telephone rang. I sighed and put my fork down, shooting a warning glance to the cat who was hungrily eyeing the ham in my salad.

"Hello?"

"Hey, Dwayne. It's Mel."

"Hi." I sounded like a dejected puppy, and I kicked myself for being so whipped.

There was a brief pause, then Melanie said, "Are you all right?"

"Sure," I said. "Why shouldn't I be?"

"You're acting weird."

"Thanks."

"Anyway," she said. "We're staying at the Renaissance downtown."

"Swanky."

"Uh-huh. You got a pencil?"

I rolled my eyes and pretended. I could Google it. "Sure."

"614-555-5050. Room 511. Jordan obligated us to go to a pre-conference bash down in one of the banquet rooms tonight, and I'll be in conferences all afternoon tomorrow. You wanna do dinner tomorrow night?"

"Hmm," I said. I flipped through my imaginary appointment book. "I'm sorry, Melanie. I can't do it tomorrow. I already have plans."

"Oh," she said. She genuinely sounded disappointed. I suspected she wanted to shuttle me off as quickly as possible so she could be with McCleary with a clear conscience. "Maybe Sunday?"

"Sure," I said. "Give me a call."

There was a long pause. "What are you, Mr. 'Sure'?"

"What?"

"You've said 'sure' about a million times. What's going on?"

"Nothing," I said. "Nothing at all."

"I'll call you on Sunday," she said warily.

"Sure," I said.

"Dammit!"

"Sorry," I said. "Bye." I hung up the phone and sat back down at the table to stare at my salad. Dexter's patience paid off as I peeled the strips of ham from the lettuce and placed them on his food dish. I tossed the rest of the salad in the garbage. I had completely lost my appetite.

*****

With the whole night ahead of me, I decided to rent some new releases from Redbox. After the excitement of the previous evening, I wanted nothing more than to stay home. I trotted down the porch steps whistling off-key and stopped abruptly when I remembered I hadn't changed the flat tire on my car. I popped the trunk and began pulling tools out, wishing I had remembered this before getting through the shower. The humidity was really piling up, and I knew I'd be soaked by the time I finished.

The Optima came equipped with no spare tire of its own, just an emergency "inflation kit." I thought that was ridiculous, so I had purchased one of those stupid, undersized spares that looks more suitable for a bumper car than a full-size automobile. The scissor jack didn't inspire much confidence either, although its small base was allegedly capable of supporting the car's full weight. I loosened the lug nuts while the car was still on the ground, then positioned the jack into the small notch behind the front tire. I almost had the car all the way up when I heard a vehicle pull into my driveway behind me. I turned to look and saw the Channel 4 news team emblazoned in living color on the sides of the white Chevy van. Antennae protruded in multiple directions from the roof, making the van look like an oversized insect. The passenger door flew open before the van had completely come to a stop. I recognized Natasha Brickman as she emerged in a camel-colored suit jacket and skirt. She was one of the station's night-time anchors and had done a human interest piece on me last fall after I had helped to catch my best friend's murderer.

She swept an errant strand of auburn hair behind her right ear and called out, "Dwayne! Hi! Natasha Brickman, Channel 4. Remember me?" She offered her hand, and I suspiciously took a step backward.

"Yes, Natasha, I remember you. What's going on?" I asked. I could see someone pulling camera equipment from the back of the van.

"We wanted to get your comments on the serial killer. I understand you found the body of the latest victim," she said.

"Oh no, no, no, no," I said, shaking my head vehemently. "I've got nothing to say."

"Oh, come on, Dwayne," said Natasha, cocking her head to the side and winking. "Don't you think I did a nice story on you last year?"

"Well sure, but—"

"The public is going to want your take on what's happening," she said. Her cameraman, now fully armed with his equipment, sidled up beside her and positioned his camera on his shoulder. I could hear the hum of electronic storage, so I clammed up completely. I wasn't going to have Special Agent Crockett on my ass again.

"This is Natasha Brickman with Channel 4's Crimebusters," said Natasha into the microphone the cameraman handed her. "We're here with

Dwayne Morrow, who you may remember as a featured Crimebuster last fall—"

I was already walking away. I hurried up the steps to the porch while Natasha and her cameraman tried to keep up.

"Mr. Morrow," she appealed while I went inside the house and closed the door. "Just a quick word—"

I ignored her and went upstairs, trapped inside my own house.

*****

It was another two hours before I felt safe to go back out to finish changing the tire on my car. Upon examination, I discovered a sizable nail embedded in the rubber. I lowered the car to the ground, replaced the jack in its little home in the trunk and tossed the flat tire in on top of it. With transportation restored, I headed east on Orin Way.

It was nearly three o'clock, and I was ravenous. I had bypassed lunch earlier after Melanie's phone call had soured my stomach, but now it was vocalizing audibly. I figured I could kill two birds with one stone and have the tire fixed while I grabbed a bite to eat in the mall. I connected to I-270 from Georgesville Road, going north toward Tuttle Crossing. Discount Tire Mart had its own free-standing building at the front of the parking lot.

After dropping the car off, I walked across the lot and entered the mall through JCPenney. They were having a spectacular Winter clearance sale, but I couldn't be bothered at the moment. I was drawn to the food court, where I purchased a heaping pile of boneless almond chicken served over fried rice with an egg roll on the side. I spent the next twenty minutes in a state of mindless delirium, consuming every last bite in the Styrofoam container. If I had been by myself, I would've licked the container clean.

With that done, I strolled around the mall, basically killing time. The attendant at Discount Tire Mart had told me it would be about an hour before my car would be ready, and I didn't have anything else to do. I was surprised at the number of vacant storefronts. Apparently, the American public was beginning to sour on the centralized and completely overpriced mall concept. The tiled corridors were bustling with teenagers up to no good, elbowing their way through in loud groupings. They weren't here to spend money; the mall was merely a hangout. Some women clutched their purses tightly to their bosoms, their suspicious eyes alert for trouble as they dart from one store to the next before retreating to suburban safety, packages in tow. Some men challenge the reign of the teens, offering a subtle, "Get a haircut" or "Get a job" or "What are *you* looking at?" The rest of us fall somewhere in between, aware of both extremes yet choosing to keep our opinions to ourselves. It was safer that way; some of today's teenagers carry guns.

I was passing McNavitt's Jewelers when I saw a familiar face and groaned. Brady Garrett had spotted me simultaneously, and he pardoned himself from a svelte platinum blonde who was hovering over the glass showcase and was seemingly attached to his elbow. His great big smile was firmly in place when he stepped up to me and offered his hand. "Mr. Morrow!" he enthused. "Imagine running into you here."

I ignored his hand. "Oh, gee, what a surprise," I said dryly.

His smile faltered, but only momentarily. "Surely you don't think I was following you, do you? That's my fiancée, Nikki." He indicated the willowy blonde. "We're looking at engagement rings."

"Yeah, just think of the size of the one you can buy once your stories about the killer go national," I said.

He sighed. "Look—it's Dwayne, isn't it?—what is it you do for a living? Something with computers, right?"

"That's right."

"I assume you put forth your best effort when you're on a job, right?"

"Well, obviously, but what I do doesn't sensationalize anything, it—" I pressed my lips firmly together. This was exactly how he had gotten information out of me the last time. I wondered how it was he knew what

51

I did for a living. Had I mentioned it? It appeared as though Brady Garrett had done his homework on me, but why?

"That's all I'm doing, man," he continued. "I've wanted to be a newspaper journalist since I was old enough to hold a pencil. It ain't easy to break into the big time here in the Midwest. You have to be on top of the news when it happens. You have to be creative to maintain an edge."

"But at what cost, Brady? You just put every family who is missing a teenager through hell, wondering if that was their baby hacked to pieces in the alley. What difference can a few hours make?"

He laughed at my apparent naiveté. "It's the difference between *The Columbus Dispatch* and *The Washington Post.*"

"I get it. All ambition, no ethics. Nikki's a real lucky girl to catch you."

Brady shook his head and retreated back to the vacant blonde who was impatiently glaring from inside the jewelry store. Truthfully, I understood what he was trying to convey. Nonetheless, I wasn't about to be manipulated again in order to advance Brady's career. There was no such thing as off-the-record with him. It was an issue of trust, and I found him to be wholly untrustworthy.

I glanced at my watch. Almost an hour had passed since I had left my car at Discount Tire Mart, and I had run out of stores to wander through. Frankly, I'm not much of a browser. When I shop, I know what it is I'm after before I ever head to the store. Once inside, I get it and get the hell out. It drives my sister wild; she could spend whole weeks thumbing through racks of merchandise only to walk out of the store at the end of the spree with nothing at all. I say that qualifies as a colossal waste of time.

As I went back through JCPenney and neared the exit door, I saw a storm had broken while I was inside, and rain was falling in sheets, splashing up from the pavement. When I opened the door, I was greeted by cool air, signaling the end of the unseasonably warm temperature. I stood under the overhang, waiting for a break in the rain before heading across the parking lot, but none came. If anything, the intensity of the storm increased. Dark, ominous clouds rolled in from the western horizon, spitting frequent bolts of lightning punctuated by thunderclaps.

Impatience overrode common sense, and I sprinted out into the parking lot toward Discount Tire Mart. Thick thunderheads turned late afternoon into premature dark. The vapor lights in the parking lot had kicked on but hadn't swelled to full luminosity, and I darted like a shadow between headlights and water puddles. By the time I reached Discount Tire Mart, I was completely drenched and took a minute to shake off like a dog before entering.

A pimply-faced kid with shocking red hair and a name tag which read "Randy" manned the customer service counter, his angular features contorted by intense concentration as he studied his computer terminal. I dripped on his counter and waited for him to acknowledge my presence, but it wasn't until I cleared my throat that he finally looked up.

"Can I help you?" he asked with no enthusiasm whatsoever.

"Is my car ready?" I asked. "It's a red Optima. Dwayne Morrow."

The kid thumbed through a stack of work orders arranged alphabetically in a sorter by his computer monitor. He looked up uncertainly and gave me a vague smile, then started at the beginning of the file and worked his way to the end. "Dammit, no one knows how to do anything right around here. The paperwork isn't here. Hold on, let me check the computer," he said and began slowly pounding on the keyboard with his index fingers.

He stared at the screen for a minute and then looked up, smiling weakly. "Can you hold on just a minute?"

"Sure," I said.

He hurried out from behind the counter and disappeared into an office on the left. I paced the waiting area and watched the storm's fury intensify. A moment later the kid was back, following a smiling, pot-bellied man in suit pants and a tie. His meager supply of gray hair had been carefully arranged from behind his right ear across his balding pate. His smile was of the manufactured variety that can be found on anyone fielding customer complaints.

"Dwayne Morrow?" he asked.

I nodded.

"I'm Tom Alexander, service manager," he said, offering a large hand which I firmly shook.

"Is there a problem?" I asked.

"Apparently so," he said with a sheepish grin. "Your car was already paid for and picked up, not fifteen minutes ago."

CHAPTER SIX

Mall security arrived first, taking a description of my car before heading out into the parking lot to scour about. The Columbus PD arrived next, speaking first to me then to Tom Alexander. Brady Garrett arrived last, his inquisitive eyes shining like a kid's at Christmas.

"What's going on?" he asked, sidling up to me as if we were old friends. "I saw all the police and—"

"Calm yourself, Brady," I said. "It's not murder. Someone stole my car."

"Oh," he said, sounding disappointed. "What happened?"

"Somebody came in and said he was me. Paid for my repair and took my car," I said.

"The clerk didn't realize it wasn't you?"

"Obviously not," I said.

"Hmm," he said, reflecting. "I never gave it much thought, but I don't recall ever being ID'd when I've picked up my car from a service station. That's quite an interesting racket."

"Yeah, if you hurry, you can probably throw together an exposé on auto theft in Columbus for tomorrow morning's edition," I said.

"Would you give me a break?"

I wouldn't *give* him anything. If he wanted a break, he would have to earn it by doing a decent impersonation of a human being for a while. "Where's your girlfriend—Bunny, is it?" I asked.

"Nikki. She had to go back to work," he said. "She works at the cosmetic counter in Sephora."

"Ah."

"Don't they have video surveillance here or something?" asked Brady.

"Nope."

"Doesn't the clerk remember what the guy looked like?"

"The kid who rang him out was talking to his girlfriend on the phone at the time. He reeks of marijuana and barely remembers the transaction at all."

"Nice."

Tom Alexander had finished with the police officer and ambled over to where I stood. "I can't tell you how sorry I am about this, Mr. Morrow. Never in a million years would I have thought that someone would do something so brazen."

I nodded curtly. I wanted to get in his face and vent some steam, but I was too angry to be coherent. "In the future, you need to ask for a driver's license before releasing a vehicle," I said.

"I know, and I've already instructed all of our clerks," he said.

"What about the signature on the work order?" Brady asked.

I turned to face him. "What are you talking about?" Tom Alexander looked distinctly uncomfortable.

"You had to sign a release for them to work on your car, right?" asked Brady before turning to Alexander. "Doesn't a person have to sign when they pick the car up? Wouldn't your people notice that the signatures didn't match?"

Alexander shrugged his shoulders. "In a perfect world, yes, but my people dropped the ball. I don't know what else to tell you. There was no second signature on the form at all."

"Next time I need a new car, to hell with financing," said Brady. "I'll just pick one up here."

Alexander decided to ignore that remark and shifted toward me. "Is there anything else I can do for you, Mr. Morrow? Do you need a way home?"

"What I need is my damn car," I said. "But in lieu of that, yeah, you could call me a taxi."

"Don't bother," said Brady. "My car's right outside. C'mon. I'll give you a lift."

What a wonderful set of options. Wait an hour for a cab in the lobby of Discount Tire Mart staring at the idiots who lost my car or accept a ride from Columbus's very own Woodward or Bernstein. If it hadn't been raining, I would have walked.

The indecision must have been evident on my face, because Brady added, "Off the record, of course."

I sighed. "Fine."

*****

The rain continued to pound the earth, and the sun had completed its descent to the west. As we were leaving, a police officer barely old enough to grow peach fuzz handed me a copy of the police report to file with my insurance company. The irony was that I only had liability coverage on the Optima; my insurance company couldn't care less. The car was paid in full, and I figured I could eventually afford another car with the money I saved in premium. I wished I could re-think that.

Brady drove erratically on the interstate, warping down the wet tarmac and darting between cars as if we were fifteen minutes late for a five-minute interview. I clutched at the armrest and frequently used the imaginary brake pedal at my feet. The whole thing reminded me of the last time I rode with Melanie. She can't drive worth a damn either.

What in the hell did she see in Jordan McCleary? Prestige? McCleary was a college professor. Melanie came from less than auspicious beginnings. She had been raised in a staunchly religious home where virtually every one of life's pleasures was considered sinful. Her father had died when she was young, and her stepfather had repeatedly violated her and her sisters. I was amazed she had turned out as well as she had. She was pretty and clever and I never wanted to be with someone so much in my life.

I hated Jordan McCleary.

"You're awfully deep in thought," said Brady, glancing across at me.

"I suppose so."

"Must be rough finding a mutilated body like that."

I shot him a warning look, and he grinned.

"You get ruffled easily," he noted.

"Knock it off," I said.

"Fine. You don't want to talk about the serial killer, I do, so listen. You might be interested. You want to know why this thing is such a high-profile case?" he asked.

"I would guess because people are being butchered by a madman?"

"Nope. I mean, that's *part* of it, but that's not all. The third victim? She was a Fed."

"You're shitting me," I said. "Someone working the Eviscerator case?"

Brady shook his head. "I don't think so. I'm not certain. Name was Dorie Carpenter. According to the official release, she worked a clerical position at the local field office. I'm getting word she was undercover on something unrelated. Stumbled into this. Talk about bad timing."

"Getting the word? What word?"

He looked offended. "I've got sources on the street. I know how to push for information."

I regarded him with disdain. "So why haven't you printed any of this?"

"Because I can't fully substantiate it. I feel like I'm on the precipice of something really major in my career. I don't want to ruin my reputation before I even have one."

"Oh, I'm sure you've got a reputation," I said.

"You know, I don't get you. We're not that different, you and me. You're out to become a private detective, aren't you?"

"How do you know so damn much about me?" I asked. "I don't recall telling you my name when I saw you at my brother's apartment complex. I don't recall telling you what I do for a living. Yet you know I work on computers, you know I want to become a PI—what the hell is going on?"

Brady laughed. "For God's sake, settle down! It's no big mystery. You had a business card wedged in the back glass of your car when you parked at your brother's. I took a look around the car before I pulled up beside you. I knew you had seen something downtown. I saw the police and the Feds grilling you. I also knew you looked familiar. After I saw your name on the business card—which also advertised your computer consulting business, by the way—it all came together. I remembered seeing the story about you on *Crimebusters*. I don't only see my *own* work, you know. I was intrigued by the way you applied yourself to that murder down south. I believe you mentioned in that piece you were working toward becoming a private eye. And that's my entire point. I would think your instincts would be drawing you into this, just like mine are. I want to see this bastard caught as badly as anyone else."

"But you don't have a problem with making a name for yourself in the process," I said.

"You say that like it's a crime. Think about it. If you were to solve a case of this magnitude, your path to becoming a private eye would be smooth scootin'. You'd have business winding around the block."

"This is way beyond my means. I mean, if you want the truth, luck had more to do with my solving that murder than skill," I said.

"Hey, that's life," said Brady. "You'd be surprised at how many successful people got their break just from being in the right place at the right time."

I grimaced. "It turns my stomach to think of this as an opportunity."

"Well, I guess that's where you and I differ," he said.

We were nearing the Georgesville exit, and I instructed Brady to turn right off of it, although I suspected he already knew where I lived. Why not? He seemed to know everything else about me.

The rain had slackened to a drizzle, and the temperature was substantially cooler than it had been in the afternoon. Traffic was heavy exiting the freeway because of the movie theater in Georgesville Square—it was nearly show time. Once we made it through the traffic light, we continued west toward Norton Road.

"So, what are you going to do about your car?" Brady asked.

"I guess I'll rent one for a few days, wait and see if mine turns up," I said.

"Do you need a ride to pick one up?"

I looked at him suspiciously. "I don't get this. You're acting like we're best friends. I suspect there's more to it than that."

Brady sighed. "Fine. I'm working on a sort of proposal, something that might mutually benefit both of us."

"What kind of proposal?"

"I thought we might work together on catching this bastard," he said, and my laughter drowned out the tail end of his sentence.

"You have *got* to be kidding," I finally managed.

"Hear me out."

I shrugged and indicated for him to go on. I figured it would be good for another laugh—something I sorely needed on this miserable evening.

"After I saw you leave the alley last night, I knew you had found the next victim. It was as plain as the nose on your face. You might want to keep that in mind. If you're going to be a successful private detective, you're going to have to learn to mask your emotions better. I'll bet you're a terrible liar."

"That's what Melanie says," I grumbled.

"Who?"

"Never mind. Go on."

"So, I started thinking what a great piece it would be to have the horrors of the evening come from the person who discovered the body. I figured it would put a more personal spin on everything. People have become amazingly desensitized when it comes to violence. I suppose it's all those slasher films and graphic TV shows. I thought I might be able to approach the story from an angle where it would really hit home with the readers. It could have been their son/daughter/sister/mother/brother found in that alley, you know? So that's why I decided to follow you. I didn't have any idea who you were although, as I said earlier, you looked vaguely familiar.

"Once I saw the business card in your back glass, everything fell into place. I remembered the *Crimebuster* segment on you and was really patting myself on the back about then. I thought your recollection of what had happened would be more credible than some hysterical pedestrian who had just stumbled over a dead body."

"You must have been disappointed when I refused to talk."

"You gave me enough to meet my deadline," said Brady.

I shot him a disgusted look. It didn't take much to remind me of what a worm this guy truly was.

Brady continued. "So, all night long I tossed and turned, trying to figure out a new spin on the story. Some way of approaching it differently than any other reporter might."

"Turn left on Norton, then take the first right at Alkire," I said.

"Then I had an inspiration," he said, following my instruction as he spoke. "What if you and I were to collaborate on this piece? What if you were to investigate the murders while I documented your progress? It would be like an insider's guide to catching a serial killer. I'm thinking big numbers, big numbers."

"Well, you might want to get all those numbers out of your head, they're fucking with your brain. First of all, the likelihood of me voluntarily working with you for any length of time is slim-to-none. Secondly, what makes you think I can do a better job of tracking this whacko than the FBI? They have experience and resources I can't even begin to imagine. All I have to my credit is one solved case—and I already told you that was just dumb luck."

Brady shook his head. "It wasn't dumb luck. You may not have known exactly how to go about solving the crime, but you knew what to do with the information once you had it."

"I'm telling you, it was luck."

"And I'll tell you the main reason I want to do this: You don't have to follow the same set of rules the FBI does."

I laughed. "The FBI doesn't have to follow any rules they don't want to."

"They have to follow the one that blacks out information to the press."

"Ah," I said. Now we were getting somewhere. No agent in his right mind would agree to have Brady Garrett tag along during a covert operation. He was the definition of information leak. "So, what's your big plan, Brady? Are we going to set an elaborate trap to draw the killer out?"

"Exactly!" said Brady, snapping his fingers sharply. "We come up with a scenario and invite him in."

"Just pick up the phone and give him a ring?" I rolled my eyes and saw Orin Way go whipping by on the left. "Whoa! Whoa! That was my street back there. Turn around."

"I've got information on the first three killings that hasn't been released to the general public," said Brady.

"And just how did you manage that?" I asked.

"A good reporter's got sources," he reminded me. "I'm not sure that all of it checks out, but it makes for some interesting reading."

"Is the FBI aware of this 'information?'"

"I'm sure they are," said Brady, turning into a driveway on the right side of the road before backing his Saturn out and turning back in the direction from which we had come.

"You're really something else, you know?" I said. "You honestly think that we could set a better trap than the Feds?"

"In some ways, yes. Killers seem to have a sixth sense about sting operations. I think we might be able to slip underneath the radar."

"*What?* You mean we keep the police—turn right! Turn right!—we keep the police completely out of whatever it is that we're doing?" I realized that I was speaking as if I was interested. Not a good sign.

"I seriously doubt they would appreciate our assistance."

"So why aren't you tackling this by yourself? You strike me as the type who would want all the glory for himself," I said.

"The truth?" he asked, and I nodded. "This is the first murder case I've ever reported. I'm a little gun-shy trying to set a trap by myself."

"So, you thought of me?"

"Well, not immediately," he admitted. "But after I went back and read the piece *The Dispatch* did on you last fall, it dawned on me that we might make a good team."

I sighed and shook my head. "I don't know about this, Brady. I'm on contract to complete a computer upgrade at Dial-Tech in Dublin. My days are pretty full."

"But you *are* interested," he persisted.

"Hell yeah," I said. "But not for the same reasons you are. I want to see that bastard caught. If I wind up getting some PI business as part of the fallout, so be it, but that's not my driving motivation."

"Sure," said Brady. "A regular saint you are. Look, I don't have my files with me, but I could stop out sometime tomorrow if that's okay and show you what I've got. I'd like your take on it. There's some computer stuff involved, and it's all Greek to me. Maybe you could shed some light on it."

"I'm going to have to think about this," I said.

"What's there to think about? It's a great opportunity!"

I stared at him dumbfounded. How in the hell could he view four grisly murders as a 'great opportunity'? And how could I work with someone whom I so completely distrusted? I was sure Brady would offer his own mother to the serial killer if he thought it would net him a story. The way his eyes glistened with excitement while he prattled on was enough to make me sick. Earlier, I had decided catching a serial killer was police work. That was before I had stumbled across the fourth victim and seen the butchery of this madman firsthand. I wasn't deluding myself that I was more capable than the FBI. But as the old saying suggests, aren't two heads better than one? I had more or less been resting on my sleuthing laurels since last fall. Sure, I had convinced myself that target practice and exercise were an adequate first step toward my new career. In reality, I was still doing pretty much the same things I had always done. I had spent long hours at Dial-Tech Labs upgrading hardware and installing new software, and I had even tried to discourage Geneva Carter when she had come to me with the proposition of tailing her husband around town. Was it really because I was unlicensed? Or was it because I was chicken-shit? I had one of my wrists broken and a tooth knocked out last year, physical damage that has since healed (or remedied with a cap, in the one case), but what did that do to me psychologically? Life is full of witty wisdoms, like 'When you fall off the horse, you have to get right back on.' That's all well and good unless the horse has kicked you in the mouth and tried to kill you.

"I'm just not sure," I said.

"What are you waiting for? Another corpse?"

"That would make you damn near orgasmic, wouldn't it?"

"We're on the same side," said Brady.

"Speaking liberally, yes," I said. "But I don't trust you, Brady. You're seeing your name in big, bold print. You're talking about a plan that could potentially cause me to put my life in your hands and vice versa. How can I do that when I don't trust you?"

He looked offended. "You don't have to be an ass," he said. "I'm just trying to do my job."

"But your job sickens me!" I said. "Or at least your perception of it. I don't know. Let me think it over. Bring the files by tomorrow and let me see what you have."

"I don't want to share my information with you if you're going to turn me down. You could run to Channel 4 or *USA Today*—"

"I guess we're on the horns of a dilemma," I said. "I don't trust you, and you don't trust me. It has all the makings for a fine, fine partnership. My house is coming up on the right."

Brady sighed. "Okay. You're right. We've got to start somewhere. I'll be by tomorrow with my files."

"Good," I said. "And for what it's worth, even if I don't agree to go forward with this harebrained scheme, I'll keep my mouth shut about what you've got."

"Oh, you'll go through with it," Brady said with a smile. "I can tell that it appeals."

"Don't be so sure of yourself."

"Hey," said Brady, slowing to turn into my driveway. "It looks as though you have company."

I looked up, hoping I would see Melanie waiting for me on the porch, Jordan McCleary having dumped her at the banquet for some silicone-breasted society girl. No such luck. The porch was dark and empty. As the Saturn's headlights pierced the darkness, illuminating the sedan which was parked in the driveway, I swallowed hard and began fumbling with the latch for the seatbelt.

The car parked in the driveway was my Optima.

CHAPTER SEVEN

"Isn't that your car?" asked Brady, shifting his car into park.

I was already halfway out the door. "Yes."

I scanned the yard for any signs of life. There was nothing to see. Water droplets fell to the ground from the rain-soaked leaves overhead—nature's leaky faucet. The house stood dark and silent, save for the foyer light which I had left on. My house had been broken into and vandalized last year and in the time since, I had a state-of-the-art security system installed. I didn't hear the telltale sounds of the alarm's sonic scream, so I didn't think anyone had gone inside. Still, having gone through the personal violation of a housebreak once, I was automatically on guard.

I approached the Optima slowly from the rear. In the illumination of Brady's headlights, the passenger compartment appeared to be empty. The car looked none the worse for wear. I edged up to the back glass and peered inside. Empty. My keys were dangling from the ignition, but the doors were all locked. Thanking God for keyless entry, I went around to the driver's door and punched in my code. A satisfactory thunk sounded as the lock on the door disengaged. I opened it and slid in behind the wheel, examining the car's light beige interior for any clues as to who may have taken it from Discount Tire Mart. I didn't find anything out of the ordinary underneath the meager dome light.

Brady stepped up beside the open door. "So, what do you think? Practical joke? It's just the sort of thing we would have done to someone in college."

"I don't know anyone who would find this funny," I said. I reached for my cell phone and the police report the young officer had given me. I called in and asked that a message be relayed to let him know that my car had turned up.

"Is there any damage?" asked Brady.

"None that I can see."

"I guess you won't need a ride to the rental place tomorrow," said Brady. "You want me to stick around while you check the house?"

I shook my head. "Thanks, no. I've got it." I didn't need him prying through my personal belongings while I inspected my premises.

"What time do you want me to stop by tomorrow?"

"Huh?" I wasn't really listening to him. The darkened shrubbery which lined the wide porch was teeming with natural shadow; the perfect place for an intruder to hunker down and blend with the earth.

"With my files. What time?"

"Oh, sometime after noon would be fine," I said, retrieving my keys from the ignition and getting out of the car. "Thanks for the ride." I walked slowly toward the porch, all of my senses in a heightened state. My hearing seemed so sharp I could've probably heard my neighbor break wind a mile up the road.

As I ascended the steps to the porch, I could tell there was no one hiding behind the bushes. Dexter was on the windowsill in one of the panes which overlooked the front lawn, watching me disinterestedly from the other side of the glass. I figured it was a good sign. If someone had actually broken into the house, he would be hiding underneath my bed; he wasn't wild about strangers. When my house had been vandalized the previous fall, I had found him standing amongst broken glass on the porch. It had been an early indicator that something was amiss. He was an indoor cat and had no reason to be on the porch. Judging from his current wide-mouthed yawn, he wasn't disturbed by anything at the moment, so I stepped up to the door and inserted my key.

I turned and saw Brady standing by his car, shuffling on his feet as if unsure of what he should do next. "It's fine," I called. "I'll see you tomorrow."

He didn't look convinced, but he got behind the wheel of his car and backed out of the driveway, heading slowly back in the direction from which he had come.

I turned back to the door and twisted the key. As I opened the door, the high-pitched tone of the alarm sang its warning bleat, a reminder to deactivate the system before the fat lady *really* started to sing. I punched in my code on the control panel and the system gave one confirmatory beep before going silent. I locked the front door and began a thorough sweep of the premises, turning on every light as I passed through. There was no one lurking in the closets or underneath the beds. There were no madmen in the basement. There was no sign that anyone had entered the house at all.

I plopped down on the sofa where I puzzled over the strange event. Maybe Matt or Sheila had decided to do this as a surprise—but that was a stupid thought. First of all, neither of them knew I had a flat tire. Secondly, they wouldn't have left me stranded at the Tuttle Mall without a clue as to what had happened to my car. The next thought which crossed my mind almost made me nauseous.

Brady Garrett.

I had run into him inside the mall. He could've been following me again. His girlfriend, Nikki, conveniently returned to work between the time I saw them together and when I discovered my car was missing. He could have taken her over to Discount Tire Mart and paid for the car, collecting the keys and passing them off so she could bring my car here. He could be picking her up somewhere along Orin Way this very minute. But why? What could he possibly have to gain by pulling a stunt like this? It didn't make sense.

And that was precisely why I shouldn't even consider working with him. If I so obviously distrusted him, what kind of partnership could we form? Having someone watch your back was no good if you thought he may be the one who would ultimately stick it to you.

The light on my answering machine was blinking insistently. I pulled myself off of my sofa and crossed the room and pressed the playback button. The mechanized voice announced, "You have four new messages. First message, five p.m., Friday."

"Hey, Dwayne. It's Sheila. Matt and I are thinking about having your folks up next weekend to tell them the good news. I thought we could turn the whole thing into a cookout. Maybe you could bring Melanie if she's available. Call me."

Bring Melanie. Sure. Should I bring Jordan McCleary too?

"Second message, five-ten p.m., Friday."

Whoever called didn't leave a message but didn't hang up, either. I could hear the breath whistling in and out of whoever's nostrils. After about fifteen seconds, the line disconnected.

"Third message, five forty-eight p.m., Friday."

"Dwayne. Nina Crockett. Thought we might have a late dinner tonight if you feel like it. I should be around until nine or so. 614-555-4911. Bye."

I couldn't help but grin. Maybe the running was doing more for my body than I realized. And what the hell? Melanie was undoubtedly occupied by her professor. "Fourth message, five fifty p.m., Friday."

Ragged and rapid breathing sounded from the machine, as if the caller had run a very long way to make this call. After a few seconds, the breathing dissolved into anguished sobs, before drying up in one long, wet snort.

"You bastard. You've ruined everything. Twenty—[*nose blow*]—fucking nine *years!* I'll make you pay for what you've done. Do you hear me? Do you *HEAR ME?*"

The receiver was slammed down. The voice belonged to Geneva Carter. Dumbfounded, I stood and stared at the answering machine. I knew

Geneva was upset with me, but I had no idea she had gone completely psychotic. It was obvious from the tone of her voice she had been drinking. I half-expected her to come roaring through the adjacent cornfield in her two-ton Buick, giving her horn a quick toot before barreling through the wall of my kitchen.

Was it possible that Geneva Carter had brought my car home?

I disregarded the idea quickly. I didn't think she knew where I lived. From the sound of her message, she was three sheets to the wind at approximately the time the car had been taken. The clerk at Discount Tire Mart may not have remembered specifically who picked up my car, but I suspect that Geneva Carter, drunk and furious, couldn't have stood out more if her entire head was on fire. And why would she bother pulling such a relatively harmless prank?

Alan Carter?

I was sure he wasn't thrilled with me. I had no idea how much information he had pumped out of Geneva before packing up and heading out. Still, after observing him for a while, he didn't strike me as the particularly vengeful type. Of course, Geneva hadn't shown *her* true colors until recently either.

I shrugged it off and picked up the telephone, dialing the number Special Agent Crockett had left on the answering machine. She answered on the second ring.

"Crockett."

"That's how you answer your home phone?" I asked.

There was a momentary silence, then she said, "May I ask what this is in reference to?"

I laughed out loud. "This is Dwayne Morrow. I'm returning your call. You still hungry?"

"Oh! Sorry about that. I thought you were selling something. I hate telemarketers," she said. "Yeah, I'm still free. Where did you have in mind?"

"Have you ever been to the Winking Lizard?" I asked. "It's up north near Polaris." Along the northern outer belt, Polaris was one of the busiest shopping and dining areas in town. Perhaps I already subconsciously realized it, but there was little to no chance we would run into Melanie so far from downtown.

"I've never been," she said. "But I've heard good things about it. Can you give me a about an hour or so? I have some work to do before we go."

"Sure. Where are you staying?"

"I'm at the Renaissance, downtown. You know where that is?"

I groaned inwardly. Columbus isn't exactly small, so what were the odds that Nina would be staying in the same hotel as Melanie? According to my luck, the smart money would have been on it all along.

"I've got the address," I said.

"I'll meet you in the lobby at quarter past eight. Sound good?"

"I'll see you then." I hung up the receiver and headed up the stairs. I needed to take another shower if I was going out—I still had grime on my hands from changing my tire earlier. The mystery of the vanishing Optima was going to have to remain unsolved for the time being.

*****

I showered and dressed casually, checking myself in the mirror for any noticeable defects. Finding nothing too unsightly, I glanced at my bedside clock and saw only twenty minutes had passed, which left almost an hour before I had to leave. I decided to catch up on my own business.

I've worked for myself for the past eight years, and I don't think I could ever rejoin the nine-to-five squad. I've had a taste of freedom, and I won't go back. There's nothing like padding down the stairs in your stocking feet to put in a little time sorting bills, processing invoices—all the bullshit that keeps me fed, clothed and square with the IRS—pausing whenever I feel like it to take in a quick sitcom or grab a nap. Of course, fieldwork is another matter. It would be entirely unprofessional to show up whenever I felt like it in my stocking feet. Still, I know what I'm in for before I ever accept an assignment, and I can always refuse one that I feel isn't compatible with my own needs. It provides a tremendous amount of freedom. There's always someone who needs his computers tweaked.

I pulled my leather chair up to my desk and grabbed the stack of mail I had been ignoring for the past several days. There was a tremendous amount of junk. I am on the mailing lists of every computer wholesaler and retailer in the continental US as well as every training facility that has ever been Microsoft-certified. I subscribe to a fair number of industry publications. It's necessary in my field to stay abreast of emerging technology. It appeared one of every title had arrived, and I set them aside in a separate pile to take with me to the bathroom. Okay, that may have been a little more than you wanted to hear. However, men do our best reading while sitting on the toilet. The regular envelopes were a real grab bag. Credit-card pre-approvals, utility bills, a payment from one of my best clients, MGDC.

For a moment, any anticipation I felt for going out with Nina Crockett sank into the murky gray. I knew I was only doing it because Melanie was with that Jordan asshole. Maybe she would see me pick up Nina at the Renaissance. Maybe she would understand a little of what I was feeling. It wasn't fair to go out with Nina under false pretenses.

Shit! Listen to me. It wasn't like we had a date at the altar, for God's sake! It was dinner. She had already seen me naked and hadn't run screaming into the night. Hell, I might even get lucky.

I turned on my computer and returned to what was left of the mail to integrate it into my filing system while my computer booted up. Once it had loaded, I checked my email and was surprised to see I had thirty new messages. Five to ten I could imagine, but *thirty*? As the messages piled into my electronic mailbox, I could see a pattern quickly developing. In the subject line of over twenty of them, I was guaranteed the best cyber-sex I had ever experienced. None of them contained viruses—I have scanning software for that—but most of them triggered pop-up boxes with body parts flashing before my eyes at the speed of light.

I growled while I put a block on each sender and deleted all of the unsolicited pornography. Electronic junk mail is more difficult to kill than cockroaches and nearly as aggravating. I mean, what if Jasmine, Melanie's eleven-year-old, had been using my computer and seen this filth? Just two months ago, she was prowling the internet looking for games, and—

I stopped myself before I could think any more about it. I had a date to prepare for.

I shut down my computer and headed upstairs to give myself another cursory inspection in the mirror, looking for dried toothpaste at the corners of my mouth or renegade strands of hair which had defied my attempts at taming. I flicked on the television in my room before passing through into the attached bathroom to run a damp brush through my hair. It didn't look bad, but it didn't look good, either—it was somewhere on the right side of mediocre.

The television was on Channel 4, and I could hear Natasha Brickman introducing herself and *Crimebusters* to the television audience. I paused in my preparations to sit on the edge of the bed, curious at how successful I had been in dissuading her efforts earlier that afternoon.

"A serial killer is on the loose in the streets of our city," Natasha began earnestly, her practiced expression reflecting somber urgency. "A fourth victim was discovered in an alleyway last night in the brewery district, here between High and Third."

Stock footage loomed like déjà vu, showing the crime scene in progress. I saw myself toward the rear of the picture, in the process of being interrogated by Nina Crockett while police officers warded away passersby and cordoned off the area with bright yellow tape. The whole scene seemed unreal, as if it had been cinematically rendered for optimum effect.

"The victim has been identified as Tina Barlow, a twenty-two-year-old native of Worthington."

That was news to me. At last count, the identity of the victim was still being kept under wraps. Oh well, it was bound to break sooner or later. Natasha continued by recounting the details of the earlier homicides, using appropriate adjectives to convey the viciousness of the crimes while family photos of each victim flashed across the screen. The third victim's identity had been added to the gruesome roll call, although there was no mention of her affiliation with the FBI. As I watched their faces play across the screen, it occurred to me how diverse the victims were. The first, Gigi Garson, was a white, heavyset housewife whose children were all grown and gone. She was moderately well off, but we're not talking Rockefeller or anything. The second, Paul Nicholas, also white, was a well-respected geographer who had authored or co-authored a dozen books on various subjects. His opinions were considered preeminent in his field (possibly because of the sheer volume of research the man had amassed in his short career), and those who shared his interests considered his murder no less devastating than that of John Lennon. The third, Dorie Carpenter, was a thirty-something black woman with sharp, patrician features and deep set, intelligent eyes. What Natasha had to say about the fourth victim was difficult to hear.

"The crime against Tina Barlow was particularly heinous. Ms. Barlow was paralyzed from the waist down in an automobile accident when she was ten years old. She was working toward a major in social sciences at Otterbein, living in handicapped-accessible student housing off of Cleveland Avenue. Despite security lights and an on-duty doorman, the killer was able to gain entry to Ms. Barlow's apartment undetected. Imagine the horror of being trapped inside your own body, unable to fend off the advances of a knife-wielding madman—"

As if the mutilations themselves could be any worse. Yet the killer had targeted a victim who had no real chance of fighting back. What seemed sick before had impossibly twisted into something even more perverse. My attention was pulled back to the screen as I heard the sound of my own name.

"Now, federal agents are consulting with a local hero," Natasha said into her microphone. A horrible black-and-white picture of me sprang to the screen, taken at some point during the interviews I had given after Ryan McGregor's murder. My mouth was partially opened, and my eyebrows were knit together as if in complete befuddlement. I would have guessed my IQ in the single digits based on the image.

"Dwayne Morrow was observed in lengthy conversations with federal agents, although his role in the matter is not clear. Earlier attempts to elicit a statement from Mr. Morrow were unsuccessful."

I watched a replay of this afternoon's videotape in which Natasha chased me up the steps to my porch while I hurried away. At least Nina wouldn't be able to bust my balls for any indiscretion *this* time. They hadn't captured a single word from me. Still, I didn't suspect the Feds would be too thrilled with the aftertaste that Natasha's story left. It was as if they had exhausted all of their meager resources and had turned to me (expert that I am) out of desperation.

I sighed and flicked the TV off with the remote control. What was the point in avoiding the media? Natasha didn't get the story she wanted, so she made one up, painting my involvement in sweeping generalities based on nothing but assumptions. My parents should catch the rebroadcast at eleven o'clock, since Channel 4 out of Columbus was the only NBC affiliate broadcasting in Lymont. Great. My mother would have herself worked into a frenzy by the time she called.

I gave myself another once-over in the mirror and decided I was presentable. Remembering the falling temperature, I grabbed a lined jacket and headed down the stairs.

I was nearly at the bottom when I heard a tune floating up the hallway from the rear of the house. I paused and cocked my head, listening. It sounded like electronic carnival music, gaily jangling through a series of bars before looping back on itself and beginning again. It was coming from the den.

Adrenaline coursed through my veins with the delicacy of a runaway train.

I glanced at the front door and could see that the deadbolt was still in place. Dexter appeared near my ankles, looking up at me questioningly. I absently bent down and scratched the top of his head while I continued to listen.

The clock over the mantel in the living room was the only other sound in the house. The hallway at the foot of the stairs was well lit and empty. My living room, which occupied the entire front half of the first floor, was also in order. The kitchen and dining room, which occupied the east rear corner of the house, were also empty. I stuck my head through the doorway to ensure that the deadbolt was still in place on the back door. It was. That only left the bathroom and the den, both of which were down the hall and to my right.

Scanning for a weapon, I grabbed a pair of scissors from the kitchen and started down the hall, listening for any change in the idiotic melody. Fortunately, the first thing I had done upon entering the house was turn on all of the lights so my progress was unimpeded by ominous shadows and the unseen things lurking within them. Still, I was cautious. The business with my car had left me justifiably edgy.

The bathroom was clear, and by the time I reached it, I knew for certain the sound was coming from inside the den. I eased up to the doorway and peered inside.

The room was as empty as when I had left it.

The electronic music was emanating from my computer speakers while a buxom redhead gyrated on the screen. She played peek-a-boo with her bra, exposing round full breasts one at a time with a mischievous wink of her eye before finally tossing the garment aside completely and grinding her hips in a slow, circular motion. When the music looped around, the girl magically found her clothes and started her naughty dance all over again.

Funny. I thought I had turned my computer off.

CHAPTER EIGHT

I arrived at the Renaissance at exactly eight-fifteen. Traffic was moderately heavy as there was an arts festival on the riverfront, but I found a spot near the front entrance. I pulled up to the curb, and Nina Crockett stepped out from the lobby doors. I was preparing to get out of the car to open the door for her, but she had already bridged the distance and was lowering herself in, waving me back into my seat.

She was a striking woman, more handsome than pretty, with dark hair and dark eyes, an angular nose and squared jaw line. She wore a light blue satin dress with thin straps stretched over her broad shoulders. Despite her height, which was well over six feet, she had elected to wear tall black heels, which should put me at eye level with her chin. She pulled and tugged self-consciously at the hem of the dress as she adjusted the passenger seat of the Optima into a more comfortable position. I had a feeling she would've been a lot more comfortable in jeans and a sweatshirt.

Before I pulled away from the curb, I guiltily scanned the sidewalk. There was no sign of Melanie nor Jordan McCleary. Good.

"So, you live in Columbus?" I asked. I admit, I pretty much suck at small talk. Throughout life, we meet new people, and at some indistinguishable point they stop being strangers. Although many people are good with conversation both before and after this transition, I have a little trouble with the early stage. I think most of what I say is pricelessly inane and judging from some of the reactions I've gotten in the past, I suspect I'm not entirely off the mark.

Nina shook her head. "Pittsburgh. I'm just here to help see this thing through."

I nodded and fell silent for a few minutes. "This is really some weather, hunh?" I winced as the last of that fell from my lips.

"Mmm," she said, and then turned sideways in the seat. "Can I ask you a question?"

"Sure."

"Who were you looking for back at the hotel?"

"Nobody."

"I saw you."

"Really. It was nobody," I said. "I've never seen the Renaissance up close. It's really beautiful."

Nina was silent. Then, "You're a terrible liar, you know."

"I've heard that before."

We drove the rest of the way to the Winking Lizard in uncomfortable silence, broken occasionally by polite occupational questions to each other. It was obvious Nina didn't want to talk about the Eviscerator case, so I kept my questions procedural to be safe.

When we arrived, we were seated relatively quickly and had soon placed our orders. Nina cleared her throat and asked, "So, who is she?"

"Who?"

"Come on, Dwayne. I saw the way you were watching the hotel. You weren't looking at the building. You were looking *for* somebody. You knew the way to the hotel readily enough and yet claim to have never really seen the place."

I turned what she had said over in my mind for a moment, looking for a loophole that wouldn't make a complete asshole out of me, but in the end, my mouth opened and out came, "Melanie McGregor. I think I'm in love with her. Hell, no—I *know* I'm in love with her."

"Then what's the problem?"

79

"She's staying at the Renaissance with someone else. Her goddamned English professor, would you believe? Jordan McCleary." I grimaced in disgust.

This is a point in the story which I have elected to condense. There are many reasons why, but the most important is I don't look so good in it. I continued to prattle on and on about Melanie while Nina took it all in surprisingly good humor. She was a very good listener, probably from all her years of FBI training. Somehow, I suspect she didn't think she'd find herself playing Dear Abby to a whiny, thirty-four-year-old baby. I didn't bother to ask for any more background about Nina because I was too busy filling the room with my own words. I was animated, agitated, and articulated—boy, did I ever articulate.

As I was finishing my dinner, I realized Nina had stopped eating some time ago and was sitting across from me with her chin resting in her upturned hands. She hadn't spoken a word in a considerable amount of time, although I couldn't be precise because I hadn't been paying attention.

"Oh, my God," I said, sudden mortification overwhelming me. "I'm such an asshole."

"Hey, I asked," she said. "And I was worried all you would want talk about would be the case."

"Nina—I don't know what to say. I've been inexcusable."

"Yes, you have," she said, but she said it calmly with a sly, sideways smile. "But really, it's okay. It wouldn't have worked out, you know. You seem pretty rooted to Columbus. I don't plan to leave Pittsburgh anytime soon. Do you know the kind of chance a relationship like that has?"

"Still—"

She leaned across the table and winked. "Truth be known, I was after your body, anyway."

My mouth dropped open, and she laughed for the first time that whole evening. "I *am* sorry," I said.

"Don't worry about it."

I suddenly caught sight of something over Nina's left shoulder, something black and curly that ducked away sooner than I could get a fix on it. "Excuse me," I said, easing out of the booth and walking quickly down the aisle toward whatever it was.

Sure enough, tucked into a corner near a potted plant was Brady Garrett, smiling sheepishly at me. "Hey," he said.

"What in the hell are you doing here?" I asked.

He raised his eyebrows and scowled. "Eating, I think. Isn't that what you do in a restaurant?"

My eyes narrowed. "This is *bullshit*, Brady. You're following me."

"Hey, I can't help it. I've got a nose for the news. When I realized you're hooking up with the FBI Amazon over there, I figured it might be in my best interest to see what you're up to."

"You talk to me earlier today about working together, and now you're following me around, *spying* on me? You're a real waste of skin, Brady. Furthermore, you'll be happy to know that you're interrupting us on a date—"

"A *what*? She'll break you in half."

"A *date*. There's been no exchange of classified information. She's not helping me on the side. And what's more, I'm not helping you either. Find yourself some other chump."

"Oh, come *on*, man," he protested. "Surely you can see where I'm coming from."

"Fuck off, Brady."

I went back to the table and slid into my seat.

"It was that reporter, wasn't it? Garrett?" asked Nina, and I nodded my head. She grimaced. "God, he's a weasel." I nodded again.

"I think he's eager for another victim to turn up," I said.

"That's sick."

"He's sick," I said. "Let's not talk about him. We just ate."

"Fine by me," she said. "Let's talk about you for a minute."

81

"I've been doing that all night long," I said. "I'm surprised you're not ready to call a cab."

"What I want to know is, what's the deal with the private detective business? You act as if you're interested, but it doesn't sound to me like you've done much in the way of making it happen."

"I've taken up running," I said defensively.

Nina laughed. "So do lots of overweight Americans. That isn't training."

"I've been busy with my other work. You know, the stuff that *pays*."

I satisfied the bill, and we made small talk as we returned to the car. The evening air had turned cold, but the storms from earlier in the day had completely subsided. As we pulled out of the lot, Nina said, "You know, it's time to either shit or get off the pot, so to speak."

"What do you mean?"

"If you really want to become a detective, you need to start working aggressively toward it. Do you even know Ohio's requirements for obtaining a PI license?"

I shook my head.

She laughed again. "So, you're *not* serious about becoming a PI?"

"No, I'm serious," I said. "I just haven't gotten that far."

"You're a procrastinator, aren't you?"

"I thought we all were."

"No, not all of us," she said. "I'll tell you what—are you free tomorrow afternoon?"

I squirmed a little. After all of the emoting I had done over Melanie, I didn't think Nina would be interested in going out with me again. I didn't want to lead her on. I knew she and I had no possibilities together, at least not anytime soon.

"Not a date," she said, reading either my expression or my mind. "A tutorial."

"A tutorial?"

"That's right. I can dig up some information that might help you," she said, adding, "That is, if you really *are* interested in becoming a detective."

Since I had told Brady Garrett to take a hike, my Saturday afternoon was suddenly open. I *was* curious about whatever it was he had wanted to show me, but I couldn't stand the thought of working with him.

"That'd be nice."

We drove back to the bright lights and tall buildings, and I had the good fortune to find a parking spot directly in front of the hotel. I eased up to the curb.

"Thank you for an interesting evening," she said, unfastening her seatbelt.

"Would you like me to walk you up?"

She smiled and shook her head. "You don't want Melanie to see us, remember?"

I grimaced and apologized again.

"I'll call before I head out tomorrow. What time?"

"Any time after noon," I said. I am, by nature, a night owl. I don't function well at all in the A.M. hours.

She waved and headed for the lobby door.

*****

The rest of the evening was uneventful. There were no more angry messages from Geneva Carter on the answering machine. As a matter of fact, there were no messages at all. Dexter reminded me I hadn't given him his evening nibbles, so I filled his plastic food dish with dry food and freshened his water bowl. He mewed favorably and settled down to feast upon the crunchy bits of dehydrated chicken.

I turned on the television just in time to see a replay of Natasha Brickman's earlier report on the Eviscerator. I saw myself walking away from her, waving her away as I entered my house. It struck me as odd that

I was receiving so much publicity out of all of this. I doubted those who had discovered the previous victims were still being pursued by the media. Of course, my background *did* invite a little of it, I supposed.

I was surprised I hadn't heard anything from my mother. She was born to worry. All it would take would be the most subtle suggestion I was working on this case, and she would be all over me about responsibility and safety and other such nonsense. She must have missed the news today.

I watched an old Alfred Hitchcock movie, *Shadow of a Doubt*, and fell asleep on my overstuffed sofa with my cat perched on top of my head.

*****

I was up at ten and on Orin Way by ten-fifteen, stretching my legs for my daily run. The cold front which had caused the previous day's turbulent weather had settled in. The brilliant blue sky overhead belied the temperatures which had dropped into the low sixties. The weather report said to expect a steady decline all the way into the forties over the next twenty-four hours. Spring in Ohio could be so completely unpredictable. We would probably still have another big snow before the season was out.

I looped around the circuit and made pretty good time doing it. As I trotted up my front steps, I stooped over and grabbed *The Dispatch*. I let myself in the front door, tossed the newspaper on the couch and headed up for the shower. I was a weird blend of hot-cold from the sweat pouring down my body mingling with the crisp morning air. I turned the water in the shower as hot as I could bear and stood there long enough to lose all concept of time.

Dexter was messing around outside the bathroom door, waiting impatiently for his morning vittles. I scooped him up off the ground and nuzzled his belly, something he pretends to despise but his throaty purring belies. I put him down on the hardwood floor of the upstairs hallway and he trotted toward the staircase, looking over his shoulder to make sure I was following.

I paused long enough to slide on a pair of jeans and a navy t-shirt and went down to the kitchen. Breakfast for me was a ham-and-cheese omelet. The cat got whatever that ground stuff is in a can. We were both content.

I retrieved the paper from the living room and spread it over the table as I finished my coffee. The front page contained nothing new about the killings. Instead, there had been another bombing in Iraq and a sizable drug bust off Livingston on the east side. The Eviscerator must have taken the weekend off.

I had almost successfully gotten my mind off the whole thing when I came across Brady Garrett's commentary buried in the back of the first section. A picture of Nina Crockett and me at the table in the Winking Lizard, under which was the caption, "FBI considering all avenues. Agent Nina Crockett confers with P.I. Dwayne Morrow."

I groaned. First of all, I *wasn't* a P.I. Could I get in trouble for that? I didn't think so. *I* wasn't the one who made the claim. Secondly, Nina's superiors weren't going to be thrilled by the implication, as if I were the next step above their team of trained experts. I couldn't believe that Brady had done this. He seemed so genuine with his proposal that we work together. Genuine enough that I probably would have done it, if I were to be completely honest.

I couldn't even begin to explain why I was felt so compelled. She had been someone's daughter. She had been paralyzed from the waist down, unable to run, unable to hide. Now she was so much worse than dead. No words I could string together could ever begin to describe the horror.

The opportunity to lend a hand, no matter how inexperienced it may be, was something I couldn't dismiss lightly. I didn't want free advertising, as Brady had suggested. I wanted to be secure in the knowledge that a crazed maniac capable of dismembering someone so thoroughly was no longer stalking the streets of my city.

85

I cleaned up my breakfast dishes and glanced at the clock on the kitchen wall. It was eleven-thirty. Nina should be calling soon. I realized I hadn't checked my answering machine and went into the hallway to check the machine. Two blips.

The first was my mother.

"I just got the paper this morning, Dwayne. What's going on? You shouldn't be running around playing with the police. I thought you learned your lesson. Call me. Your old mom's worried."

I knew the news blackout couldn't last forever. I'd return the call later. The next was a surprise.

"Hey, Dwayne. It's Mel. I was hoping to catch you in today. We really need to talk. Please call me when you get in. I should be free pretty much all afternoon."

Countdown to destruction.

I couldn't bring myself to call Melanie even if I wanted to. I could picture her calling from the phone on the bedside table, turning to Jordan McCleary with a quick shrug before hanging up the receiver and resuming the non-stop lovemaking in which they had engaged since arriving in their room.

I continued down the hall and entered my den, dropping like dead weight into my leather chair and absently flicking the power switch on my computer. I was going to have to deal with Melanie sooner or later. Tonight. I would call her tonight and get it over with.

The telephone rang. I reached across the desk and picked up the receiver.

"Hello?"

"Hey-a, Dwayne. It's Jaz," said the small, high-pitched voice. Jasmine was Melanie's eleven-year-old daughter. She and I had developed a sort of mutual respect after her father died. She was extraordinarily perceptive for her age, and I think she appreciated the fact I recognized it. She often talked to me about things she would be too embarrassed to discuss with her mother. I suddenly realized if Melanie and I stopped seeing each other, I wouldn't be a welcome party to Jasmine's life any longer. My heart sank to new depths.

"Hey, kiddo," I said, doing my best to keep it upbeat. "What's up?"

"Is Mom there?"

"Huh-unh. I haven't seen her since yesterday when she stopped by with—"

"Professor McCleary? He's neat. He's been helping me with my science fair project. He doesn't even *teach* science."

"I guess that makes him real smart, huh?"

"Yeah, super smart. Mom likes him a lot, too. She says she doesn't know if she could get by without him."

Ouch. From the mouths of babes and all that shit. "Well, I'm sorry, kiddo, but I haven't seen your mom. Do you want me to have her call you if I see her?"

"Yeah, wouldja? I want to spend the night at Suzie Brubaker's, but Gramma won't let me on account of I didn't clean my room. I keep trying to tell her that Suzie and I are going to study, but she's not buying it."

"Studying on a Saturday night? Your grandma's a smart lady."

Jasmine giggled. "S'pose so. I'm surprised Mom isn't there. She's not in her room. I wish she'd get a cell phone, but she says there isn't enough coverage down here to make it worth it. I figured she would spend all of her free time with you."

"Your mom's a busy lady," I said. "Maybe she hasn't had any free time yet."

"I guess. Okay, well, I'm going to go. Don't forget."

"I won't."

"Thanks. You coming down anytime soon?"

"You'll be the first to know."

"Later tomater." She giggled again and hung up the phone.

My computer had loaded, and I logged on to my email. I did a double take when I saw that there were 494 messages pouring into my inbox. I watched the pornography rush in like dirty rainwater, promising titillation of unprecedented proportion—MasterCard and Visa welcome! Body parts flew from the screen in animated 3-D, and it took me a minute to do anything more than just sit and stare. All of the senders' names were bogus, things like, "Hot Sex@cum.com" and "Horny Bitches@fuckme.com." No two were the same, and none of them were the senders I had blocked yesterday.

I began the arduous process of deleting the messages and blocking the senders, being careful not to accidentally purge legitimate mailings. Nestled within the 494 messages were nine actual emails intended specifically for me. Most were business related, a couple were from friends, but one stood out specifically. The sender was GCarter@barleynet.net. The subject line was blank. I clicked the message with my mouse to open it.

"Mr. Morrow:

You won't get away with this. I promise you.

Geneva Carter"

Short and to the point. At least she wasn't misspelling vulgarities in a drunken stupor. Could she be responsible for all of the pornographic material pouring into my email? Geneva was competent with a computer, but it would take some extra know-how to do something like that, not to mention the type of personality that would do such a thing. Geneva was turning out to be a real surprise. She had seemed so level-headed, so rational when we had shared lunch at Dial-Tech Labs. She had been personable and funny. I had never seen her in so much as a bad mood before this. It struck me as funny; the first irrational thing she had done was to "hire" me.

I had expected some sort of contact from Alan Carter, but what sort I didn't know. If someone had been trailing me for days, I would likely be pissed. But maybe he realized I was only doing what his wife had asked.

Maybe he realized any anger sent my way would only be misdirected. He had been living with Geneva for many years. Just because he wasn't having an affair didn't mean he couldn't use a break from his wife. She had told me that their two children, a son and a daughter, both lived out of state. Out of mommy's grasp. Go figure.

The doorbell sounded and snapped me from my reverie. I had expected Nina to call before coming out, but maybe I had misunderstood. I turned the monitor off, not wanting Nina to think I was a total pervert (as I hadn't been able to delete all of the pulsating body parts yet). I went to the front door and pulled it open, the smile falling from my face when I realized who my visitor was.

It was Brady Garrett, a briefcase tucked under one arm, and a cheesy grin spread like margarine across his weasel face.

"What's for lunch?" he asked, opening the storm door and stepping inside.

CHAPTER NINE

"What in the hell are you doing here?" I demanded.

"What? You told me to stop by after noon," Brady said, depositing his briefcase onto my sofa and plopping down with his legs stretched out in front of him. "It's after noon."

I narrowed my eyes and glared, my hand still holding the front door open. "You're kidding, right? After the shit you pulled last night, you still thought I'd be willing to work with you?"

Brady shrugged. "I don't see why not. My proposition is still valid, isn't it? You still want a piece of the action, don't you?"

I didn't respond. The image of the fourth victim continued to tug at my consciousness, surprising me at odd times with quick mental snapshots of the gruesome aftermath. I had forced myself to start thinking of Tina Barlow as "The Fourth Victim" because I was having trouble with the reality of her murder. She was in a wheelchair, for God's sake! The anger that surged in me was a living thing, growing stronger each minute. Anything would be better than remaining idle, but to intentionally align myself with Brady Garrett? I would be swinging with the monkeys first.

"I think you should go," I said, indicating the open door.

"Hey, okay, maybe last night was a poor judgment call on my part," said Brady. "How did I know you were on a date with Xena, Warrior Princess?"

"You certainly knew after I *told* you," I said. "But you still managed to twist it all around for the morning edition. I saw your commentary. Get out."

90

"Oh, *that*. That was nothing," he said, dismissing it with a wave of his hand.

"*Nothing?*"

"Candy for the public."

"You're repugnant."

Brady unfastened the clasps of his briefcase and flipped the top open. "I brought what I felt was pertinent—"

"What you felt was *pertinent?* You're editing my copy before I even get a chance to see it! This is not going to work, Brady. I'm serious. Get out."

"Okey-dokey," he said, retrieving a handful of flash drives from his briefcase before closing it again. "But I'm leaving this with you to take a look at. It's the computer stuff I was telling you about."

"What kind of computer stuff?"

"I don't know. If I knew, I wouldn't be asking you."

"Where did it come from?"

"I know this really hot girl in Records at Quantico, legs up to her eyeballs and limber as—"

"Oh, no!" I said, pulling my hands away from the drives as if they were electrified. "You lifted this from the FBI?"

"I wouldn't exactly call it *lifting*, I just—"

"Take your stuff and get off my property. You're playing with fire, Brady, and I'm not going to be the one who gets burned."

Brady looked at me as if I were from Mars. "What in the hell is wrong with you? What kind of fairy tale are you living in? The only way to get to the bottom of this is to dig. Dig deep. Sometimes rules have to get bent. You better get used to it if you really intend to be a PI."

I clamped my lips together in silence and guided Brady through the door. He was still protesting when I closed it in his face. What if Nina had shown up while Brady was there and realized the drives were classified? What kind of implication would that have been? Not a very good one, that's what. I realized the validity of his "Bent Rule Theorem" but was reluctant to make an enemy of the FBI so early in my career.

The phone rang. I crossed to the extension in the hall and picked up the receiver. "Hello?"

"It's Nina. By my watch, it's twelve-fifteen. Are you awake?"

*****

Nina sat at my kitchen table, placing a brown leather satchel in front of her. She began retrieving sheets of paper from within, stacking them in orderly piles after giving them a cursory inspection.

"Do you want something to eat? Something to drink?" I asked.

"Do you have any beet juice?"

"Any what?"

Nina sighed. "Do you have any juice at all?"

"I think there's some orange juice in there. I'll have to check the expiration date, though." I began rummaging through my refrigerator, pushing aside leftovers I could no longer identify. I run a clean kitchen as far as surfaces go. Unfortunately, my refrigerator might be mistaken for a time capsule because I'm too cheap to throw leftovers out though I rarely eat them. They tend to accumulate and grow spores. Maybe I could've helped Jasmine with her science fair project after all.

"How about some water?" she finally asked when I hadn't produced the OJ after a minute or so.

I retrieved a glass from the cupboard and filled it with ice and water from the refrigerator before sitting across the table from her. She looked comfortable in blue jeans and a beige knit sweater, a vast improvement over the stiff mini dress and ice pick heels she had chosen for the previous evening.

"Nice picture in the paper, huh?" She didn't look up, her voice neutral.

"I'm sorry," I said automatically.

"Sorry? What's to be sorry for? You didn't take the picture. It was that pond scum, Garrett."

"I hope it didn't cause you any trouble."

Nina lightly massaged her temples. "No more than usual. The Director's pulled me from the case."

"*What?* That's ridiculous! You had nothing to do with it. We were only eating dinner, for God's sake!"

"I should've had the foresight to see how it might look."

"So, FBI training also includes mind-reading?"

"No, really, Dwayne. It *is* my fault. I knew Garrett was tailing you. I could see the slant this whole thing has taken with the media."

"Slant? What slant?" I asked.

Nina grinned at me, looking up from her collection of paperwork. "The media likes you. You photograph well. You are, my dear sir, what we call a media darling." I instantly remembered the horrific black-and-white photo of me that was shown on *Crimebusters*. That was a *good* picture? I'd hate to see a bad one.

"How so?" I asked.

"Strong public reaction to your adventure last fall. That little girl would have been killed if it hadn't been for you."

I squirmed uncomfortably. "I had a lot of help. A PI in Lymont actually deserves the credit, not me."

"Doug Boggs, right? From what I understand, he wouldn't know his ass from a hole in the ground."

"You've been doing a lot of checking up on me," I noted.

"Of course. We've been checking up on anyone connected with the Eviscerator's crimes. You didn't expect any less, did you?"

I folded my arms across my chest and scowled. Although I understood the reasoning, I still felt invaded.

Nina continued, "*The Dispatch* will sell a lot more copy if they emphasize your alleged participation in this investigation. Garrett knows this. He's disgusting, but he's not a fool. I really shouldn't be here now. He's liable to come popping up out of a bush somewhere. But I promised you I would drop this information off." She indicated the papers she had spread like solitaire across my table.

"God, that's a lot of paperwork," I said, craning my neck to read upside down. "I figured I had to pay a fee, take some target practice, but *man!*"

Nina nodded, pulling a piece of paper to the top of the stack. "Requirements for licensure vary from state to state, so I've put together a summary that applies specifically to private investigation in Ohio. It's all spelled out in Ohio Revised Code, Section 4749."

I began scanning the material. There were three licensure classifications. Class A covered an individual who does both private investigation and security services, while Class B was specifically for private investigation. Class C applied only to those interested in being rent-a-cops. I stumbled when I got to the prerequisites.

"It says here I would need a degree in criminal justice. I didn't even finish school for what I'm doing now," I said with a frown.

"The University of Toledo has online courses that would make it more convenient with your schedule," Nina offered.

"It also says I have to work more or less as an apprentice for two years before I can even apply for my own license."

"That's right," said Nina. "You could either work for a licensed PI or take a job as a night watchman."

"Where am I going to find the time to do that?"

"That's your problem."

After high school, I had bypassed college because I was too impatient to see it through. I'm very stubborn about learning things on my own terms, and that philosophy seems to pretty much conflict with the general rules of etiquette at most universities. My current career was built through self-study and hands-on experience, and I really thought I was finished with higher education. I never dreamed I would have to clock so many hours before I could even *apply* for my private investigator's license. Shit.

I couldn't begin to guess the cost of tuition, but the fees associated with the process itself weren't too bad. The examination fee was $25, with an annual licensing fee of up to $375. I would have to complete a firearms basic training program that would include twenty hours of handgun training and five additional hours of training in the use of any other firearm I may choose to use while working. Since I had purchased my gun, I had been going to Vince's Lodge almost weekly to use the range for target practice. I could see now this was going to involve more than tightening the pattern I blew through the little paper man at the end of the string.

When I looked up, Nina had settled her chin onto her clasped hands, and a smug smile was in place. "More complicated than you thought?"

I sighed and nodded. "I'm going to have to think about this some more. I don't know how I can maintain my consulting business while I take classes and punch a clock as a guard or investigator for two whole years."

"Maybe your friend, Doug Boggs, could use an apprentice. The hours would probably be more flexible than those in security," suggested Nina.

I laughed. "I'd sooner eat my own foot."

Nina pushed her chair back from the table and stood. "It's up to you. You might not have to put in two years if you pled your case to the director of commerce. You do have some real-world experience that should apply."

I shrugged. "I'll have to go over the rest of this and see."

"For what it's worth, I think you'd make a fine detective."

"Thanks," I said as warmth spread through my cheeks. Compliments generally embarrass the hell out of me. "So, I guess I won't be seeing you again."

"You might. I'll be sticking around to support the team awhile longer," said Nina. "But if you find yourself licensed someday, you now have a contact inside the FBI."

"Really?"

"Don't get all excited," she said. "It's not like I'd divulge information that would compromise a case, but I'd help you if I could."

"Thank you," I said, reaching out to offer a handshake.

She responded by taking my hand and pulling herself close, glancing a kiss off my cheek. "Good luck," she whispered.

The heat which had been contained in my face spread to the tips of my ears, as well as to other mindless portions of my anatomy. I pulled back and heard a sound at the front door. I turned my head, looked through the hallway and into the living room. I had left the door open, and through the glass of the storm door was Melanie, staring with her hands on her hips. She had a copy of *The Columbus Dispatch* clutched in her right hand, folded back to Brady's editorial with the damning picture of Nina and me peeking out from underneath her thumb.

I literally leapt away from Nina and hurried to the door. "Melanie! I didn't expect you to drop by."

"So, I see," she said stiffly. She wore blue jeans and a plaid flannel shirt, but somehow managed to look both sexy and elegant. Her blond hair was pulled back into a ponytail, and her emerald eyes were furiously aglow. She thrust the paper at my chest when I opened the door. "I was going to ask you what the hell this was, but I guess I can see for myself. Asshole."

The paper fell to my feet as Melanie turned and stormed back to the white Lexus parked cockeyed behind Nina's car. Jordan McCleary's white Lexus. I stooped to pick up the paper and watched her slam the car into gear and roar backwards onto Orin Way. She overshot the berm, and the rear tires landed in a shallow ditch. With appropriate pressure on the gas pedal, she managed to bulldoze her way back to the road. She disappeared in a plume of gravel and dust.

Nina stepped up behind me. "Melanie?"

"Melanie."

"She's pretty."

"Yeah."

"Why aren't you going after her?" she asked.

"Because she's seeing Jordan McCleary."

"How do you know this?" she challenged. "I listened to your whole story last night, and you never once told me you had *asked* Melanie about Jordan."

"Well, I *haven't* exactly, but I can see what's going on."

Nina rolled her eyes and headed for her car. She opened the driver's side door, then turned to face me. "What are you, thirteen? You're about to lose something important to you, all because you're too scared or stupid to ask about Jordan McCleary."

I was offended. "I just don't want to hear it out loud, that's all."

"So, you aren't even going to *ask*?" She shook her head in bewilderment and got behind the wheel. "I guess I was wrong. Maybe you won't make such a good detective after all." She pulled her door shut and backed out of the drive.

*****

I went back to the envious task of deleting the pornography landfill my email inbox had become. Fifty new messages had piled in, all of them XXX. I knew unsolicited email, also known as SPAM, was unavoidable, but this was like a concentrated assault. Was someone specifically feeding my email address to these sleaze sites? Instinct suggested Geneva Carter. I continued to block the various senders as I deleted the messages, hoping on a day in the not-too-distant future, I might finally stop receiving the damned things.

Nina was clearly off target about Melanie. I had convinced myself that Melanie had a hell of a nerve coming over to give me grief about Nina when she was shacked up in the Renaissance with her professor. It helped to stay angry. I really thought Melanie and I had a good thing going, and it isn't often I have a good thing going. Had we gone too slowly? Was that it? I

97

hadn't wanted to rush Melanie after the loss of her husband. Had she finally gotten bored waiting for me?

I had just deleted the last of the emails when a solitary new one popped in. It was from my friend, gcarter@barleynet.net. The subject was, "A PRESENT FOR YOU." I opened the message, which had no text beyond that in the subject line. A bright, yellow paperclip in the upper right corner indicated there was an attachment. I right-clicked my mouse over the paperclip to view the attachment's name before opening it. A word to the wise: This is how viruses often spread. Never blindly open attachments unless you are expecting them. What I found was the Fun Love virus, ready to attack the program files on my hard drive. I deleted it immediately, unopened.

Well, that was it. This had gone way beyond ridiculous. I rummaged through my organizer and found Geneva's phone number, then grabbed my cell phone. I tapped my foot impatiently while the phone rang at the other end. Soon, Geneva's husky voice came on the line. "Yes?"

"Geneva, this is Dwayne Morrow. What's the big idea?"

There was a long silence at the other end. Finally, Geneva said, "I don't have any idea what you're talking about. If you don't stop harassing me, I'm going to call the police."

I couldn't help but laugh. That was rich. "You emailed a virus to my computer. I'm pretty sure that's against the law."

More silence. "I don't know anything about a virus." Tonight, her voice was flat, emotionless. I couldn't figure out the rugged geography of her moods. "If you don't stop harassing me, I'm going to call the police."

"Yeah, you already said that," I said, disconnecting the call.

*****

I spent the evening working on my finances. I wrote checks for bills that were due and scheduled new ones on my calendar. I would be returning to work at Dial-Tech on Monday, and I longed for the assignment to be over. Thomas Baldwin would be in a foul mood because of the water damage to his building and would take it out on everyone around him. Even though he had laid me off for a week, he would no doubt find me responsible for the subsequent delay in completing the hardware upgrade. As if that weren't enough, I would undoubtedly run into Geneva Carter time and again for the duration of the project.

I picked up the telephone a half dozen times or so to call Melanie but replaced the receiver each time before dialing the entire number. What would I say if Jordan McCleary answered the phone? And why wouldn't he be there? He had made his intentions clear.

I decided to return my phone messages instead. First, I called my mother and reassured her I had not done anything foolish with respect to the serial killer. After listening to fifteen minutes of uninterrupted lecture about how my irresponsibility was going to inevitably cause her a stroke one day, I worked my way off the line. My next call was to Matt, to try and confirm availability for the get-together he and Sheila were planning for the next weekend. I got the answering machine and decided against leaving a message. I didn't want to explain to a machine why I wouldn't be bringing Melanie.

I grabbed James W. Hall's *Rough Draft* from my bookshelf and burrowed into my overstuffed sofa. The next couple of hours were lost in literary detachment. At some point, Dexter had worked his way onto my lap and curled into a contented, rumbling ball. I absently scratched his shoulder blades as I read, pushing all thoughts of Melanie McGregor aside.

It was almost ten when I was startled by a knock at my front door. I certainly wasn't expecting anyone else. I disrupted Dexter's slumber and marked my book, struggling to my feet to find one of my legs had fallen asleep. Invisible pins and needles prickled at my flesh as I hobbled across the hardwood floor. My front door used to be a multi-paned glass affair that would have allowed me to identify my visitor from across the room.

After my house was broken into, I had replaced it with one that looked like wood but was made of steel. It had a peephole, two deadbolts and a door guard. So much for safety in the suburbs.

I peered through the peephole and saw a thin man with wispy blond hair and skin so pale it was almost translucent. His eyes were downcast, watching his feet, occasionally flickering up but never quite even with the peephole. I opened the door, leaving the guard on. "Yes?"

"I'm sorry to bother you, Mr. Morrow. I know it's late," apologized the man. His eyes continued to study his well-worn dock shoes. He was dressed in khakis and a pale blue pullover, his lanky frame propping the clothes up as if they were on nothing more than a hanger.

I had never seen the guy before in my life. I looked at him quizzically and waited for him to continue.

He cleared his throat nervously and dared to make momentary eye contact. "I was hoping you might have a few minutes to speak with me. My name is Jeffrey Carter. Geneva Carter is my mother."

CHAPTER TEN

For a brief moment, I wondered if Jeffrey Carter had come to seek revenge on behalf of his mother, but his nervous demeanor and less-than-menacing stature indicated otherwise. I unfastened the door guard and invited him in.

"I really am sorry to come so late," he said. "I promise I won't stay long."

"It's all right, Mr. Carter," I said, opening the door and allowing him to enter.

"Jeffrey," he corrected, his thin lips playing at a smile before giving up the cause. "I am aware that my mother asked you to follow my father. I'm also aware she's not happy with the outcome."

"I hope you're not here to pile on," I said. "I'm really not in the mood."

"Oh, no, not at all," he said. "Quite the opposite, in fact. I wanted to apologize for my mother's erratic behavior. She's been under a terrible strain."

"Have you spoken with your father since he moved out?" I asked.

"Moved out? He didn't move out," said Jeffrey.

"That's what Geneva told me," I said. "She blamed me for the whole thing."

"He took a few days to think things over, that's all. Sometimes Mother can be a handful. I don't know how he's managed all these years. You see, she suffers from a bipolar disorder. She takes medication to keep the mood swings under control, but sometimes her body chemistry shifts, and the medicines are no longer as effective. The doctors will come up with a new cocktail, and she'll be good as new for a while. In the meanwhile, Father asked me to come by and beg your indulgence. He would have done it himself, but he thinks he'd have a hard time being civil to you. He *knows* you were only doing what my mother asked, but it still bothers him that he was being followed."

"I suppose I can understand that," I said. "I thought Geneva told me you and your sister lived out-of-state."

"My sister does," he said. "Trina lives in Kansas with her husband, Charlie. I've been away for a while but recently returned home when Father told me what had happened. I've decided it's best to stay close to Mother for the time being, at least until they get her medication sorted out."

"You're staying with them?"

"Of course. I figured that Father could use the help. This episode of Mother's has been more severe than usual," he said. I noticed how formal he was when referring to his parents. It would indicate a breeding I hadn't expected from Geneva Carter's children. "I wanted to apologize for any inconvenience. Mother's simply looking for someone to blame. I'm afraid you're it."

"Well, she's clogging my email with junk, not the least of which was a virus. I don't want to have to change my email address. I use it for my business," I said. "If she doesn't stop, I'll have to report it."

"She'll stop, Mr. Morrow, I assure you." He turned and headed for the door, and I followed him to the porch. He turned before stepping down and handed me a business card. "If you have any more difficulties with her, please don't hesitate to give me a call."

"Thanks," I said, taking the card and watching him return to his sporty red BMW. He didn't look back again as he started the car and backed out of my drive, turning down Orin Way and disappearing into the night.

The card proclaimed Jeffrey Carter an independent financial consultant and listed a business phone, a cell number and an email address. There was no physical address attached to the business, which I guess by definition made him truly independent.

I was about to go back in the house when I spotted a small, square package tucked under my porch swing. It was wrapped in brown mailing paper and had no markings whatsoever on the outside. I picked it up and held it to my ear. The package was relatively light and refrained from ticking, so I carefully unfastened the clumsy tape job from both ends and removed the outer wrap.

It contained the flash drives Brady Garrett had tried to hand off earlier.

I immediately scanned the horizon, expecting federal agents to storm-troop across the field, seize the pilfered data and lock me up for their trouble. All I heard was an airplane passing far overhead.

Damn Brady! He *knew* I didn't want anything to do with this information! I went back inside and placed the package on an end table, reaffixing the outer wrap with fresh tape. I would return it untouched, but it would have to wait until later. It was almost eleven, and I was exhausted.

*****

I didn't do a thing all day on Sunday, trying to unwind before I had to return to work, but I wasn't entirely successful. I couldn't get the image of the dead girl out of my mind.

Monday morning snuck up and pushed me out of bed. A quick look at the alarm clock confirmed I had slept too long and couldn't spare the time to run before heading to Dial-Tech. I showered and dressed in heavy corduroys and a dark sweater. The temperature was still dropping, and I figured we might see snow if the trend continued.

I chased Dexter around the kitchen and finally cornered him by the washing machine, where I scratched between his ears and worked him into a state of undeniable bliss, throaty purrs rumbling from his voice box. Afterward, I cracked open a can of foul-smelling food and deposited it in his food dish. This routine had developed early in his eight years with me. Wouldn't you know, my own cat was a "morning person." Traitor.

Traffic was as traffic is during rush hour. I-270 was packed with cars tailgating each other, defying the person in front to stop suddenly. I took my place in the chain of automobiles and drove north to Dublin, where Dial-Tech Labs was headquartered. After tangling with city planners over special zoning, Thomas Baldwin had built the six-story concrete structure on land that his family had owned for generations. It was tucked away from the rest of Dublin, its fifty-acre grounds preventing other neighbors from cozying up too closely. I wasn't exactly sure what they did at Dial-Tech. I believe it was chemical research for consumer products, but I couldn't swear to that. Thomas Baldwin was absolutely paranoid about security, and I didn't want to ask too many questions, or I would soon be answering to him about my motivation. Simple curiosity as an explanation wouldn't suffice.

The entrance, a ribbon of blacktop stretching deeper into the property, was marked only by a simple concrete flagstone baring "Dial-Tech Labs" in engraved letters. It almost looked like a gravestone in its solemnity. About halfway up the blacktop, I arrived at a security checkpoint and was asked for identification from a stocky man I would guess to be in his mid-fifties. He was square-shouldered and grim-faced, with the residual imprint of military training etched into the lines of his face. He scowled at my temporary ID and glanced at a clipboard he had tucked under his arm.

"Is there a problem?" I asked through my open window.

"Mr. Baldwin would like to see you in his office right away."

Woo-hoo! That's exactly how I wanted to start the week. Baldwin was bound to put pressure on me to finish up more quickly than humanly possible. I would have to explain the impossibility, listen to him threaten to fire me, remind him what the job would cost him in the real world—*shit*.

I acknowledged the request, retrieved my ID and continued down the blacktop until it spilled into the employee parking lot. The lot was already half full, and I saw Geneva's beige Malibu at the far end. This was going to be a day in hell. I parked, steeled myself and walked across the lot to the enormous plate glass doors of the main entrance.

Theresa, Dial Tech's cool and distracted receptionist, looked up from filing her nails as I entered. "Mr. Baldwin wants to see you. Pronto." She didn't like me much and seemed pleased I was in the hot seat.

"I've heard," I said, continuing through the tiled lobby to the bank of elevators along the back wall. I punched the button and willed the elevator to hurry to save me from Theresa's smirking scrutiny.

I stepped in the shiny chrome cube and pressed the top button. Thomas Baldwin kept his offices on the sixth floor of the building, like an overlord watching his evil empire. He also had a small apartment there for those times when he didn't feel like going home to Mrs. Baldwin. I had only met her once before, but I could understand his motivation.

The elevator slid to a stop, and when its doors whooshed open, I thought for a moment I had gone blind. Everything in the lobby was white, and no matter how many times I had conferred with Baldwin, I was always ill-prepared for the ocular assault. The reflex was to peel my shoes off and ask for latex gloves, but to date, I had managed to resist the temptation.

"Mr. Morrow," said Vivian, Baldwin's long-time secretary. She was expertly dressed in a black business suit, her silver-gray hair swept up and held by an antique silver comb. Her voice contained no emotion whatsoever, and I again had the creeping sensation that I was among robots. "I'll tell Mr. Baldwin that you're here."

I had barely entertained the notion of lowering myself onto the pristine white sofa when the door to Baldwin's office opened a crack. Vivian turned to me and said, "You may go in now."

I opened the door to find Thomas Baldwin easing himself back into the enormous, faux-leather chair behind his enormous, faux-wood desk. He was knocking at sixty's door, thick and burly, with a built-in sourpuss that made him look as if he were experiencing a perpetual fart. He wore thick-

105

rimmed glasses, and his bald pate was dotted liberally with liver spots. He was focusing all the energy of his grimace in my direction.

"You wanted to see me?" I asked.

"Sit down," he said, indicating one of the burgundy pleather chairs across from him. The inside of the office was a stark contrast to the outer lobby. In here, dark colors pervaded. Rich, paneled walls with built-in bookcases were adorned with paintings and other interesting decorative pieces, all related to the manly sport of hunting. You almost expected Baldwin to wear safari gear. Instead, he continued to study me from behind his thick glasses.

"If you're wondering about the impact the water break had on completion time—"

He waved my words away. "No. This is a little more serious."

I raised an eyebrow. "Would you care to enlighten me?"

He cleared his throat and shifted forward, leaning his elbows on his desktop blotter. "We have decided not to continue your contract, Mr. Morrow."

I sat there for a moment staring at him. I wasn't sure I had heard that correctly. Had he just *fired* me? That simply wasn't possible, was it? I finally found my voice again. "Was my work unsatisfactory?"

His eyes shifted away from me uncomfortably. I had never seen Thomas Baldwin at a loss for words, but he clearly didn't want to discuss it.

"I think the least you could do is explain," I persisted.

He finally looked at me. "Look, I don't know what it is that gets you off, but I'm not going to have a sexual harassment suit played out here. You're a subcontractor. I can terminate your contract anytime I want."

I shook my head, trying to follow the nonsense that was spilling out of his mouth. "Did you say sexual harassment?" I asked.

He looked at me as if I were diseased. "It shouldn't come as a surprise to you. She said she warned you that you wouldn't get away with it. I just can't imagine you hitting on someone so much *older.*"

Geneva Carter. The bitch. What was she orchestrating?

"She told me if I cut you loose, she wouldn't press charges against the company or you. So, count yourself lucky, you sick fuck. Your ass is going to stay out of jail because of my generosity." He leaned back in his chair and turned to his computer monitor.

I was completely dumbfounded. I had never been fired from an assignment before. *Never.* Not even from a nasty old bastard like Thomas Baldwin. But to realize this had all happened because Geneva Carter had developed a misguided death wish for me?

Almost as an afterthought, Baldwin added, "Security will see you off the premises, Mr. Morrow. Good day."

*****

I was so furious I nearly ran down the guard at the security booth. He leapt out from in front of my speeding car, and I tossed the temporary ID out my open window at him, hoping the pin would catch him in the eye.

Geneva Carter must be stopped. She was wrecking my life. I didn't know what, if anything, Jeffrey Carter might be able to accomplish in the taming of the shrew, but I felt I owed it to him to at least forewarn him I was about to file a civil complaint against his mother. I couldn't have her maliciously ruining my reputation. My business was built on word-of-mouth. It could just as easily be destroyed by it.

With my day unexpectedly abbreviated, I returned home, plotting revenges both practical and ridiculous. I thought it might be a good time to take my gun to Vince's Lodge and release some frustration by riddling some paper corpses.

Instead, I sat at my desk and laid down my head. Even though I knew I had done nothing wrong, I couldn't help but feel a little ashamed. I had just been fired. Dexter was sensitive to my mood and jumped into my lap offering support. The paperwork Nina Crockett had left for me was stacked underneath my face, and I eventually found the strength to lift my head and focus on the material.

Two years of continuous employment in investigation or security. It might as well be ten-to-twenty.

I turned on my computer and waited for it to load. Once I was logged in, I checked my email, dreading the onslaught of pornography which I fully expected to pour in. I was pleased to see I had only received three emails, all of which were from friends. Maybe Geneva was winding down, her work finished now that she had gotten me fired. One could only hope.

I flipped through my Rolodex and located the business card that Jeffrey Carter had given me the previous evening. I tried both the business and cell phone numbers and got no answer, not even an answering machine or voicemail. That was odd. I couldn't imagine a successful financial advisor being completely out of reach during business hours. I decided I'd try him again later. I flipped the Rolodex back and retrieved another business card.

I stared at the phone, and it stared back at me. I knew if I thought about it too long, I wouldn't do it, so I snatched the receiver off the hook and punched in half the phone number, realized what I was doing and hung up. I rocked in my leather chair and continued to stare at the phone. I tried again, completing the number but hanging up after one ring.

"Do you really want to do this to yourself?" I asked aloud. When no one protested, I sighed and dialed the number again. Before I had a chance to reconsider, the call was answered.

"Boggs Investigations." I recognized the shrill voice as belonging to Doug Boggs's secretary and mother, Loretta. Loretta didn't care much for me. She was holding a grudge because I had beaten the tar out of her son when we had a disagreement during Ryan McGregor's murder investigation. Doug was over it; I wish she'd get there.

"Hi, Mrs. Boggs," I said, forcing smarmy cheer into my voice that fooled no one. "This is Dwayne Morrow. Is Doug in?"

There was a stiff pause during which I could hear hot breath huffing through Loretta's nostrils. Finally, she said, "And what, may I ask, is this regarding?"

"Business," I said.

"What kind of business?"

"The kind of business that earns Doug money," I said, resisting the urge to tell her whatever business it was, it wasn't any of hers. "I'd like to make an appointment to come and see him."

I heard papers riffling in the background as Loretta flipped through Doug's appointment book. Much of what Loretta did was for show, trying to give the illusion Boggs Investigations was a bigger outfit than it actually was. I figured Doug was probably in his office taking a nap.

"We're pretty booked up this week," she said. "I might be able to squeeze you in—"

I heard a gruff voice in the background, but Loretta's hand slid over the mouthpiece so I couldn't hear what was being said. The exchange was heated and getting hotter, then there was a sudden quiet. For a moment I thought Loretta had hung up, but then her hand slid away from the mouthpiece, and I could nearly hear her hot breath in my ear once more.

"Please hold, I'll connect you now," she muttered.

There was a click followed by a hint of Muzak, then Doug Boggs picked up the phone. "Boggs."

"Hey Doug, it's Dwayne Morrow," I said, knowing full well he knew who was on the other end. He enjoyed playing his part, and who was I to rob him of the pleasure? I had a favor to ask, and it was going to hurt like hell. May as well keep him in a good mood.

"Good to hear from you, buddy," he said. I could tell he was chewing on the butt of a cigar from the way he formed his words. I also knew the cigar wasn't lit, because if it were, his mother would be raising all kinds of holy hell. "Long time no see. What can I do ya for?"

"I was wondering if I might be able to stop by for a few minutes tomorrow," I said.

I could almost see Doug sit bolt upright in his chair. "What's going on? You got some work to throw my way? Something that needs the ol' Boggs expertise?"

"Maybe," I said. "It's more of a business proposition, but I'd rather wait until tomorrow to get into it. What time?"

"Aw, any time after eleven, I guess," he said. "I have to admit, business ain't been too good. I could sure use anything you could throw my way."

"We'll talk tomorrow," I said. "Thanks." I replaced the receiver, my hand lingering on the handset. What had I just done? Doug Boggs may have saved my life once, but to be his protégé? It was really an issue of competency.

I let my head drop back onto the blotter.

*****

I tried Jeffrey Carter at one o'clock, three and again at five. There was still no answer at either of his numbers. I wondered if maybe Geneva had gone completely insane, and the family was spending a quiet day having her committed. That would be too good to be true. I sent a short email to the address on his business card asking him to call me at his earliest opportunity.

I figured I should call my attorney, Sally Sheaffer, and let her know what had happened at Dial Tech, just in case I needed to do something to prevent Geneva from doing any more damage to my reputation. It probably wouldn't hurt to get my side of the story on the record before Geneva started running to the Dublin police (or worse yet, the press) with her wild accusations. Still, I couldn't bring myself to make the call quite yet. I didn't want to have to actually admit I'd been fired.

I wandered around the house straightening up a bit—nothing too heavy duty. When I bought the farmhouse, the realtor had assumed I was raising a large family. Why else would I want such a large house? There are five bedrooms and a spacious bathroom on the second floor. An enormous living room extends the entire width of the front of the house, one end of which I've converted into a dining room. Beyond that is the hallway which bisects the house, leading to your choice of the kitchen, my den or the other full-service potty. There's also a leaky, musty basement which we will not discuss. My furnishings leaned towards overstuffed, second-hand pieces which I grouped for comfort, not aesthetic appeal. As I collected socks I had discarded at the foot of the couch, I spotted the brown-wrapped package with the flash drives sitting on the end table. I muttered a string of curses and headed for the phone in the hall.

After locating the number for *The Columbus Dispatch* in the phonebook, I called the switchboard and asked for Brady Garrett. I was immediately transferred to his voicemail. After the tone, I said, "Brady, this is Dwayne Morrow. You left something at my place that I think Nina Crockett would be very interested in." Then I hung up the phone. I wondered if it was even possible to make him sweat.

After doing everything I possibly could without the use of an electrical appliance, I went to the kitchen to heat up a bowl of tomato soup for supper. Dexter coiled and twisted at my feet, determined to obtain his own reward or throw me to the floor trying. I finally relented and poured some odd-smelling, crunchy nuggets into his bowl. I had just retrieved a Pepsi from the refrigerator and taken my seat at the small table in the kitchen when I heard a knock at the front door.

More cursing.

I crossed the hallway and went into the living room. Through the large window behind the dining area, I could see the white Lexus parked in my driveway. It seemed Melanie wouldn't be satisfied until she had actually ripped my heart into pieces. I opened the door. She stood with her arms folded defiantly, her eyes liquid fire, her chin jutted out, her foot tapping impatiently. Just over her shoulder was Jordan McCleary, and if I wasn't mistaken, he was smirking.

CHAPTER ELEVEN

"Aren't you even going to invite us in?" asked Melanie. Her blonde hair spilled freely over her shoulders, and she tucked a few errant strands behind each ear.

"Sure," I said, stepping aside to allow them entry. "Come in."

Jordan hesitated, then said, "I'll wait out here, if that's all right. I'm allergic to the cat, remember?"

"I forgot," said Melanie, turning to him and placing a hand on his arm. "Are you sure you don't mind? This shouldn't take long."

"It's fine. I'll be right here if you need me." Jordan crossed the porch and deposited himself onto the swing at the far end, brushing imaginary flecks of dirt from his expensive navy slacks. He wore a steel-gray sweater that I didn't suspect was from Walmart. I didn't like the implication of his words, as if I might pose some physical threat to Melanie. My response was just short of a growl. I wanted to wipe the smirk right off of his face.

I followed Melanie into the living room and closed the front door. I didn't see any reason to share our conversation with McCleary. The room was silent for a moment, Melanie lingering in front of the fireplace, her back presented to me. She was beautiful when she was angry, and at that moment, she had never looked better. She wore a pale blue sleeveless sundress underneath a cream-colored knit wrap, which she hugged to herself to combat the dropping temperature.

"So, what's up?" I asked, stepping up behind her.

113

She whirled around and slapped me, knocking my bottom teeth into my upper ones. "How dare you do this to me," she hissed. Her voice was frightening in its steadiness. "I *trusted* you."

I massaged my throbbing jaw. "You trusted *me*? What about *you*?"

"What in the hell are you talking about?"

I indicated the porch with a wild, sweeping gesture. "Your boyfriend. Jordan McClearasil."

"Real mature."

"I don't feel mature right now."

Melanie sighed. "So, you ran right out and hooked up with the first woman you could find, never mind that she looks like a circus mutant?"

"Nina Crockett does *not* look like a circus mutant!"

"She looks rather horse-like to me."

"How about Mr. Ivy League out there? Could you go for anyone *older*, Mel? I mean, good Lord, he could be your *father*," I said, instantly regretting it. Melanie's childhood had not been good. Her stepfather had physically and sexually abused all five of his children, and as Melanie was the oldest, she was usually the first to suffer his indignities.

Melanie's face twisted in a valiant effort to keep her emotions under control. "If you know what's good for you, you won't say anything like that ever again," she warned. "Jordan McCleary is my English professor in college. We're attending a writer's convention together, just as I told you."

"I've never heard of a convention that requires you to spend the night with your professor in a hotel," I said.

"What makes you think we spent the night together?"

"McCleary made his intentions clear," I said.

She rolled her eyes and a strangled sound of exasperation passed through her clenched teeth. "So that must be the way it is, huh? Just because Jordan said so? You've just *assumed* we shared a room. Why didn't you *talk* to me? We've been through this before—if you want an answer, ask a question. Don't you dare try to guess what's going on inside my head!"

I didn't know how to respond. I struggled for a defense, anything to maintain my dignity. It didn't register immediately she was telling me there was nothing between her and her professor.

"So how long have you been seeing her?" Melanie asked.

"Who?"

She looked at me with disappointment. "Don't play games with me."

"Nina? I went out with her once."

Melanie's laugh was half-hearted. "Just the one time, huh? And on that one date, you managed to get your picture in the paper. How stupid do you think I am? I'm tired, Dwayne. Maybe it'd be better if we just let things go."

Suddenly, everything was crystal clear to me. In this particular scenario, I was the mustachioed villain. I had leapt to conclusions that were about to come true if I didn't make the correct move and quickly.

I reached across to softly touch Melanie's cheek, but she winced and pulled away. "I'm sorry," I said, my hand still hanging helplessly in midair. "I was wrong. I should've talked to you. And I really did only go out with Nina once. I spent the whole evening talking about you. If you don't believe me, you can call her right now." I offered my cell phone to her.

Melanie shook her head, and I could see excess moisture collecting at the corners of her eyes. "We've waited so long for the timing to be right. Do you really think so little of me? Did you think I was that impatient?" She again turned her back to me, but not before I saw a tear escape and roll down her cheek. "After what Ryan did, the thought of you cheating was more than I could bear."

Her late husband had not only been unfaithful but had sired a child with another woman during the course of his infidelities. For Melanie, this was a violation of two of the most basic of civilized concepts, honor and integrity.

I placed my hands on her shoulders. She tried to pull away, but my gentle grip was firm. I turned her around and looked deep into her wounded eyes. She was trying to remain composed, but her lower lip was trembling, and the floodgates were cracking. My remorse was an instantaneous collection of bile in the back of my throat. I cupped her chin in my hand and said, "Please believe me, I would never intentionally hurt you."

Her chin quivered, and her broken voice said, "You didn't even try to follow me last night. It was like you didn't even *care*—"

I felt about two inches tall. It had never occurred to me to visit things from Melanie's perspective. "I've never cared about anything more," I said solemnly. I pulled her toward me, and this time she came, her small frame wracked with sobs she could no longer contain. My own eyes began to mist over as I felt her body convulse in my arms, and I knew how very deeply I had hurt her. Her arms were locked around my waist, holding me tightly. I buried my nose in her hair and smelled strawberries. I found myself repeating my apology softly, over and over, hoping to undo whatever damage I had caused.

We stood together in front of the cold fireplace until Melanie's hiccupping sobs faded. She took a step backward, nervously dabbing at her nose and eyes, embarrassed by her display of emotion. She rarely wore makeup, so there were no black trails of mascara to blot. The tip of her nose was red, as were her swollen eyes, but the emerald irises shone in the waning daylight. She was the most beautiful woman I had ever known. I used my thumb to wipe away the last of her tears, my eyes on hers. We stared at each other in silence, my hands stroking her soft cheeks, her hands on my hips.

When our lips touched, it was a soft, gentle convergence. We had only kissed once before, in the middle of a crowded dance floor. It had been a kiss borne of lust and alcohol. Now, we touched each other gently and carefully, almost reassuringly. In her eyes, I saw the need reflected in my own. It wasn't a physical need, but an emotional one reminding me of how delicate and frequently unappreciated human relationships are. This was more than a passing fling; Melanie and I belonged together. Trust was essential if we were going to make it.

We reluctantly stepped apart, but our fingers remained interlocked. "I hate it when I cry," Melanie said.

"I hate that I made you cry. I'm so sorry, Mel."

She nodded her head. "I know."

"Let me make it up to you."

Her face lightened. "How?"

"Stick around and find out."

There was a soft peck at the door, and we were suddenly reminded we had left grim-faced Jordan McCleary on the porch for quite some time. I didn't feel the enormous sense of victory I had expected. Instead, I felt a little sorry for the professor. As I glanced at Melanie, I certainly understood his motivation.

"Oh, God," she said softly. "What am I going to say to him? I didn't even know he was interested."

I had no advice to offer. She extracted her hand from mine and crossed to the door, opening it and stepping over the threshold. She pulled the door shut behind her, and for a moment, I was afraid she was leaving. I could hear the cadence of conversation, but I forced myself to behave and grant them a moment's privacy. I couldn't help but sneak an occasional glance through the living room window, however. I have to admit, McCleary took the news well. There was no arguing nor was there an unpleasant scene. McCleary was betrayed only by the slight droop of his shoulders after a moment. I watched him smile earnestly before returning to his car.

Melanie opened the door and came in, her eyes freshly damp. "Now, I don't want you to be upset with him. He really is a sweet man. I don't think his intentions were bad. And we still have the rest of the conference to attend together."

"This won't hurt your grade, will it?"

Melanie waved my concern away. "No way. He's not that type—"

Tires skidded in gravel and angry horns dueled in front of my house. I went to the door and threw it open, expecting to hear the crunch of metal at any second. Melanie was right behind me, and we crossed to the edge of the porch.

They could have only missed by inches. McCleary had backed out of the driveway blindly, pulling right in front of Brady Garrett's red Saturn. Brady had jumped from the driver's seat and was pacing a territorial line between his car and McCleary's. I could see Brady's mouth flapping from where I stood, his words erupting like gunfire. McCleary had rolled down his window and was nodding his head, agreeing with whatever Brady was saying and waving a hand in surrender. He shifted his Lexus into drive and pulled forward, but Brady stalked along with him, his mouth spewing obscenities at extraordinary velocity.

"Hey! Garrett!" I shouted, and Brady's head whipped around to fix on me. "Leave the guy alone, will ya? You've got more important things to worry about."

Brady gnashed his teeth together, pivoted and stalked back to his car, backing up and pulling exaggeratedly away from the side of the road to allow McCleary a wide berth.

"I'll see you tomorrow, Jordan, okay?" Melanie called. Jordan nodded, his pallor almost completely gray. He waved weakly before driving off.

After McCleary had passed, Brady whipped his car into the driveway and cut the engine. He got out of the car and stormed across the lawn toward the porch, his curly black hair bobbing with each step.

"Who's this joker?" Melanie asked under her breath.

"I'll catch you up in a bit," I said. I turned toward Brady. "What's the matter, *dude*? You seem agitated."

Brady tromped up the stairs and glowered at me, his face a deep crimson. "Let me get my heart rate back to normal, for God's sake! Who was that asshole? He pulled out right in front of me!"

"Let it go, Brady," I said.

"Tell me you didn't give those drives to Nina Crockett," he said. He noticed Melanie and gave her an appreciative head-to-toe, smiling crookedly. "And who's this?"

Melanie extended a hand. "Melanie McGregor. And you are?"

"Brady Garrett," he said, taking her hand and making a big spectacle of himself by kissing it. "I'm a good friend of Dwayne's."

I laughed, which broke his distracted gaze and returned his attention to me. "Yeah, right. Good one."

"Tell me you still have the drives," said Brady.

"I told you I didn't want anything to do with them," I said. I was enjoying watching him squirm, and boy, was he ever squirming. His mouth twitched nervously in and out of a smile, his eyes glistened under furrowed eyebrows.

"If you gave those drives to Crockett, you will have cost a very nice person her job," he said.

"I won't have cost her anything," I said. "I wasn't the one who copied government property and distributed it unlawfully. The FBI is probably better off without her."

Brady's mouth pressed together in a frustrated grimace. "I would have never given those to you if I thought I couldn't trust you with them."

I laughed again. "Now isn't the time to be lecturing me on ethics, Brady. You shouldn't have had that data in the first place. What's more, I *told* you I didn't want anything to do with it, and you came back and left them on my porch anyway. Anyone could've gotten them."

I watched him struggle for something else to say, some other way to justify his actions, but for once, he seemed at a loss for words. He sat down hard on the top step of the porch. "I could really get in a lot of trouble for this," he said.

"I suppose you could," I said. "If I had actually turned the drives over to Nina. Lucky for you, I didn't. Now take them and get them away from me."

Relief flooded over his features as he leapt to his feet. I led the way across the porch and into the house, Brady following close at my heels and Melanie bringing up the rear.

"I hate to interrupt," she said. "But I'm completely lost. What drives?"

Brady turned and offered one of his patented smiles. "Ms.—McGregor, did you say it was? Why does that sound familiar? Oh, yes! Ryan McGregor was your husband, wasn't he?"

Melanie cocked her head quizzically and nodded. "How did you know?"

"From all of the publicity Dwayne received at the time," he said. "The story was quite big up here, hometown hero and all. I must've read your name a couple dozen times."

Melanie smiled. "The drives—?"

"It's nothing, Melanie," I said. "You don't want to know."

She looked at me and scowled. "Of course I do. Didn't I just ask? Brady," she said, ignoring me and turning to Brady. "Tell me about the drives."

Brady made himself comfortable on my sofa while Melanie perched on a chair across from him. I sighed, relegated to touring the room and turning on lamps; the sun had almost completely set, and long shadows had fallen over the living room.

"Have you been following the news about the serial killer?" asked Brady.

"The Eviscerator? Of course. I think everyone in the tri-state area has heard of him," she said.

"I'm a reporter with *The Columbus Dispatch*," he said. "I've been following the Eviscerator story very closely. Many of the articles you've read were probably mine. I've been trying to get an inside angle on the story, present it in a truly unique way. Dwayne seems to be of the opinion that I'm merely grandstanding, and I must admit, I wouldn't mind the exposure. But what I really want to do is catch this bastard before he kills anyone else."

"I'm not really following," said Melanie. "What does this have to do with the drives?"

"Bear with me, kind lady," said Brady, with another dazzling smile. I groaned and rolled my eyes. Brady continued, "I was hoping to enlist Dwayne's assistance, but he doesn't seem to be interested in doing his civic duty."

I aimed a finger at him. "Now that's bullshit, Brady, I—"

"Enlist his assistance how?" asked Melanie.

"I have some information on those drives, file backups from the computers of each of the victims—"

I cut Brady off. "I don't want to hear any more about this! Melanie, this stuff he's talking about is classified. It belongs to the FBI. He's got a source on the inside that leaked this out to him, and I don't want it in my house!"

"Why do you think this information is valuable?" Melanie asked Brady, completely oblivious to my protest.

"I'm looking for some kind of link," said Brady. "Something that might tie the victims together in a way that's been overlooked. To tell you the truth, I'm not even sure if the term serial killer applies. The victims don't fit the standard profile for a serial killing. There isn't an obvious common thread."

"Don't you think the FBI has computer specialists looking over this same information?" asked Melanie.

"Maybe—probably—I don't know. Admittedly, it's a shot in the dark, but I've discovered some similarities that I don't know enough about computers to explain. That's why I hoped Dwayne would look at them."

I shook my head. "No way."

"What kind of similarities?" asked Melanie.

"Folder names that were identical on each of the machines," said Brady.

I laughed. "That doesn't mean anything. There would be plenty of matching file names on the computers if they were running the same operating system. I'm assuming they were Windows?"

"Three were, one was a Mac," he said.

I frowned. I wasn't overly familiar with Macs, but I wasn't as cocksure about my easy explanation anymore. Would there be similar folder names between different operating systems? I honestly didn't know.

"Each had a hidden file folder named 'Moo'," said Brady.

"Moo?" repeated Melanie. "You mean like a cow?"

Brady nodded. "Do you know of any program that would generate that particular file folder?"

I sat down in the bucket chair across from the couch. I had to admit, I was intrigued. I didn't know of any software that created a folder called, 'Moo.' "Did you look inside these folders?" I asked.

"Yeah," said Brady. "They were all empty. It really didn't make sense to me." He looked at me expectantly.

I debated for a moment, wrestling with the notion. If I were to get caught with the drives in my possession, I could get arrested. If I were arrested, I would forego any possibility of obtaining a private investigator's license—remaining felony-free was also a prerequisite. But if I could find a pattern that might help find this guy, stop him before he kills anyone else—*wasn't* it my civic duty? I looked to Melanie, but her face was neutral.

"I'm going to have to think about it, Brady," I said. "I really don't want any trouble."

Brady pursed his lips and nodded slowly. "That's all I can ask, man. I'm going to leave the drives here with you. That way, if you decide to look at them, they'll be right here. Don't wait too long. We might really have something here."

"I'll call you tomorrow evening," I said. "I'm tied up all afternoon."

Brady nodded and let himself out. The package with the drives mocked me from where it sat on the end table.

The phone rang just as Melanie was about to start grilling me for details. I said a silent thanks for the small reprieve and ducked into the hall to grab the cordless. "Hello?"

"Good evening, Mr. Morrow. Jeffrey Carter." The thin voice was sharp and unfriendly.

"Hi, Jeffrey. I've been trying to reach you all day but couldn't leave a message. I wanted to talk to you about your mother and what happened today."

"Yes, well, I don't think it would be advisable for us to discuss the matter without the presence of our attorneys," he said.

My words dried up, and my mouth dropped open. "Excuse me?" I finally managed.

"I didn't realize the validity to Mother's complaint, Mr. Morrow. Had I known, I would have never visited you in the first place. You need professional help."

I couldn't believe what I was hearing. Geneva had apparently convinced her son I had sexually harassed her. Why was that so easy to believe? I was beginning to get a complex. "I didn't do anything, Jeffrey. She's telling everyone I did something that I didn't do—"

"I really don't think it's appropriate for us to be discussing this," he said stiffly. The line went dead in my ear.

"Who was that?" asked Melanie.

We moved into the living room and sat next to each other on the sofa. I recounted the Geneva Carter fiasco, omitting only the part in which I found the mutilated victim in the alley. I didn't want to think about that, much less talk about it. When I finished, Melanie's eyes were ablaze with fury.

"How can she get away with this?" she demanded. "This is ridiculous! It would have to be her word against yours. There can't be witnesses to something that never happened."

"I'm getting a little scared," I said. "I think I should call my attorney in the morning."

"That would probably be wise," she said.

"I've never been fired before," I groused. "It was humiliating."

Melanie stroked the side of my face, cocking her head to the side and studying my features. "You look tired," she said.

I grinned. "This has been the most exhausting day I've ever lived through."

"Why don't you take me back to the hotel," she said. "I've got a workshop in the morning, and you need to get some rest."

My grin faltered. "I thought you were going—I mean, I thought we—"

She smiled. "What do you say we make a date," she said.

"A date?"

"Uh-huh," she said, getting to her feet and pulling me to mine. "Tomorrow night, let's go have a nice dinner, catch up on everything that's happened the past few months, maybe a little dancing—"

"I don't dance."

"I seem to recall you do okay," she said. "Then we'll come back here, light a fire in the fireplace—"

"And?"

"Who knows?" Melanie's smile was slightly wicked.

*****

We drove into town in comfortable silence. Melanie was fascinated by the city traffic and the downtown architecture. She stared at the Leveque Tower with the wonder of a child, and I realized I had never taken her on a proper tour of the city. Columbus isn't the biggest city in the continental United States, but compared to my hometown of Lymont, it is enormous.

We decided it was best to drop Melanie at the curb in front of the Renaissance so as not to exacerbate Jordan's discomfort. As she slid out of her seat, Melanie asked, "Are you going to do it?"

"Do what?"

"The drives."

"I don't know yet."

She nodded. "I think you should consider it."

"I will," I said. She smiled, leaned across the seat and kissed me. "I'll call you tomorrow."

"You better," she said, trotting off toward the hotel entrance.

I drove home in a state of semi-bliss. All of my anxieties about Melanie had evaporated, and I hoped I might finally get a good night's sleep.

It was only a little after ten, but it felt much later. I wanted to try and get an early start to Lymont in the morning. If I was going to actually try and partner up with Doug Boggs, I was going to have to do it before I had a chance to reconsider.

When I pulled into my driveway, I sensed immediately something was wrong. I distinctly remembered turning the porch light on before Melanie and I had left. It was almost automatic since my house had been ransacked the previous fall. Without the porch light, my house stands alone in a sea of shadows, something I don't much enjoy coming home to. The porch was dark now, and odd shapes leapt across the facade of the house as my headlights swept its width. I had left a light on in my living room, and it still burned behind the curtain, casting a small square of light onto the wooden floor of the portico.

I approached the porch slowly, feeling a little foolish. The bulb had probably just burned out. That was all. My ears, however, remained alert, scanning for any unusual noises.

Other than night sounds, there was nothing to hear.

125

As I neared the porch, I saw a small bundle at the base of the screen door. From where I stood in the yard, it looked like a rabbit, hunched up and frozen with fright, its ears pressed back against its body so as not to protrude. It couldn't be a skunk, could it? I paused, weighing the option. I didn't think so. The shape was all wrong. It wasn't right for a cat or a dog and was looking less and less like a rabbit the closer I got. It wasn't until I climbed the steps that I could actually determine what it was.

It was a foot.

CHAPTER TWELVE

Red and blue lights pulsated, pushing back the night with garish frequency. I had waited outside for the authorities to arrive, calling them from my cell phone. I wasn't about to go in the house until I'd been given an all clear. From an aerial view, my property looked as if it were under siege. Policemen and FBI agents swarmed, searching for clues—and for the rest of the body. I had already been questioned by a handful of investigators but didn't have much to contribute. Although no one had come right out and said it, there wasn't a doubt in anyone's mind this was the work of the Eviscerator. The severed foot appeared to be female, but it was hard to be certain. The prints had been seared from each toe as well as the pads on the bottom of the foot. The only indication that it had once belonged to a woman was the bright red polish on the toenails. None of the previous victims were missing any body parts, so the implication was clear. The Eviscerator was accelerating.

Nina's successor, a grim-faced man named Arthur Steele, had spoken with me briefly and watched my responses intently. It was like an unspoken accusation, as if finding a body a few days earlier and now a body part was entirely too coincidental.

Ten minutes after the police arrived, Brady Garrett pulled into my driveway, his eager eyes surveying the scene. He must have heard the report on the police scanner and headed over. In an odd way, it was a relief to see someone I knew, even if it was Brady.

"What's going on?" he asked.

"After you left, I took Melanie back to her hotel downtown. When I came home, I had a present waiting for me on the doormat," I said. I knew whatever I told him would appear in the paper, but I was too tired to care.

"What kind of present?" he asked.

"A human foot," I said, and Brady visibly blanched.

"Have the cops found—anything else?" he asked.

I shook my head. "Not so far."

Brady started networking the scene, sticking his nose into private conversations and gathering tidbits of information to include in his story. As I watched him get ejected from one conversation after another, a dark thought came to me. Just two nights ago, Brady had deposited the parcel with the flash drives on my porch. He could've easily repeated the performance tonight, only with a different type of parcel. Of course, that would mean Brady Garrett was a cold-blooded killer, an accusation that can't be made lightly or without some substantial proof. I would've never considered the possibility if I hadn't seen the gleam in his eyes as he pursued his story. He wanted to make a big name for himself. Was he willing to manufacture the news to accomplish his goal? When my car had been taken from Discount Tire Mart, I had considered the possibility Brady was behind it and still couldn't be sure he wasn't.

Brady had just looped the perimeter and was walking toward me when I noticed two of Columbus's finest exiting my house through the front door. The one on the left had a small, brown-wrapped parcel in his hands, holding it away from his body.

"That isn't what I think it is," muttered Brady from behind me.

Shit! I winced and nodded almost imperceptibly.

"Mr. Morrow?" said the nameless officer who was holding the package. "There may not be any reason for alarm, but this was in your living room on an end table. There's no address on it, even though it looks as if it's been prepped to mail. Do you know anything about it?"

Thank God! They hadn't opened the package. By nature, I'm a miserable liar. I tend to sabotage my own efforts with conflicting stories that won't stop pouring from my lips. The pressure to perform was high; if I screwed this up, I could kiss any chance I had of becoming a PI goodbye.

"Um, yes," I said. "It belongs to a client of mine. I hadn't gotten around to addressing it."

"Do you mind if we have a look inside?" the officer asked, giving the package an exploratory shake.

"Why?" I asked, and I thought the word came a little too quickly. "I mean, it's just some flash drives with hardware drivers and backup files."

"Then you won't mind if we take a look," said the officer. He already had a finger tucked into the mailing paper and was prying the tape away from the flaps. I chanced to look at Brady, but his anxious expression did nothing to calm my nerves.

The brown mail wrap fell away, revealing a small cardboard box. The policeman pulled the carton tape from across the top and reached in to extract the flash drives. My breath caught in my lungs and refused to budge, one way or the other. He examined the drives from all angles.

"Sorry," he said with a half-hearted nod. He tucked them back into the box and handed it to me before walking away with his partner to rejoin the others in the house.

A fine trickle of cold sweat needled its way between my shoulder blades, and I finally exhaled. Brady looked uneasily at me. "That was close," he said.

Looking into the box, I could see each was marked with an unintelligible code, written in precise, black fine-line marker that could have meant anything at all. I don't know what I expected. Secret FBI Data Drive 1, 2, 3, etc.? Still, the experience had taken another layer from the lining of my stomach, and I could still taste the bitter acid burning the back of my throat.

Brady darted off again, in search of an informant—*any* informant. I leaned against the hood of my Optima and watched the officers work like an army of ants, scouring for any clues that might lead them to this monster.

*****

By the time I made it to bed, the digital clock read 3:23 AM. Despite my exhaustion, I stared at the ceiling, unable to sleep.

Special Agent Steele had spoken with me briefly before he left. There was no sign of forced entry nor any indication the house had been entered. There were no footprints, fingerprints or tire tracks. It was as if the killer had floated down to make his grisly deposit before flying away.

There was no sign of the rest of the body, either.

Steele left me his card with a special hotline number and asked me to call him with anything I thought might be relevant. He warned me in a curt, no-nonsense monotone there was a possibility I was being targeted by the killer. He didn't believe it was an accident the foot had been left at my door—and I didn't believe it, either. My name and face had been in the papers since I had discovered the body of Tina Barlow. A car would be patrolling the area at regular intervals until they felt it was secure. In the meanwhile, it was probably a good idea if I stayed indoors after dark, keeping the door bolted and the security system armed.

And I was supposed to sleep?

*****

I finally drifted off as the sun began to rise. The alarm clock began its shrill scream only three hours later, and I dragged myself like a zombie to the shower. Once inside, I stood under the heavy stream of water, the temperature as high as I could tolerate. I slowly worked my way to consciousness as the last of the shampoo ran out of my hair.

I was pleased to note there were no new body parts on my porch when I crossed to my car. Narrow bands of clouds strolled through the brilliant blue sky, and it was almost possible to pretend the grisly discovery of the previous evening had only been a dream. The temperature had now dipped into the forties, and I wore a navy barn coat over my sweater. It was the closest thing I had to a trench coat, and Doug Boggs was big on optics.

My hometown, Lymont, is a hundred miles southwest, bordering on the Ohio River. The economy seems to slide downhill as you drive south along US 23, the towns smaller, the cars older. People don't drive the same in rural areas as on the interstates, either. Everything is slow and steady, with a high frequency of sightseeing. Once you've adapted to city traffic, the frustration is nearly enough to cause a stroke.

The geography undergoes a dramatic shift south of Chillicothe, the flat land of Northern Ohio giving way to rolling hills which extend to the state line and beyond. Despite the relative poverty of the area, the landscape is, at times, extraordinary. This was not one of those times. It was March, and the trees were still huddled in naked groups, waiting for spring to come and redecorate their limbs.

As if in ominous prelude, the narrow band of clouds I had admired earlier widened into dismal gray blankets which shrouded the rest of the sky. By the time I reached Waverly, a light drizzle had begun to fall. I turned on my headlights and set my wipers to intermittent. Once I turned west on US 52 in Portsmouth, the rain had turned to a downpour, and thunder rumbled through the hills and valleys.

I finally reached Lymont and headed straight for the small downtown district, which consisted of a handful of limping businesses and more its share of empty buildings. I drove along Dennison, counting the numbered streets as I passed. When I reached Second, I turned right and eased to the curb in front of a shabby, two-story building which was home to three separate addresses. The last time I had been here, there was a realtor in the slot on the right, but the space now stood ironically empty, a FOR RENT sign in the window with another realtor's number below it. On the left corner of the building was Reminger's Bouquets, a family-operated business which had been in Lymont for generations. There was a recessed entrance in the middle of the building, opening on a narrow staircase leading upward. A tacky, illuminated letter board was parked on the sidewalk, pointing its flashing arrow at the doorway. It read, *Doug Boggs, Master Detective, Spy on your Hole Family! Ask About My Groop Rates! Walk-Ins Welcome.*

I sat with my hands clenched on the steering wheel, staring at the ridiculous sign. I have a real problem with public displays of illiteracy. If you're going to go to all the trouble of hanging a sign, shouldn't you take a minute and make sure all the words are spelled correctly first?

And I was going to ask this guy for a job. I needed to have my head examined.

There was no imminent break in the rain, so I raced across the sidewalk to the cover of the recessed doorway, managing to sink my foot into a large puddle along the way. Cold water splashed upward and soaked my right leg. So much for staying dry.

I climbed the stairs, which deposited me into a narrow lobby with only one door to choose from. Doug's name was painted on it in military stencil, its alignment a little off-center. I could hear the steady clatter of typewriter keys striking the platen as Loretta occupied herself on the other side of the frosted glass. I steeled myself with a deep breath and went inside.

Loretta's fingers froze on the keyboard as I entered the small, drab outer lobby. Her eyes narrowed as they glared up at me from within the folds of her face. Her lemon-colored hair was piled in an awkward lump atop her head, whole sections of which were held in place by nothing more than gallons of hair spray. Her makeup was a thin Play-Doh mask covering her entire face from forehead to drooping jowls. Her ample frame was barely contained by a lime green polyester pantsuit, the seams stretching in silent screams.

"Good morning, Mrs. Boggs," I said, nodding at her and smiling. "I believe Doug is expecting me."

Loretta arched an eyebrow and regarded me coldly. Without a word, she picked up the receiver of her phone and dialed Doug's extension. "The Morrow boy is here," she said and hung up the phone. She turned to me and said, "I'm callin' the po-lice at the first sound of trouble. You hearin' me?"

I grinned sheepishly. She was never going to let me off the hook for kicking Doug's ass. Fifty years from now, she'll still look at me with the same contempt, the same maternal rage. If I were to partner up with Doug, she would technically become my receptionist. My stomach clenched, and for a moment, I thought I might lose control of my bowels.

I crossed to the inner door which led to Doug's office. Inside, Doug sat behind his desk with his scuffed shoes propped awkwardly on the top. He was chewing one of his unlit cigars, oblivious to the shower of wet tobacco that had sprinkled his chin. His black hair dusted the top of his head in a never-changing military cut. He was a former classmate who had evolved from a nerdy, scrawny teenager into a barrel-chested, stocky blowhard. He had always been preoccupied with anything having to do with guns or artillery, so his career choice hadn't come as a complete surprise to anyone. His preoccupation with protocol was distressing, however, and his endless stories, which were intended to be self-congratulatory, always turned out to be unintentionally self-deprecating.

"Dwayne," he said, with a curt nod of his head. "I have to admit, you got my ear when you called yesterday." He swung his feet back to the ground, severing his gnawed cigar in the process. The wet stub landed in his lap before rolling underneath his desk.

I sat in one of the ugly orange bucket chairs positioned across from Doug. I cleared my throat, hoping I could actually manage the words without becoming physically sick. After a few false starts, I began. "I have a business proposition for you."

Doug leaned forward, his expression comically serious. "I'm all ears."

"Have you ever thought about expanding Boggs Investigations?" I asked.

"I'm always lookin' for ways to bring in new business," he said. "Did you see the special I'm runnin' on the board outside? I thought that would bring people in droves, but so far, all I've got is a bunch of punk kids who rearrange the letters every night to say, 'Pee On Your Entire Family' or 'Ask About My Poop Rate.' Wish I could catch one of those little bastards in the act. I'd—"

"Not like that," I said, shaking my head. "I'm talking about expanding your coverage, taking your business to the next level."

"And how would you suggest I do that?"

"By opening a branch office in Columbus," I said. "The population's higher, so you'd have more clients to choose from—"

"I'm sure competition's higher, too," he interjected.

"Sure, but I think that percentage-wise, you'd still have a bigger slice of the pie than what you have right now in Lymont," I said. "And you'd still be getting your normal business from here, so what would you really have to lose?"

"I can't very well be in two places at the same time," he said. "The nature of the business requires me to be available at a moment's notice to some clients. I don't see where you're goin' with this."

"Where I'm going is this: I propose you open a branch office in Columbus with me handling things at that end." I sat back in my chair and waited for his response.

Doug chewed at his bottom lip while deliberating. "What's in it for you?" he asked. "I thought you were a computer geek."

I scowled a bit. Being called a geek by one who most certainly *is* a geek is a little hard to tolerate. "I still have my consulting business," I said, generously omitting the fact that it was performing quite well financially, unlike Doug's one-man enterprise. (Although Loretta acted as Doug's

134

receptionist, I didn't really count her as an employee because she was also his mother.) "But after everything that happened with Ryan McGregor last year—well, I think I'd make a pretty fine detective."

"And I think I'd make a pretty fine brain surgeon, but I ain't about to go practicin' on my neighbors," Doug said.

"C'mon, man," I said. "I know what I'm up against."

"It ain't simple like that," he said. "I can't just have you runnin' around, doing things any ol' way you please, all in the name of Boggs Investigations. You'll ruin my reputation."

I forcibly suppressed the urge to enlighten Doug about the true nature of his reputation. "I'm not an idiot, Doug. You know me well enough to know that."

"I also know you well enough to know that you ain't got a clue what you're doing. Why, if I hadn't been there when the shit hit the fan awhile back, we'd all be visiting you in Lymont Memorial Cemetery."

This was coming dangerously close to begging, and I was certain the contents of my stomach would not abide that. "I know, Doug, and I appreciate it. But I want to do this. I want to earn my license. I need your help."

"So, you're lookin' to intern with me without actually bein' here, then, right?" he asked, and I was surprised he actually saw through my thinly veiled master plan.

"Well, yeah, kinda," I said.

He pressed his lips together and began shaking his head again. "I really don't think I can help ya out, ol' buddy."

"Why not? It wouldn't cost you any money. I would supply the storefront in Columbus," I said.

"I'm a solo act," he said. "I can't be worryin' about coverin' my back and yours, too. It'd throw me off my game. And I can't just turn you loose on the city of Columbus by yourself. That ain't what they mean when they talk about gettin' two years on-the-job experience. And when I think of what it could do to the name of Boggs Investigations, the business I built with these two hands—"

So far, I was bombing out big time. Why I continued to persist, I don't know. Doug was probably doing me a favor I was too stubborn to recognize.

"First of all," I said, "I never meant to give the impression I was looking to become a freelance vigilante. I'm relying on your expertise to learn the trade—" Maintaining my composure wasn't easy; as I've indicated, I'm not a good liar. "—and I think it would only be fair if you were to take the lion's share of any money I brought in. You could visit your Columbus office anytime you saw fit, but you wouldn't be chained to it."

"Well, of course I'd get the lion's share!" he said. "I'm the owner of this here establishment!"

Loretta promptly burst through the door, her fists clenched at her sides. "Did he hit ya, Dougie? Cause if he did—"

"Everything's fine, Ma," he said. "Dwayne's just making me a business proposition. Thinks I should open a Columbus office and put him in charge of it. Whaddaya think of that?"

Loretta's guffaw emerged from somewhere deep within her rotund body, making her oblong breasts jiggle disconcertingly atop her extended belly. "That'll be the day," she said, wiping a tear from the corner of her eye. She retreated, pulling the door shut behind her. I could hear her laughter continue long after she had gone.

"Ma doesn't think it's such a hot idea," said Doug.

"Do you do everything your mother tells you to? *C'mon!*" I had just about had enough. There was only one thing left to say, and as much as I didn't want to, I wasn't about to walk away empty-handed if I could help it. "I need you."

Doug sighed and readjusted his position in the chair. "At least I agree with you on that much," he said. "*If* I were to do this—and I'm only saying *if*—what kind of profit split did you have in mind?"

"Seventy percent to you, the rest is mine," I said.

He laughed. "No way."

"That's more than fair!" I protested.

"Not even close," said Doug. "I wouldn't even consider it unless I worked hands-on with you for a while. Once you figure the money I'd lose doin' *that*—"

"What kind of split were you thinking?"

"I was thinking of something in the five-to-ten percent range for you."

"That's robbery! You *know* I'd pull my own weight—"

"I don't see that you have a lot of room to squabble," he said. "I was runnin' this business just fine yesterday without Dwayne Morrow. I'll run it just fine tomorrow without him, too."

The urge to crawl across the desk and seize him by the throat passed after I silently counted to ten. "So, what do you say? Are you interested or not?" I asked.

His fingers formed a steeple, the tip of which he placed beneath the end of his nose. "I can't rightly say. I'm going to have to take this under advisement."

"Under advisement? With who, your *mother?*"

He chose to ignore me. "I'll get back to you after I've sorted through it, but understand, any partnership we form will be on my terms and my terms alone. I've got a helluva lot more to lose than you do." He stood, signaling our conversation had just ended.

I got to my feet and dropped a business card onto his blotter. "My home phone and cell number are there," I said. "Let me know when you decide. I really think we could be a great help to each other, and I certainly would appreciate the opportunity to learn from someone I know and—am comfortable with." I had almost said, 'Someone I know and respect', but there was no way *that* was going to escape my lips.

I waggled my fingers in Loretta's direction as I crossed through the outer lobby, and she growled something unintelligible. I trotted down the narrow staircase and stepped back out into the afternoon rain which, if anything, had intensified. I ducked into my car and started the engine, heading north with the distinct feeling I had just wasted my entire afternoon.

CHAPTER THIRTEEN

When I got back home, I had three messages from Brady Garrett, each wondering if I had come to a decision about the flash drives. The disembodied foot had pretty well made up my mind; I planned to look at them in the morning. I started to call Brady to let him know, then decided to leave him hanging for the night. I was still a little pissed about having the damned things thrust on me in the first place. And I had plans for the evening.

I arrived at the Renaissance at seven-thirty. This time, I did the proper thing and went up to Melanie's room to collect her. I was wearing black slacks and a slate blue ribbed V-neck. Never one to wear much cologne, I was hoping I hadn't overdone it (as was my tendency). I thought I looked pretty good, but when Melanie opened the door, my breath was taken away. I had never before seen her look so beautiful. It was a simple, red sleeveless dress which hugged every contour of her well-toned body. She wore no makeup, nor did she need any. Her blonde hair spilled down her back in a careless waterfall cascading midway down her back.

She folded her arms underneath her breasts and leaned against the doorframe, smiling. "You really *have* been working out," she noted, her eyes traveling to my tightened abdomen. Other parts of me were tightening as well. Her grin broadened as I squirmed.

"Thanks for noticing," I said. "So where do you want to have dinner?"

"This is your town," she said. "You choose."

Melanie looked good enough to take to any restaurant in the whole damn city, and I knew I would feel the stares of a thousand jealous so-and-sos throughout the course of the evening. We ended up at a cozy Italian restaurant called Fernando's in Upper Arlington. I didn't want a thousand guys staring at Melanie. Tonight, I wanted her all to myself.

We ordered white wine and made small talk while we waited to place our orders. The tables were cozy, and the ambient lighting was reflected in Melanie's sparkling eyes.

"So, how's the conference?" I asked.

She sipped her wine. "Good. I've met some really interesting people."

"Good," I said. "Is Jordan okay?"

"He really is a sweet man. I'm sure he's fine," she said. The waiter arrived, and we both ordered lasagna.

"You seem to really be into this whole writing thing," I said.

Melanie smiled. "Yes. I think the 'whole writing thing' is pretty fascinating."

"So, what is it that you write?"

"Mostly children's fiction. I used to make up stories for Jasmine all the time. Now I'm putting them down on paper. Jordan thinks they show great promise. So do several of the people I met at the writer's conference."

"Very cool," I said.

"That's kind of what I wanted to talk to you about when I came up," she said. After realizing she wasn't interested in Jordan McCleary, I had forgotten there had even been something she had wanted to discuss. "It's so hard for us to do this thing long distance, you know? I was thinking about checking out some of the schools up here. I've never really been out of Southern Ohio before. I think it would be good to broaden my horizons."

"That'd be wonderful!" I enthused. "How does Jasmine feel about it?"

"I don't know," Melanie said. "I haven't asked her yet. I know she's wild about you, but it isn't like we'd be living with you. She'd have to make

140

all new friends and go to what I can only assume is a much larger school. It'd be a lot of changes for her."

"Changes for both of you," I said.

"I'll find something that pays the bills, get a little apartment somewhere," she said. "It'll be tight until I get through college, but I think the experience would be great. Besides, if you and I are going to get serious, we have to correct this whole geographical situation."

"I want to go with you when you look for an apartment," I said. My first apartment in Columbus had been a fiasco. It was a simple, brick townhouse on the east side of town, just off of Livingston. Shortly after moving in, I found I was surrounded on all sides by teenage gangs, all of whom liked to use the basketball court behind my apartment. My car had been used as bleachers, with as many as twenty foul-mouthed, disrespectful punks parked on it at any given time. I could yell at them all I wanted, but they just laughed and showed me their favorite finger. Once, I called the police to break up the congregation. Four days later, all of my tires were slashed. I didn't want Melanie and Jasmine to unwittingly find themselves in a similar situation.

"That'd be great," she said. "I thought that after I get done with the conference, I would sit Jasmine down and bounce the whole thing off of her. I hope she'll be excited. I don't know what I'll do if she doesn't want to go."

"One step at a time, Mel," I said. "I think Jasmine might surprise you. She already senses there are bigger things beyond Lymont's city limits."

A shadow fell over the table, and I turned to find Brady Garrett grinning down at us, his hands stuffed in his pockets, teetering back and forth on the balls of his feet. "Hey, folks!" he said. "Fancy seeing you here."

"For shit's sake, Brady!" I said, raising the eyebrows of a few nearby patrons. "Can't you see we're on a date?"

The waiter arrived with our lasagna, and Brady stepped back to allow him to put the hot plates on the table. As he started to leave, Brady grabbed his elbow and said, "Bring me one of those, too, wouldja?" Without waiting for an invitation, he pulled a chair up to our table, turned it backwards and straddled it, leaning on his elbows. He was grinning apishly at Melanie, and I could tell she was amused. If you ignored his rodent-like persona, Brady had his own sort of physical charm, I guess.

"So, what brings you to our table, Mr. Garrett?" asked Melanie.

"Brady," he corrected, grinning lasciviously. "Please."

"All right," she said. "Brady."

"I'm going to be sick," I said. "What are you doing, Brady?"

"Hey, I just wondered what you decided about the you-know-whats. I've been trying to reach you all day, but you never called me back," he said.

"I had other things to do," I said. "And I'm busy at the moment, so if you don't mind—"

"Oh, not at all, man," he said. "But hey, since I'm here and all, why don't you fill me in on what happened last night after I left. Did they find any more of the body?"

"*Body*? What body?" Melanie asked. I hadn't mentioned anything to her about the previous evening. I didn't want to spoil what was supposed to be a perfect night. I shouldn't have worried about it. That's what Brady was for.

"Oh, yeah," he said. "Dwayne found a foot on his doorstep. Didn't you say you had just gotten back from taking Melanie to her hotel?" He glanced at me just in time to receive a dirty, rotten glare that both begged and warned him to shut his blithering yap.

Melanie shifted her attention to me. "You didn't say anything about a foot. What's going on? Is it this Eviscerator thing?"

"I think it's pretty coincidental," said Brady. "Especially since Dwayne found the last victim. It's almost like he's singling Dwayne out." I winced.

Melanie's mouth was slightly open in disbelief, her eyes locked on mine as she awaited my response. "I didn't want to upset you," I finally said, and she rolled her eyes.

"So?" asked Brady.

"So what?" I asked.

"Did they find anything else?"

"The FBI doesn't report to me. Now get lost!" I said. "I'll send your food over when it comes."

"How 'bout them drives?" he asked, rising from his chair.

"All right! All right! I'll look at the damn things in the morning," I said. "Now go away!"

Brady leered at Melanie and kissed her hand in another of his ridiculous displays of gloppy affection, then he retreated to the corner of the room where he took a seat at an empty table.

"Is this Brady guy stalking you?" asked Melanie.

"I think so," I said. "It seems like every time I turn around, there he is."

"Do you really think you can help him?"

"I doubt it," I said. "I can't imagine I'll find anything the FBI hasn't already found."

"You never know."

"And that's the only reason I'm going to do it."

Melanie tilted her head and studied my face under the warm ambience of the golden wall sconce. "It must have been awful," she said, her eyes looking beneath my surface. "Are you okay?"

I tried to nod, but the mutilated image of Tina Barlow leapt unbidden into my mind, and I only managed to stiffly jerk my head up and down. "I'm not wild about the idea that this guy has somehow chosen me to be the one to find all his handiwork."

"Why would he do that?" she asked.

"He's a psychopath. He can do any damn thing he wants."

"Did you know any of the victims?" she asked.

The waiter chose that moment to arrive with Brady's lasagna. I allowed him to put it on the table and breeze away before surgically separating the middle layers and adding a thick, secret coating of crushed red pepper. I reassembled the dish when I was satisfied with my work. I then beckoned to another waiter and forwarded the dish to its intended recipient. It's the little things that pick me up.

"No, I didn't know any of them," I said. "The whole thing's very screwy. The victims don't seem to fit any particular pattern. Different ages, sexes, races—it's like he's circumventing all the standard rules of serial killing. Tina Barlow, the girl I found, was paralyzed from the waist down. She was literally a sitting duck. What kind of sick bastard does this type of thing?"

Melanie shook her head, swirling her fork in her dinner. Somehow, conversing about mutilated corpses tends to put a damper on the old appetite. I had already pushed my plate away.

I smiled broadly when I heard Brady jump to his feet and bellow for a glass of water.

"I went to see Doug Boggs today," I said, changing the subject. I was finished with the dead-speak while trying to consume a dish that floated in red sauce.

Melanie's expression soured as if she were smelling fermented eggs. "Ew. Why?"

"Hey, Doug's not so bad," I said. "It's his mother who needs to be locked away."

"You didn't have a good word to say about Doug Boggs until he saved your life."

"Reason enough to reassess anyone, don't you think?"

"I suppose so," she said. "Still, why did you go see him? Did you think he might have some suggestions on how to catch the Eviscerator?"

I laughed. "Good Lord, no! Actually, I was proposing to him we form a business partnership."

Now, it was Melanie's turn to laugh and boy, did she ever. "You've got to be *kidding* me! Was there a reason for this or were you running a high fever?"

"If I'm going to get my PI license, I need two years hands-on experience. As my consulting business is my livelihood, I can't very well apply for a regular position with a PI in Columbus. I'm hoping I can sort of align myself with Doug but not have to see him too awfully much," I said.

"Good luck," said Melanie, sipping her wine. "But from what you've told me, he's too much of a control freak to stay out from underfoot. I'll bet he'll be popping up everywhere, second guessing your ideas, overruling you with his ownership vote."

"I doubt it will be much of an issue," I said. "I don't think he's going to agree to it. He has this ridiculous notion he should actually be *present* while he is acting as my instructor."

"So, what are you going to do?"

I shrugged. "I don't know. Maybe I can find someone here who's flexible with hours."

"Maybe you shouldn't become a PI," said Melanie. "Maybe it's a sign."

I looked at her curiously. "I don't give up that easily. I'm surprised you even suggested it. Do you have a problem with me becoming a private investigator?"

Melanie dabbed at the corners of her mouth with her napkin, but I knew she was buying time to properly formulate her response. "No—it's not that," she said. "I knew you wanted to do this last fall. It's just that—" Her voice trailed away, and she ended up just shaking her head.

"It's just what?" I persisted.

Melanie sighed. "Before, it was something you were *planning* to do, you know? *Someday.* But now that you've actually taken steps towards it, everything you touch seems to turn to shit. Your first unofficial client has gone bonkers and gotten you fired from your consulting assignment—and may still yet bring you up on charges of sexual harassment. In the meanwhile, a sadistic madman who's roaming the streets of Columbus has decided to appoint you town crier, leaving you a rather unusual doorstop as a calling card. Everything's moving so quickly—it scares me a little."

145

"It scares me a lot," I admitted.

"Then why do you want to do it?" she asked.

I pondered the question, trying to bring words together which might describe my motivation. Answering was like trying to describe the color orange to a blind man. "Did you ever do logic problems in puzzle books?" I asked.

"You mean the type where they give you a couple paragraphs of narrative, then expect you to figure out whose first and last names go together, what it is each did, and so on?"

"Yeah," I said. "I fell in love with those as a kid, and I've done them ever since. Working on computers is a lot like that. When a computer system is messed up, the factors must be analyzed logically. If you've done the job correctly, you come to a resolution, and *presto!* The problem is solved. Private investigation is just another form of puzzle. You line up all the little pieces and find there can be only one solution. It's like going to the next level."

Melanie shook her head. "Only on this level, all of the little pieces are armed," she said.

"I don't think what's going on now is representative of how the whole business works," I said. "Doug told me he spends most of his time tailing cheating spouses. I suspect he spends the rest of his time playing solitaire and scratching his ass."

"Doug also lives in Lymont, population 18,000," she said. "Statistics alone indicate he wouldn't run into as many whackos as you would."

"Are you saying you wish I wouldn't become a PI?" I asked. I have to admit, I was surprised by Melanie's hesitancy. When we worked together last year, she seemed to enjoy the pursuit as much as I did. Of course, it was personal then, and maybe that made all the difference.

Melanie slowly exhaled. "I would never ask you to give up something that was important to you," she said after a lengthy pause.

"But it bothers you," I said.

"Of course it bothers me!" she said. "You've got someone breathing down your neck who specializes in dismembering people!"

"I didn't go looking for the Eviscerator," I said. "He came looking for me. I can't sit around doing nothing if there's some way I might be able to help."

"I know," she said with resignation. "But it's going to be hard to sit through my conferences wondering if you're safe, wondering if the Eviscerator has decided to do more than leave you a present."

"My house is secure. After the break-in last fall, I had a state-of-the-art security system installed. It detects forced entry, broken glass—pretty much anything but motion," I said.

"Why not motion?" asked Melanie.

"Dexter would set it off every time he jumped onto the back of the couch," I said. "But someone would have to get inside before motion-tracking would be effective anyway, and no one's going to get inside. I have replaced all of the old, wooden doors with mighty steel ones—the place is nearly a fortress," I said.

"I'm glad you sound so sure," she said. "Because the Eviscerator made it all the way to the other side of that steel door undetected. He walked right up and put a foot on your doormat. That scares the hell out of me."

When put so bluntly, my confidence crawled away like a slug, leaving a cold, slimy trail down my spine. The waiter returned, wondering if we had saved room for dessert. We had barely eaten half of our dinners, yet we both shook our heads and patted our stomachs as if we'd gorged ourselves.

As the waiter glided off to tabulate the final damage to my wallet, I caught the sounds of an animated, one-sided conversation occurring at the edge of my periphery. I turned my head in time to see Brady Garrett jump to his feet, overturning the table in front of him. His airborne lasagna landed in the lap of a startled woman at a neighboring booth. His glassware and dinner plate fell to the floor where they would have broken had it not been for the thick carpeting. The lip of the overturned table came down hard on an older gentleman's foot who sat directly across from Brady, and he howled like a wounded animal. Brady stood stiff as a board, his face bloodless, his cell phone pressed against his ear. He was oblivious to the melee he had caused and the curses which were floating free and easy around him. He wasn't saying anything at all, but the voice on the other end of the phone apparently required no response.

"What's going on?" asked Melanie, as a rescue team of kitchen help emerged from the back to try and restore order to the dining area. "Is Brady having a seizure?"

I shook my head and watched Brady's complexion continue to wax and wane. His knuckles stood out white against his dark, curly hair, clutching the phone as if it were the one thing holding him to this earth. His head began to nod slowly, but he remained silent, listening. Then, his grip on the phone was abruptly lost, and the small, black piece of plastic wizardry dropped to the ground. He half-stumbled, half-ran from the room, making a beeline for the exit.

"Something's wrong," I said. I tossed a credit card on the table. "Pay for ours and Brady's, then meet me in the parking lot."

I got up from the table and cut a path through disgruntled patrons, some of whom were still trying to clean tomato sauce speckles from their garments. Brady had already left the building by the time I worked my way to the exit, but I could see him in the parking lot, getting into his red Saturn. His expression was one I'd never seen before. His eyes were widened, and his mouth hung stupidly open; he looked completely shell-shocked. I hurried out into the parking lot, waving my arms wildly overhead. Dammit, where was Melanie? If she didn't hurry up, I was going to lose him!

As it turned out, I needn't have worried. He started his car and threw it into reverse in one gear-grinding motion, rocketing out of his parking spot and plowing into the trunk of a silver Ford Crown Victoria, which happened to be backing up directly behind him. A befuddled oldster emerged from the Crown Vic, scratching the top of his snow-covered head in bewilderment. Brady tried to pull the car forward, but his rear bumper had become one with the bumper of the Ford, and all he managed to do was spin his tires. He got out of the Saturn and repeatedly slammed his hands against the roof of his car, screaming unintelligible nonsense. The owner of the Crown Vic took a hesitant step backward, afraid Brady's assault may not be limited to the top of his own car.

I bridged the gap between us, increasingly alarmed by Brady's bizarre behavior. The color had returned to his face in full force, his cheeks so flushed I thought his head might explode. More distressing than that was the wetness around his eyes, shining in the dim haze of the sodium arc lighting.

Brady spotted me, and words flew from his mouth in a tangled heap. "I've got to *GO!* I was supposed to call, but I didn't—and then they called, and—Oh, my *GOD!* It's all my fault, all my fault—"

Melanie appeared behind me, her breath visible as it floated heavenward. "What's going on?" she whispered, and I shook my head.

I grabbed Brady by the shoulders and shook him firmly. His eyes seemed to focus briefly before clouding over again. "She wasn't supposed to do that, you know—I've told her a million times, but she won't—"

"*BRADY!*" I put as much force as I could into the word and launched it three inches from his nose. "Calm down, man. Tell me what's going on. Maybe I can help."

His face contorted grotesquely before sobs exploded from deep with him. He doubled over, and I had to physically hold him up.

"Will you take me? *Please?* I have to go." His voice was like a frightened child's, something I never expected from the pompous newsman. His eyes pleaded with me desperately as fresh waves of tears lapped at the shores of his cheeks.

"I don't understand, Brady," I said. "Where? Where do you want to go? What's happened? Who is 'she'?"

For a brief moment, he found a small, internal reservoir of composure and pulled himself together. "Nikki," he says. "My fiancée. They want me to come and identify—her body."

CHAPTER FOURTEEN

I squirmed in the driver's seat as we drove to the Franklin County Coroner's Office. Brady sat glassy-eyed and slumped in the passenger seat, his face turned to the window and shining from tears spent. His mouth continued to move, although rarely did any sound escape. I didn't know what to say. How can you comfort someone in a situation like this? Especially someone you don't particularly like? I wouldn't suggest it might not be Nikki; that would be too cruel. If the police had reason enough to call Brady, they must be pretty sure.

I had so many questions I wanted to ask. I already knew the answer to my first. If we were going directly to the Coroner's Office, I doubted this was an accident. But when did it happen? Where was she found? Who found her? Did the Eviscerator do this to her?

I feared I already knew the answer to that one as well.

Melanie had stayed behind at Fernando's to sort out the mess with Brady's car and the confused elder gentleman's Ford. She told me she'd catch a cab back to the hotel, and she'd call me after tomorrow's workshops. The evening certainly wasn't turning out anything like we had hoped.

"Make sure Brady gets home okay," Melanie had said before we left. "You boys can squabble some other time."

It seemed somehow fitting I would see Brady back to his door after he had done me the courtesy when my Optima had been "borrowed." Then we would be even, and it wouldn't feel like I owed him anything. But when

I looked at him staring blankly out the window, his lips moving soundlessly, I knew the rest of the evening was going to be a shared hell, and no matter how I felt about the man, I wouldn't make him face it alone.

*****

Indeed, the body (or what was left of it) belonged to Nikki Sanders. The identification wasn't easy; the corpse had been mutilated and burned. It was possible (although I prefer not to believe) Nikki was alive when much of this damage had been inflicted. The only thing which remained untouched, looking obscenely pure against a backdrop of charred flesh was her right eye and the area immediately around it. It was if the killer took special precaution to preserve this ghastly effigy, a single staring eye, its startling clarity unchallenged even in death. It was the eye that let Brady know it was her.

He went completely batshit right about then, kicking over shiny metal trays of sterilized instruments, screaming in an inhuman voice that tied my throat in a lump the size of a bowling ball. Brady's grief swept across the room, encircling everyone in its path, and we all just froze for a moment. Doctors came with tranquilizers, but Brady vehemently refused, batting them away and frightening the usually unchallenged medical staff. A guard finally settled the issue, stepping in from the corridor and taking Brady into a bear hug from behind. A wiry doctor with salt-and-pepper hair and a grim look of determination sank the needle home in the meat of Brady's arm. Brady howled and thrashed for a few more moments, but then he began to wind down, his eyes glassing over. Somehow, they looked more dead than those of the woman on the table.

Did I mention Nikki was missing her right foot?

*****

Special Agent Steele had arrived shortly after Brady's tranquilizer kicked in. Brady remained amazingly responsive, but his speech was an unaffected monotone, and his eyes remained glassy and unfocused. It was as if every ounce of emotion had been entirely suppressed. Maybe it was a good thing. It surely had to be better than what he was feeling before.

Special Agent Steele took Brady's statement in a small, private room somewhere in an administrative suite. I wasn't invited, left behind in the cool, sanitary hallway to stare at the cold tile floor and try to pretend corpses weren't neatly filed away in drawers in the rooms that branched off to either side. Truthfully, I didn't know where the bodies were stored, but my imagination was supplying me with endless possibilities.

According to Brady, Nikki had left Columbus Monday afternoon to visit her parents in Perma, PA, a small township outside of Pennsylvania. It was her parents' fortieth wedding anniversary, and Nikki had wanted to surprise them with an impromptu visit. They wouldn't have known anything was amiss when she didn't arrive because they weren't actually expecting her. She had no other family in the Columbus area. The police had contacted Brady when they found his phone number in the wallet that was considerately left behind by Nikki's killer.

The killer was undoubtedly the Eviscerator.

A little over an hour later, we were back in the Optima, the heater set to high yet still unable to dispel the chill which had settled over both of us. Brady was nearly asleep, the body's natural defense mechanism coming to his aid. My head pounded like a son-of-a-bitch, and the onslaught of approaching headlights was like looking directly into the sun. We were going to an address on Hayden Run, a narrow two-lane blacktop, which acts as a vague border between Hilliard and Dublin. I'd been there before, and the comparison to my own neighborhood is unavoidable. Large farms are spaced far apart on acres of property with gardens of corn, soybean and tomatoes stretching off to the horizon. It wasn't at all what I expected of Brady, whom I figured would occupy a one-room flat with leaky pipes and bars on the windows in a rundown flophouse somewhere downtown. It wasn't that I thought Brady couldn't afford better; I knew he was a moderately successful journalist. I just assumed he would stay close to where the action was, renting as modest a dwelling as possible since he always seemed to be on the road, sniffing out the latest scandal.

In the cloudless night sky, the moon was full-faced, its luminescence frosting the nightscape with delicate shades of silver. The air was cool, but I kept the window slightly cracked, allowing the passing wind to sting my cheeks and keep me alert. Along the right-hand side of the road, I finally found the mailbox which advertised the address Brady had given me. Beside it was a gravel drive that stretched back several yards before dipping below the horizon, and I couldn't see a trace of the house from the road. Brady was asleep, his head bobbing in time with the ruts in the road, and he took no notice that we had arrived at our destination. I eased the car onto the drive and continued forward as pebbles crunched underneath my tires.

As we descended the dip in the driveway, the house finally came into view. It was a modest, one-story cottage tucked beneath the distended fingers of weeping willows. It looked as though it had been there for a hundred years. I didn't know it at the time, but the house was only ten years old. Brady had gone to a lot of trouble giving it the worn look of a structure that has weathered many a storm. The siding had been sealed and stained and left to fade under the scrutiny of the sun. It was now the mottled gray of abandoned tobacco barns which are scattered throughout the vanishing farmlands of the Midwest like tombstones. Lights twinkled from the two windows that peered out from the front of the house, giving the illusion of occupancy to any passing thieves who might think the empty house was an easy target. A bright security light kicked on as we passed underneath, illuminating the remainder of the driveway and the front of the house, as well as chasing away most of the shadows which wrestled underneath the tree limbs. I could hear the sound of rushing water whispering from beyond the line of pine trees at the rear of Brady's property, and I could smell the fresh water of a creek riding the night air.

The downward slope of the driveway leveled off when it was even with the yard, widening to form a miniature parking lot directly in front of the house. I cut my engine and gently prodded Brady's arm. "You're home," I said.

Brady's head snapped up, his eyes wide but uncomprehending. His head swiveled from side to side, taking in everything yet seeing nothing. He showed no recognition for the place that should have immediately been familiar, and I wondered what the hell kind of sedative the doctor had given him. I had a prescription for more in my pocket, as well as a few sample tablets to administer if Brady needed one before the pharmacies opened in the morning, but I was reluctant to give him any more. Their calming effect had at first been a godsend, but now Brady's withdrawn behavior was freaking me out. When I looked at him, I couldn't even imagine the man who would have crawled in sewers and picked through garbage if the end result was a Pulitzer. What I saw now was a very scared and lonely child, trying to detach himself from the world and everyone in it, as if the pain would go away if Brady refused to participate.

"Where are we?" he asked dazedly.

"You're home," I repeated. "Let's get you inside, okay?"

Brady nodded dumbly, and I got out of the car, crossing to his side to help him out. Thankfully, I was too occupied to consider the Eviscerator might be waiting inside the house or even in the yard, under the ample cover of shadows too deep for even the security light to banish. Once I got Brady to his feet, he leaned heavily against me, his legs still wobbly in the pharmaceutical afterglow.

"Billy," he muttered. "Need to—Nola won't—eh?" I ignored his babble and concentrated on guiding him to the front walk. It was a narrow ribbon of cobblestones leading to a small, covered porch. There were no steps to negotiate, and I considered that a small blessing; Brady's feet were unreliable, and I was almost carrying him to his door.

"We're almost there, big guy," I said.

He shook his head, nearly throwing me off balance. "I can walk, man, let me go." He shrugged away from me and nearly fell, but he managed to wobble the remaining steps to the front door unassisted. He didn't even attempt to use his keys; he simply thrust them at me. He leaned against the doorframe with his eyes pinched shut as I tried one key after another. On the fourth try, the deadbolt released.

I've always been amazed at the insight that comes from visiting someone's home. The single table lamp which had beckoned from the window illuminated a tasteful if somewhat small living area. A small worktable with computer gear had been tucked discreetly into the far corner, behind a beige sectional which formed an L at the room's center. There was no flashy entertainment center. Where it might have been were built-in bookshelves, which spanned the entire western wall. Volume after volume filled the space, the raw number of books unimaginable.

I expected to see self-congratulatory clippings framed and pasted to the walls, examples of Brady's journalistic brilliance. I expected to see diplomas or photographs of Brady accepting awards for his various achievements. There was no evidence of any of that. The house could as easily have belonged to a vacuum cleaner salesman. What I didn't expect to see were family pictures on the walls. Brady with a big-eyed, dark-haired girl, resplendent in her wedding gown. A bright, pink baby with an angry tangle of fuzz exploding from the top of his head. There was something about him that didn't look quite right, but I couldn't put my finger on it. As my eyes traveled the perimeter of the room, I watched the child mature, and soon I could see what hadn't been immediately apparent. The boy was handicapped. In what appeared to be the most recent pictures, I could see the metal brackets of his leg braces showing at the bottom edge of the picture. A closer examination of the room revealed a wheelchair tucked against a wall.

In the meanwhile, Brady had crossed the room and picked up the telephone, entering a number that was obviously familiar. When he spoke, his voice was almost normal. "Nola? Hi, it's me. I'm sorry to call so late. I hope I didn't wake Wendell—Oh, that's good. I know you were expecting to see me, not hear from me, but I've got something pretty big going down, and I was wondering if I might impose a favor? Would you mind keeping Billy tonight? I'm afraid I'm going to be awhile, and I'd hate to move him after he's—Oh, that's great. Great. Thanks, Nola. You're my favorite." He replaced the receiver and deflated, sinking into the nearest chair.

"I didn't know you had a son," I said. "How old is he?"

"Ten," said Brady as he rubbed his hands over his tired features. "I'm getting a drink. You want one?"

"No, and you can't either," I said. "Drug interaction alert. Is Nola your wife?"

Brady smiled. "No. Nola is a gracious gift from God. She and her husband, Wendell, are old family friends. They're retired and frequently watch Billy for me. I'd never get by without them."

I crossed the room and gently touched the beautiful face of the olive-skinned woman who had stood so happily beside Brady in that frozen moment suspended on the wall. "Then who—"

"*IS THIS GODDAMNED FIFTY QUESTIONS?*" he roared, his eyes suddenly wild and a little frightening. The rage almost immediately subsided, as if this retched day had nearly stolen all of Brady's energy, and he couldn't sustain anything for long. His head dropped into his hands, and he began to cry again. "I want a goddamn drink," he whined.

I wished Melanie were with me. She would know the proper thing to say to comfort Brady. My mouth is a loose cannon in situations such as these. The less I say, the better for everyone involved.

"It's all my fault," Brady said through his fingers.

157

"How can this possibly be your fault?"

"Don't you see?" Brady was suddenly looking at me, twitching from side to side in a disconcerting fashion. "The Eviscerator has zeroed in. He's found a new game, and we're it. He's turned everything around— he's—he's—"

I couldn't ease his concerns; I more or less agreed with him.

"Who's safe now?" Brady asked. "Is my little boy safe? How 'bout Nola and Wendell?"

"You're getting hysterical, Brady. I—"

"How 'bout that cute little blonde of yours?"

"*SHUT UP!*" It was my turn to snap. My breath huffed in and out, and I slowly became aware I was digging my nails into my palms. I stubbornly refused to follow the natural progression of his theory.

"Nikki and I were supposed to get married," he said softly. He couldn't make it any further than that, and I began to feel extraordinarily claustrophobic. It was time to shut Brady Garrett down for the evening. I needed to be away from this place, away from this viscous cloud of all-consuming grief. I searched for the kitchen, finding it at the rear of the house, and got a glass of water from the tap. I returned to the living room and presented Brady with the water and two of the pills the doctor had given me.

"What's this?" he muttered.

"Take it," I said. "It isn't much, but it might help." I expected resistance, but for once, Brady was compliant. He swallowed both pills simultaneously and washed them down with a slug of water. He groped to his right for a pack of Kools on an end table. He pulled one out and lit it, leaning back to stare at the ceiling while the smoke formed clouds overhead. It was more than I could take. I reached across and snagged one for myself, lighting it and barely noticing the horrid menthol taste. A moment of staring at the ceiling had its appeal for me, as well.

*****

Brady had nodded off by the time I finished the cigarette. His was still dangling between two fingers, so I retrieved it and stubbed it in the ashtray on the end table. He didn't look at all comfortable tucked into his chair, but I certainly wasn't going to try and move him. It was past midnight, and I was more than ready to go home.

A cordless telephone sat in a base beside the computer, and I took the receiver back to the kitchen to place a quick call to the Renaissance. After everything that had happened, I needed to hear Melanie's voice and know she had gotten back to her room safely.

"Hello?" Her voice was guarded, and her anxiety spanned the network of wires between us.

"Hi," I said. "Are you okay?"

"Yeah, I'm fine. What happened?"

"Brady's girlfriend was killed by the Eviscerator."

There was silence on the other end.

"Melanie? Are you still there?" There was panic in my voice, because in my mind, she had just been snatched away from the phone against her will.

"I'm here," she said. "I just don't know how to respond. Are you absolutely certain it was the Eviscerator?"

"Yes."

"Is Brady okay?"

"No, he's not, but who would be under the circumstances? He's blaming himself. He thinks the Eviscerator would've never selected Nikki if it hadn't been for her relationship with him," I said.

"What do you think?" she asked.

"I don't think it's Brady's fault, but I do think his reasoning is sound. You have to promise me you'll be extra careful, Mel. Maybe you should lay low for a while," I said. "Maybe you should go back to Lymont."

159

"You think he'll come after me next?" Although I could detect fear in her voice, Melanie wasn't one to buckle under pressure. She just wanted the facts, and since there was a legitimate cause for concern, I thought she should have them.

"Yes, I'm afraid that might happen," I said. For a moment, I was back at the morgue, staring at the mutilated corpse of Nikki Sanders—only this time, the eye staring blankly from the ruined face was Melanie's.

"Well, I won't turn and hightail it back to Lymont," she said. "I've still got three more days of the conference."

"Melanie, this is serious," I said.

"You don't think I know that? But I'll be damned if I'm going to let somebody keep me from something that is important to me," she said.

"The conference really means that much?"

"Yes, it does," she said. "And so do you."

I sighed. "If you insist on staying, then you need to take steps to protect yourself. Get some mace to carry in your purse. Don't go anywhere without Jordan. If you even suspect someone is following you, call the police."

"I can handle myself," she said.

"I know you can handle yourself with rednecks, but this guy ain't no redneck," I said. "He's a monster."

"I know," she said. "I drove Brady's car back to the hotel. I hope that was okay."

"That's perfect."

"Where are you now?" she asked.

"I'm still at Brady's, but I'm going home," I said.

"Listen to your own advice and be careful," she said.

"I will."

"I love you."

Even after the evening's tragedy, I managed to smile. It was the first time she had ever said that to me. "I love you, too," I said, and we disconnected.

I went back to the living room and returned the phone to its base. I rooted around until I found a pen and a piece of paper. I hastily jotted a note to Brady, letting him know I'd call in the morning to see if he needed anything. He hadn't moved an inch since I had left the room, and I suspected mental exhaustion would keep him under for hours.

I set the button on the doorknob to lock behind me and let myself out. I couldn't double-bolt it, but I really didn't think Brady was in any immediate danger. The Eviscerator was orchestrating a scenario for us, and it seemed unlikely he would kill off one of his players so early in the game. Besides, the bastard was probably still in the afterglow of his most recent conquest.

Still, my senses remained heightened as I traced the path back to my car. An owl hooted overhead, and I nearly dropped a load in my trousers. I used my key fob to unlock the doors, which also caused the overhead light to come on. I peered into the backseat before getting in, promptly relocking the doors after sliding behind the wheel. I had the engine started and the car in gear in a matter of seconds; a moving target was harder to hit than a sitting duck.

Bleary-eyed, I worked my way back to I-270, driving south towards home. Dexter was *way* past his dinnertime and would be loudly complaining, but I took my time, steeling my nerves. Even at that time of night there were still cars on the roadway, and for once in my life, I was happy to be on the interstate with fellow non-maniacal citizens. Even if the Eviscerator was two lanes over, he wouldn't do anything here.

It wasn't until I took the Georgesville exit and proceeded west that traffic dissipated, leaving me on my own to find my way safely. Even though there were no phantom lights trailing me, my unease grew as the populace dwindled. By the time I reached Orin Way, I was wide awake, scanning my surroundings for oddities.

Under the light of the full moon, there were many oddities.

Shadow fingers stretched across the road from the bare branches of tall treetops, obscuring familiar surroundings and infusing me with a deep sense of dread. I began to wonder what the Eviscerator may have left for me tonight. A kidney? A lung? A human head?

I pulled into my driveway and turned the engine off. I stared at the long facade of my farmhouse and listened to the sound of my heart pounding in my ears. Although nothing appeared to be amiss, I no longer trusted my senses. They had been overpowered by adrenaline, and everything I saw seemed to promise something horrific. I don't know how long I sat there, thirty feet away from my own front door but reluctant to leave the safety of my car.

I had bought the house because I wanted property and privacy, and yet these were the very things which paralyzed me now. I never in a million years thought I could feel this way about my own home.

CHAPTER FIFTEEN

I let myself in, disarmed then rearmed the security system. I snapped the deadbolt into place and swung the hasp of the door guard over its bolt. I then made a sweep of the first floor, checking the lock on each window and peering into every conceivable hiding place. First the living room, then the kitchen, the laundry room behind the kitchen, the hallway, the bathroom, the den. I moved quickly and without deliberation. I wasn't going to let every little creak in the house put me on the edge of my nerves. After I finished with the first floor, I moved to the basement, throwing the switch at the top of the stairs. Light flooded the cinderblock room from a naked 100-watt bulb suspended in its center. As large as the rest of my house is, I have never used the basement for storage. It is musty and dank, and stuff is more accessible in the upstairs bedrooms anyway. Mercifully, that made what could have been one hell of a spooky place easily assessable. All clear. That only left the upstairs.

A few moments later, I was back on the main floor. Perimeter secured. I cracked open a can of cat food and quieted the roaring beast at my ankles. I put a pot of coffee on and wandered back to my office to fire up my computer. Soon enough, I was seated at my desk with a piping hot cup of Hills Brothers black, reaching for the package with the flash drives Brady had asked me to look at.

The drives were labeled in a bizarre code of Brady's own creation, assumably for the purpose of throwing off "The Fuzz" if he should get busted. The first one was labeled 1W101gg. The next was marked

2M201pn. The next 3W301dc. After a moment, I realized that the first digit indicated the victim number, and the two lowercase letters at the end were his or her initials. A little after that, I determined that the W stood for Windows and the M stood for Macintosh, so I placed the drive containing Paul Nicholas's computer brains aside. I didn't have a Macintosh machine, and even if I had access to one, I wasn't familiar with the common filenames of that operating system. I focused on the drives from Gigi Garson and Dorie Carpenter.

Using Windows File Explorer, I looked at the contents of each drive, starting with Gigi Garson's. I had brought Word up so I could easily transcribe any information or thoughts that seemed important into a word processing document. I had already enabled viewing of hidden files and folders in File Explorer, any of which would appear as slightly grayed out. Many of the folders I saw were the common creations of a normal Windows installation. I didn't immediately find the hidden folder Brady had referred to, the one called 'Moo.' It wasn't until I got into the subfolders that I found it. Sure enough, a folder named 'Moo.' I opened the folder and found nothing inside it. What good could an empty folder possible be to anyone? It occurred to me to open the system's registry editor and do a keyword search on 'Moo.' I immediately found a registry hive with the same name in the HKEY_CURRENT_USER node. There were several keys and subkeys listed in the hive. They served a specific purpose for the program that called them, but I had no idea what that program might be.

Moo.

What a stupid name for a folder. I examined the remainder of the Garson drive and made several notes, but many of the folder names I didn't recognize I was able to easily eliminate from consideration by examining the contents of the files within them or by consulting Google. There didn't seem to be anything sinister in the works.

I extracted the inbox of what had been Gigi Garson's email program. There were hundreds of messages inside. She must have saved every one she received. I began poring through her personal correspondence, gaining a mental image of this woman who was no more. She had many friends who wrote frequently, sending pictures of themselves and their children as well as jokes and web sites that might have been of interest. A good bit of the mail was unsolicited ads. The *New York Times* headlines had been received each morning. I guess I was looking for a message from a secret admirer who had requested a meeting, but there was nothing to be found. I progressed through each of the folders of the email program, yielding exactly zip.

Moo (moo) To emit the deep, bellowing sound made by a cow; low.

What the hell kind of name is that for a folder?

By the time I progressed to the drive containing the contents of Dorie Carpenter's computer, the sun was beginning to creep up in the east, and my eyes were beginning to creep down to the south. I needed to get some rest, or I was liable to overlook something important (if there *was* anything important).

I shut down the computer, packed the drives back into the box, and as an afterthought, tucked the box inside the cold hearth of my fireplace. I still didn't care for the thought of having stolen government property in my possession.

I discarded my clothing one piece at a time and fell into bed, startling Dexter who had been sleeping on one of the pillows. I was asleep beside him in no time at all.

*****

I woke at one the next afternoon, still groggy after what could only have been six hours of sleep. I forced myself to face the chilly and dismal afternoon, pulling on sweats and a t-shirt to run my three-mile circuit.

165

Healthy habits are hard for me to form, and I was afraid to miss another day. The wind was building, making the temperature feel even colder than its current fifty-three degrees.

As I ran, I reflected on the events of the previous evening. I needed to check on Brady. Understandably, he was upset—but *how* upset? I didn't know him well enough to guess. I could only imagine how devastated I would be if it had been Melanie. I wished I could make her return to Lymont. I would feel so much better if she wasn't anywhere in the vicinity of this psychotic bastard. Her writer's conference was important, but was it worth her life? Or was I overreacting?

I had actually *seen* Nikki Sanders's mutilated body—I wasn't overreacting.

I needed to look at the drive from Dorie Carpenter's computer. I was surprised at how long it had taken to sort through all of the folders that had once resided on Gigi Garson's computer hard drive. My list of unusual folders was narrowing, and 'Moo' was still at the top, primarily because Brady had already told me there was an identical file on each of the victim's computers.

As I neared my house, I decided Brady topped my list of priorities. His erratic behavior had left me unsettled, and I didn't think I would accomplish much else until I saw he was all right. A phone call wouldn't cut it; it was the hollow look in his eyes that left me spooked. I had already offered a ride to pick up his car, anyhow. It would only take an hour or so, then back to the flash drives.

Another car waited in my driveway as I huffed toward my house. It was a metallic blue Chevy, totally unrecognizable to me. A petite and businesslike woman was knocking on my door, her dark hair pulled back into a tidy chignon. Her attire was immaculate in its tailoring, a beige skirt and matching blazer that followed the graceful lines of her own body. The sound of my footsteps on the sidewalk alerted her to my presence, and she turned, showing me a smile that only comes from lots of practice in the mirror. She wore horn-rimmed glasses that immediately brought to mind Wonder Woman's dowdy secret alter ego, Diana Prince.

"Mr. Morrow?" Her voice was like music, my name ending in a smooth, upward lilt. I nodded. She came forward with her hand extended. "Hi. I'm Barbara Dugan."

I took her hand lightly and was surprised by her strength. "Do I know you?" I asked.

"Oh, no. Of course not," she said. Her other hand was suddenly thrusting papers at me, and my reflex was to grab them. She simultaneously let go of both the papers and my hand and smiled sweetly. "Considered yourself served, darlin'."

I stared after her dumbly as she trotted back to her Chevy and got in, waving once before backing away and driving off. I looked down at the paperwork in my hands.

Geneva Carter had filed a sexual harassment suit against me.

*****

I had never quite gotten around to calling my attorney, so I had some catching up to do. Sally Sheaffer was a one-woman operation, extending her services to a select clientele. She didn't take cases she couldn't win and was a piranha in the courtroom. I knew this by reputation only, as I had never seen her in action. I had helped her with a network client configuration problem that had stopped her business cold. She was unable to access client files days before an important trial. I had saved her bacon and in return, she offered her services should I ever need them. I never really thought I would take her up on the offer.

"This Carter woman sounds insane," she said, after listening to my end of the story. I heard her making notes as I briefed her.

I paced my office, clutching the summons and complaint in one hand while I kept the phone cradled against my neck. "Her son, Jeffrey, seemed to understand she was acting abnormally. But then, after she had me fired, his attitude changed. It was as if he decided I'd actually harassed his mother after all. Good God! She's old enough to be my *own* mother!"

"You should have called me Monday," she said. "We could've filed our own action for illegal termination of your employment."

"I wasn't employed," I said. "I was sub-contracted. That's one of the dangers of the business. You can be let go with little or no notice."

"How in the world did you get mixed up with someone like this Geneva Carter?" she asked.

"I don't know. She seemed normal at first. We ate lunch at the same time, so we saw each other every day. Eventually, we made small talk— you know how it goes. Then she was offering an opportunity to do a little detective work. I thought, what the hell?"

Sally sighed. "Although I know your first inclination is going to be to contact her or a member of her family, it is absolutely out of the question. We are now beyond the stage where you might smooth things over with quick reasoning—they aren't listening to you anyway. I will file an answer to the complaint and see if I can talk some sense into her attorney—who is it?"

"Morton Jennings, III," I said.

She groaned.

"What?"

"Nothing," she said. "The guy's a complete perv and a pompous gasbag. Any contact at all with him makes me want to scrub my skin off with a wire brush."

"Sorry."

"What must be done must be done," she sighed. "Are you absolutely certain there weren't any incidents at Dial Tech that may have been misinterpreted by others?"

"Unless you count having lunch with the woman," I said. "I guess that might have started some really sad tongues wagging—but why bother?"

"Do you know much about Geneva's home life?" she asked.

"I know she thought her husband was cheating on her—which he wasn't. They have two children—Jeffrey and a girl, although her name doesn't spring to mind. Both lived out of state until recently when Jeffrey returned to stay with his mother. He said she was bipolar."

Sally sighed again. "I can't believe even Jennings would take on such an obvious stinker. There must be something else."

"I couldn't even guess what that might be," I said.

"I'll call you after I get a handle on what we're looking at," she said.

"Thanks."

"Yeah, yeah. Email me the complaint." She disconnected the call. It felt good to leave some of the burden on someone else's shoulders.

*****

It was nearly three o'clock by the time I got underway to Brady's. I had called to let him know I was coming, but the line was busy. I think that disturbed me more than anything. A reporter's phone is never busy.

I turned down the sloping driveway, finding it much more easily than I had the previous evening. Tall, yellow grass waved on both sides of the drive, providing a natural shield to the residence below. It was an interesting cottage under the light of day—infinitely less threatening. I stopped the car in the gravel parking area. The front door was standing slightly ajar, and my heartbeat kicked up a notch.

Call the police?

Don't be stupid. It was the middle of the afternoon. Brady had most likely opened the door himself.

But his line was busy.

So, he didn't want to talk to anybody. Big deal. As an interesting afterthought, it occurred to me Brady was probably being besieged by

169

fellow journalists, all of whom were after the inside story on the Eviscerator's latest victim.

I got out of the car and approached the front walk. The creek burbled away behind the house, lending the scene a special tranquility. It seemed impossible anything bad could happen in such a peaceful setting. I knocked on the storm door, and when I got no response, poked my head inside.

"Brady?"

Nothing. All of the curtains were still drawn except for a large vertical blind that covered sliding glass doors at the rear of the house. A rectangle of daylight spilled through, shrouding the remainder of the interior by contrast. I looked around the living room, but it was empty.

"Brady? It's Dwayne," I said, stepping into the room. The little hairs on the back of my neck were beginning to prick up. I crossed the living room and peered down the dark hallway to the right, which led to what I guessed would be bedrooms. To the left was a dining alcove which housed the sliding glass doors. Further left through the swinging latticework door was the narrow kitchen.

As I went into the alcove, I noticed that the sliding doors were not completely closed as it had originally appeared. The vertical blind ruffled to reveal a small gap, and I stepped up to the glass, peering through.

The view was breathtaking. An enormous redwood deck had been attached to the back of the house, offering different elevations from which the backdrop could be viewed. I noticed immediately all of these levels were accessible by ramps, allowing Billy to go wherever he pleased in his wheelchair. The deck jutted out from the house and was supported at its ends by stilts. It afforded a view of the gently sloping landscape that rolled down to the bank of the industrious stream. In a few months, the foliage of the trees would all but obscure the view of the creek, but its soothing voice would still filter through.

Brady was at the tallest of the three elevations, sitting on the railing with his legs dangling over the side. He wore a t-shirt and underpants, and I guess I was thankful for that much. His wild curly hair danced in the wind, bringing to mind images of mad B-movie scientists. His back was to me, and he didn't seem to notice when I slid the door on its track and stepped out onto the deck. He was hunched slightly forward, his hands locked onto the railing on either side of himself, as if they were the only things keeping him from plunging headlong off of the deck. His legs swung loosely, like a child on a swing whose feet can't touch ground. I had the idea that if I scared him, he would lose his grip and fall.

I approached him in a wide arc, making sure he saw me in his peripheral vision. He turned his head to look at me, and I was startled by what I saw. He hadn't showered or shaved. The skin around his eyes was puffy and dark, but it was his eyes which frightened me. They looked completely empty.

"Brady?"

He cocked his head, waiting for me to continue.

"You wanna come down from there?" I asked. "Look, I'll give you a hand—"

Before I could finish the thought, he shook his head and waved me away, and for a second, I was sure he was going to go over the side. I don't think it would have killed him but breaking a bone or two wasn't out of the question. At the last opportunity, Brady righted himself and ambled down the ramp toward me.

He was completely looped. He zigzagged like a circus clown, his head bobbing like a bladder on a stick.

"You're tanked," I said.

"What of it?" he countered.

"How much have you had to drink?"

"Drink? Yes, I'd like a drink," he said.

"No. How much have you had already?"

"I haven't had a drop."

"Bullshit."

"Swear to God on my dead little Nikki's grave," he said, mushing up some of the softer consonants. "I took them pills."

The pills. That's right. The doctor had given me enough sedatives to get Brady through until I could get the prescription filled. I hadn't filled it yet, but Brady must have found the remaining pills I had left behind. Thankfully, there had only been two left. I could see that Brady was having a hard time keeping his eyes open. He loped into the house and headed for the living room, where I heard the distinct clatter of bottles.

I followed him, hitting a few of the light switches along the way. "Get out of the booze, Brady."

"I said I wanted a drink, and I'm havin' one. You want one?"

"No, and I repeat, neither do you. Drug interaction alert, remember? What are you trying to do, kill yourself?"

He turned toward me, his face completely vacant. A chill ran through me as I realized how deeply this man was contemplating my question.

"Knock it off, Brady," I said. "You've got a little boy who depends on you. You can't just bail on him."

Brady sat down wearily in one of the recliners, his attention momentarily distracted from the liquor cabinet. "Billy deserves better than me."

"You're feeling sorry for yourself, and it's nauseating. You're supposed to be this badass reporter. Tough as nails. What in the hell are you doing? I don't know about you, but I want to catch this son-of-a-bitch more than ever. I can't tell you how sorry I am about Nikki—I really am. You shouldn't have to go through something like this. But how are we ever going to feel safe about anyone close to us? We need to pull together and try to catch this bastard."

I expected Brady to at least respond to my pep talk, but his face remained impassive. "I don't know," he said. "I don't know right now. I want a drink."

"You can't have one," I said. "But I will give you a little time to clear your head. You need to get some more rest, bud. But no more pills after this. I'll come back this evening after I get finished looking at the flash drives. We can figure out what we're going to do from there—"

Brady was snoring. Great. I looked around, trying to figure the best way to move him back to his own room and decided it wasn't worth the hassle. He would probably just wake up and demand a drink. Even if he didn't wake for hours, he was liable to head straight for the liquor cabinet when he finally did. With that consideration in mind, I transferred the contents of the cabinet to the trunk of my car, knowing that Brady would be furious, but it would be best in the long run. He was drowning himself in chemicals, hiding from his problems, and it wouldn't solve anything.

Brady had shifted positions, burrowing deeper into the chair, by the time I had taken the last of the alcohol from the house. I spotted the combination telephone/answering machine on an end table, its receiver askew in the cradle. Without thinking, I put it on the hook, and it rang immediately. I was so startled, I snatched it up, wanting to silence it before it wrenched Brady from his slumber.

"Hello?"

There was a brief pause at the other end. "Is this 614-555-7988? I'm calling for Brady Garrett."

"This is Brady's, but he can't come to the phone right now. May I take a message?"

There was another pause. "May I ask with whom I am speaking?"

"Dwayne Morrow." I only briefly paused before my next white lie. "I'm a friend of Brady's."

"Can you please ask Brady if he could spare a moment? His son wants to know when to expect him."

I searched my memory and came up with a name. "You must be Nola, the one who cares for his son."

"That's right," she said, pleased by my recognition. "I've been trying to reach Brady all morning, but the line's been busy. I was giving it one last try before I came over. I've got a meeting at the church this afternoon, and

I'll cancel if he needs me to, but I need to know what to do. Can he come to the phone?"

Brady stirred in his sleep, babbling nonsense before turning over and drifting off again.

"I'm afraid not, Mrs.—"

"Caudill. But please, call me Nola."

"Thank you," I said. "And if it isn't too much trouble to rearrange your afternoon, I'm sure Brady would appreciate it. His son really shouldn't see him this way."

CHAPTER SIXTEEN

After assuring Nola that Brady was not physically hurt, I told her it would be better if I could explain in person. I was afraid of waking him, and he desperately needed rest. She agreed readily enough and gave me concise directions to her home. As I drove, the bottles in my trunk clinked and clattered with every bump and jolt.

Nola and Wendell Caudill lived in a small ranch house in a quiet, suburban Hilliard neighborhood where houses were arranged on tidy patches of grass and the mailboxes all looked like little wooden birdhouses. I pulled into the driveway which was barely deep enough to accommodate my car. Nola met me at the door, her face lined with obvious concern.

"Please come in," she said, ushering me past her into the small living quarters. The room was done in warm and inviting blues and beiges. A long sofa stretched against the wall with a coffee table squatting in front of it. A matching chair was off to the side, aimed at a television mounted on the opposite wall. The house smelled of potpourri and bleach, and not a speck of dust could be seen anywhere.

Nola was the stereotypical grandmother. Her short hair was like cotton on her head, framing a round face that looked like it belonged on a package of oatmeal cookies. She wore a pale-yellow cotton dress with a frilly white apron tied around her. She stared at me through bifocals that were perched on the end of her pudgy nose.

"What's happened?" she asked, guiding me to the sofa.

"Is Billy—?"

She shook her head. "I told Wendell to take him out for a while. It sounded serious."

"I'm afraid it is." I recounted the previous evening's events and watched Nola's face absorb the details with growing horror.

"Oh, that poor man," she said as I finished. "First Teresa, now this."

"Teresa?"

Nola nodded. "She was Brady's wife. Billy's mother. She died several years ago in an automobile accident."

"I didn't know," I said.

"It doesn't surprise me. He doesn't like to talk about it. He always thought he was to blame."

"How so?"

Nola sighed. "It was just one of those things, you know. Terri told him one of the tires on the car was worn. Brady said he'd have it replaced on his way home from work, but he got sidetracked and never got around to it. That night, Terri used the car to pick up some things at the grocery. The tire blew out, and she lost control of the car. She went off the road and hit a tree. Now, the impact shouldn't have killed her—she wasn't going too fast. But she wasn't wearing her seatbelt, and the way her head struck the steering wheel—I guess it just hit the wrong spot, I don't know. Next thing you know, we're all sitting at her funeral. Billy was devastated, of course. But Brady—he's always felt that he was to blame. If he replaced the tire, it never would have happened."

I grimaced. It was a really shitty break. There was no way to comfort someone in Brady's position. No matter what anyone said, he would ultimately know he might have been able to prevent his wife's death if he had simply taken a little time out of his busy schedule. I couldn't imagine the burden.

"And that would be bad enough if it were all," continued Nola.

"What do you mean?"

"Wendell and I were friends with Brady's parents since we were all a bunch of teenagers," she said. "Brady's father, Jack, enlisted in the service same time as Wendell. Sylvia, Brady's mother, and I lived in army housing right across the street from each other. I've literally known Brady since the day he was born." She smiled wistfully.

"You've never seen a child so ambitious!" she continued. "Brady was always determined to become a reporter, just as far back as I can remember. You know how kids are—one minute, they want to be a police officer, the next, a fireman. But not Brady. He only wanted to be a reporter. He used to keep notes on all of his little friends, and more than once, it got him into trouble. He wanted his parents to be proud of him, and believe me, they were."

"I'm sure they were," I politely agreed, feeling awkward at having invaded Brady's personal history. Nola seemed to have no qualms, however, and appeared to be in the middle of a lengthy dissertation, so who was I to stop her?

"When Brady got his first front page credit for a community paper in some little Indiana town, he was just as proud as punch. This was before he was married and a father himself. He had gotten a raise and felt like he was on his way. We always knew he would make it. Someone with that kind of drive is *bound* to succeed. As a thank you for years of support, Brady bought a vacation package for his parents, who were then retired. Two weeks in Hilton Head, all expenses paid. They were stunned, tried to refuse, but Brady said the tickets were non-refundable." Nola pressed her eyes together, and I detected the beginnings of moisture welling at the corners.

"What happened?" I asked.

"There was a malfunction with one of the airplane's engines," she said. "It went down in North Carolina. There were no survivors."

"Oh my God," I said. Brady's history read like a never-ending obituary. First, his parents then his wife, now his fiancée—if anyone had good reason for feeling suicidal, it was Brady Garrett. The burden of responsibility was unimaginable.

"Wendell and I never had children of our own," said Nola. "When Terri was killed, we moved here, knowing that the Lord would want us to keep an eye over Brady and Billy after all that they've been through. Brady really is like a son to us."

"I was hoping you might be able to keep Billy for another night or two, if it's not too much of an imposition," I said. "Brady's not doing so well right now, but hopefully, I can get him to snap out of it."

"Of course, we can keep Billy," said Nola. "I'll call Dr. Clark—he's Brady's psychiatrist—and ask him to give Brady a call."

"Brady sees a shrink?"

"Every week since Terri died," she said. "Dr. Clark will know what to do."

I got up and worked my way toward the door. I handed her a card as I opened the door. "In case you need to reach me," I said.

"Thank you," said Nola, taking the card and tucking it into one of her apron pockets. "I'm glad Brady had a friend with him last night."

I winced. Brady wasn't my friend. I didn't know he *had* any friends. At least now, the people who were his family were aware of what had happened and could be there for him. It felt hypocritical trying to fill the position.

As I returned to my car, a red Ford pickup truck pulled parallel to the curb. A lumbering man in overalls, liver spots sprinkled liberally across his jovial face emerged. He nodded a cautious greeting before rounding the front of the truck and opening the passenger door. He reached in and scooped a small boy into his arms, turning and closing the door with a quick kick. He ambled up the stairs, and I got my first look at Brady's son.

Billy favored his father in many ways. His hair was the same thick, dark ringlets, covering his small head and almond-shaped face. His mouth and nose were smaller versions of Brady's, too. His eyes and skin tone, however, were from his mother. I recognized the similarities from the portraits on Brady's walls. He was thin and small for his age, his back curved by scoliosis into a lazy S. His legs, which were draped across the older man's arms, looked like sticks underneath paper-thin skin, only thickening at the kneecaps where they were swollen.

"Hello," he said, smiling crookedly.

"Hi," I said. "You must be Billy."

His grin broadened, delighted I knew his name. "This is Papaw Wendell."

"Nice to meet you," I said. "I'm Dwayne Morrow. I'm—a friend of your dad's."

Wendell nodded politely. "C'mon young William," he said. "Let's get you inside. You're so heavy my arms are about to fall off." He hurried the boy into the house, still unsure of whether I was friend or foe.

*****

I spent the next several hours back at my house, pouring over the contents of Dorie Carpenter's computer from the one of the drives Brady had given me, looking for common threads which might connect her with the other victims. Anything I had ever read regarding serial killers suggested the victims would often share physical traits such as gender, race and age. The Eviscerator had neatly circumvented the stereotype, culling his marks from each corner of the demographic spread. It seems ridiculous that any rules should apply when dealing with a psychotic mind, and although statistics backed these expert opinions, I wondered if I was on a wild goose chase, trying to find a connection where there was none. Other than system folders, the only unique match on the entire drive was the folder called 'Moo.'

Moo - To make the throat noise of a cow.

179

The folder was empty, like the others. There were more of the anonymous registry entries that meant nothing to the casual observer—or to me, for that matter. Were all of the victims part of a mutual bovine appreciation society? Ridiculous. But it had to mean something. I own four different computers: three desktops and one laptop. None of them had the mysterious 'Moo' folder anywhere on their hard drives—I checked.

I noticed from her browsing history Dorie had frequented several internet chat sites, which moved my mind along another path in the same direction. Suppose the victims had never actually *seen* their killer, at least prior to the murder. Suppose they had met in a chat room on the internet and had agreed to a secret meeting. Stories of fatal attractions formed through internet chatting were somewhat commonplace. As an electronic lonely-hearts club, chatting allows the user to become anyone he wants to be—rich, good-looking, or maybe even someone famous. What difference does it make? The person at the other end will never know, and odds are pretty damn good he is lying his ass off, too.

I barely had enough time to build enthusiasm for the idea before it was dashed. I checked the Garson drive and found no inclination for chat, personal or otherwise. So much for that idea.

I gave myself a fifteen-minute break, stretching my legs and wandering out to the kitchen for a glass of water. I intended to pay some long overdue attention to my cat, but as it turned out, Dexter hadn't missed me at all. He had found a plastic grocery bag and was quite occupied, diving on it like a kamikaze bomber before darting off as the plastic crinkled its protest.

The telephone rang as I was filling my glass with water. I set the glass on the counter and grabbed the extension mounted on the wall by the refrigerator.

"Morrow Consulting." The greeting came automatically during normal business hours, but a quick glance at the clock told me I was off the mark. It was almost six.

"May I speak to Mr. Morrow, please?" The voice was male—deep, resonant and soothing as a tranquilizer.

"This is he," I said, mentally connecting the dots before confirming my hunch on the Caller ID screen. "You must be Dr. Clark."

"Yes," he said. "I left Brady's house just a little while ago, and Nola Caudill asked me to call you. She says you were with Brady when he was notified of his fiancée's passing."

"Yes," I said, marveling over the good doctor's smooth ability to derive 'passing' from 'brutal murder.' "How is Brady?"

"I really can't say," he said. "He seems very withdrawn, which is certainly understandable. I wanted him to come with me, check into the hospital for a few days of observation and counseling, but he steadfastly refused. I was hoping I could persuade those closest to Brady to keep an eye on him for the next couple of days. Can I count on you?"

"Well—sure," I said, surprised the doctor would ask for my assistance. It seemed like something that would be requested of family not an outside acquaintance. "You should probably know that Brady and I aren't exactly close."

"That's really no surprise," said Dr. Clark. "Brady doesn't let anyone get very close to him. But I think it's especially important he be surrounded by others now. Too much time to himself will only deepen his depression."

"I don't mean to sound insensitive," I said, "but is Brady's reaction normal in this situation?"

"Normal is a very subjective term," he said. "Brady is reacting as I would have predicted."

"Nola told me about Brady's wife and his parents—and their deaths. Does Brady blame himself for all of it?"

"I'm not at liberty to divulge any specifics from Brady's sessions but suffice it to say we were making tremendous progress," he said. "The death of his fiancée is a devastating setback."

My first reaction was to be offended. I'm sure Nikki Sanders's parents thought her death was more than a mere setback. I had to remind myself that physicians form clinical detachments as an essential part of maintaining sanity.

"What am I supposed to do?" I asked.

"Just be supportive. Try to coordinate with Nola so someone will be with Brady at all times for the next few days."

"What about Billy?"

"Nola and Wendell are keeping him. I will be checking in regularly to see how Brady is progressing. Thank you for your generosity, Mr. Morrow," said Dr. Clark.

We exchanged pleasantries, and I replaced the receiver, realizing without explicitly being told, I had just been drafted for a suicide watch.

*****

My head was splitting. I had been staring at my computer monitor for another couple of hours, making notes and crossing ideas out when they proved useless. I was back down to 'Moo.'

I vigorously rubbed my eyes with the backs of my hands and pushed myself away from the desk. The clock on my computer showed it was almost eight-thirty, and I had told Nola Caudill I would check in with Brady at nine. She and Wendell were taking turns staying with him until then, and she had asked if I would relieve them for a couple of hours. They were going to the airport to pick up a foreign exchange student who would be staying with them while attending the Christian academy at their church. Billy was still with whichever one wasn't watching Brady, but he was growing anxious to see his father. Dr. Clark had indicated it would be good for Brady to have his son around, and Wendell planned to take him home and spend the night with them.

I had nearly pressed the sequence of keys that would shut my computer down when a thought occurred to me. I opened the web browser and typed "www.moo.com" in the address bar. I sighed with frustration as a commercial website offering instructional manuals materialized on the screen. The instructional materials were computer-related with no ominous overtones whatsoever.

I then clicked the 'Search' button on the browser and typed, "Moo" into the search path. As the results filled the screen, I was surprised at what I read.

MOO was an acronym for 'MUD, Object-Oriented'. Great. But what did that mean? I searched the definition of MUD, discovering it was an acronym for Multiple User Dimension/Dialogue/Dungeon. In other words, a MOO is a type of virtual reality. It is role-playing for the electronic age with members from around the globe competing or conversing in a fictional arena defined by the creator of the MOO. Themes were widely varied, although enchanted elves and mystical wizardry seemed to abound.

It was too much information to absorb quickly, and I needed to relieve Nola of Brady. I clicked the 'Print' button like mad, sending pages of text to my laser printer from the various informational sites I had found. As many years as I have worked with computers, I had never heard the terminology before. MOO was a way for users to interact outside the normal methods of chatting.

I was finally on to something.

*****

It was quarter to nine by the time I made it to the car, so I coaxed the Optima along ten miles above the given speed limit. I was going to be late, no matter how quickly I drove, so I grabbed my cell phone from where it had nestled in the passenger seat amongst a stack of freshly printed paperwork. I dialed Brady's number and after a couple of rings, Nola answered.

"I'm sorry," I said. "I'm running a few minutes behind."

"Oh, dear," said Nola in a hushed voice. "Nalia won't know what to do if we're not there to meet her. How far away do you think you are?"

"Fifteen minutes."

"I think we can spare five," she said. "Brady's lying down. Do you think we would be all right to leave him for just ten minutes?"

"I don't know," I said. "How has he been acting?"

"Like you'd expect," she said. "He's been sleeping a lot."

"I don't think ten minutes will hurt anything," I said. "He was alone all morning before I went out and found him on the deck. He'll probably sleep right through."

"I feel terribly guilty for leaving him, but this is our first exchange student. I want everything to go smoothly."

"I'm sure it will be fine."

We disconnected, and I sped up, realizing I had just placed my neck in a noose. What if Nola and Wendell left Brady alone and in those ten minutes, he slashed his wrists or shot himself or—

My cell phone chirped again.

"Hey."

"Hey," I said. I wished Melanie was beside me in the car instead of just a voice in my ear.

"Any progress with the flash drives?" she asked.

"Maybe," I said, flashing my brights in protest at an oncoming car whose own were blinding me. "I'll know more in a little bit. I'm headed over to Brady's to try and distract him with what I've found, maybe get his brain working again. I have a lot of information to pour through and could use the help."

There was a long silence at the other end.

"Melanie? Are you still there?" It was annoying to note the trace of panic in my voice.

"Yeah, I'm here," she said. "I just don't know that you should be going out to Brady's."

"Huh?"

"I don't know, this may be really off-base, but hear me out. I was telling Jordan what happened last night, and when I mentioned Brady Garrett, the name struck him as familiar."

I eased off of I-270 at the Tuttle Crossing exit and turned left at the end of the ramp. "Of course it sounded familiar," I said. "Brady's something of a local celebrity. Even people in Lymont read *The Dispatch*."

"That's what I thought, too," she said. "But he seemed surprised to learn that Brady was a reporter. It nagged at him all day, but then it finally came to him as we were returning to the hotel."

"And?"

"Six years ago, Brady Garrett was implicated in the murder of his wife."

"He *what*?" I was stunned. Why hadn't Nola mentioned this? Or even Dr. Clark? It surely wasn't within the scope of his confidentiality. It would've been a matter of public record.

"I don't know any of the details," said Melanie. "Jordan didn't put it together until very late, and I haven't had a chance to go over to the library and look at the old newspapers—"

"No," I said. "I don't want you going to the library after dark."

"Relax," she said. "They're closed. I can't do it until tomorrow anyway. I'll go after the convention, while the sun is high in the sky. I don't even know if it's true. Jordan may be completely wrong—but if he's not, Brady may not be the kind of person you think he is."

"I'll call you tomorrow," I said. "I promised Nola Caudill I'd stay with him for a couple of hours."

"Nola who?"

"I'll catch you up later," I said.

185

"Call me when you get home tonight," she said. "I want to make sure you get back safely."

"It'll be late."

"I don't care. I love you. Be careful," she said.

"I love you, too."

I put the phone back in the passenger seat and absorbed this latest information. I didn't know for certain what kind of person Brady was. I didn't care for the type I *thought* he was, but a murderer? I had considered it once before, when my Optima had been taken from the lot of Discount Tire Mart. Maybe my first instinct had been correct.

I cruised down the sloping driveway towards Brady's cottage, reminding myself I didn't have any confirmation of this alleged crime. Nola had indicated Teresa Garrett had died in an accident. Brady's negligence was unfortunate—but accidental.

If she was telling the whole story.

I stomped on the brake pedal, bringing the car to a skidding halt in the gravel as my headlights washed over the porch. Whatever kind of person Brady was, I had a feeling I was about to find out. Illuminated by my headlights, Brady stood frozen, just under the overhang at the edge of his porch. His eyes were fixed on me, looking out from swollen and darkened flesh. His lips were moving slowly, almost trancelike.

Clutched tightly in his right hand, swinging ever-so-slowly back and forth at his side, was a long, wooden-handled ax, its blade glistening in the beam of my headlights.

CHAPTER SEVENTEEN

I can't imagine what my face looked like, but my bladder sure wanted to let go. Brady leaned forward, shielding his eyes against the glare of my headlights. His lips were still moving slowly, his eyes glistening darkly from underneath his cupped hand. He took a tentative step forward, the ax still clutched tightly in his fist.

He was still thirty feet away from the car, so I quickly rolled my window down and called, "Brady!" I stuck my head through the window, rethought the wisdom of the maneuver and pulled it back inside.

He stopped and squinted harder, trying to peer through the windshield. "Who's there?" he called.

"It's Dwayne Morrow," I said. "Can you do me a favor and put down the ax, please?"

Brady looked at the ax as if he hadn't noticed it before and quickly dropped it. It did nothing to soothe my shattered nerves. He could pick it back up and lop my head off before I got halfway across the yard.

"What are you doing there, buddy?" I asked.

"Needed wood for the fireplace," he said. "Woke up cold. What are you doing here?"

I got out of the car and joined Brady on the porch, casually kicking the ax aside as I passed. "I just wanted to see how you were doing. You weren't yourself when I was here earlier."

Brady grunted and scooped up the small pile of wood at his feet. "I thought you were that goddamned bastard," he muttered. "Be glad I didn't have a gun."

I trailed inside after him, making myself at home on the sofa while he piled the wood over a faintly glowing bed of embers. He stoked the fire to a roaring blaze, then stood close to the hearth, shivering against a chill I couldn't perceive. He looked even worse than he had that morning, which I didn't think was possible. After a few moments, he crossed to the recliner and flopped heavily down onto it.

I fidgeted on the couch, trying to think of conversation that might pass two hours, conversation that wouldn't drift to the topic of his murdered fiancée, but I was drawing a complete blank. Our entire association had been formed on the basis of the Eviscerator's killing spree. What else was there to discuss? Should I ask him what *really* happened to his deceased wife, Terri?

I ended up turning on the television. We sat in silence and watched *Gunsmoke* on MeTV, although it was doubtful either of us followed the plot. I watched Brady discreetly, wondering if the man across the room may have murdered his wife before launching an entire campaign of terror. He sat glassy-eyed, his mouth hanging slightly open, staring vacantly at the screen. His lips occasionally fluttered, but that distressing habit seemed to be settling down.

Although I had brought the printouts to read while at Brady's, I had left them in the car in my haste to distance Brady from the ax. Now, I was glad I had left them there. I wasn't ready to share my newly discovered find with Brady, at least not yet. If there was any possibility whatsoever that he might be the Eviscerator, I would be playing into his hands if I let him know I had found what he had dangled in front of my eyes.

The slowest evening of my life passed. *Gunsmoke* gave way to *I Love Lucy*. *The Bob Newhart Show*. *Alice*. I nearly ran out the door to meet the Caudills when they finally arrived.

*****

I slept amazingly well that night, perhaps from sheer exhaustion. My eyes had recovered, temporarily at least, from the strain of the previous day's computer work. I had no further obligation to check in with Brady, and that was just fine with me. Nola and Wendell planned to fully man the watch themselves. I had no idea what kind of baggage Brady was carrying around, but I intended to find out before I cooperated with him any further. Brady could be the Eviscerator. I couldn't substantiate his whereabouts for the earlier crimes, but he was present the night I had discovered Tina Barlow's body. Good journalists have sources who give them the inside track on major events—I know this. But what if Brady knew where to be because he had just deposited the body in the alley? Probable or not, it was definitely *possible*. Brady had conveniently shown up at Fernando's while Melanie and I were dining. It was there he was notified of Nikki Sanders's murder. He could have killed her before coming to the restaurant for a quick spot of dinner. It was *possible*.

I had called Melanie on my way home to let her know Brady hadn't murdered me during my visit. I told her I would meet her at the library when she went to research the old newspaper articles about Terri Garrett's death. After spending the evening with someone who may or may not be a ruthless and savage killer, I was nervous about Melanie wandering around downtown by herself, even during the daylight.

My late morning run passed in a blur, my mind occupied by the tidbits of information I had absorbed about MOOs. If the Eviscerator was an internet stalker, it would explain the lack of consistency in his victims. A physical association couldn't be made from only a series of electronic whispers from a keyboard. Or could it? If these virtual realities allowed people to assume roles, maybe there was a physical similarity in the description of the roles. I needed to find out which MOO created this common folder on the hard drives.

This might be profiling for the new millennium.

Of course, there was a downside to all of this. Even if I was able to confirm this or any other theory based on the information I found on the flash drives, I had no easy way to get it into the hands of the proper authorities. To do so would probably expose Brady's source, even if I mailed the drives to the FBI anonymously. The drives had to have been leaked somehow. Despite my sincere reservations about the official competency of Brady's source, I didn't want to be the reason she lost her job. Oh, well. I figured I'd cross that bridge when I came to it.

I was invigorated by the time I got back to the house and took a five-alarm shower. I emerged pink-faced in a cloud of steam, feeling almost completely recovered from the exhaustion of the last several days. As the last of the water spiraled down the drain, I heard the answering machine beep, and a muffled voice leaving a long-winded message. I was dripping on the tile floor and had just discovered a patch of shampoo I had missed, so I elected to let the machine keep the call.

After rinsing out the last of the soap, I dried off and pulled on jeans and an OSU sweatshirt. I went down the stairs and stopped at the telephone table in the hall. I had two messages waiting. The first was a piece of welcome news. I wouldn't be unemployed for much longer. Donna Nelson, office manager for MGDC Distribution, had called to tell me I could come and finish a job I had started several months before. There had been a fire in the office of MGDC, wiping out most of the computer system and all of the customer service cubicles. I had restored the computer system in a makeshift work area so they could continue to operate while the building was repaired. Now those repairs were done, and they were eager to have all the equipment moved to permanent locations. It wouldn't be a long job, probably not even a week, but with the money from it, I could pay my mortgage and buy a few weeks' groceries.

The second message was from Sheila. Her voice was shrill and angry, and I had a sudden pang of empathy for my brother and what would surely be the longest months of his life. "Dwayne. It's Sheila. I told you to call me about this weekend. I haven't heard a word. Typical. Matt and I have already confirmed with your parents, and they are coming all the way up from Lymont. Do you think I can just run to the store at the last minute, based on whether you decide to come or not? Give me a call. I need to know if you're bringing that girl or not. I'll have to pick up more steak. I mean it. *Call me*."

I rolled my eyes. Like I had just been standing around doing *nothing*.

I returned Donna's call first, confirming my availability for next week.

"Oh, good," she said. "Marti's eager to have the lunchroom turned back into a lunchroom. I was afraid you'd still be tied up at Dial-Tech."

I laughed. "Fat chance of that. I got fired." There. I'd said it aloud, and my head didn't explode or anything.

"*Fired?* What happened?"

"One of the employees accused me of sexual harassment. *Me*. Can you believe that?"

"*What?* Oh, that's absurd. I've known you for years. You've worked numerous assignments at MGDC. If you were going to sexually harass anyone, I'd hope to God it would be me," she said.

"The woman's insane," I said. "She's actually filed a civil complaint against me. I can't believe it. It really shakes me up when I misjudge someone so badly. Geneva Carter seemed perfectly normal to me—"

"Geneva Carter?"

"Yeah. You know her?" I asked.

"Well, no, I don't know her personally, but I know *of* her. You shouldn't have any problem discrediting her. She's nuts," said Donna.

"How do you know this?"

"We're both members of the country club, although we run in completely different circles," said Donna.

"Why, Donna," I said. "I didn't figure you for the country club type."

"Shut up," she said. "Al's law firm makes all the partners join. I get dragged off kicking and screaming every so often, so I can stand at the end of Al's arm like the trophy I am. It's my kind of fun, let me tell you. People like Geneva Carter rub me the wrong way. I work hard for a living and enjoy the people at MGDC. Geneva toddles off to Dial Tech to mingle with the commoners, soil her fingertips with a little toner residue—and all the while, she's looking down her nose at everyone, satisfied she is of a higher caliber than anyone else in the room."

"Sounds like you've got a pretty good handle on her," I said. "But you said I wouldn't have any problem discrediting her. What did you mean?"

"She's lawsuit-crazy," said Donna. "She must have filed ten complaints in the last year alone. She sued her hairdresser because her permanent turned out lopsided. She sued the city because she didn't authorize the inclusion of chemicals into her drinking water—just after she had sued them because the blacktop on her street wasn't level. The woman's a complete crackpot. If your lawyer is any good at all, you shouldn't have any trouble having this thing dismissed."

"Well, that's a relief," I said. "I can't tell you how much better you've just made me feel, Donna. I'll see you Monday morning."

We disconnected, and I debated long and hard about returning Sheila's phone call. I doubted she'd had enough time to decompress, and I couldn't stand the thought of her speaking to me as if I were a naughty four-year-old. Procrastination—my old friend. If I waited until later, I might catch Matt and avoid speaking to Sheila altogether. I wondered if I could avoid speaking to her for the duration of her pregnancy.

*****

The rest of the afternoon consisted of exploring different MOOs. It was an almost addictive experience, exploring fictional realms with

192

dungeons and secret corridors and enemies behind every corner. I was correct in the assumption that a user profile was created when joining, and the information was, of course, at the ultimate discretion of the user himself. I could be a 78-year-old obese black woman, and no one would know the difference. There was a form of user etiquette involved upon which I didn't bother to learn, and I found myself getting repeatedly killed in the early stages of many of the games. A kindly gnome informed me of my repeated faux pas, and I corrected my behavior immediately. I stumbled across a really terrific murder mystery MOO, but before I could really get into the plot, my character was assaulted from behind and shoved over the parapet of the third-floor balcony to be impaled upon the wooden slat fence below. It was jolting.

All this, and still no 'Moo' folder appeared on my hard drive. There were literally hundreds of these MOOs, and it would take a while to explore them all. I knew time was of the essence, but I could only work so fast, and I had a lot of ground to cover. I needed to settle my mind one way or the other about Brady Garrett. If his wife's death was even remotely suspicious, I would have a hard time trusting him with anything I had discovered about the MOOs. Otherwise, I could really use his help exploring these alternate realities. If Melanie didn't have any plans after we were finished at the library, I would try to induct her help, too. With three of us working, we might be able to find something before the Eviscerator killed someone else. Unless, of course, Brady *was* the Eviscerator.

Dammit!

I didn't trust—hell, I didn't even *like* Brady Garrett, but I had a hard time believing he was responsible for the horrors I had seen the last few days.

*****

Going back to the library was like déjà vu. Had it only been a week since I had followed Alan Carter here?

The large, square structure was Roman classic in style, reminiscent of old-fashioned government buildings in larger US cities. It was built in 1903 courtesy of an endowment from Andrew Carnegie, then expanded and renovated most recently in 2016. Special care had been taken to preserve the antique feel of the building while adding computers and other modern conveniences to the facility. I didn't go to the main branch often (mostly because I avoid downtown completely, if at all possible), but I loved the big, sprawling building with its smell of musty books and murmur of hushed conversation. Coming from a town as small as Lymont, I found the building almost overwhelming in scale.

It was five-thirty when I met Melanie at the front entrance. We went inside and consulted the attendant at the information desk, who directed us to the library's media center. There we would have access to microfilm containing old newspapers and magazine articles. We found a table near the readers and sat down.

Melanie listened intently as I brought her up to speed on the events from the previous day. When I finished, she sat back in her chair and tugged at her bottom lip, absorbing the tragedies that comprised Brady Garrett's life. Judging from her tired eyes, she hadn't gotten much sleep overnight.

"You really think he could have killed his own fiancée?" she finally asked.

"I don't know. I suppose so," I said. "We need to find out about these allegations about his wife. I can't work with him anymore until I know what happened."

"Did Brady live in Columbus at the time?"

"I don't know. Nola didn't say specifically, although she did mention that his first front page story appeared in a small Indiana newspaper before he was married. I tried using Google, but I didn't find anything other than articles Brady had written recently," I said.

"How far back did the dates on those articles go?" asked Melanie.

"I don't know. I wasn't really looking at the dates. I was scanning for information related to his wife's death."

"Give me your cell phone," said Melanie, and I obliged. She crossed the large room to the area where the telephone directories were stored and retrieved the phone number for *The Columbus Dispatch*. She punched in the number and waited.

"Yes, human resources, please," she said, her voice coming more through her nose than her mouth. "Closed? Oh, dear—maybe someone else could help me. My name is Meryl Brittany with Consumers Choice Lenders. Mr. Garrett has some paperwork in progress with us, and our processor overlooked a couple of things—nothing major, nothing confidential like salary—I just need to know how long Mr. Garrett has been with *The Dispatch*—Yes. I understand. Do you think there might be anyone else with whom I could speak? Mr. Garrett is supposed to close on his loan tomorrow, and I would hate for there to be a delay over something so trivial—Oh, that would be wonderful. Yes, I'll hold."

Melanie grinned at me while she waited, and I nodded approvingly. Melanie was quite good at improvisation.

"Hi—I'm sorry, I didn't catch your name," said Melanie. A librarian shot us a stern look from across the room and Melanie tried to lower her voice without making herself sound suspicious. "Mr. Edwards? Oh, thank you so much for speaking with me—oh, no, nothing like that. We've already confirmed Mr. Garrett's financial portfolio. This is so stupid; I can't believe it was overlooked. I hate to bother you with it, but frankly, my rear-end's on the line. Can you tell me how long Mr. Garrett has been with the paper? Uh-huh—uh-huh. And before that? Oh, no—I wouldn't expect you to pull his personnel file. I might be able to get by with what you've told me. Thank you so much, Mr. Edwards, and should you ever need a loan or advice in planning your finances, please keep Consumers Choice and Meryl Brittany in mind." She jotted notes as she spoke, and while she was still possessed by the spirit of Ms. Brittany, I leaned across the table to see what she had found.

Melanie handed the phone back to me. "Ms. Brittany thanks you for the use of your phone, sir. Brady must have moved to Columbus after his wife died. This Edwards guy told me Brady's been with *The Dispatch* for about five years and although he didn't know his exact previous address, he did remember Brady mentioning Elnora, Indiana upon occasion."

"You are brilliant," I said. "Let's see if we can find an available computer and figure out exactly where Elnora is. We could also Google to see if Elnora has a local paper. If not, we can see which major city is closest and check the newspapers from there."

"That would also explain why you may not have seen the story back when it was printed. Jordan reads an extensive number of newspapers in the college library. He may have been reading one from outside our area when he came across Brady's name."

It was a place to start, and soon, we were huddled together in front of one of the library's computer screens. We discovered that Elnora was a very small town approximately 100 miles southwest of Indianapolis. I attempted to obtain the articles by searching the archive on the website of *The Indianapolis Star*, but that part of the site was temporarily unavailable due to maintenance. Undeterred, we requested microfilm of the paper for two years prior to Brady arriving in Columbus and manned adjacent microfilm viewers, working in tandem. It was almost three hours later before Melanie came across the first pieces of the story.

"I've found the report of the accident," she said. "It's not much of an article. It mentions Brady and his son, who was four at the time. It doesn't say anything about foul play."

"What's the date?" I asked.

She indicated the top of her screen, and I replaced the microfilm I had been viewing with material from after that date. We continued to scan the viewers, although we decreased our speed, examining the pages even more thoroughly.

"I can't find anything that would indicate the police thought this was a homicide," said Melanie.

"Ah," I said, my eyes locating an interesting item on my own screen. "I don't believe it was the police who thought there was a problem. Look at this."

Melanie leaned over and read the headline aloud. "'A Mother's Grief, Tragedy in a Small Town.' What is this?"

"Read on," I said.

The article was more public interest than news, detailing the devastating loss of Maureen Stiltner, a 52-year-old schoolteacher in Elnora. Maureen had been widowed at the age of 19, three days after her honeymoon, but not before the brief union had resulted in her pregnancy. Teresa Stiltner—Terri, to her friends—was intelligent, beautiful and ambitious. Maureen's whole life was built around her only child, and she had worked two jobs to make sure Terri had everything she needed. Then Terri had met Brady Garrett, a troublemaking delinquent from Bloomfield, who had spent more than a few nights in jail for drunken and disorderly public conduct in his college days. After an extremely brief romance, the two had married and soon, a son was born. Unfortunately, Billy Jack Garrett came into this world with spina bifida, a condition in which the vertebrae do not completely develop to provide adequate cover for the delicate spinal cord. There are varying degrees of the condition, but Billy's was severe, and doctors knew he would never be able to walk without braces and crutches. He would, in all likelihood, ultimately be confined to a wheelchair. Four years later, Terri was killed in an automobile accident which Maureen was quoted as saying, "—happened *clearly* through Brady's negligence. He knew about the tire and handed her the car keys on the night she died. Terri and Brady constantly argued. Terri told me Brady had a vicious temper, especially when he was drinking." The article concluded with the fact that

197

Maureen Stiltner had filed a civil complaint against Brady for negligence in the death of her daughter. Ultimately, she was seeking custody of her young grandson, whose life she felt was in grave danger were he to stay with his father.

"This is all speculation," said Melanie. "Obviously, Maureen didn't win the case, or Billy wouldn't be with his father now."

"True," I said. "But that doesn't mean Brady didn't kill his wife. When Terri told him about the worn tire, he might have purposefully avoided having it replaced."

"That's not a very good plan," said Melanie. "The tire could've blown just as easily when Brady was driving the car."

"But otherwise, there would be no reason for the police to suspect murder. The tires weren't slashed or compromised in any other way."

"We shouldn't take Maureen Stiltner's account as gospel," she said. "She's the grieving mother of the victim. She was looking for someone to blame."

"Ah, but we shouldn't completely discount Maureen Stiltner's opinion, either. We barely know Brady," I reminded.

"So where does that leave us?"

I sighed and slumped back in my chair, massaging the beginnings of another headache at the base of my skull. I had been hoping to find answers about Brady's mysterious past. Instead, my list of questions was merely growing.

CHAPTER EIGHTEEN

"The library will be closing in fifteen minutes," whispered a timid, female aide before scurrying off to the next of the remaining library patrons.

Melanie pushed away from the table and stood, stretching her back in a chorus of audible pops. "So, what now?" she asked.

"Dinner," I said. "But first, I want to gather just a few more pieces of information."

Melanie cocked her head quizzically, then followed me to the librarian kiosk where I returned the microfilm. I sidestepped the current newspapers and periodicals, filed alphabetically and suspended horizontally on hooks, their spines impaled by long rods. These were the editions published within the last year, not yet transferred to the more storage-friendly format of microfilm. I sat at the computer we had used earlier and pulled up the internet. I went to *The Columbus Dispatch*'s website and searched for articles on the Eviscerator and was instantly rewarded with the information I needed: Family names of the victims as well as cities and states in which they lived. Directory assistance could do the rest. I deposited change into a slot and requested printed copies of the screen. If only the articles from *The Indianapolis Star* had been as easy to find.

"Are you planning on visiting the families?" asked Melanie. "You'll be driving all over the place."

"I hope not," I said. "But I do plan to make a few phone calls. I need to know if anyone knows anything about these MOOs. If someone under your roof was really into something like that, don't you think you'd know about it?"

"Maybe, but I guess it depends on the type of MOO it is," she said. "Sometimes the point of an alternate universe is to escape the one you live in."

"Point taken," I said.

We gathered our things and headed for the exit. I was deep in thought and nearly collided with Alan Carter in the door frame. He stepped back with a chuckle, brushing imaginary flecks from his dark gray coat, then his eyes focused on my face and recognition dawned. The smile was gone in a flash.

"Mr. Morrow," he said, disdain creeping across the sagging flesh of his face. "I had certainly hoped you had discontinued following me."

I stood like a fool with my mouth open. It shouldn't have surprised me to run into him at the library. I'd certainly followed him here often enough. After a moment, I finally found my voice.

"I'm not sure I'm allowed to speak to you without my attorney present," I said.

He sputtered. "Your *attorney*? There's no need to get bent out of shape, Mr. Morrow. I understand what happened last week. I'm frankly embarrassed by the whole matter. But surely Geneva has requested that you cease your observation of me."

I exchanged a puzzled glance with Melanie.

"You are aware that your wife has filed a lawsuit against Dwayne," said Melanie.

Alan's eyebrows leapt up, and his whole body jolted as if he had received a short burst of electricity. "A lawsuit? Whatever for?"

"She's claiming sexual harassment," said Melanie.

"Oh, for heaven's sake!" he muttered, nervously rubbing a finger below his bottom lip.

"I'm confused," I said. "You didn't know about this?"

It seemed as though Alan didn't hear me. His brow knitted in private reflection, his head slightly lowered. His attention returned abruptly, and his head snapped up. "Eh?"

"The lawsuit," I said. "Surely you knew about it."

He shook his head. "Geneva's nephew is an attorney. I suspect she initiated this through him, the greedy little bastard. Allow me to assure you, Mr. Morrow, I will see to it that this matter is resolved immediately. I hope you will be most gracious in your patience."

I was completely stunned. Again, déjà vu, with the elder Mr. Carter reiterating the position of his son back when I had first met Jeffrey Carter. Of course, Jeffrey's stance had changed dramatically since then. Would Alan's position reverse the next time I saw him? I was highly uncomfortable with this exchange and wished Sally Sheaffer was present.

"What exactly is going on?" asked Melanie.

"I don't believe I know you, miss," said Alan.

"Melanie McGregor," she said, offering nothing more yet still waiting for the answer to her original question.

Alan waffled for a moment, adjusting his coat and glancing around as if he were looking for someone off in the distance. He cleared his throat and said, "Geneva is not a well woman. She suffers an imbalance that causes her to be—difficult, at times."

"Jeffrey told me she was bipolar," I said.

His eyebrows arched again, this time in mild surprise. "I wasn't aware that you had spoken with Jeffrey."

"He came to see me several days ago," I said. "He was asking for my patience, too. As a matter of fact, he told me he had come on your behalf."

Again, the eyebrows went up. Then he chuckled. "That's just like Jeffrey. He was trying to smooth things over for his mother. He tries so hard to protect her. He's had the most difficult time adjusting to her illness."

"His opinion about me seemed to change shortly after that," I said. "I called him about a bunch of junk email I was receiving from Geneva, and he refused to talk to me. Said we should speak through our attorneys. The next thing I know, I'm served with a lawsuit."

Alan sighed, slowly and deliberately forming his next words. "There was a time not so long ago when Geneva was much different than she is now. She was a good wife and a good mother for many years. The manifestation of her condition was unusually sudden. Trina—she's my daughter—had already married and moved away. She has her own family to tend to now. Jeffrey, however, has always been his mother's boy. He has a hard time disbelieving the things that come from his mother's lips. Above all else, she is his mother." His smile was pleading, urging us to understand.

"Geneva also pressed this issue with Dial Tech Labs and had me removed from my job," I said.

Alan's already cheesy complexion waned even more. "Oh, dear. I'm sure we can straighten this out, Mr. Morrow. I will call Geneva's boss tomorrow morning and explain everything. I have to anyway because it's obvious she won't be able to work for a while."

"You're getting her some help?" asked Melanie.

He nodded stiffly. "I cannot apologize enough, Mr. Morrow. I certainly hope it isn't too late to salvage your position at Dial Tech. And while I run the risk of planting the idea in your head by telling you this, I sincerely hope you'll contact me directly about any personal losses you may have suffered through the course of this—you know, before speaking to an attorney. I know what an incredible favor that must seem under the circumstances, but I want you to understand, the expenses of Geneva's illness have been enormous. And Jeffrey—well, you won't have to worry about him, either. Once Geneva is under medical supervision, I'm sure he will be returning to Pennsylvania. No real harm done, eh?"

"I got the impression he had relocated here permanently," I said.

"Oh, no. He only just took a leave from work. Came in last Saturday. Very busy man, you know," said Alan. "But once he is away from his mother's influence, he will see how ludicrous this whole situation is. Truthfully, Jeffrey and I have never gotten along very well. I don't think he'd be comfortable staying unless his mother was present."

"From what I've read, bipolar disorder is often hereditary," I said. "Has Jeffrey ever been tested?"

I could see from the look on Alan's face that he was offended. "Of course not! Jeffrey means well, he just has trouble separating fact from fiction where his mother is concerned. I hardly think I need to rush him off for psychiatric counseling."

"He may actually benefit from it," said Melanie, and Alan's glare shifted directions, landing squarely on her. She continued, "I don't mean to offend, but if Jeffrey is having a difficult time dealing with his mother's illness, he may need someone to talk to. Since the two of you aren't particularly close, I doubt he'd come to you."

"Ms. McGregor, I would appreciate it if you would mind your own business," snapped Alan. "Have you even met my son?"

"Well, no. But—"

"Then I would thank you to keep your opinions to yourself," he said.

"There's no need to be rude, Mr. Carter. Melanie's only trying to help," I said.

Alan took a deep breath and massaged the bridge of his nose. "I'm sorry, I'm sorry. I'm under a terrible strain. I'll see to it that this lawsuit nonsense is stopped. I'll speak with Geneva's boss on your behalf as well. Again, I'm so sorry."

The timid little library worker scuttled back over to gently but urgently reiterate that the library would be closing soon. I smiled and nodded an acknowledgement, but by the time I turned around, Alan Carter had already gone.

*****

The final day of Melanie's conference was tomorrow, but she didn't have to check in quite as early, so she volunteered to wade through MOOs with me for as long as she could keep her eyes open. On the way back to my house, we stopped at Steak and Shake off of Georgesville for a late dinner. We ordered Frisco melts, cheese fries and milkshakes, chocolate for Melanie and strawberry for me. We barely spoke while we crammed food into our mouths. It had taken longer at the library than either of us had anticipated, and we were completely famished.

"Thanks for helping me search for the MOO," I said, pushing my plate back as I came up for air.

Melanie laughed. "Don't say that so loud. People will think you're developmentally disabled. And you should be forewarned, you'll have to show me exactly how to go about this. I've barely used the internet, much less explored chatting or role playing."

"It's not all that difficult," I said. "Each one has its own criteria, which you read before becoming a user. Then, as a character on the screen, you interact with other people who are logged into the MOO at the same time. You do different things, depending on the point of the MOO. I'll help you with the etiquette, too. It'll keep people from killing you quite so quickly."

Melanie's eyes widened. "It sounds ridiculous."

"Well, that's your opinion," I said. "Some people find them very fascinating."

"Some people? You?" she asked, her eyebrows arching.

I took a pull off my straw and shrugged. "Maybe. I walked around in some that were interesting."

"'Walked around'? You've got to be kidding me."

"You'll see," I said with a grin.

"Well, at least you've gotten something accomplished today. It would appear the Geneva Carter business is under control," said Melanie. "That must be a relief."

"I'll believe it when I get a copy of the dismissal," I said. "I've never met a family quite so odd."

"You had no idea whatsoever that Geneva was disturbed?"

"None," I said. "She reminded me a lot of Sarah." Sarah McGregor was Melanie's mother-in-law. My cell phone suddenly shrilled at my belt, and I answered.

"Oh, sweet merciful God, are you coming or not?" The male voice was familiar and desperate.

"Matt?"

My brother groaned. "Sheila is driving me *insane* about this damned cookout on Saturday. You would think we were entertaining European royalty, not just Mom and Dad and my stupid brother—that is, if my stupid brother is coming. What's with you? I know Sheila is over the top, but you could've at least called to let her know for sure whether you were coming or not."

"Oh, God! I forgot!" I said, smacking my forehead. "I got her message this afternoon and then got distracted. Tell her I'm sorry—"

"Huh-unh. You can apologize for yourself. I'm currently not speaking to her. I know it will pass, but I feel it's in both of our best interests if we just stay clear of one another for the rest of the evening. That, by the way, is thanks to you. Are you coming or not?"

"Yes, yes. I'll be there. Hang on a sec." I covered the mouthpiece of the phone and looked up at Melanie. "My brother and his girlfriend are having a cookout on Saturday. Wanna go?"

Melanie grinned. "Sure."

I went back to the phone. "Melanie's coming, too. Hey, I'll tell you what. How about if Mel and I come early to help Sheila get ready for the arrival of Mom and Dad?"

Melanie's face immediately registered alarm. "Your *mom*? Oh, no. I'm not going. She hates me."

"She doesn't hate you—not you, Matt, I was talking to—never mind. What time on Saturday? Okay, we'll see you around eleven."

Melanie was shaking her head as I disconnected the call. "You tricked me."

"I didn't trick you. What's the big deal?"

"The big deal is that your mother hates me. She still blames me for getting you involved with the police last year."

"It wasn't *entirely* your fault," I said with a smile. "And she doesn't hate you. She just doesn't know you. I think it's time we corrected that."

*****

It was almost eleven by the time we got back to my house. Dexter met us at the door, irritable and vocal, protesting my absence and resentful of Melanie's presence. He was in a mood to hiss. I quieted him with a can of tuna—the real stuff, not the ground meat and ash combination to which he was accustomed. He seemed appropriately appeased.

Afterward, Melanie and I set up shop in my den. I cleared a corner of my desk and dragged in a chair from the kitchen table so Melanie would have a place to sit. I took my laptop from its carrying case and hooked it up so Melanie could use it on the opposite side of the desk from where I sat. I showed her the basics, and then we began the tedious process of joining MOOs and checking the hard drives, waiting for the elusive 'Moo' folder to appear on either the laptop or the desktop computer I was using.

Hours drifted by with no luck. I had visited more enchanted forests than I could count, as well as a couple of whodunits and a few virtual cafes. As it neared two o'clock in the morning, I looked up to find that Melanie had fallen asleep with her head on her outstretched arm. My eyes were dry and stinging, and I was ready for sleep myself.

I shut down my computer and stood, yawning and stretching. I went around the desk and shut off the laptop, then gently scooped Melanie out of the chair and into my arms. She slept undisturbed, her head drooping against my chest and her arms instinctively finding their way around my neck as I tucked an arm underneath her bent knees and lifted. I carried her to my bedroom and eased her onto the king size mattress, stepping back to gaze appreciably at this sleeping angel, perfect despite the slight snore that rhythmically escaped her lips. I pulled my comforter around her as she folded into a fetal position and then kissed her gently on the forehead.

I went downstairs and stretched out on one of the big, overstuffed couches in my living room, exhausted after a long day. My last thought before finding sleep was that Melanie's first overnight visit hadn't gone at all as I had hoped.

*****

I had to forego my morning exercise. We had overslept, and Melanie was running late for her conference. She used all of the hot water, and I was forced to acknowledge the brutal truth about cold showers on portions of the male anatomy. We fumbled over each other as she raided my closet, trying to find a shirt she could wear with the jeans she had worn the previous evening. She hadn't thought to bring a change of clothes and didn't want people at the conference to think she didn't bathe. She settled on a white button-down shirt from the back of my closet, one I only wore to weddings and funerals. She looked like a little girl wearing her father's shirt. In the bathroom, Melanie blow-dried her hair and my face as I leaned in to brush my teeth.

"I don't suppose you have an extra toothbrush," she said as she turned the hair dryer off.

"'Fraid not," I said.

"Oh, well," she said, taking my toothbrush from my hand and loading it up with toothpaste. "Ahll buy oo unuther," she added with toothpaste foaming at the corners of her mouth. I didn't really mind.

I tossed some dry cat food down for Dexter as we raced through the first floor. I returned the flash drives to the box from which they had come and placed them back inside the cold hearth of my fireplace.

"What are you doing?" asked Melanie.

I shrugged. "I don't want to leave the drives laying around. I'm not even supposed to have them."

I armed the security system and locked the door behind us before we went to the car. It was almost nine-thirty when I pulled up to the curb near the entrance of the Renaissance.

"Call me when you get finished," I said. "I could use more help trying to track this MOO."

"Hopefully, you'll have it figured out by then," she said. "I'm supposed to check out of the hotel today. Would you mind if I stayed with you again tonight?"

I grinned. "You can stay with me any night you want."

Melanie softly stroked my cheek with her fingertips. "Be careful when you speak with the victims' families," she said. "The wounds will still be fresh."

"I will," I said. "And remember, don't go off anywhere by yourself. There's good reason to believe the Eviscerator might have an eye on you."

"Are you planning to talk to Brady?"

"Not if I can help it," I said. "Not until I feel I can trust him and frankly, I didn't trust him much even before we heard about the death of his wife."

"I know it's only instinct, but I don't think Brady's the one," she said. A car horn sounded angrily behind me, reminding me that others wanted to use the curb as a drop-off point, too. Melanie leaned over and kissed me. "I'll call you when I'm done. Good luck."

She got out of the car, and I watched her as she half-walked, half-jogged toward the hotel. Despite another desperate bleat from the car behind me, I waited until I had completely lost sight of her before putting my car in gear and pulling away from the curb.

*****

I could see my breath in front of me as I walked down the driveway to retrieve my mail. The temperature had continued on its downward spiral, and the weatherman was threatening snow in the forecast. I flipped through the assortment of junk and utility bills, sorting as I went. I absently unlocked the door and disarmed the security system, tossing the junk mail aside as I shed my coat and headed through the living room into the hallway and to the den beyond. I dropped the bills in the wood grain inbox on the corner of my desk and stretched across the top to push the power button on my computer. It was time to get back down to business and find myself a MOO.

While the computer booted, I went back out into the hallway and pressed the button on my answering machine as I passed. Only a few messages. The first was Sally Sheaffer, letting me know that Morton Jennings, III, had officially filed a dismissal on behalf of Geneva Carter. Well, thank God! That was one fire out. Sally's subtle reminder that a bill was on its way was the only downside, and I was just about feeling cocky enough to forward it to Alan Carter for all my trouble. It was a momentary consideration—if I never saw another Carter again, it would be too soon. The second was a message from Jordan McCleary, sounding quite uncomfortable as he asked if Melanie might still be here.

"You didn't mention that you would be spend—uh, I mean—uh—it's a little after nine, and I just wondered where you were. If you get this, call my cell," he said, addressing my machine as if it had no affiliation whatsoever with me. "I really am worried about you, Mel." Beep.

209

The next call was a hang-up, and the machine began to rewind. I had hoped that it would be Doug Boggs, calling with his decision about our partnership. I had expected him to call by now and could only assume that he was delaying the bad news. Either that or his mother didn't allow him to make long distance calls.

I had continued into the living room and crossed to the fireplace. I extended my arm into the cool mouth and felt my way up the sooty interior of the chimney for the inner ledge where I had stashed the drives. My fingers made contact with the shelf, but not the box. I slid my arm back and forth but found nothing more than charred soot and cinder. My heartbeat echoed in my ears as I tried one more time to locate something that simply wasn't there.

Someone had been in my house.

I pulled my arm out of the fireplace abruptly, as if there might be something with huge jaws waiting for me in the darkness of the chimney. My feet were rooted to the spot, but my eyes and ears were already in overdrive, looking and listening for anything out of place. The blanket I had used overnight still lay strewn across the back of the sofa. Stacks of magazines and junk mail that always seemed to spontaneously grow was still scattered over the large, square coffee table in the middle of the room. Its order seemed undisturbed, although it would be impossible to be certain, as it hadn't been arranged in any particular way in the first place. I could hear the refrigerator humming busily in the kitchen, the grandfather clock ticking in the upstairs hallway, a *creak*—but, was it only the house settling?

Dexter wandered into the room and sat on his haunches, watching me curiously. The alarm had been on when I came home—I was sure of it. I had been sorting through mail, but distinctly remembered deactivating it. What I didn't remember, however, was reactivating it. Shit. I had left the front door standing wide open. Anyone could have followed me in. Anyone could still be here. A cold sweat broke out on the back of my neck.

I was fifteen feet from the door. I could just go. I could grab my keys and be out the door in no time, call the police from far, far down the road. But what could I tell them? The only thing I was sure was missing was something I shouldn't have had in the first place. How could I explain being in possession of government information?

One step at a time. I couldn't seem to think anymore. I was hearing noises I knew were in my head because the cat didn't react to them. I needed to get outside, check the situation from there. My house is relatively isolated. It was doubtful anyone had walked or ridden a bicycle. There should be a car nearby if someone was still in the house. Yes. That's what I'd do. I'd see if there was an abandoned car along the road. If there was, I'd get in my car and make use of my cell.

I grabbed my keys and phone and took long strides toward the door. I punched in the alarm code and reactivated the system. If anyone was still in the house, he couldn't get out without setting it off. They were only pieces of a plan, but it was better than nothing. I stepped out onto the porch and pulled the door closed, locking the deadbolt with my trembling fingers.

Pocketing the keys, I turned around and ran right into Brady Garrett.

CHAPTER NINETEEN

"What in the hell are you doing here?" I demanded, my voice sounding oddly high in my own ears.

Brady was doubled over, his lungs gasping for the air I had so rudely dislodged. He held his forefinger up while his diaphragm found its rhythm again. He still looked like hell. His eyes were puffy and cupped by dark rings that were prominent against his ashen complexion.

"I stopped over to see if you figured anything out about the flash drives yet. You haven't called," he said. He seemed more like himself than he had since the night Nikki Sanders's body had been found.

"I see you got your car back," I said, not wanting to discuss the missing drives. His Saturn was parked in the driveway behind my Optima, and from where I stood, I could barely see the damage to its back end.

"Nola took me downtown. I picked up the keys at the Renaissance," he said, straightening and drawing in a deep, clean breath.

"You saw Melanie?" I asked, alarmed. If Brady had picked up his car keys, then he now knew where Melanie was staying. I couldn't remember if I had mentioned it before, but I didn't think so. If there was any possibility at all that Brady was the killer, Melanie was no longer safe there. Thank God she was checking out that afternoon.

Brady looked at me in bewilderment. "What is *with* you, man? You act like you're about to jump out of your skin."

"You didn't answer my question."

"Did I see Melanie? No, I didn't see Melanie. She called me yesterday and arranged to leave the keys at the front desk. What's the big deal?" he asked.

"Just stay away from her," I said, the words coming out before I could even consider them. He was either amused by my challenge or thought I was completely insane, but I couldn't read his expression through my own anger.

"The *flash drives*," he repeated, shrugging it off. "What have you found?"

I shifted from foot to foot, unable to meet Brady's penetrating stare. "I'm still working on it," I muttered.

"*Still working on it?*" He began pacing, and I casually moved away from the door and closer to the edge of the porch. "I thought you knew something about this type of shit, or I would have never left them with you. How many more people have to die before you get off your ass and do something?"

"Hey, I've *been* doing something. I've poured over those drives and cross-referenced files and cataloged messages and invaded personal correspondence. Don't blame me if I haven't found a link. There may not even *be* one," I said.

"Then what about this 'Moo' folder? Isn't it a little coincidental?" asked Brady.

I debated what to tell him. If Brady was the killer, he had brought me the flash drives with the sole purpose of drawing my attention to the folders named 'Moo,' leading me to the next stage in his twisted game. Otherwise, he was genuinely curious, and my current behavior was bewildering. I hated this.

"It's pretty coincidental," I noncommittally confirmed.

Brady stopped pacing and turned on me, his eyes furious. "Why are you acting like this? It's like pulling teeth to get anything out of you. My gut tells me that common folder is more than important. If you're not going to help me, just give me the goddamn drives back and stop dicking me around. I'll try to find someone else. I have a score to settle with the bastard who did this to Nikki." His eyes darted from side to side. Was he lying or was he trying to keep his emotions in check? Was he trying to force me to admit that the drives were gone, something he already knew since he had just stolen them? A good detective would be able to tell the difference, so what did that make me? All I wanted was for Brady to leave.

"Look," I said. "I've got an appointment, and I'm late. Let me give you the short version. A MOO is an online environment that allows users to interact. I would assume each of the victims belonged to the same one, because the folders that were generated on the hard drives were identical. However, none of the MOOs I have explored has created a 'Moo' folder on my hard drive. I'm still searching."

"Interesting," said Brady. "Are there a lot of them? MOOs, I mean."

"Hundreds," I said. "I'll let you know when I have something more concrete."

"Why don't you show me what to do?" asked Brady. "I could be checking out ones you haven't tried."

"I don't have time right now," I said, stepping off the porch and willing Brady to follow. "Like I said, I'm late for an appointment."

"Goddamn it!"

"I'm sorry, Brady, but I've got responsibilities of my own to deal with," I said. "I'll call you later."

"Sure you will," he said. "This is bullshit." He stuffed his hands into his pockets and stormed off in the direction of his car. He was off in a spray of gravel.

My tension seemed to evaporate as I watched the crumpled back end of his car disappear down Orin Way. For all I knew, someone could still be inside the house, but I didn't think so. The timing of Brady's arrival was entirely too coincidental. But why would he want the flash drives back? What possible reason could he have for stealing them from under my nose?

Unless, of course, the purpose was to shake me up, make me unsure of the security of my own home.

Before going back into the house, I decided to drive the length of Orin Way as I had originally planned, making sure there were no empty vehicles within walking distance. The alarm was still set, so if anybody tried to get out of the house, it would be screaming bloody murder by the time I returned. Orin Way was empty, and when I returned, all was quiet.

I went into the house and locked the door behind me. After rearming the system, I toured the house for intruders, again struck by déjà vu. Admittedly, the effort was only halfhearted. I didn't believe there was anyone in the house. For reasons unknown, Brady Garrett had come back to retrieve the drives. Was he the Eviscerator? Probably. Did I have one shred of evidence? Nope. But if the hairs along the back of my neck served jury duty, Brady Garrett would be going away for a long, long time.

Okay, so the flash drives were gone. Did it matter? Not really. The only common file shared by the two computers I examined (and presumably the third, which I couldn't examine because it was a Mac) was the 'Moo' folder. I felt that I was on the right track in my investigation, and I didn't need the drives to continue. If the MOO was out there, I'd find it eventually.

But my queasy stomach told me I needed to get my suspicions about Brady into the hands of someone who might be able to do something about it. But who? Nola and Wendell Caudill? I couldn't subject them to this kind of conjecture. I certainly couldn't call FBI Agent Steele. What would I tell him? Someone had stolen my bootlegged government info? I'd serve jail time and kiss my chances of becoming a private detective goodbye.

Nina Crockett.

She had called herself my contact at the FBI. Was it too soon to utilize her?

*****

215

"Why are you acting so fidgety?" asked Nina. She blew steam from the top of her coffee and sipped, then returned the cup to its saucer on my kitchen table. "What's going on?"

I was pacing the floor furiously, sure I had made an enormous mistake. Nina Crockett was still an FBI agent, after all. There was no type of attorney-client privilege here. If she didn't like my story, she could haul me off to jail just as easily as Agent Steele. After the way I had treated her on our "date," she would probably enjoy the experience. But I had come this far, and I didn't think she'd buy it if I told her I'd asked her over just to see how she was doing.

"So, how've you been lately?"

She scowled and propped her chin on her elbows. "You're miserable at this."

I raised an eyebrow.

"Yes, you," she confirmed. "If you need to say something, just come out and say it."

"I'm afraid you'll arrest me."

"Have you done something illegal?"

"Maybe."

Nina pursed her lips. "You're really starting to concern me."

I pulled a chair up to the table and sat across from her. "Okay, how about if I were to give you a hypothetical situation."

"Hypothetical?" she asked.

"Exactly. Because there's not one shred of proof to anything I'm about to tell you, and it would be your word against mine, and I'd deny I ever said a thing," I said.

"You've got my attention."

"Suppose someone were to get his hands on some classified material—say, evidence in a high-profile murder investigation—nothing like the murder weapon or anything. More like information. For example, let's say

216

the contents of the computers of each of the victims," I said, watching her expressionless eyes for any sign of the quality of reception.

"And how would someone gain access to such information?" asked Nina tonelessly.

"Let's just say someone else forced it on this person, and he thought he might be able to help. And he may have. He may have discovered something that was overlooked on the computers, something that might provide a link between the victims and the Eviscerator. But see, he can't tell anyone about it because he never should have had this information in the first place—not that he meant any harm."

"Are you talking about the MOOs?" asked Nina, and my jaw dropped.

"You *knew*?"

"Of course we knew," she said. "What kind of computer guys do you think we have? The best. Don't get me wrong, I'm not trying to denigrate what you do, but these guys are geniuses. You can't get anything by them. They had that figured out within hours."

"So do you think that's how the Eviscerator met his victims?" I asked.

"It looks likely," she said. "Of course, I'm not working the case any longer, so I've lost touch with the most recent developments. It certainly makes sense, though. It would explain the lack of common physical characteristics between the victims."

"So which MOO was it?" I asked.

"That's classified," she said with a crooked grin. "And speaking of which, how did you get this information? If there's a leak at the Bureau, I need to know."

"And I couldn't agree with you more," I said. "But in all honesty, I have no idea who leaked it."

"Then how did you get it?"

"Brady Garrett brought over a box of flash drives," I said.

Nina groaned. "I should've known. Mr. Garrett is the biggest pain in my ass."

"That seems to be the consensus. If you want to plug the leak, you should take a look at your female clerical staff, specifically anyone who might find Brady's peculiar charm appealing."

"No names, though?" she asked.

"Sorry. Dammit! I thought I had stumbled onto something that might actually help the investigation," I muttered, thinking of all the wasted time and eye strain that had gone into my MOO research.

"So where are the flash drives? I should probably relieve you of them before you get yourself into trouble," said Nina.

"They're gone," I said.

"*Gone?* Gone where?"

"They were stolen from my living room this afternoon," I said.

"I don't like this," said Nina, slowly shaking her head. "Was anything else stolen?"

I shook my head. "Not that I could tell. I have a theory to bounce off you, though. I just don't have anything to back it up."

"I'm all ears."

I relayed my story, leaving nothing out. I started with how I had seen Brady just before my car had been 'borrowed' from Discount Tire Mart and finished with my growing unease of him and his unusual family history.

"That's pretty speculative," Nina said after I had finished.

"I told you it was," I reminded her. "Has the FBI ever done a background check on Brady?"

"We've never had any reason to," she said. "But I think I'll do a little probing, see if I can get a better handle on his past. Of course, since I'm not officially working the case, it'll take a little time and a lot of discretion."

"Was Nikki Sanders a member of the MOO?" I asked.

"No," she said. "But that's not particularly surprising. Like many serial killers, the Eviscerator enjoys the press he's received. You've been prominently featured in his stories of late, and I suspect he's not happy about that. It's changed his motivation. The game with your car, the foot at your doorstep—his recent moves suggest his victims are chosen for effect. Let's assume Brady Garrett is innocent. It stands to reason that Nikki Sanders might have been chosen to punish Brady for shifting the focus of his articles."

"But a sudden change in pattern—" I said.

"Means he's beginning to unravel—whoever he is," she said. "You should be relieved to know your house has been under regular surveillance since Nikki's foot turned up."

"Then why didn't they see someone breaking into my house?" I asked.

"There are officers patrolling the area every half hour or so," said Nina. "It's not like they've set up an outpost in your barn."

"More reason to suspect it was Brady who took the drives."

"What reason would Brady have for stealing the drives? He gave them to you in the first place," said Nina.

"It could be part of his game—I don't know."

"Be cautious," she said. "You're making great leaps and bounds about Brady's involvement without an ounce of substantive proof. Innocent until proven guilty, remember?"

"I know, I know," I said.

"If you're wrong—and I'm willing to bet you are—you're pushing Brady away when he needs his friends most of all," she said.

"Brady and I aren't friends," I said. "He's been as much a pain in my ass as yours."

"Even so, you can't accuse him of murder without some kind of proof. He doesn't need that on top of everything else."

"Well, that shouldn't be a concern," I said. "I plan to avoid him entirely."

"That may not be possible," said Nina. "You can't control when he might stop by. If he's not the killer—and I'm willing to bet he's not—he's going to want the drives back. You can't put him off forever. In the meanwhile, I'll see if I can clear up what you've told me about his background just as soon as possible. If nothing else, it might give you peace of mind."

I leaned back in my chair and crossed my arms over my chest, scowling. "Isn't there some way you could slip me the name of this MOO? I've been working on it for days, and I—"

Nina firmly shook her head. "Huh-unh. No way. Your investigation ends here. You shouldn't have had that information in the first place. If the drives show up again, I expect you to forward them to me immediately. No minor league heroics. Got me?"

"So, I'm supposed to just sit here and wait for a psychopathic killer to make his next move and hope like hell it doesn't involve me or my family?"

Nina sipped her coffee, replaced the cup in the saucer and shrugged. "I don't know what else to tell you."

*****

I locked the door and rearmed the security system, a recent paranoid routine that had become amazingly robotic. I detested living under a shroud of insecurity. I wanted to be able to leave my door standing open if I desired without worrying about what might creep in from the neighboring fields. In the summertime, I sometimes fell asleep right on the porch swing. Would I ever do that again? I had worked too many long hours to afford this place, and I was damned if someone was going to ruin it for me.

I went to the den and sat in my leather chair, staring at my reflection in the empty surface of the computer monitor. After a few moments of deliberation, I decided I would continue as if I hadn't spoken to Nina. Frankly, I didn't like what she had to say. I didn't understand her reluctance to cast Brady Garrett into the role of psycho killer. He was an ambitious reporter, hoping to win accolades for his groundbreaking work. What better way to propel his career forward than to invent a murderer and document his killing spree? I knew it was farfetched, but isn't any motive for murder? It was plausible enough to require further examination, for heaven's sake!

I was worried about Melanie. If Brady knew she was at the Renaissance, he could easily intercept her at any time. Of course, while the convention was still in session, she would be safe with Jordan McCleary. I found it ironic that I hoped Melanie stayed next to him all day long.

I retrieved the legal pad I had scrawled upon at the library. I had listed the victims' family names along with where each lived, and I began calling directory assistance to get phone numbers for each. I had thought it was a stroke of genius at the time, but I quickly learned that contacting the families might be more difficult than I had originally hoped.

Gigi Garson's obituary from *The Scranton Times-Tribune* had listed Donald Garson as her husband. I was frustrated to learn there were three Donald Garsons in and around the Scranton area, but I diligently plowed on, dialing one after the other. My frustration grew after learning that none of them was the Donald Garson I was trying to reach. I moved on to the next name on the list.

Paul Nicholas's mother, Anita, was listed as his only surviving relative. I groaned aloud when directory assistance in Albany, New York, provided eighteen names, all either Anita Nicholas or A. Nicholas. A caustic young bitch reminded me (after an exaggerated sigh) that it would be easier to get the correct number if I knew the proper address. She refused to give me all eighteen names, stating she was only permitted to give out two numbers per call. I slammed the phone in her ear after receiving the first two, then made eight more calls to get the others. Fortunately, I didn't have to speak to the same operator again.

As it turned out, I only needed the first three. The elderly woman who answered the phone was not Anita but her sister, Marlene. I quickly learned more about the Nicholas family than I ever needed to know, and all without asking a single question. Unfortunately, it was all useless information.

221

Marlene Briggs had just returned to the area from Arizona, where she had spent the last thirty years with her recently deceased husband, Ralph. When Paul was killed, Anita had completely fallen apart, so Marlene had decided to move in and care for her. She had only been back in New York a little over a week when Anita had a stroke. She had lingered in a coma for two weeks before finally drifting away, leaving Marlene her house and her remaining possessions. No, she had barely known Paul, much less known anything about his computer hobbies. Why? Did I want to buy some of his junk? Did I know he was a famous writer? Oh, nothing fun like V.C. Andrews—just textbooks and stuff.

The third name on the list was Dorie Carpenter. Her obituary also listed her mother as her only surviving relative, a woman by the name of Velma Wright. She lived in Granville, which was beyond the far east side of Columbus. Her number was listed with directory assistance, and she answered on the second ring.

"Hello," I said. "I'm looking for Velma Wright."

"You've found her," she said, her voice noncommittal. "If you're selling something, save your breath."

"No, no—I'm not selling anything," I said. "I was hoping I might be able to talk to you about your daughter."

The silence grew heavy on the line.

"Ms. Wright? Are you still there?"

"I'm here," she said. "I'm about sick and tired of all you news people. How many times do I have to tell you I don't want to be interviewed?"

"I'm sorry, I've given you the wrong impression," I said. "I'm not with the media. My name is Dwayne Morrow. I'm—looking into the murd— investigation." My tongue was tripping me up at every turn. Dorie Carpenter had only been dead for a little over a week. In typical fashion, I hadn't really considered what I was going to say to these people if I actually got through. I have a horrible tendency to be blunt as a sledgehammer in these situations, and I didn't want to upset Ms. Wright. She was certainly under no obligation to speak with me at all.

"I've already spoken with the police and several of Dorie's fellow agents," she said stiffly. "I don't know what more I can offer."

"I'm not a police officer," I said. "I'm looking into this investigation independently." I noticed that Ms. Wright had referred to her daughter as an agent, although Brady Garrett had told me she held a clerical position with the Bureau. I wondered if perhaps Dorie embellished the facts a bit for her dear old mom.

"Why?"

"Pardon?"

"Why? What's in it for you?" Her distrust was evident, and I suspected she still thought I was a journalist.

"Uh—nothing, I just thought—"

"That's ridiculous. Nobody does something for nothing, Mr.—I'm sorry, your name again?"

"Morrow. Dwayne Morrow. And really, I—"

"Wait a minute," she said. "I've heard that name before. You've gotten messed up in all this yourself, haven't you? I've read it in the paper."

"Yes," I said, relieved to hear the ice begin to melt in her voice. "That's right. I suppose if you're looking for my selfish motivation, it would be that I want this maniac to leave me alone."

"What makes you think I can help?"

"Because Dorie was your daughter. I didn't have the privilege of knowing any of the victims, but I'm sure there was a common link. I only have a few questions, if you wouldn't mind."

There was another long pause. "No," she finally said. "Not like this. If you really want to speak with me, you'll have to come here."

"I'm sorry?"

"To be honest, Mr. Morrow, I don't know if I trust you or not," she said. "I judge a man by what I see in his eyes. If you're serious about speaking with me, you'll have to make a little more effort than dialing a phone."

"Sure," I said. "That's fine. When would be convenient for you?"

"Any time. I don't get out so much anymore." She gave me directions that involved a lot of landmarks, and I added them to the legal pad.

"It's almost two o'clock," I said. "I'm in Grove City, so it will take me a half-hour or so to get there."

"I'll be here," she said. "But one last thing, Mr. Morrow. If you're pulling my chain in any way, I'll set you out on your ear. If you *are* working for a publication or a television program, I'll file a lawsuit that will cost your employers a great deal of money. Reporters may be my least favorite of the human variety."

"Believe it or not, Ms. Wright, that's one thing we truly have in common," I said.

CHAPTER TWENTY

Velma Wright lived in a small rural area that was actually closer to Columbus than it was to Granville. Whoever had designed the neighborhood had little imagination; all of the one-story block houses were identical in construction, the only distinction being the color of the walls. Most of the yards flowed contiguously together, unfettered by fencing or geography. A group of laughing children ran from one to the next in an animated game only they understood. I missed the simplicity of those days.

I parked along the curb in front of Ms. Wright's house, a pastel pink stucco affair. Empty flowerbeds lay underneath heavy, opaque plastic, promising a floral kaleidoscope come spring. Small wooden craftworks adorned the yard, adding a touch of personality and warmth to the potentially sterile landscape. An ancient Ford sedan was parked underneath the carport, its glossy paint shining as if it were brand new. Everything I saw indicated Ms. Wright subsisted meagerly, but it was equally obvious she took great pride in her possessions, old though they may be.

I knocked on the front door and waited, hoping I looked trustworthy. If Velma Wright didn't talk to me, I was back to square one, pouring through my list of MOOs. Of course, if she didn't have anything useful to tell me, I might be doing that anyway. I think I sensed her more than anything else, peering through the peephole in the heavy wooden door. After a second, I heard a chain slide back and the deadbolt release.

Velma Wright was a short, round woman with probing, intelligent eyes. Her short gray hair was like a dusting of snow, her skin so dark it nearly

225

deflected the light of the sun. The sharp lines of her nose and brow suggested she had Native American somewhere in her lineage. She wore a simple cotton housedress that had been laundered until only a suggestion of its original blue color remained.

"Good afternoon, Ms. Wright," I said, extending a hand. "I'm Dwayne Morrow."

She blatantly evaluated me before taking my hand. "It's *Mrs.* Wright," she corrected, stepping aside and allowing me to enter.

Her living room was small but cozy, full of knick-knacks and pictures, many of which were of Dorie. I recognized her patrician features from the segment of Natasha Brickman's *Crimebusters* I had seen several days before. The furniture was old but serviceable, with tangles of ivy and green-tinted flowers fading into the upholstery. Thinning olive carpet bore the fresh tracks of a vacuum cleaner, and the scent of laundry detergent floated through the air while the washing machine worked noisily somewhere in the background.

"Make yourself comfortable," she said, shuffling in slippered feet to an afghan-covered recliner.

I waited until she had lowered herself into the chair before taking a seat on the sofa. "Please accept my condolences, Mrs. Wright," I said. "I wish I didn't have to intrude on you under these circumstances."

She nodded stiffly, her gaze firmly riveted to my face. Apparently, she hadn't made up her mind about me yet. "The Lord does work in mysterious ways," she said. "I put my faith in Him and try like hell to let the anger go."

I smiled, instantly liking this woman. The years hadn't been particularly kind to her body, but it was obvious her spirit was still intact. "How have you been holding up?" I asked.

A smile tugged at the corners of her own mouth before dropping away. "That's funny," she said, more to herself than to me.

"What?"

"All of the people who paraded through my house—policeman, federal investigators—a million questions and not a-one of them asked me how I was doing," she said, shaking her head. "I have my good days and my bad ones." She shifted in her chair and folded her hands in her lap. The look on her face was different now, and I realized the key to earning her trust was simply extending common courtesy. Well, whaddaya know?

I nodded. "I wish I could offer you some words of wisdom, but I'm honestly not that wise and would undoubtedly put my foot in it before it's all said and done. But I am truly sorry for your loss."

A brief laugh rumbled through her lips. "Thank you, Mr. Morrow. I do appreciate it. Now tell me, what is it you think you can accomplish that the Federal Bureau of Investigation cannot?"

"I don't really know. Maybe nothing. But I have good reason to believe the killer is either targeting me or toying with me, and in either case, I can't just sit around and wait for him to show up. The FBI won't tell me anything other than that they're watching my house, and yet still someone managed to break in and steal some flash drives. It's the content of the drives that you may be able to help me with."

Mrs. Wright's expression changed, if only slightly. "Flash drives, huh? Well, go ahead and ask your questions, Mr. Morrow. I reserve the right to refuse answering any one of them."

"Thank you," I said. "First, can you give me some insight into Dorie's work with the FBI? I had been given the impression that she did clerical work. Is that right?"

Mrs. Wright's eyebrows shot upward. "Why clerical? Just because she was black?"

I was flustered. It never occurred to me Mrs. Wright might find my question offensive. "No, no—not at all. That's what I was told."

"By whom?"

"A reporter," I said.

"Brady Garrett?"

227

The air in the room congealed. My mouth was slightly open, but there was a lengthy pause before I could manage words. "Do you know Brady Garrett?" I asked.

"Not really," she said. "Dorie did."

"How did Dorie know him?"

"I don't know exactly, but it had something to do with this Eviscerator mess. He claimed he was trying to get an inside angle, but he was just using Dorie," she said, the words dripping bitterness.

"So Dorie *was* working the Eviscerator case," I said, thinking aloud. Brady had indicated to me that Dorie's involvement had been purely incidental.

"Not officially," Mrs. Wright was quick to interject. "She had found something that she thought was significant, and it had something to do with computers. Shows you how much I know. I thought she was talking about cows at first."

MOOs. Bingo!

"Didn't Dorie report her suspicions to her superiors?" I asked.

Mrs. Wright paused before pressing her lips together and shaking her head. "No, she didn't. I kept telling her she should, but she was—reluctant."

"Why?"

Mrs. Wright sighed and shifted positions in her chair, her eyes glossing and threatening to spill over. "My Dorie was an ambitious girl. She worked hard to earn the respect of her bosses. Last year, she went undercover to help take apart a drug ring. She got some bad information and passed it on without checking it out first. It was an ambush. One of her fellow agents left the scene in a body bag. She never forgave herself for it, even though there was no formal action against her or anything. When Dorie came across something on this Eviscerator she didn't want to say anything without being sure. She wasn't involved in the investigation in any way. If she was wrong again, she was afraid it would hurt her career—maybe even end it. It all happened so fast. One night, she's excited and nervous and the next, she's secretive and spending a lot of extra time with her door closed. Then, she goes off and doesn't come back."

"Did you tell the FBI about this?" I asked.

"Of course," she said. "I want them to find the son of a bitch who did this to my daughter."

"What did they make of it?"

She chuckled. "They didn't exactly share their opinions with an old lady. They were most interested in what she was doing on the computer."

"Do you know what she was doing?"

"Not exactly," she said. "I left Dorie alone to do her work. She surely didn't need me hovering over her shoulder. But I did see the screen once or twice. It looked like a bar."

"Excuse me?"

"She was typing away on the keyboard, and words were running up the right side of the screen, but there was this picture of a bar, you know, with stools pulled up and cartoon people milling about."

"Like maybe a singles bar?"

Mrs. Wright paused, chewing her bottom lip while deliberating her phrasing. "Dorie was a good-hearted, selfless woman. She would go hungry herself to make sure her friends and family were fed. But Dorie's beauty was inside. She didn't have a lot of social graces with men. She was lonely."

Her meaning was suddenly clear to me. Dorie hadn't been investigating the Eviscerator case at all. She had been logged in to a virtual singles bar, trying to meet someone on the other side of the looking glass. Somehow, something she had encountered had alerted her to the possibility this was how the Eviscerator was meeting his victims. From within such an environment, the killer could assume any identity, whichever gender he desired. It all fit. But what could have alerted Dorie?

"What part did Brady Garrett play in all this?" I asked.

"I wish I knew," she muttered. "I never trusted that beady eyed little man from the moment I set sight on him. Dorie didn't seem to care for him much, either. He knew she was on to something, and he was trying to tag along."

"How would he know she was on to something?"

"How should I know? As I've said, I always left her alone to do her work."

"Did you tell the FBI that Brady had been in contact with Dorie?" I asked.

"Agent Crockett didn't seem at all surprised. She said Mr. Garrett had been trying to approach many people about the murders," said Mrs. Wright.

It seemed odd Nina hadn't mentioned Brady's prior relationship with one of the victims. Of course, she hadn't really offered much in the way of information, hiding behind a shield of professional confidentiality. In retrospect, Nina was also very quick to dismiss Brady as a suspect. Even though she had said she was going to dig up some background on him, she had seemed rather halfhearted about the endeavor. I wondered if Nina knew Brady better than I realized. Could she be protecting him or was I becoming completely paranoid?

"Did you ever speak to Brady yourself?" I asked.

"Other than introductions, not much," she said. "I have to say, I wasn't surprised when he turned up the day after Dorie was—found. I guess he still got his headline, one way or the other."

Her choice of words sent a chill up my spine. "Did you speak to him then?"

Mrs. Wright shook her head. "Mr. Garrett showed up in the middle of the wake. The house was full of family, and he was trying to pump me for information—can you believe that? My brother's boy, Jamar, had to escort him out of the house after I found him going through Dorie's things."

I was taken aback. I knew Brady was unscrupulous, but to violate the sanctity of a bereaved family? That was a new low even for him. "Did Brady take anything?" I asked.

"Not that I could tell, but I didn't keep an inventory of my daughter's room. I suppose there are plenty of small items he could have made off with, and I never would know the difference."

Like flash drives. Brady hadn't gotten the drives from some doe-eyed security hazard at the FBI. He had stolen them from Dorie Carpenter's room during her wake. She might have had access to the hard drives of the first two victims' computers, and if she had uncovered the relevance of the 'Moo' folder, it was possible she might have also made a mirror image of her own hard drive just in case something went wrong. Or maybe Brady was more proficient with a computer than he had ever let on and had loaded the drives himself, pushing them off on me just to drag me into this whole mess. But then why steal them back?

*****

The return trip was on autopilot. I was deep in thought, listening to my inner voice whisper Brady's guilt again and again. I no longer trusted Nina Crockett to provide honest information about Brady's past, and that was downright irrational. I couldn't help it. The memory of Nina's vigorous defense of Brady Garrett—and by now I'd convinced myself it *had* been vigorous—was building a ball of acid in my stomach.

I had hoped the visit with Velma Wright would provide further insight into the MOO her daughter was using. All I wanted was that one little piece of information. I had been hoping for some little scrap, something small to chew on, not a spotlight on Brady Garrett. Everything I knew related to those damn drives, and I still couldn't tell Agent Steele about them. Hell, I couldn't even prove they had ever existed now. I had already told Nina, but what good had it done? Nina seemed curiously disinterested in pursuing anything that might incriminate Brady Garrett.

My cell phone rang, startling me back to the present. I reached into the passenger seat and retrieved it from where it was wedged.

"God! Where have you been?" The voice was somewhat breathless.

"Melanie?" I asked, tensing immediately. "What's wrong?"

"I've been trying to reach you for hours. Don't you carry that damned thing with you?" she asked.

"I left it in the car. Are you alright? You're scaring me, Mel."

"Yes, yes—sorry. I'm fine. Everything's fine. Everything's great. I *found* it," she said, and I realized her breathlessness was due to exultation.

"Found what?"

"The *MOO*," she said. "I've got it."

"You mean you know which one?" This was the information I was originally after. Even though Mrs. Wright had narrowed the focus of my MOO quest, she hadn't been able to supply me with the actual name.

"Uh-huh. And guess what?" She could barely contain her excitement.

"What?"

"I think I've found the Eviscerator, too."

*****

Driving into Columbus was an exercise in frustration. A semi-truck had jackknifed on I-70 near the junction of I-71 and S.R. 315, backing traffic up for miles. I had to resist the urge to get out of the car and run the remaining distance, which would have undoubtedly been faster. Finally, I arrived downtown and pulled into a premium parking garage, sliding my battered red Optima between a shiny black BMW sports car and a pearl Lexus sedan.

I had told Melanie to lock herself in her room and not to answer the door for anyone except me. She reminded me she had already checked out of her hotel room and was currently at the library, her suitcases in tow. I didn't like the thought of her being so exposed. She thought I was being overly cautious, but I didn't want to take any stupid chances. If she had, in fact, initiated contact with the killer, then it had all happened too easily. The FBI had known about the MOO for some time. They would have had agents monitoring the site since first becoming aware of it. For Melanie to have stumbled across the murderer on her first attempt—it was hard to swallow. Of course, if Brady Garrett was behind the murders, this would only be the next move in his increasingly personal game. He could be keeping tabs on Melanie from a discreet distance, waiting quietly in the wings for his moment of opportunity.

Melanie was at one of the tables positioned near the main entrance. Her eyes were dancing with excitement, and she stood as I drew near.

"I thought you'd never get here," she said, kissing me quickly before turning to clear the table of the magazines with which she had been passing the time.

"Traffic," I said, stooping to pick up her suitcases. "Where's Jordan?"

"He went back to Portsmouth," she said. "He seemed anxious to return, and I didn't see any point in keeping him."

I lugged the bags through the main exit and wrestled my way through a throng of students ascending the front stairs. It was rush-hour on a Friday night, and pedestrian as well as vehicular traffic was heavy. Melanie jogged along beside me, her breath pluming out and dissipating at regular intervals. She was so pleased with herself she was almost skipping.

Once we were in the car and safely underway, I said, "So, fill me in." I hadn't wanted to discuss anything over the cell phone earlier. My current state of paranoia now also included the possibility of wiretapping, apparently.

"The conference ended early today, just after one," she said. "I didn't have anything else to do. I had already checked out of the hotel, so I was hauling my luggage everywhere I went. I decided to go to the library and continue our search. I found it at about two o'clock. Boom! There was the 'Moo' folder on the hard drive. It's like a singles bar or something. It's called, 'Sweet Meet.' Catchy, huh?"

"Why didn't you call me?"

"I thought you were going to be tied up with the victims' families," she said. "And then I kind of got into what I was doing and lost track of time."

I knew exactly what she meant. Hours pass as minutes when I'm deeply engrossed in a computer project.

"You said you thought you found the Eviscerator."

Melanie nodded. "I started a dialogue with someone who called himself Odin. Very creepy. Claimed to live close to Columbus. He was into ancient mythology in a big way."

"Odin? Is that supposed to mean something to me?"

"He's the Norse god of war."

"How original. Why is that psychos always feel compelled to go for the goofy crap?"

Melanie shrugged. "I don't know. Maybe it appeals to something primal."

"That's bullshit."

"Of course it's bullshit," she said. "We're talking about a man who literally shreds his victims. What kind of logic are you looking for?"

"Sorry. The whole thing is just so cliché. Bet you money that when this bastard is caught, we'll hear all about his abusive mother, his alcoholic father," I said.

"Voices in his head, too."

"So, what makes you think this Odin is the Eviscerator?" I asked.

"He said that he had been absolved by the blood of St. Nicholas and worn the crown of thorns of the carpenter."

"What?"

Melanie sighed. "Paul Nicholas and Dorie Carpenter. It seems like a pretty direct reference to me," she said, disappointed I hadn't immediately understood.

"Maybe," I said. "But he could be paying simultaneous homage to Santa Claus and Jesus."

"Ha-ha."

"Well," I said. "I guess the only thing to do is log in and try to find him again. Maybe we can turn the tables and lure him to a rendezvous of *our* choosing. Wouldn't that be a kick in the pants?"

"Shouldn't we call Arthur Steele?" she asked.

"What for? We don't have anything conclusive to tell him—other than what we *do* know we culled from stolen federal property."

"How about Nina Crockett?"

I pursed my lips and shook my head. "I'm not comfortable with her anymore."

"What?"

"I asked her to check out Brady's past," I said. "She was too quick to jump to Brady's defense."

"In what way?"

I chewed on my bottom lip. "Well, nothing specific. She just kept telling me I was overreacting. Do you think she might be sleeping with Brady?"

Melanie laughed. "That's out of left field."

"I just can't understand why she's so eager to dismiss Brady as a suspect."

Melanie groaned. "What is it with you and Brady Garrett? He's not the Eviscerator."

"I may have to disagree," I said. I then recounted what I had learned at Velma Wright's house earlier. Melanie was quiet after I spoke, digesting all of the oddities of the story.

"Do you really think Nina Crockett might be involved with Brady?" she finally asked, and I couldn't help but grin. My suspicions may be nothing more than paranoia, but it was nice to have company. Then she added, "And if so, do you think she's involved in the murders, too?"

That hadn't occurred to me. My imagination had fed me a story that involved Nina Crockett falling hopelessly in love with Brady, willing to lie if necessary to keep him out of trouble. If she was his partner in crime, her job with the FBI gave her unique insight into the progress of the investigation, even if she wasn't working directly on it.

"I don't know," I said. "But we have to keep our eyes open. Everybody is starting to look suspicious to me now."

As my house appeared in the distance, I noticed a car already waiting in the drive. This was turning into a regular occurrence. I had never had so many uninvited guests, all willing to camp in my driveway until I eventually returned. I was pleased to see that it was not Brady Garrett's maroon Saturn. I recognized the red BMW sports car, but it wasn't until Jeffrey Carter emerged from the driver's side that I connected the dots.

"Who's that?" asked Melanie, studying the man's pallid countenance, tinged bright red at the cheekbones.

"Jeffrey Carter," I said. "Geneva and Alan's son."

And judging from the way he approached, he was *pissed*.

CHAPTER TWENTY-ONE

I motioned for Melanie to stay in the car while I got out. I quickly scanned the horizon, wondering where in the hell the cavalry was. I expected federal agents to come storming out of the tall grass bordering my yard, weapons drawn in my defense. They didn't know Jeffrey Carter from Adam, but his approach was undeniably aggressive. For all they knew, he could be the Eviscerator, come to claim his next two victims. The tall grass waved listlessly in the gentle breeze, a sure sign I was on my own.

"Mr. Carter?" I said, my perplexity evident in the way the last syllable of his name twisted up the scale. He was literally *huffing*, his shiny red cheeks pulling the cold air in and out in a furious cloud of exhaust. His hands were thrust into the pockets of his custom-tailored beige overcoat, and I could see his knuckles clearly outlined against the straining fabric of his pockets.

"Well, are you happy *now*?" he shrieked—and when I say he shrieked, I mean like a hysterical woman. He had stopped about two feet in front of my face, his wild eyes searching my reaction. I had no idea what in the hell he was talking about.

"Hey, calm down, Mr. Carter," I said. "I'm not sure what's going on, but—"

"*LIES!*" He nearly perforated my eardrum with that one. "You hated her, and you lied about her, and you *HATED* her!"

"Hated who? What are you talking about?"

"*MY MO-MO-MOTHER!*"

I kept the car door between myself and Jeffrey, not at all sure what he was blithering on about. I thought the whole Geneva Carter fiasco had been put to rest. Alan Carter had assured me of as much. Sally Sheaffer had received a dismissal of the complaint. What more could there be?

"I don't understand, Mr. Carter," I said. "The case was dismissed. Your father said—"

"My *father?* Well, I should have known," he muttered, shaking his head ruefully. I was thankful he had returned to a level human ears are capable of receiving. "You got to her through him. I see."

"You're not making any sense," I said. "I didn't do anything to your mother, I swear to you. Not ever. I have no idea why she would make up such a story except she was pissed at me because your father found out I was tailing him."

"You can go to hell with your lies," he hissed. "It really doesn't matter anymore, does it? She's gone."

"Gone? She left your father? Where did she go?"

He shot me the funniest look, as if I'd dare pretend I didn't already know. "She didn't *go* anywhere. She *killed* herself."

"*What?* Oh, my God!" The past week had shown me Geneva Carter was unbalanced, but I had attributed her behavior to a pathetic cry for attention. She certainly hadn't seemed the type to kill herself, but then again, I don't know if I would have recognized the signs if they had been right in front of my face.

"Father was planning to have her committed," he spat. "No doubt because of the things you told him. Mother took an entire bottle of sleeping pills."

"Oh, God," I said. "I'm so sorry. I—"

He stopped my flow of words with the sheer contempt in his eyes. "I only want to know one thing," he said. "Are you happy now? She's dead, and you murdered her."

I pressed my lips together tightly. Did I? Did I really murder her? Were my actions what pushed her over that final precipice? Impossible. I was caught in one of her self-scripted psychodramas. I had done nothing more insidious than eat lunch with her. When she had asked me to follow Alan all over creation, I had done it because I liked her. I had felt sorry for her. If her husband was cheating, I thought she was entitled to know. Still, nothing I could say now would dissuade Jeffrey from believing the words that flowed from his lips like venom.

He waited for a response, his accusing eyes burning into me. I said nothing, returning his glare evenly. I wasn't about to accept responsibility for this, not just so Jeffrey could unload some of his angry grief on me. He eventually shook his head in disgust and returned to his car, firing up the engine with an exaggerated roar. He nearly clipped my door as he backed haphazardly around my car, finding his way back to the road and disappearing in an angry cloud of dust.

Melanie had gotten out of the car as Jeffrey drove away, and she watched until his taillights disappeared on the eastern horizon. "You know this isn't your fault," she said.

"I know. I just can't believe it. Geneva Carter—dead? It doesn't seem possible."

Melanie stepped around the trunk and insinuated herself against my side, wrapping an arm around my midsection. We walked to the house in silence, her head resting against my shoulder.

Dexter met us at the door, yowling his familiar greeting, which translated loosely to "Get me my dinner, you bastard." I tossed my coat aside, then stooped down and scooped him up, nuzzling him into a purring frenzy as I carried him into the kitchen. I automatically activated the answering machine as I passed, noticing it was blinking but not bothering to tabulate the message count.

The first two calls were hang-ups. The third was Nola Caudill.

"Dwayne? Hi, this is Nola—Brady's friend? I was hoping you might be able to call me later. My number is 614-555-3567. It doesn't matter how late. Thank you."

Hmm.

The fourth was from Doug Boggs.

"Dwayne? I'm sorry it took me so long to get back with you. I—uh, I've been giving your proposal a lot of thought, discussing it with my people—" (By people, he meant his mother.) "—and I have to admit, I find it interesting. Unfortunately, I don't really think I'm in a position to expand the business right now. Maybe someday we could give it a whirl, but right now...Anyway, feel free to call me if you need something. Any of your friends or family need someone followed, you know who to refer 'em to."

Well, shit. I knew it was coming. I knew Loretta Boggs would never allow her son to collaborate with me. Still, the rejection was a disappointment. I would have to reformulate my plan for getting a PI license, and short of abandoning my consultant business, I had no idea how to proceed. Oh, well. It was a problem for another day.

The answering machine signaled it had reached the end of messages, and Melanie asked, "Do you want me to reset the messages?"

"Yeah," I called, scooping a malodorous ground concoction into Dexter's food dish. He dove in, chomping noisily as his throat continued to softly rumble. I went to the living room and grabbed the cordless, dialing Nola Caudill's number.

"Hi," I said when she answered. "Dwayne Morrow, returning your call."

"Oh, Dwayne. Good. Thanks for calling me back," she said. "I'm sorry to bother you, but I wanted to talk to you about Brady."

"Is something wrong?" I asked.

She paused. "I'm not really sure. He—he's not been himself. Of course, I suppose that's only natural considering what happened to Nikki. I'm not really sure why I called you. Maybe I'm looking for some kind of reassurance. Have you seen Brady lately? Has he seemed like himself to you?"

The last time I had seen Brady was when I believed he had stolen the drives from my house. "Nola, I should probably tell you that Brady and I aren't exactly friends," I said. "I only met him for the first time last week."

"Oh," she said, clearly surprised. "When you were there after Nikki had been—I thought—I guess it doesn't matter what I thought."

"What makes you think Brady is acting unusual?" I asked.

"He's been talking to himself quite a bit. I know there are plenty of folks who do that on a regular basis, but not Brady. He's usually quite deliberate when he speaks," she said. "But he's mentioned Terri more than once, and I'm afraid he's going to end up upsetting Billy. Billy's an amazing little guy, very resilient. But I don't know how much of his father's nonsense he can take before it eventually affects him, too."

"He hasn't been abusive, has he?"

"Oh, heaven's no! Brady wouldn't hurt a fly. But he's asked me to keep Billy with me almost non-stop since Nikki—died. It's not that I mind, don't get me wrong. Wendell and I love having a child in the house, and Nalia, our exchange student, thinks Billy's adorable. It's just not *normal*. Brady is famous for asking us to watch Billy on short notice. It's the nature of his job. But he never leaves him for long or for so much consecutive time. He's barely seen his son at all since—" Her voice trailed away.

If Brady was the Eviscerator, then he had been a very busy man the past few days. He wouldn't have had time to play responsible parent while advancing his evil. Of course, if he *wasn't* the Eviscerator, he could be afraid to keep his son near him, afraid the killer might again exact vengeance on his dwindling circle of family. On the other hand, if Brady *was* the Eviscerator, and Melanie had, in fact, initiated contact with him, he might already be baiting a trap for her. All that bullshit about St. Nicholas and the blood of the carpenter. It was too easy. It even smelled like a trap. He could have been sitting right behind Melanie in the library, watching her as her excitement grew, feeding her line after line to raise her suspicions. I needed more information about Brady, and I needed it yesterday.

"Is Billy with you now?" I asked.

"Yes," she said. "Brady said he would be tied up all evening. Why?"

"Nothing," I said, trying to sound nonchalant. The realization that Brady Garrett was loose in the night, his whereabouts unaccounted for, had a startling impact, and I found myself glancing around the room, checking each window, expecting Brady's grinning mug to be framed in any one of them. "I just thought I might stop by and visit him, make sure he's doing all right."

"Well, you'll have to wait until tomorrow. He said he was going to be out of town overnight."

"I'll do that," I said. "I'm sorry I can't give you greater peace of mind. I'm sure Brady's just coping with things. Has he been to his psychiatrist?"

"Dr. Clark? Other than right after Nikki's murder, I don't think so. I keep telling Brady he should go, that he needs someone to talk to, but he just smiles and shakes his head. It just breaks my heart."

"I'm sure everything will work out," I said, but the words were hollow in my own ears. "If you want, I can call you after I see him."

"Oh, that'd be nice," she said. "I'd appreciate it. I'm very worried about him."

"Try not to dwell on it," I said, opting for the inane after finding nothing sage. "I'll call you as soon as I can."

We disconnected, and I turned around to find Melanie perched on the arm of my couch, waiting expectantly. I paused, then turned back to the phone, dialing Brady's number. It rang four times before the answering machine picked up. Judging from the length of the musical interlude before the signifying beep, Brady hadn't checked his messages in some time. I hung up without leaving one.

"C'mon," I said, grabbing my coat. "We've got some investigating to do."

242

"Oh, we do? What's going on?" asked Melanie as she slipped back into her own coat. I was prowling the living room, digging through piles of junk mail and old newspapers. "What are you looking for?"

"My camera," I said. "I know I left it around here somewhere."

"Why do you need your camera?"

"To take pictures."

"Smart ass. Are you going to tell me what's going on or just keep me guessing?" she asked, nudging with her toe a small pile of clothes I had left near the end of the couch. I bent to scoop them up hastily, embarrassed that she had gotten a glimpse of my more slovenly side.

"Nola Caudill is a family friend of Brady's. That was her on the phone," I said, still scanning the room's surfaces for my camera.

"Tell me something I don't know."

"She's been concerned about Brady's erratic behavior."

"Would you expect his behavior to be anything other than erratic?" asked Melanie, casually dragging a finger through a layer of dust that I had apparently repeatedly missed on the mantel. Dammit! "Whether he's the killer or not, his life has changed dramatically in the past few days."

"Yes, and it's the uncertainty about him that's driving me crazy," I said, kneeling in front of the sofa and peering underneath. Nothing but a pair of my own underpants. God, I was a pig! I pushed them farther back, hoping Melanie wouldn't notice. Where was my damned camera? "Nola said that Brady was going to be away overnight. I want to take a look at his house, see if the drives are there. I need to know if he took them. I want to take the camera in case we stumble onto anything else that might interest the FBI."

"Are you sure you left the camera here?" she asked. "Could it be in the car?"

I shook my head. "I had it the last day I followed Alan Carter. I remember leaving it in plain sight in the living room, hoping it would remind me to get the film developed so I could forward the pictures to

Geneva. She paid for the pictures, so I figured she should have them. Then all this shit started up, and I forgot all about it. Guess it doesn't matter now."

"How are we supposed to get into Brady's house?" she asked.

"I'd rather not talk about that right now," I said, and Melanie nodded her head once in silent understanding. I knew we would have to break in, yet another illegal activity I could add to my résumé. At this rate, it didn't matter that Doug Boggs had shunned my partnership offer. I wouldn't be eligible for a PI license anyway, not with my continuing casual disregard for the law. Still, I needed to know.

*****

The night air was bitterly cold, but the Optima's engine was still warm, and the blower dumped enough powerful heat into the floorboards to cause our feet to nearly burst into flames.

I was irritated. We had to make a pit stop at Kroger to pick up a cheap disposable camera because I hadn't been able to find mine, and the camera on my cell phone was practically useless. That damn camera was brand new, and I had spent a small fortune on it. I hadn't even figured out what half of the buttons were for. I could have sworn I left it in the living room, but after a thorough-to-the-point-of-redundant search, I had allowed I might have transferred it to the car, meaning to drop the film off to be developed. I cursed myself again for choosing film versus digital. Turning the car inside out produced nothing more than forgotten change and a Lifesaver or two. I didn't have time to dig any further. I didn't know how long Brady would be away from his house, and we were still twenty minutes away.

"Are you ready to tell me how we are getting into the house?" asked Melanie.

"Let's hope he left the front door unlocked."

"Yeah, right."

As we descended the gravel driveway, I was relieved to see that Brady's bungalow was dark except for a porch light. His red Saturn was nowhere to be seen, and I realized I had been holding my breath in anticipation.

"What if he comes back while we're inside?" asked Melanie.

"I don't know."

"What if there's an alarm system?"

"I don't know."

"What if he's already inside?"

"For God's sake, Melanie!" I snapped. "We're going to have to take this as it comes."

Out of the corner of my eye, I saw her jaw extend slightly, a sure sign that I had just pissed her off.

"I'm sorry," I said. "I didn't mean that to sound like it did."

She nodded but didn't speak, and I knew it would be a few moments longer before she would again be willing. I almost sighed, but stopped on a dime, realizing it would only piss her off more.

I parked my car at the mouth of Brady's sidewalk, killing the lights and shutting off the engine. The wind had picked up, and temperatures were heading south. I could hear bare branches from the tall trees by the creek gnashing together in protest.

"Should you leave the car here?" asked Melanie. "It's right in plain sight. If Brady comes back, he'll know we're here."

"I know," I said. "We'll have to take the chance. If there's any type of surveillance going on at my house—and I'm not entirely convinced there is—they might be watching Brady's house, too. I want to get in, but I don't want it to look like we're breaking in."

"But we *are* breaking in."

"If we have to."

"Then what difference does it make?"

245

"If we tried to hide the car and some FBI guy comes across it, he'll *know* we're up to something. He'll make a beeline for the house, but not after calling it in. At least this way, we might stand a chance. We could say we were stopping by to check in on our old buddy," I said.

We got out of the car and approached the porch. A closer inspection of the premises confirmed that the place was, indeed, empty—unless, of course, Brady was hiding in complete darkness, waiting for us. I shuddered inwardly and pushed the thought away. I had already grown paranoid enough without paralyzing myself with such mental imagery.

I tried the doorknob, but of course, it was locked. I tugged at the two windows which overlooked the porch to no avail, their frames held securely in place by brass hasps and layers of paint. I turned and did a quick, guilty scan of the horizon, ensuring that we were still alone.

"What now?" asked Melanie.

"Stay here," I said. "I'm going to check the other windows and the sliding glass door in back. If you see anything at all, scream like crazy."

Melanie shivered in the cold. "All right. Hurry."

I went around the side of the house, testing each window as I passed. All were securely fastened. The rear of the house was less accessible. The landscape drifted down toward the creek bed below, providing no access to the deck upon which I had once spoken with Brady. But—lo and behold—I could see the sliding glass door that opened out onto the deck was standing slightly ajar. I guess Brady didn't worry so much about this entrance since it was twenty feet above the ground. None of the nearby trees were close enough to use as a ladder, and I doubted my own ability to shimmy up the stilted legs of the deck; climbing up was out of the question. On the plus side, I was fairly certain Brady didn't have an alarm set, because it would be screaming like a banshee with the sliding glass door open. I continued around the house, climbing back up the craggy hillside to examine the windows on the far wall. Like all the others, they were shut tight.

"No luck?" asked Melanie as I returned to the front of the house.

"The sliding door's open, but I don't know how I can get to it—unless—" I reached up and easily cupped my hands over the eave of the porch. I clamped down and tried to pull myself up, my legs flailing wildly as I tried to plant my elbows over the edge of the low roof. Running had done wonders for my midsection but nothing, unfortunately, for my upper body strength. I scrambled hopelessly and eventually lost my grip, landing squarely on my ass on the concrete sidewalk.

"*DAMMIT!*" I screamed.

"Well, if anyone's watching the house, they surely heard *that*," said Melanie, offering a hand to help pull me back to my feet. "What were you doing? Going down the chimney?"

"I'm not Santa Claus!" I said irritably, getting up and dusting off my backside. "The sliding glass door opens onto a deck out back. I can't get to it from the backside of the house because the yard slopes down, but if I can get on the roof here, I could go over the top and drop down onto the deck."

"Boost me."

"What?"

"I'm smaller than you, lighter than you," she said. "Boost me."

She handed me the disposable camera, and I stuffed it into my pocket. She went up easily, lithely scampering across the tiled roof and disappearing over the slight crest at its center. Again, I scanned the horizon, my ears magnifying every whisper of the night. After a moment, I heard a soft thud, the sound of Melanie's feet making contact with the wooden deck. After another moment, the deadbolt clicked, and I was inside.

Melanie started to turn on one of the standing lamps in the small living room, but I stopped her hand. "We can't turn on the lights. They'll show through the windows."

"Well, we can't see in the dark. Did you bring a flashlight?"

Dammit.

"Turn on the kitchen light," I said. "It's in the back of the house and won't be so noticeable. It should still throw some light our way."

Melanie felt her way through the gloom and reached around the corner, fumbling for the light switch. A moment later, a rectangle of light spilled down the short corridor from the kitchen and into Brady's living space.

I crossed the room to the small computer workstation in the far corner. I saw them halfway across the room, three flash drives scattered haphazardly beside the mouse. I dragged my finger across them, recognizing the strange codes I had seen, identifying the origin of each drive's contents. I didn't really know what to do. I stared at them for a moment in silence and nearly jumped out of my skin when Melanie placed a hand on my elbow.

"Find something?" she asked. Her voice was on edge as well, as if she already knew I had. She hadn't really thought Brady was capable of these horrible murders, and as the evidence glistened in the reflected light, I realized I hadn't really believed it either. I didn't want to accept I had repeatedly been in contact with someone so unspeakably evil.

"Uh-huh," I said, stepping aside so she could see the flash drives underneath my fingertips. "He was the only one who could have taken them."

I fumbled in my pocket for the disposable camera, and my eyes came to rest on the shadows across the coffee table. Laying on its side with its hinged back open was my camera, its empty guts coldly eyeing me.

"I guess I see what happened to my camera," I said, picking it up and closing the cover. I turned it over and examined it for damage, but there was nothing discernibly wrong with it, except that its roll of film had been removed. I strapped it around my neck and pulled out the disposable, snapping a few pictures of Brady's work area and the resting beside the mouse.

"What now?" asked Melanie.

"I'm going to search the place," I said. "This is enough for me, but it doesn't directly tie Brady to the murders. There has to be something else in the house. I want you to go back out on the porch and stand guard. I don't want Brady to sneak up on us."

"All right."

Melanie crossed the room and placed her hand on the doorknob. My cell phone chose that exact second to shrill, scaring the hell out of both of us. I snatched it from my belt and hurried to answer it.

"Hello?"

"Dwayne, honey?" It was my mom. Of all times.

"Mom, I can't really talk right now. Let me call you back tomorrow," I said.

"Honey, I need to speak with you for a minute. It's urgent."

"So's what I'm working on, Mom. *Please.*"

"I don't know how to tell you this, but something's happened. Your father and I can't get there for a couple hours, and I think you really need to go."

"Go? Go where?"

"To Riverside, sweetheart. Something's happened to Sheila."

My mind went blank for a minute. Sheila? Sheila who? Melanie remained at the doorway, her hand on the knob, her eyes fixed on my face. I was afraid Brady would turn the knob from the other side at any moment. I needed to be off the damn phone!

"Sheila?" I said, my voice hollow and detached in my own ears. The fog suddenly lifted. "Matt's Sheila?"

"I'm afraid so," Mom said. "She was attacked when she left work tonight."

CHAPTER TWENTY-TWO

"Is she all right?" The plastic casing creaked in protest as I unconsciously tightened my grip on the phone. My internal temperature had plummeted.

"I don't know. She was hurt pretty badly, and I guess she's in surgery. I don't know much more than that, but I don't think your brother should be alone. He was hysterical."

"Of course, of course," I said. "I'll go right over." I disconnected the call and headed for the front door, my mind racing, and my vision blurred. My subconscious was whispering things about too much coincidence, but I didn't want to accept that; to accept it would be to take responsibility.

"What?" asked Melanie as I stepped past her. "What's going on?"

"My brother's girlfriend was attacked tonight. She's in the hospital." She scrambled after me as I hurried past her.

"Attacked? What happened?"

"I don't know anything. Let's just go," I said, holding the door for her as she crossed the threshold to the porch. I pulled the door shut, my mind still insisting that the timing of this wasn't right. I slid into the driver's seat and slipped the key into the ignition.

Time crawled like sludge as we crept across town toward Riverside Hospital. I kept telling myself everything would turn out all right, it always did, but it seemed ridiculously futile. That's the sort of nonsense we teach our children to ward off nightmares. In real life, things rarely play out by the numbers. I felt guilty that my last exchanges with Sheila had been less than pleasant. I knew her short temper had mostly been due to hormonal changes, but it hadn't stopped me from taking offense, avoiding her simply because I wasn't willing to be the object of her witty putdowns, even though I *knew* they were meaningless. Oh my God. The baby. Was the baby all right? The baby *had* to be all right. This was my brother's child, my future niece or nephew, my—

I hadn't even realized my eyes were leaking until Melanie reached across and gently wiped my cheek with her fingertip. "It'll be okay," she whispered, but there was no sincerity in her voice. She was the widow of a murdered man, for God's sake! She knew firsthand there was nothing fair in life.

We finally arrived at the hospital, and I curbed the tire hard as I careened into the parking lot, screeching to a halt in a no-parking zone. I defiantly challenged anyone to slap a ticket on the windshield as I dragged Melanie toward the emergency entrance. Melanie struggled to keep pace with my longer stride. I pushed through non-ambulatory waiting room drones, heedless of their potential frailties, until I finally found the nurses' station.

"Morrow," I said with no preamble of any sort. I was greeted with the vacant stare of a young woman with pursed lips, trying to pull the English out of what I had just said. "Morrow, dammit, Morrow! Sheila Morrow!" I thumped my palm against the countertop, and she shot a quick glance to the security guard who was standing near the entrance. I took a deep breath and forced myself to relax, soften my tone. I tried again. "Can you tell me where I can find Sheila Morrow? She was brought in after an attack—of some sort."

The nurse typed a few keystrokes into her computer and stared with her big dumb eyes at the flickering screen. "I'm sorry, there's no one here by that name."

I was dumbstruck. Could Mom have been mistaken? It took a moment for the dust to dissipate, and I remembered that Sheila and Matt weren't married. But what was her goddamned last name? It was at the edge of my periphery, just beyond my grasp—

"Barker," supplied Melanie from over my shoulder. "Sheila Barker."

I turned to face her in amazement while the nurse entered the new information on her keyboard. "You've never even met Sheila," I said.

"You've mentioned her before. Her last name stuck with me, like Bob Barker from *The Price is Right*."

"Yes, we have a Sheila Barker," said the nurse. "She's still in surgery. I'm afraid I don't know anything about her condition."

"My brother is here waiting," I said. "Can you tell me where I'd find him?"

"Go down the hall to the elevators on your right. Go to the fourth floor and check in at reception. They'll direct you to the waiting lounge."

I grabbed Melanie's arm and dragged her along toward the elevators. I jabbed impatiently at the buttons, contemplating the expediency of the stairs when one of the cars finally arrived. The elevator was near capacity, but I wasn't above nudging a few of the occupants into sharing a closer proximity so Melanie and I might fit in as well. The car stopped at every damn floor on the way up, exchanging occupants but never really reducing the overall number of disgruntled passengers. Finally at the fourth floor, we escaped.

The next sequence of events is a blur. I had nearly reached the nurses station when I saw Matt pacing the far end of the corridor. I hurried toward him, but he was too lost in his own horror to notice. I had nearly reached him when his eyes finally focused on me. I saw recognition.

Then anger.

There was no hesitation in his stride. I didn't even see his feet moving across the shiny, off-white tiles. He was suddenly on top of me, knocking me backward. My head snapped back only to be stopped by the wall, and the whole world went fuzzy for a moment.

"THIS IS YOUR FAULT!" Matt screamed, spittle flying from most of the consonants.

"Wha—?" I managed before being slammed into the wall again. I knew Melanie was saying something, but I couldn't pick out the words. I saw her trying to hold Matt's arm, but he brushed her aside effortlessly.

"Your goddamn *Eviscerator* did this to Sheila!" he spat. "If you could keep your fucking nose where it belongs, none of this would be happening!"

He slammed me against the wall again, jarring my teeth in my head. I did nothing to defend myself; the weight of his words was only just sinking in. It was true, then. He was getting to me through my family. The thought had crossed my mind when I warned Melanie not to travel downtown by herself, but even then, it never really seemed *truly* possible. But the bastard was actually *doing* it.

"Do we have a problem, gentlemen?" Hospital security had appeared in the form of Hulk Hogan, or someone bearing an uncanny resemblance. He inserted himself between us like a knife through soft butter.

"Let's go, Dwayne," urged Melanie, tugging at my elbow.

My lips were numb as I moved them. "I should stay—"

"So help me," hissed Matt, straining over the shoulder of the security guard. "If Sheila doesn't pull through, if anything happens to our baby—"

"C'mon now, sir," said the guard, taking Matt firmly by the shoulders. "You're not doing anyone any good like this. Let's go back to the waiting room." He guided Matt away, and although Matt allowed it, he continued to stare at me with the most ghastly blend of hatred and accusation. My inner voice was whispering its concurrence with my brother, who looked at me as if he wished me dead. I was utterly unprepared for this. I've always been close to my brother. We'd never had more than the customary sibling disagreements, the same stupid squabbles that occur in any family. Nothing of substance—nothing like *this.*

"Let's go," Melanie repeated, slipping her arm around me. The sounds and smells of the hospital were suddenly overpowering my senses. I needed fresh air. I allowed Melanie to direct me back toward the elevators and out of the hospital while my brain locked up and refused to process even one more shred of thought.

*****

"Are you all right?" asked Melanie, gently stroking my cheek. The Optima's engine was off, the car still nestled in a shadowy corner of the parking garage. I desperately wanted a cigarette. Who gave a shit if I died of lung cancer? A slow, agonizing death was exactly what I deserved.

Still, I nodded remotely. I was far from all right, but there wasn't much I could do about it. I had no idea how Matt related Sheila's attack with the Eviscerator, but I knew if he believed it, he must have good reason. Why hadn't I *warned* them? With the placement of Nikki Sanders's foot, the game had taken a distinctly intimate turn. Not only should I have warned Matt and Sheila, but Mom and Dad, my sister Gina, and—

"It's not your fault," said Melanie, taking my chin in her hand and turning my face toward her. "This is one sick guy. There's no reasoning in what he's doing."

I opened my mouth, but there weren't any words in the wings. My throat made an odd sort of squeak, and then she was holding me, pulling me close and whispering gentle comforts that flowed so effortlessly from her lips.

*****

It was almost nine o'clock when Melanie and I returned to my house. This time, no one waited in the drive, nothing lurked in the shadows other than more shadows. We went inside, and I rearmed the alarm and bolted the door. I sank into one end of the sofa, and Melanie snuggled up beside me. I stared at the pictures on the wall, lost in my own sense of responsibility. Despite Melanie's reassurance, I knew Matt was right. If the Eviscerator—oh, let's just call him Brady, shall we?—hadn't fixated on me, Sheila would be home right now, bitching at Matt about the size of her ankles or some such shit. She and Matt would be preparing for the big cookout tomorrow, preparing to inform my parents that soon they'd be grandparents. Oh, God. Every avenue of thought led back to the unborn baby, possibly already lost. I felt completely helpless. Things would never be the same between Matt and me again.

Brady Garrett.

Was he doing this to Sheila as Melanie and I nosed through his cottage? How many times had he been standing here in my living room, leading me by the nose toward whatever was on those drives? He could have killed me at any given moment, but apparently that would have been poor sportsmanship. I deserved to suffer, and Brady had found a hell of a way to make it happen. I hugged Melanie so tightly it was a wonder she didn't cry out in pain. Although I would never say it aloud—never even let the thought form consciously—I was selfishly relieved it wasn't Melanie who was attacked. It was the only thing that seemed more horrific to me.

"So, what now?" she asked.

"We have to stop him," I said. I got off the couch and went back to my den, turning on lights as I went. It seemed very important the house be completely illuminated, all shadowy corners dispelled. I reached down to the CPU on the floor under my desk and flipped the power switch. The monitor flickered and glowed, and Windows began to load.

The phone rang, impossibly loud in the quiet room. I retrieved the cordless, hoping like hell it wasn't my brother calling with bad news about Sheila or the baby.

"Dwayne? Hi, it's Nina. I hoped I'd be able to reach you. I heard about what happened tonight. I'm so sorry," she said.

"Do you know anything about Sheila's condition?" I asked.

"She pulled through the surgery, but I don't know much more than that."

"What about the baby?"

"What baby?"

"She's pregnant," I said.

"Oh. I didn't know. No one has said anything to me," said Nina. After an uncomfortable pause, she added, "But no news is good news, right?"

"If you say so."

"I guess you had some trouble with your brother," she said.

"Yeah. He's of the opinion this is the work of the Eviscerator," I said.

"Arthur Steele seems to think it's likely."

"How does he connect the dots?" I don't know what I wanted. Maybe I was hoping Nina would offer another alternative, a reason why I wasn't to blame for what had happened to Sheila. If it wasn't my fault, Matt couldn't hold me responsible. To hear her confirm my brother's angry hypothesis was a hammer blow to the gut, an unsettling of the bowels.

"Well, we can't be entirely certain, of course, but there was an eyewitness."

"An eyewitness? That's *great*—"

"Ah-ah—not so fast. The eyewitness didn't see enough to make her much good. What she *did* see is what makes us think it was the Eviscerator."

"I don't even know what happened," I said. "Matt wasn't in the mood to rehash."

Nina supplied the details, as best as they could be reconstructed. At approximately five-thirty, Sheila had clocked out from Brooks-Warten, a law firm in Upper Arlington where she was employed as a clerk. Her workspace was on the third floor of a sprawling building that looked more like a motel than an attorney's office. Although the building had an elevator, it was slow and rickety, and many of the employees regularly opted for the stairs. It was in the stairwell that Sheila had met her attacker. He had stabbed her at least once before Connie Eaton, a secretary from the second floor, had wandered onto the landing, her mind on a million things other than what was going on right in front of her eyes. What followed happened quickly. Ms. Eaton remembered the man turning and running, half-dragging Sheila with him. He tossed Sheila down the stairs and then bounded after her, stabbing her once more before disappearing through the exit and into the night.

"The viciousness of the attack, the persistence—he stabbed her again *after* Ms. Eaton had seen him. He wasn't interested in hurting Ms. Eaton, even though she's just a tiny little thing, hardly a match for a man with a knife," said Nina. "Combine all that with Sheila's relationship to you, it seems very likely that it was the Eviscerator."

"And this Connie Eaton didn't get a good look at him?" I asked in disbelief. How could someone witness a thing like that and not have the image burned indelibly into her memory?

"Afraid not. The stairwell is dark, and the guy wore big, loose clothes. He was in constant motion from the moment Ms. Eaton focused on him. She's only fairly certain it was even a man."

"It's Brady Garrett, Nina," I said. It was time to come as clean as I could. As long as Brady roamed the streets, the body count would escalate. "I can't give you concrete proof yet, but it's Brady Garrett. He's the one who's doing all this."

Nina sighed. "No, Dwayne, he's not. I've checked into the old records. There's nothing to suggest he was responsible for the death of his wife, other than shitty circumstances and angry in-laws. It's not all that unusual for a grieving family to try to assign blame. There was no premeditation on Brady's part."

"How can you be so certain? Did you investigate Brady's alibis for the Eviscerator murders?" I asked. Why was Nina Crockett so anxious to let Brady off the hook? I couldn't understand it. I had found the evidence in his house, proof-positive that he had stolen the drives as well as my camera, of all things. He had the gall to ask me about the drives, watching me squirm while he acted all pissed off I hadn't gotten around to analyzing them more quickly. He must have been especially pleased with himself, listening to my bullshit and knowing that was all it was.

"You need to let this go," said Nina. "You're not investigating it, remember?"

"Yeah, well—"

"*No*," she said. "There is no discussion. If you don't stay away from the investigation, Arthur Steele will have you arrested for obstruction, and don't believe for a minute he wouldn't do it. As far as Brady's various alibis, it would be difficult to determine whether he had one or not since most of the victims had been exposed to the elements for so long that pinpointing the exact time of death is damn near impossible. However, he *does* have an alibi for Number Four."

"Tina Barlow," I corrected.

"The point is," she continued, "with Tina Barlow, we were able to more accurately determine the time of death. She was—a fresher kill."

"*God.*"

"I'm sorry, I don't know a better way to say it. She had been killed within a couple hours of you finding her. Brady was with Nola Caudill the entire time."

I groaned. "She's an old family friend. She could be covering for him."

"Oh, for heaven's sake! Next thing I know, you're going to accuse *me* of bias."

I let that one go. Nina had repeatedly informed me I was a lousy fibber, and I wasn't about to counter her last statement when I half-believed it was true.

"I have to go," I said. "I want to keep the line free in case there's any news about Sheila."

"Oh, of course. I'm sorry."

"No, that's alright," I said. "Thanks. Thanks for the info."

"I mean it, Dwayne, stay out of this."

I mumbled something unintelligible and noncommittal as I disconnected the call. Melanie had been eavesdropping, saving me the effort of repeating the conversation. Wordlessly, she pulled the chair out and seated herself at the keyboard. She was in charge of this mission. She knew what to say. She knew how to act. All I could do was stand and watch her work. Her fingers flew with surprising speed across the keyboard, navigating to the MOO she had found earlier. Even as she logged in as Hot Potata, I couldn't manage a smile. All I could do was hope to hell this Odin fellow was here, and he might say something that would reveal Brady Garrett underneath. We didn't have time for a wild goose chase. We needed to set a trap and lure him in.

*****

Three long hours passed without incident. Melanie wandered through virtual reality tirelessly, peeking around electronic corners and peering into group chatter, but no user named Odin was logged in. In the event that Brady might be using another alias, she continued to plod along, trying to pick up on conversations with mythological reference, but it was entirely unrewarding.

My mother finally called at about eleven, letting me know Sheila was in critical condition in ICU. The conversation was oddly remote. We didn't discuss why I wasn't there; I assumed Matt had filled her in using big, loud words. She didn't lay blame, but I found no comfort in the tone of her voice. She didn't mention the baby, and I wasn't about to. Matt may have elected to keep that knowledge from our folks to shield them from grieving for a grandchild they would never have the opportunity to meet.

I paced restlessly, my ears tuned to the sounds of the wind against the siding. Any unusual noise sent me to the windows, peering out into the

259

cold night. A light snow had begun to fall, the tips of frozen grass catching and holding the flakes up to the moon.

Melanie persisted relentlessly. The sound of steady keystrokes was hypnotic, and after a little while, I couldn't look at the screen any longer. All the words seemed to merge together, and my patience was nonexistent. I wandered around the room thinking dark thoughts, while minutes crawled by with exasperating sluggishness. Maybe we weren't thinking this through. Maybe we should have returned to Brady's house so we could confront him when he returned. That was what I *wanted* to do. I didn't care if we could prove Brady's guilt; I *knew* he was guilty. I only wanted him to be stopped. No, that's not true. I wanted to make him pay. I wanted him to die, but slowly, and only after suffering excruciating agony. I wanted to be the one to mete out the punishment. I felt I was entitled, although I would happily share the privilege with the family members of Brady's other victims.

But it couldn't be that way, no matter how much I enjoyed the fantasy. Melanie would have no respect for me if I went blazing a path of vengeance. Dirty Harry I was not, and I doubted the authorities would be too impressed with any feat of vigilantism, even if it ended this horrible nightmare. We needed proof positive Brady was the Eviscerator, and I hoped the price wouldn't be another life.

"Are you okay?"

I was startled out of my reverie, my heart kicking out a superfluous beat. I realized the keystrokes had ended some time ago, and Melanie was staring at me. The concern in her face was sweetly evident, and I managed a weak smile. "I'll manage. I can't stand this waiting."

"Why do you think Brady took your camera?"

"Huh?" I had nearly forgotten about that. It seemed so long ago and irrelevant. Or was it?

"Brady must have had a reason to take the camera. I mean, think about your living room. What do you see—other than way too much dust? Tons of electronic equipment: TV, BluRay surround sound, stereo system—any one of which is more valuable than that camera."

I nodded. "And I sincerely doubt Brady would have a reason for petty thievery. By comparison, the crime is just too small, not worthy of his attention."

"Exactly. Maybe Brady thinks you got something on camera he wouldn't want made public. Do you recall using the camera any time when Brady was around or maybe appeared shortly afterward?"

I furrowed my brow and chewed on my bottom lip. It seemed Brady had been popping up all over the place for quite some time. Had I been using my camera at any of those instances? I couldn't remember. The camera wasn't something I constantly carried, although I had used it frequently while following Alan Carter. Had Brady been isolated in one of those frames, his guilt spelled out in great, big capital letters? If so, it was too late to worry about it. The film was gone, pulled from the insides of the camera. I could merely shrug my shoulders.

Melanie groaned and rubbed her tired eyes. I was about to suggest we take a short break when the computer suddenly chimed, as if somewhere inside a doorbell had sounded.

Odin had just logged on.

CHAPTER TWENTY-THREE

Melanie's fingers froze above the keyboard. The moment we had waited for—prayed for—had arrived, and neither of us knew what to do. We looked at each other stupidly, our mouths open as if we were each about to offer a suggestion, but the words frozen on the tips of our tongues. Eventually, our daze was broken by the sound of an electronic trumpet sounding its notes through my desktop speakers.

Odin had noticed that Melanie was logged on.

The screen read, "M'lady. It is my sincerest pleasure we meet again."

"What do I say?" asked Melanie.

"I don't know. You did just fine this afternoon."

Melanie's fingers hesitated only a moment more before typing, "I have patiently awaited you, M'lord."

"This is corny," I interjected.

"It's the way he seems to communicate," said Melanie. "What am I doing? Trying to set up a contact?"

"Yes," I said, my voice dead and emotionless. We needed to catch Brady in the act, prove irrefutably he was the one. I refused to consider the possibility of failure. My blinding need for revenge was more powerful than my common sense. It didn't matter that this lunatic had mutilated five people and attacked a sixth. I felt I could take on *two* such monsters if need be.

Melanie typed, "Can I not lay eyes upon you? A rendezvous, perhaps?"

"Where are you getting this shit?" I asked.

"Danielle Steele."

I groaned. Suddenly, Odin's words filled the screen. "On a moonlit eve, under the falling snow, we shall meet where the trains once rolled, where now the blades travel, in ye Olde Hilliard."

"What?" Melanie straightened her back and directed a puzzled gaze at me. "Hilliard?"

My mind was already in overdrive. Hilliard was a rapidly growing suburb on the western edge of Columbus, an affluent, desirable place to settle down and raise a family. The city's roots could be found along a short stretch of a longer road that connected Muirfield and New Rome. Hilliard's share of the road was predictably titled Main Street, but great care had gone into the maintenance and renovation of the area. Antique fixtures illuminated brick sidewalks, along which family businesses retained their provincial yet charming storefronts. At some point in the town's long history, a set of railroad tracks had bisected Main Street at its midsection, but as the country's reliance on its railway system waned, the tracks had been abandoned like rusting scars across the town's face. Metro Parks of Columbus and Franklin County decided to pave the tracks over, creating a smooth ribbon of asphalt that stretched through farmland and grassy flatland. The Heritage Rail Trail is about six miles in length, stretching from the center of Old Hilliard to Cemetery Pike in Plain city, it crosses Hayden Run only a short distance from the mouth of Brady's drive. What a surprise. The trail was frequented by joggers, bicyclists—and rollerbladers. The meaning of the 'blade' reference?

"When?" typed Melanie.

"In the third hour, things for you will never again be the same," said the response and a second later, Odin's name disappeared from the list of current users. He had signed off.

"Do you really think it's him?" I asked, unable to form an opinion based on the little I had seen. It seemed patently absurd. "Nobody talks like that.

How could this kind of gibberish lure anyone in, much less four people? It's stupid."

"Lonely people do strange things," said Melanie. "I don't know. I just, kind of, went with it when he started babbling. You didn't see the weird shit he said when I was at the library. All that mythological stuff, it was like he was actually *experiencing* it. He spoke of cleansing the earth, rising above, sloughing the skin."

Cleansing. What an odd word choice. There are moments when truth rushes up to greet you and completely bowls you over. This was one of those times. Brady Garrett did not believe he was killing anyone. For whatever insane reason, he believed he was freeing their tortured souls. Whatever facts may be gleaned in the days ahead, of that I was certain.

It was good enough for me.

I had to catch Brady unaware, the hunter becoming the hunted. It was just and fair. I needed him to attack me so I could go to the FBI with something substantive. I needed to crack through the armor Nina Crockett had apparently erected around Brady, and I didn't stand a chance with half-baked theorems and circumstantial postulations. I needed to capture a moment of Brady's madness irrefutably—video would be great although awkward; a few snapshots would do as well.

In the third hour.

Three o'clock. That gave me less than an hour to get my shit together and get to Hilliard.

"We'd better put a plan together," said Melanie, sliding into her coat. "I want to be prepared—"

I shook my head. "You're not going. I don't want you anywhere near this."

"If I'm not there, he might not show himself," she said, her arms frozen in midair with her jacket half on.

"That's a risk I'm willing to take. We already know it's Brady, even if we don't have any proof. That's what I plan to get. I've got a few pictures left in the disposable camera. I plan to make them count. I imagine timing is going to be tight. I won't be able to focus on Brady if I'm worrying about you."

"Maybe you need to take a minute and slow down. You should call Arthur Steele, let him know what's going on. With the victims piling up, I'm sure he'd be willing to send some sort of protection, someone to back you up."

I shook my head but offered no further explanation. I wanted to finish this myself. It wasn't a matter of headlines or heroism. It was strictly the primal need for revenge, cold and ugly, coursing through my veins. I crossed the room and kneeled in front of the cluttered bookshelf that housed every stray catalog, newspaper and piece of junk mail that crossed my door. Buried on the bottom shelf, I kept a small lockbox. Inside was the gun I had purchased last winter. I couldn't tell you what kind of gun it was; I'm not a gun enthusiast. I can tell you that it fit snugly in the palm of my hand, its grip comfortable and compatible, its cool metal casing almost clinical within my grip. I was aware of its potential and was appropriately respectful in its handling. I ensured that the safety was engaged before slipping it discreetly into my coat pocket.

"You can't go out there by yourself," said Melanie, crossing her arms and blocking my path. "I'm going with you."

"No, Melanie, you're not."

"Dammit, Dwayne! I'll go crazy sitting here waiting. I—"

"This isn't open for debate," I said, trying to sidestep her. "I'm already the cause of one casualty. I want you to stay as far away from me as possible until this thing's over. Why don't you go back to Lymont? Jasmine's probably missing you like crazy."

"That's below the belt," she said. "Don't use my daughter to saddle me with guilt! I'm not incompetent, you know."

"I know, sweetheart, I know," I said, encircling her in my arms and drawing her near. Although tense, she snuggled up to my chest, and I could

265

feel her warm breath against me. She was shivering with anger, frustration, fear and God knows what else. She held me tightly, and I wasn't sure she would let go. "Please, Melanie, *please* try to understand. I don't think you're incompetent—you *know* that. But I've seen what Brady is capable of. Remember? I found one of his victims—for God's sake, I found a severed foot on my doorstep! Sheila is barely hanging on, and I don't even know about the baby, and—"

"Shh." Melanie gently placed fingertips to my lips. My eyes implored her to understand, and it took me a moment to realize that, in fact, she had. "I want you to call me the moment this is over. I need to know that you're safe."

"I will." I patted myself down, checking my pockets. Car keys, camera, gun. Everything a vigilante needed.

As if the thought had jumped across a psychic chasm, Melanie's eyes fixed on me sharply, and I thought I heard a small gasp. "You're going to kill him, aren't you?"

My mouth opened and my jaws worked silently, but I could not find the will to lie to her.

"Dwayne, you can't do it," she implored. "It's not up to you. Bring him in. Otherwise, you won't be able to live with yourself."

"I'll get along just fine."

I kissed her deeply, silencing her protests before they could begin. Then I hurried out the door, refusing to listen to any of her well-intentioned though misdirected words of wisdom. There was no ambivalence in my mind about the correctness of my task. It was the only remaining option. The FBI was roadblocking me, and Brady Garrett wasn't going to stop killing all on his own. His next victim could be his own crippled son. Had that been the purpose of the Tina Barlow murder? Did Brady kill this handicapped Otterbein student as a rehearsal for killing his own boy? Cleansing the world of the less genetically fortunate? The parallel seemed too coincidental, and I was suddenly very afraid for Billy Garrett. Despite Melanie's warnings, my path seemed clear, and I had no qualms.

When the time came, I would have no difficulty whatsoever squeezing the trigger.

*****

Although the snow had momentarily faltered, it already coated the roads with an icy sheen that made traveling hazardous. I stopped at a Speedway and bought a tall, black coffee and another disposable camera. I wanted every opportunity to document the events of the evening. I was acutely aware of the gun at my side, its slight bulge monumental from my vantage point. I was sure each of the night owl customers in the convenient store knew I carried a means to death in my pocket.

I rejoined the highway and traveled north, taking the Roberts Road exit from 270 and turning west toward my ultimate destination. Traffic was almost non-existent as the hour neared three. Normal bar traffic had been lessened by the inclement weather, and I found myself sharing most of the trip with only my dark thoughts as company. I turned right on Rome-Hilliard Road, winding through blocks of storefronts, gas stations and fast-food restaurants. Apartment complexes were plentiful on both sides of the road, advertising move-in specials of various enticement, some even offering first month's rent free. I rolled around a last bend marked by a Dairy Queen and was on Main Street, gliding up its silent surface as once again the snow began to drift to the ground. I parked near the intersection of Main and North Center, pulling to the curb near a Chase branch office. Just as I silenced my engine and squelched my lights, a Hilliard police cruiser rounded the corner and made a slow, lazy sweep of the street. I instinctively slid down in my seat, shifting sideways and ducking my head into the passenger seat. I was fairly certain I hadn't been spotted, but I waited a moment or two before gradually peering over the dashboard. The cruiser was gone.

The wind provided stiff resistance as I opened the car door, as if it were warning me to stay inside, abandon this foolishness before it was too late, but it was already too late. I left the door unlocked in case I needed to make a hasty getaway, then checked my pockets for the millionth time, making sure I still had the cameras and, more importantly, the gun.

Antique lampposts cast pallid circles of light on the snow-covered sidewalks, their illumination obscured by the rapidly increasing snowfall. Bitter wind whipped across my cheeks and down my neck, making me distinctly aware I had neglected to dress for the occasion. The weather had been so warm lately I hadn't even considered my heavier winter coat in my hurry to get underway. The navy barn coat I wore was of little shelter against the piercing gusts, so I tucked my head down and hurried across Main, traveling west along North Center. The lampposts were less frequent as I continued down the side street, the quaint facade of the little town falling away as I stepped around the infrequent circles of light and clung to shadow. An unidentifiable business stretched along the left side of the block with a fenced-in back lot that was lightly dusted with fresh snow. Small houses faced from the other side of the street, their dark windows staring blindly at the frozen night.

I wondered if Brady was watching me approach, hiding in the same shadows I struggled to stay within. I wouldn't rate my night vision as one of my finer gifts, so every shadow distracted, pulling my attention to and fro, impeding my forward progress. It was only three blocks, but it felt like hours passed. North Center ended abruptly, with a makeshift gravel parking lot on the left for the Heritage Rail Trail and an unusually constructed building on the right called the Makoy Center. Its styling was reminiscent of 1950s roller rinks. I had no idea what purpose the building served, but its own empty parking lot had a concentration of overhead lighting that I desperately wanted to avoid. Even skirting the area would be like walking on stage. I might as well just take the gun from my pocket and shoot myself now.

My activity roused the agitated baying of a neighborhood dog. It sounded old and fat and far away, but soon, a chorus of other dogs picked up the chant, a chain-reaction of canine alarm, signaling my presence just as surely as if I had tap-danced beneath the lights I was trying to avoid. Icy sweat dribbled down my neck, and I was suddenly aware of my straining bladder. At any moment, one of the neighbors would come out to quiet his mutt. I didn't want to be seen creeping around by them any more than by Brady. In any case, the element of surprise was already shot all to hell.

I ran across the street, underneath the narrowest band of illumination I could find, through the gravel parking lot and onto the Heritage Rail Trail.

In my own ears, my feet against the dry snow and gravel sounded like stampeding cattle. I didn't stop to look back; I plunged into the dark cover found at the asphalt mouth of the trail. A little farther, the blacktop ribbon veered slightly to the left. The lights of Old Hilliard abruptly winked out, disappearing behind dense thickets of wild shrubbery. Much of it was evergreen, providing cover even in the bitterest season. Darkness swallowed me without warning. I skidded to a halt to allow my eyes to adjust, and my feet nearly flew out from underneath me. The pavement was coated with treacherous stretches of invisible black ice. Running would not be a dependable option. I felt frighteningly vulnerable standing in the middle of the path, waiting for my eyes to pierce the dark cotton, but I couldn't blunder along blindly. Alongside the evergreen were plenty of winter-stripped briar patches, and I didn't want to sprawl headlong into a nest of thorny brambles, loudly announcing my arrival as well as permanently putting my own eyes out.

I was beginning to have serious doubts. Not about my ability to mete out vengeance; of that, I was still coldly certain. It was my unfamiliarity with the surroundings that pulled at me. I was on Brady's home turf, less than a couple of miles from his own doorstep. He had chosen the

269

rendezvous, was clearly in command of the situation. The element of surprise had never been mine in the first place. Okay, so he was expecting some hapless, swooning bird to come tripping down the path and instead he gets me. Big deal. He was neither stupid nor weak. He hadn't gotten away with so many heinous acts without a little ingenuity and adaptability.

Somewhere ahead, in the swampy darkness, Brady Garrett waited for his prey, and his prey was me.

It seemed like hours I stood there in the darkness, listening for the sound of approaching footsteps, branches rustling in disruption, breathing that was not my own. The wind provided much fodder for my imagination as I braced myself for an ambush.

The moments crawled.

Finally, the shadows began to dissipate, not enough to restore a sense of control, but enough that I could again move forward.

The trail was utterly deserted. Cold snowflakes nipped at my exposed cheeks, but by then they were numb and oblivious. As if the darkness weren't bad enough, my eyes began to water in the stinging wind, blurring my vision. I carefully dabbed at the corners with fingers that were equally numb.

My breath plumed about my head as I moved forward, searching the deepest shadows for any sign of Brady. Again, my imagination was gracious enough to supply me with many false alarms, and I nearly shit myself outright when a rabbit burst through a patch of tall grass and onto the trail not three feet in front of me. First, I had to suppress a cry of alarm, then hysterical laughter.

I moved forward.

I had been walking for a while, probably almost a mile when I was startled to see a car silently cut across the trail a couple hundred yards ahead. As I approached, my eyes picked out yellow twinkling reflector lights in the distance. There was a crosswalk ahead. The road beyond it must not get much traffic; the one car was all I had seen so far.

270

More distressing was the covered shelter off the path on the left, just before the crosswalk. It was a small building squatting in the weeds, providing nominal shelter to the unlucky jogger who got caught out in the elements. Thick, perfect darkness lay inside, defying my attempts to put shape to shadow. Brady could easily be hiding within, waiting.

I checked my pocket. The gun was still there.

I extracted one of the cameras and carried it in my trembling left hand, hoping my numb fingers would be able to move quickly enough when the time came. And the time was coming soon. I could feel it.

I tucked my right hand into my coat pocket and wrapped my fingers around the icy butt of the gun. I flicked the safety off and kept my hand in the relative warmth. When it came time to use the gun, I needed more than hope. Even the slightest fumble could cost me my life.

I eased to the left, keeping on the same side of the path as the shelter. I had no doubt if Brady was in there, he had already seen me. All I could hope to do was minimize my exposure. My whole plan seemed ridiculously underbaked, but it was too late to turn back now.

I moved forward.

Frozen blades of grass crunched under my feet, loud in my own ears although undoubtedly lost in the wail of the wind. The snowfall was no longer gentle; big wet flakes rapidly piled up on the blacktop.

I couldn't see any movement from within the shelter although shapes were beginning to emerge. There was definitely something in there, squatted down, waiting, watching.

I couldn't feel my left hand at all now. My legs were slightly unsteady as the constant wind pierced the fabric of my jeans.

I crouched down and again moved forward.

I was no more than fifteen feet away from the shelter. The thing in the middle was big, bigger than a man, unmoving. Tension was winding me up tightly inside, and I was nearing the point of calling Brady's name out loud, challenging him to show himself and get this thing over with. Why didn't he *show* himself?

Another car suddenly zipped by at the crosswalk, its silent engine unnoticed until it had passed by. The brief burst of illumination cast by its headlights provided welcome relief. The thing in the middle of the crudely constructed shelter was a picnic table, and Brady Garrett was nowhere to be seen.

I straightened and breathed deeply, feeling the tightness temporarily leave my chest. It really made more sense that Brady would be waiting at the other end of the trail, closer to his own property. Didn't it?

With a renewed sense of confidence, I passed the shelter and reached the crosswalk. There was a small house tucked away on the left in the lot beyond the shelter, facing the empty rural two-lane. A prominent "Vicious Dog" sign was posted where the trail bordered the yard, but there was no sign of the beast anywhere. I was immensely grateful for that.

I stepped out onto the snow speckled tarmac and started across the street. It seemed odd that the intersection wasn't marked by overhead lighting. As I crossed, I looked up to see that there was, indeed, a lamppost, but the bulb had been shattered. For a split second, I stared at it as if hypnotized, refusing to process the possible implications. As I reached the other side of the street and rejoined the trail, I froze.

Brady Garrett was there.

About thirty yards ahead, approaching quickly. His long coat flapping in the wind, and I couldn't see his hands, but they were constantly moving, moving, moving...

The camera slipped through my fingertips and landed with a wet sound in the snowy grass to my left. Shit. My right hand tightened on the handle of the gun. I tugged at it, but the hammer caught on a ganglia of thread coiled along the pocket's seam. I tugged again, and in a burst of ripping fabric, the gun was free.

Brady's lips moving, the words carried away by the wind before they could even begin to penetrate.

My arm raised and steadied, the blunt snout of the pistol aimed toward Brady's torso. As my finger tightened on the trigger, Brady abruptly froze, his eyes perceiving the instrument in my hand.

As his eyes registered fear and his hand flew up to ward off the bullet, I was abruptly struck between the shoulder blades and sent sprawling face first to the hard pavement.

A kaleidoscope of stars filled my eyes, and a persistent ringing jangled in my ears.

Then darkness overpowered me.

CHAPTER TWENTY-FOUR

I returned to consciousness with a horrified gasp, struggling to absorb my surroundings.

It wasn't cold pavement underneath me, but instead a soft, albeit thin mattress, the type you roll up and take camping. A rough blanket had been drawn over me, and I propped myself on one elbow to examine my surroundings. I was alone in the back of a panel van. Other camping paraphernalia was strewn about: a collapsed tent, a portable grill, kerosene lanterns. I could hear the vehicle's engine running, but it wasn't moving.

I could still feel where I had been hit between the shoulder blades, a persistent throb that kept steady tempo with the pounding of my head. I pushed myself up into a seated position and discovered my ankles were linked by a pair of handcuffs. Light spilled in from the square windows in the rear doors, and it took a moment for me to realize it wasn't just moonlight trickling in. There were also flashing red and blue lights, and after another moment, I realized they must belong to a police car.

Thank God. The police. Brady couldn't have gotten away.

But why were my ankles handcuffed together?

The rear doors suddenly swung open allowing an arctic blast to rip through the cabin. Brady Garrett stared in at me, his curly hair dancing in the wind. "I think he's come around," he said over his shoulder.

Nina Crockett stepped up behind him and peered in. "Yep."

"What in the hell is going on?" I croaked.

274

They crawled into the van and pulled the doors closed behind them. I tried to back away, but the handcuffs made my maneuver awkward and futile. They stared at me curiously, as if not sure what to do with me. Why in the hell weren't the police here?

"Goddamn it!" I raged, rattling my legs and thumping them into the side of the van.

"For God's sake, Dwayne!" said Nina, reaching across and twisting me around on my ass so that my legs couldn't make contact with the metal anymore. "Settle down! You've got some explaining to do. You'll be lucky if Arthur Steele doesn't throw you in jail as it is for attempted homicide. What in the hell were you doing here tonight? What were you doing with that gun? Do you realize you almost put a bullet into Brady's head? Do you even have a license to carry that thing around?"

She was right in my face, her hands on my shoulders, shaking me with each question as if I were her disobedient child. I was so thoroughly confused! Maybe Nina didn't even realize she was blinding herself to Brady's guilt.

"Get him out of here," I said, my voice still croaking. My eyes darted to Brady, who sat cross-legged at the bottom of the mattress. He cocked an eyebrow quizzically and grinned.

"Did I do something—?"

"*GET HIM OUT OF HERE!*" I sat up and pulled my legs back.

Nina shot a worried glance at Brady and said, "You better go. I'll catch up with you outside."

Brady shrugged his shoulders, that damned cheesy grin still pasted across his face, and backed out of the van, letting in another gust of frigid air as he departed. After he had gone, Nina sat in silence staring at me, her expression hard and unreadable.

"Will you at least undo these cuffs?" I finally asked, unable to tolerate the silence stretching taut between us.

"I'm not sure if I should," she said. "You're not acting as if you're in complete control of your mental faculties."

"Funny," I said, thrusting my feet toward her.

"I'm serious," she said, shoving them away. "What in the hell has gotten into you? If you had shot Brady, it would have been cold-blooded murder. I'm sorry about your back. I didn't know any other way short of shooting you to keep you from firing. Did you even know it was him?"

"Of course I knew it was him," I said. "What I want to know is why can't you see through his act? Why do you refuse to believe Brady Garrett is the Eviscerator? Because, Agent Crockett, I've got news for you—he *is*."

Nina groaned and rolled her eyes. "Brady Garrett is *not* the Eviscerator."

"Dammit, Nina! I don't have a one thing to give you that you could actually use, but do you think I would come to this conclusion easily? Do you remember the flash drives I told you Brady gave me?"

"Ah, yes. The ones I'm not supposed to know anything about."

"He stole them from Dorie Carpenter's mother's house during the wake. Now *think* about that. Why would he be so anxious to recover them from her house? He knew there was something incriminating on them. And why would he feed them to me the way that he did? He knew I couldn't— or shouldn't—tell you about them because they were stolen property and possession of them could prevent me from obtaining a PI license. He kept after me until I gave in, reminding me of my civic duty at every turn. He damn near fed me the whole thing. He told me he had identified the 'Moo' folders on the hard drives but didn't know what they meant. But he knew. He *knew*. He was leading me into his sick game."

Her look was blank perfection.

"And then the drives were stolen from my house. Guess where they turned up?"

She continued to stare.

"Inside Brady's house," I said smugly. "I guess he was trying to shake me up, let me know someone had been inside my house, despite my extensive security."

Nina sighed. "I'm not even going to ask how you might have found something inside Brady's house, but even if you did, so what? Possession of those drives doesn't make Brady a murderer." Her face was wooden, and her words lacked conviction.

"He knew Dorie Carpenter," I persisted, astonished that Nina was continuing to defend him. I was grasping now, repeating things that should have been obvious. "When he gave me the drives, he didn't mention he knew any of the victims. That's a rather pertinent piece of information to conveniently omit, don't you think?"

"Brady is working with us," Nina said simply.

My mouth opened and closed, but no sound came out. I tried again, "Excuse me?"

"Brady has been working with us on the Eviscerator case for months," she said. "He agreed to help us control the slant of the media in exchange for first scoop. It's been a mutually beneficial arrangement."

I shook my head vacantly. "Why?"

"Most serial killers suffer from terminal vanity. They enjoy reading about their exploits over breakfast." She paused then lowered her eyes. "Subtle manipulation of news coverage can help direct the killer's next actions."

I pursed my lips; it was my turn to stare. I may be slow, but I was finally catching her drift. I had been set up. Used as bait. Dangled in front of the killer in a series of articles about Dwayne Morrow, Local Hero, instead of The Eviscerator, Population Cleanser. The FBI had wanted to draw this madman to me and my own, had conceived and executed a plan without so much as a word to me. I was speechless.

I was furious.

"And then," continued Nina, her eyes still avoiding mine, "when Brady's girlfriend was murdered, we started worrying we had made a grievous error."

"You *think*?" Bitter sarcasm dripped from my tongue.

"It wasn't my idea."

"Fine, but you knew about it, didn't you? You were probably never pulled off of the case in the first place, were you?"

She shook her head. "No. But Arthur Steele has been running the show from the start. After Brady ran the first stories, he had you followed. He figured he could protect you."

"A fucking lot of good that did Nikki Sanders—or Sheila," I said. "Get these cuffs off of me."

She bent over immediately and unshackled me. I rubbed the circulation back into my ankles and stretched my legs.

"We didn't anticipate—"

I cut her off with my glare. "This isn't some stupid game. You can't just position innocent people where you think they'll benefit you most."

"I said it wasn't my idea," she protested. "What was I supposed to do?"

"Yeah, I suppose that's fair," I sneered. "What's a life or two when we're talking about the career of Nina Crockett?"

She pressed her lips together tightly. I wasn't in the mood to be gracious and understanding, however. I had been *used*. That, alone, was bad enough, but I was also left with a feeling of residual stupidity. I had been cleanly manipulated, and the disappointment I felt in myself made me want to do something wildly destructive. It wasn't good to be in such close proximity to Nina. I eased away from her toward the back of the van, my eyes burning pinholes through her. I unlatched the door and eased out into the night.

I didn't even feel the blistering wind as it whipped by, carrying more snow down to coat the hard ground. I did notice the snow had completely covered the trail and the two-lane blacktop that bisected the crosswalk. Two unmarked sedans were pulled to the curb by the crosswalk as well as

278

an official cruiser, bubble lights undulating wildly. I was surprised they hadn't left a siren wailing. The family who lived in the small house on the corner had taken position at various windows, observing the scene with great interest. I could hear the resonant protestations of a big dog booming from inside the house, evidently the reason for the 'Vicious Dog' sign I had seen earlier. The van from which I had emerged had been pulled up into the mouth of the trail, blocking the westward path. I glanced further along and saw bobbing flashlights, combing the distance. Occasionally, the wind carried a short burst of static followed by indistinguishable monosyllabic remarks, undoubtedly from two-way radios.

I tucked my chin down against the wind and returned the way I had come, back into the dark shadows of the Rail Trail. Subtlety was no longer a concern. If there had ever been any validity whatsoever to the arranged meeting with Odin, he was long gone now. He surely wouldn't stick around after the police arrived in a blaze of multi-colored lights. It was cold, and I was tired and sore. I wanted to be home and in bed.

I had been so sure that Brady Garrett was the Eviscerator. Now, I turned the evidence over and over in my head, and I had to admit, it didn't add up to much. My intuition had been based on distrust and dislike, and I was even angrier at myself for having been so narrow-minded.

The realization I had almost shot him stopped me cold.

My hands were shaking, and it wasn't from the cold. I felt a little nauseous when the full potential of my actions was realized. If Nina hadn't struck me across the back and knocked me down, I would have killed Brady. I replayed the scene in my head, his hands moving, his words carried away on the wind. The fear in his eyes as they focused on the gun.

I doubled over and vomited, my stomach knotting and convulsing. Dry heaves followed, my body refusing to let me off the hook. I had been stupid and impulsive and had things been slightly different, I would be under arrest for murder. It was unthinkable. I felt wildly out-of-control, completely incompetent.

After my esophagus finally stopped spasming, I stretched my back and took in deep lungfuls of crisp air. I checked my pockets and was relieved to find the gun was no longer in my possession. Apparently, Nina had the good sense to relieve me of it while I was unconscious.

I finally reached the end of the trail and emerged in the parking lot. There was no sense in worrying about the streetlights now, and I plodded along sullenly through the middle of the Makoy Center lot. I was so immersed in my own thoughts that I didn't even notice Brady parked in his car until he blew the horn as I passed in front of the hood. I nearly jumped out of my skin and shot him a white-hot glare. He grimaced and shrugged, rolling down his window.

"You need a ride?" he said.

"My car's just a couple of blocks away," I said.

"C'mon," he said, stretching across his passenger seat and pushing the door open. "It's fucking cold out."

I didn't want to get in the car with Brady. Even though I knew I had been mistaken, I couldn't shake the disgust I had nurtured for him while I had convinced myself of his guilt. Knowing he had been an integral part of the FBI's plan to manipulate me wasn't helping. Nonetheless, the overriding emotion was guilt. I had almost killed him for something he hadn't done. I didn't know how I was going to come to grips with that.

I got into the car.

Brady started the engine and pulled out of the lot, turning his headlights on as we turned onto Center Street.

"My car's only a block or so south on Main," I repeated, staring out the passenger window. "This really wasn't necessary."

"Mm-hmm," he said, turning north on Main.

"Where are we going?" I asked.

"We need to clear the air."

"Nina told you?"

Brady shook his head. "When I left the van, I went around and got in the front seat. I heard every word you said."

"I should've known."

"I'm really sorry, Dwayne," he said, his eyes steady on the road. He took a right on Davidson. "I had no idea things could possibly go so wrong. You have to believe me."

I continued to stare out the passenger window, chewing on my bottom lip. I wanted to be self-indulgent and crow about the violation of my civil liberties, but I just didn't have the strength. When I looked at Brady, I was reminded he had paid a very high price for his own involvement in this. It would haunt him for the rest of his life. It could have just as easily been Melanie instead of Nikki Sanders who was killed. By comparison, I was lucky.

I sighed. "I guess I'm sorry I tried to kill you," I muttered, and we both laughed. It was a brief, hysterical moment that brought welcome relief from the tension in the Saturn's cabin.

"Why me?" I asked as we turned right on Leap.

"Arthur Steele cooked that up on the spot after you found Tina Barlow. He was familiar with your involvement with the McGregor case," he said. "He saw it would be easy to slant the news in your direction, giving the public a new angle on a story that was becoming all too familiar, while simultaneously infuriating the killer and drawing him out."

"Why didn't he just *ask* me?" I said. "Did he think I wouldn't go along?"

"He didn't want to alert the Eviscerator that this was a setup, and he wasn't sure you'd be able to continue your day-to-day life as if nothing was amiss. See, a guy like Arthur Steele spends years and years training to be a skilled investigative agent. He doesn't put much stock in guys like you. You stumbled into the McGregor case, and from what I can read between the lines, you were lucky to have come out of it in one piece. He doesn't consider you a partner in this."

I mulled Brady's words, my stubborn jaw set. It was complete bullshit. "He didn't have the right to do that. He couldn't guarantee—"

"Arthur Steele is a rock-headed, loud-mouthed bureaucrat who has risen through the ranks in a surprisingly short amount of time. His techniques are unusual and unorthodox, but his results stand for themselves. This is the first time he's ever had one really go wrong."

"And things went wrong when the killer fixated on you instead of me," I surmised. "He blamed you for misdirecting his spotlight."

Brady was quiet for a moment, his complexion pasty in the moonlight. He swallowed hard, and I knew he was thinking of Nikki Sanders. At a minimum, it would have been polite for me to offer some reassurance of some sort, but it was late, and I had left my manners at home.

"So, you did all this for a story? Was it worth it?" I pointedly asked.

Brady winced but recovered quickly. "You know, I've about had it with all this sanctimonious bullshit from you. Who are you to judge me for what I do? I have loved investigative journalism for as long as I can remember. When I was growing up, I kept steno pads full of notes about my friends, neighbors and family. It's in my blood. You know what else? I'm damn good at what I do. Yes, I want to make lots of money, and yes, I want to be successful, and why in the hell should I apologize for that? Sure, I have to be creative sometimes to get my stories, but sometimes those stories enlighten and inspire. They cause people to *think*. What a horrible thing for me to do! You want to be a *PI*, for God's sake! You'll spend most of your time crawling belly first through garbage, following adulterous spouses to the nearest E-Z Screw Motel, snapping away pornographic evidence that will ruin lives in exchange for a nice, fat check. Quite a noble profession."

I raked a hand through my hair and said nothing. I felt trapped in the car and wanted to be done with this conversation. Part of me saw the truth in Brady's words, but another part wanted to remain belligerent and combative, and I really didn't know which would win. I hate it when I'm wrong, and only through extraordinary effort am I able to admit it. It's one of my most exasperating shortcomings. Right then, I was tired and irritable, and my mind had gone on information overload. I was already struggling to insert facts over the conclusions to which I had erroneously leapt. A further admission was unthinkable.

"How did you know to be on the trail tonight?" I asked after a sullen moment.

"Steele's got constant surveillance on that MOO," said Brady. "The conversation between Odin and Hot Potata was monitored and seemed worthy of investigating. Nina and I were together and in the area when the call came through. I'm assuming you were Hot Potata."

I involuntarily flushed. "Melanie," I corrected.

"One of Arthur's guys followed you when you left your house. He reported you parked your car at the curb on Main. We knew it was only a matter of time until you appeared on the trail."

"What in the hell were you doing? You came out of nowhere with your arms flailing all over the place. I thought you had a weapon," I said.

"I was trying to ward you off. Nina's people were in position, ready to catch this bastard when he showed his face."

"You sound pretty sure that Odin is the killer," I said. "The only reason I was so sure was because I thought Odin was you."

"Thanks."

"You know what I mean."

Brady sighed. "We know Odin is the Eviscerator. The Bureau obtained log files maintained by Brandon Tinker, the administrator of that particular MOO. The logs don't contain actual conversation, but they do show users' login and logout times. Odin first contacted Gigi Garson several weeks before she was murdered. We're assuming that a meeting was arranged during one of those conversations. Odin later contacted Dorie Carpenter in the same MOO."

"But not Paul Nicholas or Tina Barlow?" I asked.

"No, but the killer may have had other screen names. Paul Nicholas was very into roleplay. Nothing much was off limits."

"And Tina Barlow?"

"We're not sure," said Brady. "She spent a lot of time on the computer. In chat rooms, she didn't have to be wheelchair-bound, you see. Raising a handicapped child, seeing the disappointment in his face when he can't do what all the other boys are doing—I can understand how virtual reality might have its appeal."

"Dorie Carpenter just stumbled into this mess, didn't she?" I asked.

"Yeah, it looks that way." He slowly shook his head. "I think she was hoping to find out that Odin *wasn't* the killer. She found all that medieval gobbledygook romantic. I can't believe she went to meet him all by herself. We know she suspected something wasn't right. God."

I had lost track of where we were going and was startled to find that we had traveled some distance, completely across Hilliard to Riverside Drive. The snowfall had dwindled, but even at this time of night, enough traffic had passed to stain and rut the fresh dusting. Brady turned right and continued driving.

"Did you really think I was capable of doing such horrible things?" Brady suddenly asked, his eyes fixing on me intently.

I shifted uncomfortably in my seat. Yep.

CHAPTER TWENTY-FIVE

It was twenty minutes after four when Brady eased his car into a Waffle House parking lot. He slid between a snow-spattered semi and a Ford Explorer mounted to gigantic wheels.

"What are you doing?" I asked as he cut his engine.

"Eating," he said, unfastening his seatbelt and opening the door. "You hungry?"

"Not really," I said, reluctantly joining him in the parking lot. The whole night had been a wash. I wanted to get home to Melanie.

The restaurant smelled of eggs and meat frying in hot oil, coating the walls with a dingy reflective film. The fixtures were made of cracking red Naugahyde that had probably been installed in the 1970s. The counter was lined with grumpy old men reading papers, sipping coffee, talking sports and politics. They were the regulars. Other late-night types chose the booths; truckers, some of the after-bar crowd, trying to sop up some of the alcohol they had consumed so they would feel better about driving home. Brady and I took a corner booth that looked out onto the oil-stained parking lot. I was suddenly aware of the vast emptiness of my stomach, which responded immediately to the unhealthy scents wafting deliciously through the air. A gum-snapping waitress with more than a few missing teeth took our orders and returned to the steady thrum of activity behind the counter.

Brady excused himself and went to the restroom, and I found myself yearning for a cigarette. Stress always has that effect on me. After a moment, Brady came back with a smile on his face.

"Spoke with someone I know at the hospital, and I thought you'd be relieved to hear that Sheila's condition has stabilized. The baby seems to be all right, too."

"Oh, thank God," I said, rubbing my tired eyes. I looked up at Brady as he slid into the booth. "Thank you."

He smiled and waved it off. "Not a problem."

"You know, one thing I don't understand," I said. "Why did you steal the drives back?"

Brady sighed and sat back as the waitress reappeared with coffee. She snapped her gum and retreated, sashaying her sixty-year-old hips like a woman half her age. "Believe it or not, I've had qualms about this plan of Steele's from the beginning. I didn't like the thought of inducting a private citizen without his full consent."

"And yet you still went along with it," I said.

Brady shrugged. "Hey, it didn't matter whether I went along or not, Steele's plan was already in action. I figured, what the hell? If it wasn't me, it would just be some other reporter."

I nodded my head slowly. It was hard to let go of the old revulsion, but Brady had made a valid point earlier. It was his job, his passion. Who was I to cast aspersions? "How does this relate to the drives?" I asked.

"Steele doesn't know about them," he said. "All he wanted me to do was point a few news stories in your direction, feed some anonymous leads to the competition with your name all over them."

"Natasha Brickman, *Crimebusters*?" I asked.

"Among others. One of Steele's profilers said this would be enough to bait a trap for the killer. Frankly, I didn't think it was very sporting of them to put you in that position," he said. "We already knew about the identical 'Moo' folders and what they meant, so I talked Nina into getting backups

CIRCUMVENTION

of the hard drives. She's not in complete agreement with Steele on his methodology either. I figured you should at least have a sporting chance."

"Why did you rifle through Dorie Carpenter's room during her wake?" I asked. "What could have been so urgent? You already had access to the contents of her computer."

He looked at me curiously. "I'm a reporter," he said slowly and simply, as if I were developmentally challenged. "It's what I do. I don't know what idea I've given you, but when I say that I made a deal with the FBI, that does not mean they gave me carte blanche with their files. Quite the opposite. I was supposed to perform my duty for them, and if the killer struck again or the police were successful in finding him, I would be pointed in the appropriate direction at the appropriate time. Beyond that, they really gave me next to nothing. I needed to get into that room and get pictures, you know, fully document her personal space. It sounds ludicrous and, in this case, fruitless, but it was *something* to do. I hadn't known Dorie long, but I liked her. If I could go above and beyond and find something useful toward catching her killer, I had to try. The more time that passed, the more people would be parading through the house and through Dorie's room. It felt like the clock was running out."

"Okay," I said, digesting the new info and seeing the pieces begin to coalesce. "So why did you steal the drives back? How did you even know where they were?"

The waitress returned with two plates heaping with glistening food, eggs and hash browns—scattered, smothered and covered. She promised she'd check back for refills and gave Brady a lingering eye, licking her cracked lips in a gesture that was, in equal parts, brazenly sexual and mildly revolting. I covered my grin and scratched my nose as she walked away.

"You really need to work on your poker face. Any time we talked about those drives your eyes would keep shifting toward the fireplace. I took them out of your house because I wasn't sure I had done the right thing anymore," said Brady, pulling me back on point. "I couldn't stop Arthur

287

Steele from setting you up as bait, but dammit, I was leading you straight into the mouth of the lion. After Nikki was found, I knew everything was blowing up in our faces. The killer's attention shifted all right, but not in the direction the hotshot FBI profiler *thought* it would. I guess I hoped if I took the drives out of your hands, you might not be able to go much further with your investigation."

I raised my eyebrows. "You're saying you took them to *protect* me?"

"You know—believe whatever you want. I'm trying to come clean here."

"All right, all right," I said. "Then what about my camera?"

He reddened to the tips of his ears. "Sorry about that," he said. "But you started acting so weird every time I saw you. You may not realize this, but your face usually reads like a book. I knew something was up, but I didn't know what. I *surely* didn't imagine you thought *I* was the killer. I thought you were trying to stonewall me because of your usual contempt for the press. When I picked up the drives, I saw the camera and snared it on a whim. I thought you might have captured something on film that related to the Eviscerator case. It was just a lot of pictures of a fat old guy."

"Alan Carter," I supplied vacantly. "I was following him at the request of his wife, Geneva. She thought he was cheating. He wasn't."

"Cool," he said, swabbing maple syrup from his plate with a forkful of waffle. "You can mail her the proof, too. I still have the prints out in the car."

"Doesn't really matter anymore," I said absently. "Geneva Carter killed herself today."

Brady looked up sharply, his fork suspended in midair.

I shook my head and returned my attention to the omelet before me. "It's all fucked up. I don't want to go into it."

"But she didn't kill herself because she thought—"

"No," I said. "Whether she had seen the pictures or not wouldn't have made a damn bit of difference. She was more than a little unbalanced, and I would really rather not talk about it right now. It's been a long day."

We ate in a more companionable silence, putting the artery-clogging meal away with surprising enthusiasm. The waitress came back with refills and another round of overt flirtation for Brady, who squirmed uncomfortably under her lustful eyes.

"So, what happened?" I asked after the waitress had gone. "Out on the trail? I saw an awful lot of officers combing that trail, and they weren't being very discreet. Did they see him out there?"

Brady shook his head. "Some hotshot rookie thought he saw him in the bushes and called out a false positive. It was a goddamned skunk. Sprayed the hell out of the cop as he was trying to order his 'suspect' out of hiding. Any shot of discretion went out the window right about then. If the Eviscerator was there, he would have heard the commotion and gotten out."

I sighed. "So, what now? Back to square one?"

Brady shrugged his shoulders. "I'm out of ideas. This was the closest we've ever gotten to him, and they blew it. Big time."

"There's got to be something else. Something that's been overlooked."

"Yeah? Like what?"

I rubbed my eyes. "I don't know. *Something.* You said that the administrator of that MOO—"

"Brandon Tinker."

"Yeah—you said that he was able to confirm from log files that Odin had been signed on at the same time as two of the victims," I said.

"So?"

"Isn't there a way to trace a connection back to its originating IP address to identify the point of origin?"

"Well, yeah, as a matter of fact, there is. I'm surprised you wouldn't know that," he said.

289

I shook my head. "Not my specialty."

"Doesn't really matter, anyway," said Brady. "The killer wasn't stupid enough to use his home computer to set up his appointments. He used the public access terminals at the library downtown. Even though there are security cameras throughout the building, the transmissions always originated from a terminal outside their scope."

I chewed on my bottom lip. When Melanie had first chatted with Odin, she was at the library. He could have been sitting across the room, trying to lure his next prey, oblivious that his partner in conversation was within easy reach. They could have been within feet of each other, each privately amused with the onscreen dialogue.

We paid our bills and left Brady's new girlfriend a nice tip. The snow had finally stopped falling, and the roads were a treacherous mess. A salt truck passed, slinging gritty pebbles onto the icy pavement. The wind still intruded in sudden, vicious gusts, and we hurried to the car.

As we pulled back out onto the road, I turned in my seat and asked, "So how long have you and Nina been sleeping together?"

Brady was visibly jolted. "How did you know?"

"Intuition," I said. "Nina did a one-eighty on you. One of the first times I spoke with her, she told me she thought your brand of reporting was loathsome. She was enthusiastically sincere. Just as suddenly, her position softened. You can see it in her expression when she mentions your name."

"I don't know if you can understand this," said Brady. "I'm not proud of it. But I had no intention of marrying Nikki. She and I had been dating regularly for a couple of years, but it was a very loose, casual relationship. We saw other people—or at least, up until recently. Nikki started pressing to get married a few months ago, and—I don't know why—I said okay. I wasn't in love with her the way you need to love the person you marry. I would've broken it off with Nikki before long. I didn't meet Nina until after Steele fed me your name. She knew me by reputation, and you're right. She thought I was a real sleazeball, at first. I guess she's changed her mind since then."

"I'd say."

My attention was beginning to drift. I wasn't trying to be rude, but I had been awake too long, and I was experiencing that odd sort of tunnel vision that coats all of reality in a thin layer of cotton batting. Something elusive niggled at me, something important, but I could no more bring it into focus than I could fly.

Brady steered toward Fishinger so I could collect my car and go home. Ah, home sweet home. I had nothing more lascivious on my mind than snuggling up next to Melanie and holding her tight while we slept.

I had nearly nodded off when Brady lost control of the car. He hadn't seen the red light until the last moment, and when he stomped on the brake pedal, the car had skidded forward, the front end veering to the left. Brady cut sharp to the right, overcompensating, and soon we were spinning round and round, the car bulldozing its way through the intersection. Thank God there was no traffic at that time of morning. We came to a sudden stop against the curb, facing the opposite direction from which we had come. Brady's knuckles were white against the steering wheel, his forehead coated with a sheen of perspiration.

"Jesus!" he gasped, jerking the gearshift into park. "Are you alright?"

I was suddenly awake, the idea that had tugged at me earlier slowly resurfacing. "Something's wrong," I said.

"What? Did you hit your head?" he asked with alarm in his voice.

"No, sorry, nothing like that," I said. "Something's bothering me about the night I found Tina Barlow. Alan Carter—the guy I was following, remember? The one whose wife thought he was cheating? He was in the habit of going to the library every day."

"So are a lot of other people. Just because this guy reads a lot, you think he's the killer?" asked Brady perplexedly.

"Good God, no! Have you seen him? He must weigh around three hundred pounds. The woman who witnessed Sheila's attack would have certainly mentioned it if the guy was obese. No. But I was following him down that alley when I found Tina's body. I wish I knew what he told the police about that night," I said.

"What difference does it make?" asked Brady.

"Well, for one thing, as much time as Carter spent at the library, he might have seen someone else who came on a regular, if not daily, basis. But that's not what's bugging me," I said. "I followed him to a pub where he proceeded to insert himself into conversation at the bar. A bit later, he came over to my table, made it very plain he was aware I was following him, and then bolted for the door. I was so surprised he had spotted me I wasn't sure if I should continue to follow him. Earlier that afternoon, Geneva Carter had made some insulting remarks about my capabilities. Maybe I thought I could redeem my reputation if I could find something useful to give to her. I don't know. I decided to follow him out into the street. By then, he had gotten a lead on me, and I'll admit, he was moving pretty quickly for a big guy, but I wasn't *that* far behind him. He went into the alley first. So, what happened to him?"

"You didn't see him at all?" asked Brady.

I shook my head. "From the moment I walked into that alley, I was alone—except, of course, for Tina Barlow. I don't think he could have made it to the other side before I got there if he had been on foot."

"You think he parked his car in the alley? That doesn't make sense—especially if you don't think he's the killer."

"No, I guess it doesn't. There were several doors leading into the rears of the buildings that butted up against the alley. I suppose he could have gone through one of those doors."

"That doesn't make much sense either," said Brady. "Think how long it would take to go from door to door, checking for one that was unlocked.

292

Unless he really lucked out and found one on his first try, the process would take even longer than running to the other end of the alley would."

"I don't suppose Nina would have any ideas about what he said when they questioned him," I ventured.

"I'm sure she knows exactly what he said, but I doubt she'd tell us," he said, then added in a comically bitter voice, "Her and her goddamned professional ethics."

"Well, then maybe we should stop by and see him in the morning," I said. "I'm at a loss for what to do next anyhow."

As we continued west along Fishinger, I sifted through my pockets, searching for my cell phone. I double-checked, then said, "Dammit, I must have lost my phone out on the trail. I was hoping to call Melanie. She's probably worried sick."

Brady reached into his coat and extracted a sleek black smartphone from his inside pocket. "Here ya go," he said, tossing his phone to me.

"Thanks." I punched in my phone number and listened to the electronic tribble at the other end. One ring. Two. Two-and-a-half and the answering machine picked up. I heard my own voice in my ear, telling me to leave a message after the tone. *Beep.* "Mel? It's Dwayne. Pick up."

No response.

"Melanie?"

Nothing.

I disconnected the call and redialed immediately. The answering machine wasn't so quick to pick up this time as it was still busy resetting. However, after eight rings, my outgoing message played again, and I felt my stomach flop.

"What's the matter?" asked Brady, who was spying me from the corner of his eye.

"I don't know," I said. "She didn't answer."

"Maybe she got tired of waiting around."

"She didn't have a car," I said. "She *couldn't* have gone anywhere. Oh God, Brady—"

"She's probably just fallen asleep, man," he said. The exit for I-270 south was approaching on the right. "Do you realize what time it is? Tell you what. To hell with your car for now. Let's just head over to your house. You can try calling back while we're on our way."

He was trying to project confidence, but his steady acceleration as he took the on-ramp and the way he gripped the steering wheel gave him away. He was as concerned as I was. I continued to press redial, my answering machine picking up every time. I felt as if I could be sick to my stomach again.

"Relax, will you?" said Brady. "Everything's fine. She's just a heavy sleeper, that's all."

"Dammit, Brady, that's not all. If anything happens to Melanie because of me—"

I cut myself short as I saw the guilty look flash briefly across Brady's face. He shook it off quickly and returned his focus to the road. I wished I could retract the words. As inhuman as I would have liked to believe Brady Garrett was, there was a haunted despair that occasionally and briefly crossed his face, just long enough for you to know he maintained a level of accountability for these tragic things that have happened in his life. He wished he could have bought his parents a cruise instead of plane tickets. If only he had placed a priority on getting that damned car's tire replaced, his wife would still be with him today. I didn't know how Brady was able to function under the circumstances, even if he wasn't really in love with Nikki Sanders. She was chosen by the killer simply to punish Brady. Her identity was a variable in the killer's eyes. It could have just as easily been Nina.

We rocketed down the interstate; a quick glance at the speedometer confirmed that we were doing seventy-five. All it would take would be a patch of black ice to send us out of control and off the road, but I didn't want him to slow down. I tried the redial button and again got the answering machine.

"Is it possible the ringer's turned off on the phone?" asked Brady.

"Not intentionally," I said. "I never turn it off. But even if it was turned off, I keep the volume on the answering machine high enough that I can hear it from wherever I am on the first floor."

Brady reached for the cell phone and punched a speed dial sequence. After a brief pause, he said into the receiver, "Hey, it's me. Listen, we might have something going on here. Dwayne's still with me, and we're not getting an answer from his house. Melanie's supposed to be there waiting for him."

I felt lightheaded as I heard him say my fears aloud. We were on the Georgesville exit, hurtling toward a red light.

"Hmm," he was saying. "Well, that's good, I suppose. We're almost there. Can you send someone this way, um, just in case?" He nearly whispered the last three words, but they stuck in my ears, nonetheless. He disconnected the call and shot an awkward smile in my direction. "That was Nina. She says they found signs the killer had been out there on the trail with us. If that damn rookie hadn't fucked up, they'd probably have him by now."

I stared blankly ahead. As we turned west on Alkire, the Saturn's rear-end lost its footing and skidded into the empty oncoming lane. Brady steered into the slide, and soon he had righted us.

"Hey, that's *good*," said Brady. "If he was out there, he can't have been here. He *can't*."

I said nothing, but I couldn't keep the thought from racing through my head. *If we had time to eat a meal, the Eviscerator had time to get here.* God. *Please.*

I could barely breathe by the time we pulled into my driveway. Every light in the house was on, radiant rectangles projected out onto the carpeting of fresh white snow. There was nothing obviously amiss and somehow, that made everything worse. Melanie wouldn't have just gone to sleep. She *wouldn't*.

Brady barely had the car in park before I was tumbling out of the passenger door. I lost my footing and went down on my knees, not even feeling the scraped flesh through my adrenaline haze. I scrambled back to my feet and moved as quickly as I could toward the porch. I could hear Brady in the background telling me to wait, but I couldn't wait any longer.

Melanie had to be safe. She *had* to be.

I fumbled with my keys, cursing profusely as they slipped through my fingers and fell to the wooden porch. I retrieved them and finally worked them into the lock, throwing the door wide open.

"Melanie?" I called, stepping across the threshold. My voice echoed throughout the utterly quiet house. Dexter appeared in the hallway, peering at me expectantly before rubbing his face against the corner of the wall. "*Melanie!*"

I passed from room to room, calling her name over and over until my voice was hoarse. Brady had entered the house and headed for the second floor, searching bedrooms while I checked the basement. When we converged on the first floor, he was already on the phone, speaking urgently to Nina.

Melanie was nowhere in the house.

CHAPTER TWENTY-SIX

I sat down heavily on the couch while Brady finished his call. I cannot begin to describe the way I felt. I was responsible for whatever happened to Melanie now. I closed my eyes tightly, wishing I could go back in time, just a few hours, make her come with me instead of staying here—no. I would have made her go back to Lymont, get herself far, far away from here. But when I opened my eyes, nothing had changed. Melanie was still gone. Brady had disconnected and was standing nearby, looking strained and uncomfortable, as if he wanted to offer encouragement but couldn't find the strength to lie.

"Nina's on her way," he said. "Should be here in about fifteen minutes." He began to pace the room, anxiety spreading like a stain across his face.

I nodded absently. Dexter sat at my feet, staring curiously at me. He could sense the heaviness in the air. I forced myself to calm down and think. I couldn't just give up. Melanie was out there somewhere, and she needed me.

I hadn't noticed forced entry when I had searched the house. That would mean she had opened the door for the bastard. Why would she do that? She had to have known him. It was the only thing that halfway made sense.

I scanned the room, looking for signs of a struggle. There was nothing more notable than my usual disarray. My eyes drifted from the front door to the dusty mantel above the fireplace, from the mouth of the hallway to the entrance of the kitchen.

297

Back to the hallway, where they came to rest on the telephone table.

A piece of paper was folded like a crude tent, propped up near the answering machine. I got up from my chair and crossed the room in three long steps, snatching the paper up and flipping it over.

"What?" asked Brady, breaking his circuit to follow me into the hall. "What is it?"

I looked up at him and giggled uncontrollably. "A note. It's from Melanie." I laughed again, a big horsy laugh bordering on hysteria. The release was bizarre but necessary, and some of my peripheral senses began to slowly come around. I clutched the paper to my chest and willed the laughter away. I handed Brady the note.

It read, *"Dwayne, Tried to call you, but (lunkhead) you left your cell phone here. You can't go through with this. Please. You'd be as bad as him. If you get back before I do, STAY PUT. I'm taking your phone with me, so you can call me. ♥ Mel"*

Brady sighed, wiping his sweaty brow with a shaky hand, a nervous twitter emanating from his own mouth. "For God's sake, call her," he said.

I grabbed the handset of my cordless and for a moment, drew a blank. It isn't often that you call your own cell phone number, and I was having trouble remembering. With exasperation, I hurried down the hall to the den. I stepped around my desk and sat in the leather office chair. I opened the top drawer to my left, a large square bin that housed hanging file folders that were alphabetized and neatly tabbed. I flipped through the folders until I found the one for Verizon and pulled it out. I retrieved the number from my last bill and punched it into the handset. Brady had followed, watching me curiously as I sat back and listened for the call to connect.

There was an unusually long pause before my voicemail kicked on, a generic female voice providing instructions for sending a voicemail, page or text message. I looked at the phone incredulously before hanging up and hitting the redial button. Again, the voicemail intercepted the call before the first ring. I canceled the call and closed my eyes tightly, holding the phone to my forehead. Any hope I had felt a moment ago vanished.

"No answer," I said through clenched teeth.

Brady stayed silent, his hands in his pockets, his lips pursed as if he were contemplating something very deep. The palpable awkwardness of the moment rendered us both unable to speak. Any encouragement Brady offered would ring hollow, and he knew it. People had been dropping like flies around him for years, and he wasn't ignorant to the way I was feeling.

I thought about Jasmine, Melanie's eleven-year-old daughter. She was at home, anxiously awaiting her mother's return from a week-long seminar. Melanie had extended her trip to help me find this psychopath. And now—

I wouldn't allow myself to complete the thought. I had grown close to Jasmine within the last year. I had met her shortly after her father had been murdered. She was amazingly tough and resilient, but I didn't think she could handle losing another parent. I didn't think she should have to. I'm not a religious man, but I found myself whispering those convenient prayers we utter when all the world has turned to shit.

Please, God, please *let Melanie be safe.*

The phone rang against my forehead, startling me so badly I dropped it. It clattered to the desktop and shrilled again. I picked it up, fumbling at the tiny buttons with fingers three sizes too big.

"Hello?" I hated the sound of desperation in my voice.

"Is this Dwayne Morrow?" The voice was male and softspoken, a little muffled.

"Yes. Who is this?"

There was a long pause, and I began to think the caller had disconnected. "Are you still there?" I asked.

"Um, yes, I'm sorry. This is very difficult."

My blood gelled. Bad news is always difficult to deliver. Brady studied me with penetrating eyes. I suspected he was straining to overhear the conversation, and I turned my back to him. Despite the situation, I wondered if he was taking notes for his next feature.

"I believe I have something of yours," he whispered. "You need to come here."

"I don't understand," I said. "Am I supposed to know you?"

More silence, a nervous sigh, then, "Please, Mr. Morrow. It is urgent that you come alone. I'm afraid your lady's life depends on it. If the police come, I can't guarantee her safety. Please promise me."

The voice was familiar, but I couldn't get my mind around it. The more I tried to identify it, the more elusive it was. The voice was pleading, and it threw me. I expected a vicious killer to be more forthright with his demands.

I lowered my voice to a whisper and walked to the other end of the room. Brady awkwardly tried to follow, but I shooed him away. "I can't very well meet you if I don't know who you are."

"Why are you talking so funny?" the voice was newly anxious, panicky suspicion adding a shrill edge to his voice. "Is someone listening?"

I suspected he was near terminating the call. "No one can hear you but me," I said quickly. "I just want to keep it that way."

"You're not alone?"

"No," I said, hoping it wasn't the wrong thing to say. "*Please.* Who is this?"

"If you tell anyone, I can't guarantee her safety," he repeated.

"Yes, I understand," I said impatiently.

"3563 Ravenswood Lane. You must hurry."

The phone went dead in my ear. A frustrated cry was strangled in my constricting throat. I repeated the address in my head and ignored Brady as he badgered me for details. I jotted the address onto a Post-It before I could forget it, then bent down to turn my computer on. My monitor thrummed with electricity and soon began displaying a series of system messages about the bios and hardware while the hard drive clicked away.

"Are you going to tell me what that was?" asked Brady, obviously annoyed with me.

300

"I'm not exactly sure," I said absently, waiting impatiently as the Windows logo flashed across the screen. After what seemed an eternity, I was able to bring up a web browser. Brady began to ease around the desk behind me, and I looked up at him sharply. "Do you mind?"

He stopped and looked at me incredulously. "You have got to be kidding me!" He backed off and began pacing the open floor space in front of the desk.

My fingers flew across the keyboard, entering the web address in Google Maps. I plugged in the street address and was rewarded with a detailed set of directions and map of Northwest Columbus, just beyond Dublin. I clicked the print button, and my Laserjet hummed, dispensing a few sheets of paper, which I quickly collected, folding and stuffing them into my back pocket. I returned my browser to its home page, then went into the options menu and cleared the computer's internal memory cache. I couldn't be sure Brady wouldn't attempt to use my browsing history to track me. The man had said to come *alone*. I powered the computer down.

"What in the hell is going on?" Brady demanded.

I had a real problem. I needed to go by myself, but how could I keep Brady from tagging along, especially considering the only car available was his? I chewed on my bottom lip as I straightened things on my desk, avoiding eye contact with Brady. Think, Morrow, *think*.

"That's it," said Brady, signaling he had reached the end of his patience. "I'm calling Nina. Maybe she can have that call traced—"

It was almost involuntary. My arm swung around and up, my fist making direct contact with Brady's nose. I heard the sickening crunch of cartilage, and his nose seemed to explode in a stream of dark, syrupy blood. His head snapped back, his eyes wide with shock, unintelligible words sputtering through the blood flowing down onto his lips. For a moment, I thought I was going to have to hit him again, but his eyes suddenly fluttered, and he went down.

301

"*Oh shit, oh shit, oh shit,*" I said, crossing to where Brady had fallen to check his pulse. I was relieved to find it strong and steady. I immediately shifted to rifling through Brady's pockets for car keys, which I found on the first try.

I grabbed my coat and glanced at the clock. How long had it been since the phone call? Five minutes? Ten? I had to get out quickly or else I'd be penned in by the police. Nina would surely want an explanation for Brady's current condition, and I doubted she would understand my reasoning. I hurried toward the door.

"Dammit, Brady," I said irritably over my shoulder as I stepped out onto the porch. "As much as I thought I would have enjoyed doing that, I really wish there had been another way." I flexed my stinging fingers and pulled the door closed behind me.

I ran-slid-walked to the car, retrieving the directions from my back pocket and tossing them on the passenger seat as I slid behind the wheel. The cabin was still warm from our earlier travels. I started the engine and backed out onto the dark country road, pointing the nose eastward. I had barely gotten off Orin Way when I passed the first cruiser, barreling silently toward my house. I accelerated, wanting to put as much distance between us as possible. Melanie's life depended on my coming alone.

Alone.

Was this what I really wanted? Working through Ryan McGregor's murder had whetted an appetite in me even I hadn't realized, yet nothing was playing out the way I had envisioned when I had decided to become a private detective. Thanks to my 'hobby,' Sheila and her unborn child were in ICU, my brother wasn't speaking to me for the first time in thirty-four years, and Melanie…oh God, *Melanie.*

The car hit a patch of black ice and skittered uneasily sideways before grabbing pavement and pulling itself back on track. I was nearing the interstate and had counted five more police cars heading toward Orin Way. Apparently, I was missing quite a party back at my place.

I tried not to think too far ahead. My stomach was already bunched up in a cold knot, and I could taste bile at the back of my throat. I kept thinking of Jasmine, asleep in her bed, oblivious to her mother's distress. I remembered the way she had looked at her father's funeral only last fall, standing solemnly at the graveside, her red ponytails hanging limp in the afternoon shower, her cheeks glistening with tears underneath all of the rain. The weight of responsibility was crushing.

I squinted my dry eyes into the oncoming traffic that was only just beginning to swell with morning commuters. I was so tired I was slaphappy. I needed to retain my focus somehow, and the steady hum of tires on asphalt was doing nothing more than lulling me toward sleep. As much as I hated losing time, I ducked into a Speedway off Broad Street and got a 20-ounce cup of scalding black coffee before rejoining the northbound traffic on the interstate.

Soon, the sun would be rising behind slate gray clouds, painting the day in funereal hues. I sipped at the coffee, singeing my lips and tongue with the liquid lava. I cracked the window, willing the bitterly cold air to seep into the compartment and drive the weariness from me. It was partially effective, and the ability to think slowly returned.

As miles passed, I became more unsettled. The killer had completely altered his routine by kidnapping Melanie. He had never taken hostages before, to the best of my knowledge. I refused to consider he may have been bluffing on the telephone, because that would mean he had already killed her. But why had he called? What could I possibly offer him that would grant Melanie her freedom? I would offer myself in a minute, but was it enough? I had a hard time believing that a psychopathic murderer could be taken at his word.

I suddenly remembered I didn't have my gun. I had either lost it or been relieved of it back on the Rail Trail. *Dammit!* Hand-to-hand combat with a crazed killer who has a penchant for cutlery wasn't what I had in mind. I mentally abused myself for a moment, because here I was again, racing toward certain danger without so much as a thought as to how I might proceed. I leaned across the seat and flipped down the panel to the Saturn's glove compartment, hoping Brady might keep something useful inside. Nothing but maps, napkins and a mangled pair of sunglasses. I slammed the glove compartment shut in frustration.

The exit for 161 was approaching on the right, and I signaled my exit. An army of salt trucks had rolled over the highway, making its surface relatively trustworthy. Once I had taken the exit and merged west, road conditions took a dramatic turn for the worse. It didn't appear that any salt trucks had passed through at all, and frequent gusts of wind blew fresh snow across the pavement in stealthy wisps. I adjusted my speed accordingly and checked the clock. I had been on the road for twenty minutes. I signaled again and took the first exit, Avery Road, merging north onto the wide four-lane. It hadn't been cleared either, and the tail end of the Saturn skidded away from me. I stomped on the brake, forgetting anything I had ever known about winter driving, causing the slide to worsen. The car glided across two empty lanes before coming to a sudden stop, the rims of its tires biting into the concrete center divider. I tried to swallow, but my throat felt like it was lined with cotton. I suddenly realized I was hearing someone shouting, cursing—and was even more startled to realize that someone was me.

Goddamn it, I'm losing it.

I rolled the window completely down and lay my head against the headrest, closing my eyes and letting the cold air wash over me.

Gotta pull yourself together, Morrow.

I opened my eyes and looked around. A small red Chevy approached slowly from the opposite direction, its two teenaged occupants gaping as they passed. After getting their eyes full, they continued on, signaling for the interstate and disappearing into the night. There were no other cars in sight. I eased the car back onto the road.

I was only vaguely familiar with this part of Dublin. Newly constructed shopping plazas lined Avery Road, brown-brick facades that blended seamlessly from one business to the next. Even McDonald's conformed to the motif, looking curiously muted in drab mud brown. I reached across the seat and found the crumpled sheets of paper that comprised the map I had retrieved from the internet. I was getting closer. I drove beyond the new construction growth that abruptly stopped after only a few blocks and Avery Road suddenly became Muirfield Drive. It wound lazily through pricey neighborhoods before finally narrowing to two lanes on the far side of the village. I was looking for a cross street named Bimmel Run, which eventually intersected with Ravenswood Lane, but anticipated several more miles of driving before reaching it. Traffic was nonexistent on this sad little patch of asphalt, and the snow had stacked into taller drifts along the berm.

Where in the hell was I going? The farther I drove, the fewer houses there were. Eventually, I found the green county marker for Bimmel Run and, since there was no one else sharing the road with me, came to a complete stop. The road, little more than a one lane path, cut east to west, looking treacherous and foreboding in either direction. I doubted that Bimmel had much of a priority with the county road crews; its surface was buried under a blanket of snow, probably three inches in depth. I was interested in the westward direction and turned my attention that way. The road meandered jaggedly back through a thicket of brush, disappearing under an arched railroad bridge. I could barely discern faint tire tracks from a vehicle that had passed through earlier in the evening, but certainly not anytime recently.

I inspected the cabin of Brady's car more thoroughly, hoping to come up with something I could use as a weapon. I was pretty sure I'd need one. A couple of empty bottles of diet soda rolled around in the back floorboard, but they were made of thin plastic—not my first choice of weaponry. I pulled out various wads of trash from between the seats: chewing gum, disposable pens, loose change and a packet of ketchup that I accidentally discharged while trying to retrieve. There was simply nothing from which to choose. I saw distant headlights crest the horizon, so I completed the turn onto Bimmel and drove slowly, listening to the sound of snow crunching underneath the tires.

I slowed as I neared the railroad bridge, noting the rusted yellow sign warning of the underpass's narrowness and height limitations. One car at a time, please. It wasn't a particularly long expanse, just lengthy enough to add an element of surprise should an oncoming car, its driver speeding or drunk, hurtle through the other end without warning.

All that was missing was a Bernard Herrmann score.

Seeing no oncoming headlights, I eased through, hurrying once I was under the cover of the block tunnel, knowing no snow or ice had collected here. The other side came quickly enough, but my nerves were beginning to shred again. Bimmel Run was nothing more than a thread, running out to the middle of nowhere. If this was Bimmel, I hated to see Ravenswood. It would probably cost Brady his car's suspension.

I was ready to turn around, sure that I'd already passed Ravenswood, when I saw a wood-burnt sign mounted on a split rail fence, incongruously emerging from the unkempt brush that bordered the majority of Bimmel. Following the directions, I turned right.

Ravenswood cut through dense woodland. Ancient trees leaned out over the road, subtly suggesting you shouldn't be beneath them in high winds. The tangle of branches overhead was so thick that even leafless, they blocked the moonlight and darkened the night.

My time for formulating a plan was quickly evaporating, yet my sluggish brain refused to produce anything useful. I thought about the note Melanie had left at my house. It was obvious from the wording that she hadn't yet realized something was wrong. She wouldn't have inducted the help of a perfect stranger, especially one traveling along a lonely stretch like Orin Way at that hour of the night. I suddenly sat upright.

Jordan McCleary?

I mulled it over for a moment. Was I just territorially pissing? Old habits die hard, and my earlier dislike for the man had yet to wane entirely. The killer's fixation on me coincided neatly with the beginning of Melanie's conference. Could it have been McCleary's jealousy? His feelings for Melanie were transparently affixed to his face anytime I saw him. I knew he lived in Portsmouth, nearly one hundred miles south of Columbus, but there was no rule stating a killer had to be native to his killing grounds. It had always just been an assumption on my part, and presumably that of the authorities and media, as well. He could own a vacation home or something out in this godforsaken wilderness. Hell, he could be waiting around any corner, burrowed down into his choice of shrubbery, leveling the infrared sight of a rifle and centering its crosshairs on my head. I sank down in the seat, willing my head to shrink.

Jordan McCleary.

It would also explain why Melanie was a hostage rather than a victim. McCleary might still think he could mend their relationship, especially if he removed me from the picture. Would he offer my dead body as a trophy to Melanie, as a symbol of his love? Were psychopathic killers even *capable* of love?

McCleary was a solidly built man, broad shouldered with the suggestion of powerful arms hidden beneath the tasteful cashmere sweater I last saw him in. I didn't look forward to tangling with him. If the killer even *was* him. I rolled down the window for another blast of cold air, knowing I should be arriving at my destination in any moment.

No weapons. No plans. The only resource I had left was my brain, and considering how sleep deprived I was, I should be dead by sunrise.

The road twisted lazily to the right, and the dense cover of trees abruptly broke, exposing an elaborately conceived fence, black wrought iron and granite block posts, topped by ornate if deadly-looking spires. I drove slowly, staring in awe as the enormous Victorian mansion appeared in a slideshow through wrought iron sections of the fence. It sat in the middle of enormous acreage, football fields of space surrounding it. As far away as it was, it still seemed huge.

As the road straightened, I found the entrance to this wonderland, a cobblestone tongue leading to a security gate. The keypad and intercom were mounted on a wrought iron post that matched the fence. It was installed in the shadow of an armless Greek statue, one of two goddesses who stood guard over the heavy black gate. An ornate headdress sat atop it, announcing the address and occupants.

3563 Ravenswood Lane.

The Carters.

CHAPTER TWENTY-SEVEN

The Carters?

I did a quick proximity check and realized I was, in fact, bordering on Muirfield, which was where the Carters lived. When I was trailing Alan Carter, I had never actually followed him all the way to his house. Once he had taken the 161 exit west from I-270 and it was apparent that he was going home, I had looped south and gone home myself. This was at Geneva's specific request; she had told me their house was on a desolate stretch of road and any surveillance I might do would be obvious to Alan.

I paused at the wrought iron gate, gaping at the structure that Geneva had called home. I hadn't imagined anything like this, even after Donna Nelson had told me of hers and Geneva's mutual membership in the country club. The snow-covered grounds were level and deep, broken only occasionally by the small, round footprints of woodland creatures. The house was a monstrosity with staggered elevations and regal ornamentation at every precipice. Gothic gargoyles perched on every turret, leaning out and staring down into the yard. There were no lights burning in any of the windows I saw, only security globes positioned strategically around the perimeter of the building.

I rolled the window down and eased up to the keypad intercom. I was about to press a button when the gate suddenly came to life, opening in an almost soundless fashion, a silent invitation to the final act of the play. I rolled through slowly, taking in the lavish surroundings as I passed through.

So, who had called me? Alan or Jeffrey? I tried to replay the call in my mind, but the voice had been intentionally muted, and I couldn't be certain one way or the other. I suspected it was Jeffrey, based simply on the fact that Alan Carter was such a large man, he couldn't possibly have attacked Sheila without his size being noted by the eyewitness. Yet Jeffrey was such a pasty little shit, it was hard to envision him as the killer either. I rolled toward the mansion with my eyes attuned to the periphery, seeking motion or activity of any kind. The building remained dark behind the cover of its exterior security lights.

The driveway led to a parking area large enough to accommodate several dozen cars along the side of the house. There were none currently in residence, and I noticed a path that cut away from the rear of the lot and led to an enormous parking structure at the back of the property. It seemed odd for the garage to be so completely detached, but after seeing the extravagances of the outdoor decor, it wouldn't have surprised me to learn there was an underground passage connecting the two buildings. I parked in the lot and quieted the engine, staring up at the structure looming before me. A marble deck had been constructed overhead, jutting out from a second-floor entrance and accessible by a winding set of stairs that twisted upwards. They, too, were wrought iron and would be hell to ascend in the snow. What choice did I really have?

I got out of the car and again longed for my gun. It was too late to worry about it now; I was going to have to wing it. I started up the stairs, fully aware that I was being watched from somewhere above. When I finally reached the top, I was startled to see that it was Alan, not Jeffrey, framed in the double French doors that led into the house. I expected smug viciousness, smirking, gloating—what I found was a very nervous man. His forehead glistened with sweat, and a nervous tic had seized control of his right eye, winking at regular intervals. His voluminous jowls were pasty under the deck's overhead lighting. I could see circular stains spreading from the armpits of his dark blue pullover.

310

"Please come in," he said, stepping aside and swinging the door wide. It was a casual invitation, no different than he might have extended to any visitor. I looked at his big hands and was relieved to see they were empty, no weapons of any sort.

"Where is she?" I said, stepping through and turning immediately to face him. "Where's Melanie?"

Alan pursed his lips and studied me for a second, fresh perspiration trickling down his forehead. "She's fine," he said. "Let's go into the library where we can talk."

"I want to see her now."

He glanced at an antique rosewood grandfather clock that stood in the corner. It was twenty after five. "Soon," he said. "We have a little time yet, and we have things to discuss." Without awaiting my response, he ambled across the room and into a darkened hallway, pausing momentarily before passing through.

I glanced around, taking in my surroundings as quickly as possible. The room in which I stood was sparsely decorated with high-backed, stiffly uncomfortable Victorian furniture, obviously authentic antique. It was impossible to discern the exact color of upholstery because none of the lights in the room were on, but I would have guessed it to be plum. Portraits of plump women splayed on settees while feasting on fruit adorned the walls, any one of which was undoubtedly worth more than I could earn in a year. Hardwood floors (the real thing, not Pergo) lay underneath oriental rugs woven in patterns of black and burgundy. A dimly lit aquarium teeming with exotic fish burbled from its position on a table in the far corner. Except for us, the house was still.

"Are you coming?" asked Alan from the darkness of the hallway. I jumped at the sound of his voice, then crossed the room, trailing behind him.

The hallway was long and wide, a half-dozen doors opening on either side before the passage took a forty-five degree turn to the right. Alan

311

waited at the threshold of the third door to the right and disappeared inside once he saw me enter the hall. I followed him into the spacious library and paused just inside the door, warily eyeing him as he lowered his girth onto a dark brown leather sofa in the middle of the room. Long bookshelves had been built into the southern wall, leather-bound volumes lining every shelf. I wasn't close enough to determine the titles, but they were undoubtedly collector's editions, lending a faintly musty odor to the room that spoke uniquely of aged paper and binding glue.

"Please," said Alan. "Have a seat."

He indicated the sofa across from him, and I cautiously perched on its edge. An ornately carved coffee table separated us, a Faberge egg collection displayed prominently in its center, undoubtedly one of Geneva's passions before she had seen fit to end her life.

"May I get you some coffee?" he asked, his eye still ticking in time with his heart.

"This isn't a social call," I said. "I want to see Melanie and I want to see her now."

Alan closed his eyes and leaned back into the couch, a sigh deflating what was left of him. He wore anxiety on his face like a mask, and I didn't understand why he was being so magnanimous. "Your Melanie is upstairs resting," he finally said.

"Is she hurt?"

"Nothing that won't heal."

"If you've touched her, I swear I'll—"

"We've got a mutual problem, Mr. Morrow," he said, cutting me short. "You must believe me when I tell you that all I want is for everything to work out for everyone."

"Fine," I said. "Give her to me. I'll take her out of here, and you won't ever hear from us again."

"If only I could believe that," said Alan, with a forlorn shake of his head. "It isn't really that easy, is it Mr. Morrow? There are—the others to consider."

"So, what do you want from me?"

Alan was silent for a long moment, his fingertips steepled together underneath his nose. "Have you ever been married, Mr. Morrow?" he asked.

I shook my head.

"Geneva and I married when we were very young, barely out of high school. We had both grown up in wealthy families and were accustomed to the very best life had to offer. I suppose we took our positions for granted, as does most anyone who is born with a silver spoon in his or her mouth. Geneva's maiden name was Ratcliff. Does that mean anything to you?"

I searched my memory, but my impatience with the situation drew a blank. "What's this got to do with anything?"

Alan continued as if I hadn't said a thing. "Geneva's father was Senator William Ratcliff, a tough old bastard from a whole line of tough old bastards. Made quite a name for himself in Congress. He really wanted a son, but Geneva was the only child he had. He spent most of his time away from his wife and daughter, taking a studio apartment in Washington while his family remained here."

"This house?" I asked.

Alan nodded. "We took possession thirty years ago, after the old man died and we had gotten married."

I did some quick calculations. "The Senator was rather young when he died then?"

Alan paused, then nodded again. "An automobile accident."

I stared at him vacantly, wondering where in the hell this was going.

He cleared his throat and cast a penitent smile in my direction. "I never really understood that corny schmaltz, 'Love is blind.' Do you?"

"I'm not sure I know what you mean."

"I always assumed it was a gracious way of explaining why the handsome sometimes marry the homely. Very righteous and selfless, you know? But I don't think so anymore. I think that it's far truer to say that love is blind*ing*."

He shifted in his seat and paused, his eye still ticking, ticking, ticking. He strained to his feet and began pacing the floor. "Our families always approved of us together, and we seemed well suited to one another. I went to work for my father's law firm, and Geneva did whatever suited her at the moment—fundraisers for the arts, mostly. Our little girl was born during our second year together."

He smiled wistfully, a pleasant rush of memories washing over his rounded countenance. "We named her Katrina after Geneva's great-grandmother. She was a beautiful child, well-tempered—slept straight through the night from a very early age. She was a gift from heaven." He paused at the window, staring out onto the darkened lawn.

"Please, Mr. Carter," I implored, unable to restrain myself any longer. "Please let me see Melanie now. I just need—"

"*Patience*, Mr. Morrow," he said without turning from the window. "We still have time. And I need you to understand. *Please*. Will you try?"

What choice did I have? I grunted in accordance and waited for him to continue, knotting my fingers together to keep my hands still. Why didn't he have a weapon? He seemed entirely too at ease with me, and it was unnerving.

"It was after our boy, Jeffrey, was born that Geneva began to suffer— her imbalances," he continued.

"Her bipolar disease," I said, more to myself than to Alan. "Jeffrey mentioned it."

He waved my comment away as if bipolar disease were no more serious than a runny nose. "Ah, yes. But in those days, it wasn't the casual phenomenon it seems to be now. Geneva was very absorbed with her new

314

baby and had become absolutely hostile toward Trina. Trina was only two years old, Mr. Morrow. I tried to smooth the waters, but Geneva seemed to have developed a pure hatred for her own daughter. I-I-I—" He broke away, staring vacantly through the window. I didn't need to see his face to know he was crying. "I just wanted our family to be normal again."

"What happened?" I asked.

"Oh, Geneva saw psychiatrists, and Trina spent a lot of time with nannies, but I guess the real breakthrough didn't happen for a few years. You see, Jeffrey was genuinely fond of Trina. It became apparent once he began to crawl, and even more so after he began to talk. At first, I feared Geneva would resent the attention Jeffrey paid Trina, but I guess it somehow made Trina more—palatable in Geneva's eyes. Everything seemed to settle down again. I finished out my career at the law firm, and Geneva began working at Dial-Tech. Obviously, we didn't need the money, but Geneva said she liked playing with real folk."

His breathing became ragged, and his shoulders visibly deflated. I allowed him the time to collect himself while I scanned the area for anything I might use as a weapon. Other than a nutcracker floating on a sea of nuts in a candy dish, there wasn't much.

When Alan turned toward me, his face was contorted with grief. His lips were parted, attempting to continue, but unable to find the right words. He dabbed roughly at the corners of his eyes with his thumbs and noisily cleared his throat.

"I'm sorry," he said. "This is hard."

I looked at him emptily, unable to sympathize while Melanie remained captive somewhere inside this house.

He began to pace again. His next words were cold and mechanical. "Three years ago, Jeffrey raped Trina. He held his own sister down and forced himself on her. Geneva and I were out of town on vacation, and it happened repeatedly throughout the week. I had no idea that Jeffrey was suffering from troubles of his own."

315

The picture suddenly came into sharp focus, and I bypassed the end of Alan's tale. "You're saying that *Jeffrey* is behind all this?" I demanded, rising to my feet.

"I don't know, *I don't know!*" His pace quickened, and he kneaded his fleshy forehead with his right hand.

"The hell you don't!" I shouted. "Melanie's here, how could you *not* know?"

"Please, Mr. Morrow, *please*," he urged, using his hands to suggest I lower my voice. "There's no need to become so animated. I'm trying to figure out what's right—the right thing to *do*—I-I-I—"

"Well, for God's sake, Alan! Whatever you do, *take your fucking time*. I don't think enough people have died yet!"

My words were a physical assault to him, and he immediately crumpled, leaning forward and taking hold of the back of the sofa. Blood rushed to his cheeks, and for a moment, I thought he was going to have a full-blown coronary. Clammy sweat rolled down his forehead, and his already ragged breathing became even harsher. I shifted uncomfortably, unsure of what to do. I was still full of rage at the sheer selfishness and stupidity of the man. How much of this could he have prevented?

When he spoke again, his voice was little more than a whisper. "Jeffrey is my *son*, Mr. Morrow. Don't you *see*? Can't you *understand*? He cannot have done these horrible things. He is my *son!*" His eyes begged for confirmation, absolution, anything and everything that I would not provide.

"Where is he now?" I asked. "Is he here?"

Alan shook his head and glanced again at his wristwatch. "No—but soon. He goes for a run every morning, trying to reach the peak of exertion as the sun rises. He says it cleanses him. He's done it every morning since he was a boy."

"*That* didn't strike you as odd?"

"Hell, no! Look at me. I'm about as far out of shape as any one man should be. I was *thankful* my boy took an interest in exercise. He was small, but it would be a mistake to underestimate his strength—" He paused as he realized the further ramifications of his words. "I'm *trying*, Mr. Morrow, I really am. It's just that I've only come to realize the truth of the situation myself. Jeffrey kept news clippings of his—handiwork. What do you think when you find something like that in your child's possession? I told myself Jeffrey had found a new hobby, morbid though it was. That night—when you were following me? He was there in the alley, getting into his car. I didn't ask him any questions, and he didn't volunteer any information. I didn't care why he was in the alley. I wanted to get away from you, and he provided an easy exit. Even after I heard about the murder, I convinced myself it was coincidence—"

"*Coincidence?*"

"Please, Mr. Morrow. When you have children of your own—"

"That's such total bullshit," I said, shaking my head.

"Tonight, everything changed. Jeffrey's never brought anyone here before. *Never*. By the time he arrived with your Melanie, she was unconscious—"

"She was *what?*"

"Unconscious, Mr. Morrow, I'm sorry. I didn't make her that way," he said. "But she was alive."

"How can you be sure?"

"Because he kept calling her Trina!" he spat. "He thinks she's Trina, and he wants to *keep* her!"

I tried to shake coherence into his words, but I still didn't get it. "What happened to Trina?" I asked.

His eyes clouded over instantly. "She's been away for years now. We had to put her in a hospital—she had a complete nervous breakdown after Jeffrey...She doesn't speak anymore, and her doctors won't allow us to see her. They say it upsets her too much. It's just as well. I don't think I could face my little girl in that condition. I only saw her once—just after—and it was *horrible*. Geneva tended to her for a while, before the doctors asked

317

that we not come, and by God, I was relieved! If I didn't have to see her, I didn't have to admit it had happened. Geneva encouraged it. We invented a son-in-law, Charlie—and grandchildren, for God's sake!" A wistful smile played at his lips. "It was as if she had grown up and moved on to her own happy life, a fantasy we could harmlessly indulge."

Harmlessly? Didn't it occur to him that his daughter might have gotten better had he and his wife continued to visit her? Their support, despite Trina's protests, could have been instrumental in her recovery. What kind of doctor would even recommend that kind of segregation for his patient? I was keenly aware of the hour, however, and didn't have time to render judgment on his own lack of it.

"We sent Jeffrey to a specialist in Sweden, a revolutionary therapist renowned for his work with—sexual deviants." The words were ugly on his lips, spilling forth like sputum. "We were virtually assured Jeffrey would return to us as he once was, all of his problems in order."

"Ain't life grand."

"Oh, but he *did*, Mr. Morrow! When he arrived, he was just as I remembered him—before the mishap, you know—soft-spoken, polite, responsible. He never mentioned Trina to us, and we were careful to do the same whenever he was around. I should've known something was wrong when he began speaking of her again. He spoke of her frequently, his desire to see her again."

"Didn't he know she was away in a hospital?"

He shook his head. "We would never let Jeffrey know where Trina is. I suppose that's the least we could do for her. But Jeffrey said he kept finding her in that damned chat room she liked so much—"

I stood expectantly. "I want to see Melanie now."

"But Mr. Morrow," he said, turning as if surprised I would want to leave his company. "We haven't decided what we're going to do."

"What is it, exactly, that you think we *should* do?"

He closed the distance between us, taking me firmly by the arms and staring intently into my eyes. "Why, we have to figure a way out of this, a way to make sure Jeffrey stays out of prison and his name stays out of the papers, we—"

I shook him off and laughed. "You have got to be *kidding* me!"

"I can get Jeffrey into a hospital," he said, his pleading voice like fingernails on a chalkboard against my ears. "I can ensure that—"

"You can ensure nothing!" I spat. "Your precious goddamn son is a whacked-out psycho killer, Mr. Carter. Time to face facts. All you're concerned about is your son's freedom and your family's reputation. How about the victims? How about their families? Your fucking son put my brother's girlfriend in the hospital tonight. He intended to kill her. He probably didn't know she was pregnant—"

"Oh, God—" Carter made a thick noise in the back of his throat.

"—but I seriously doubt it would've mattered. What do you think, Mr. Carter? Would it have mattered to Jeffrey? Does it matter to *you*?"

"Of course it does, of course it does—"

"Then here's how it goes: I'm going to find Melanie, with or without your help. We're going to get the hell out of here and as soon as we are safely away, we are going to call the police and tell them everything. Do you understand me, Mr. Carter? *Everything.*"

I could see the wheels turning inside his head, looking for some alternative way to resolve this mess, but after a brief moment of futile tabulation, he nodded grimly.

"Will you take me to her?" I asked and was flooded with relief when he nodded again. It would've taken some time to search a house of this enormity, and as we neared sunrise, I knew time was quickly running out.

Carter led the way into the hall, turning a dimmer switch as he passed, which vaguely decreased the output of the wall sconces. For the life of me, I couldn't understand why someone would have a house of this splendor and keep it lit like a mausoleum.

319

As if reading my mind, he said over his shoulder, "Jeffrey prefers we keep the lights dimmed. His eyes are particularly sensitive after his morning run."

We rounded a corner and came to a wood-paneled door with a small button pad to its right. Carter pushed the top button, and a light-duty elevator car appeared, its interior paneled to match the hallway. We stepped aboard and Carter selected the third floor, prompting the car nimbly upward.

When the door opened, I was surprised to find that the turgid stiffness of the Victorian era had been left below. This level, with its off-white and beige simplicity, was warm and inviting, with thick Berber carpeting cushioning each footfall. Where dramatic artwork of distinctive origin had adorned the walls downstairs, family portraits hung here, a testament to the Carters and Ratcliffs throughout the years. I noted extreme caution had been taken to remove Trina from any of the family pictures, erasing her from the family set as cleanly as if she had never even existed.

Carter paused at one of the doors on the left—I'd lost count of which one—and inserted a key into its glossy brass door handle. The door swung silently inward, and I could see her—*Thank God!*—I could see Melanie on the bed. Her wrists and ankles were fastened together by lengths of rope, knotted tightly enough to discolor her hands, and a knotted bandana had been inserted between her lips as a gag. My joy eroded when I realized she was unconscious, her head lolled back at an odd angle on the pillow.

"You said she was alive!" I shouted, rushing to her bedside. "You said—"

Her eyelids flickered and lifted, and she was suddenly focusing on me, her lips trying to eject the soggy rag from her mouth. I reached behind her head and gently freed the knot, tossing the gag aside.

"Oh, thank God," she cried. "Thank God."

"Hold still, Mel," I said. "I'll have you out of here in no time."

"It's Jeffrey." I flinched as she wheezed, her voice strained and raw. It left little to the imagination as to how much screaming had been done. Blood had dried on her forehead and matted her hair. "He's the one—"

"I know," I said, concentrating on the tangle of cord at her wrists. "Let me get these loose, and we'll go."

"You're not going anywhere."

I froze. That voice didn't belong here. Not *now*.

The rifle erupted like a cannon, and I dove onto the bed to cover Melanie. She went limp beneath me, and I began exploring her earnestly for damage. She was in shock but unhurt. I gave myself a quick once over, then shifted my attention behind me.

Alan Carter lay in the middle of the floor, his unseeing eyes stupidly fixed on me.

Standing in the doorway, replacing spent shells with fresh ones, was Geneva Carter. She wore a pink, fuzzy bathrobe and had curlers in her hair. Her eyes found mine as she snapped the chamber closed, and I knew we were completely fucked.

CHAPTER TWENTY-EIGHT

"Thanks for stopping by," said Geneva, stepping over her husband's body and thrusting the muzzle of the gun toward us. "Very considerate of you. Saves me some trouble."

I was reeling. What was she doing here? Jeffrey had told me that she committed suicide. He was completely distraught—*devastated.*

He was a psychopathic killer. Did I think he was above lying? But *why?* Just to compound the guilt I already felt over Sheila?

"You shot your own husband," I said stupidly, as if she didn't realize her error.

She looked at him briefly, then abruptly kicked him in the side. "Idiotic bastard," she said. "Everything would have been just *fine* if he would have stayed out of it. Twenty-nine years of quiet cohabitation, and the stupid bastard chooses now to think independently."

"What's to think about? Your son's a killer," Melanie said hoarsely.

"*YOU SHUT UP!*" shrieked Geneva, shifting the rifle's focus toward her. "You're a filthy little whore, and I'm only putting up with you because of Jeffrey." She shifted her glare toward me. "I don't have to put up with you at all."

"You never did think Alan was cheating on you, did you?" I asked, scrambling for a way to keep her from pulling the trigger, something she obviously wanted to do.

Her laughter burbled up from a very dark place. "Can you picture that? Alan Carter hasn't had a sexual thought in over a decade."

322

"Then why did you want me to follow him?" I asked. Keep her talking, keep her talking—anything to keep her from shooting.

"Jeffrey kept newspaper clippings. I tried to discourage it, but he thought it was important to remember the ones who had deceived him. Alan found the clippings, and I was afraid he might inadvertently involve the police. I wanted to know what he was doing with his days. I could keep an eye on him in the evenings."

"So, you've known all along that your son was committing these murders?" I asked incredulously. A mad fire danced behind Geneva's eyes, yet I was still having trouble accepting someone could be that inhuman.

Geneva shrugged, her hold on the rifle unwavering. "Jeffrey thought they were Trina. They weren't."

"He thought Paul Nicholas was his sister?"

She laughed again. "No. That was my doing. Jeffrey's loss of control is a spontaneous thing. It always has been. There are no victims, just accidents. The first woman, well, when he realized she wasn't Trina, he went berserk. It was only by the grace of God that no one saw him. Even though the police had no reason to suspect him, he had no alibi for the time of the murder. The best I could do was create a diversion. Paul Nicholas was that diversion. I killed him using the same MO while Jeffrey was at a fundraiser, surrounded by hundreds of witnesses who could provide him an airtight alibi. The black girl was my doing too."

"You're sick," spat Melanie.

"I am mercy," said Geneva, sending a shiver up my spine. She reached into the pocket of her bathrobe and produced a pair of handcuffs. She tossed them to me and said, "One end on your wrist and the other on the bed frame." She thrust the rifle toward me to punctuate her statement.

Melanie shook her head frantically, not wanting me to surrender my freedom, but what choice did I have? I watched her lose hope as I complied, and I was sick from the desperation on her face. I had come to save her but had failed. Now we were both going to die.

"Good," said Geneva as I latched the cuff around the bed frame. She leaned the gun against the wall and crossed the room, passing through a doorway at the far end, which led into a small bathroom. After a moment, I heard water running from a spigot, collecting in the bathtub. Geneva reappeared in the doorway, crossing her arms and leaning against the doorframe. "Jeffrey will be home soon, and I want everything to be ready."

"If Jeffrey is so fixated on Trina, why haven't you given her to him?" I asked. I was grasping at straws, trying to buy more time. "From what Alan told me, it wouldn't matter to you if Jeffrey found her."

She smiled crookedly. "Trina's been gone for a long time."

"I don't understand."

"She's not in a hospital," she said. "She hasn't been for years. When they sent her home, Alan was away on sabbatical. You see, when things got tough, Alan always ran away, leaving it for me to clean up the mess. So, you see, I cleaned up the mess. I only told Alan that nonsense about her mental state to give him peace of mind. I knew he'd never follow up with the doctors. Why would he? Geneva had taken care of everything."

Taken care of everything?

"I drowned her in this very bathtub," she said absently, her arm sweeping behind her to indicate what I could not see. "I held her head below the surface and watched her eyes swell from her head."

"What did you do with—with her body?"

"I buried her beside the gazebo near the woods about a mile from the house. Filthy little bitch. If she hadn't seduced my innocent boy, none of this would have ever happened. No one gets between me and my son, do you understand? No one."

"She was your daughter," I said.

Her eyes flared, and she charged across the room, slapping me across the face with her open palm. "Don't you ever say that! *EVER!* That— *filth* was no more my daughter than I could flap my arms and fly. She was an anchor, a curse, a—"

"You gave birth to her," I said, and this time, she balled her fingers into a fist before smashing me in the mouth. I could taste coppery blood from the split in my lip created by her enormous ring.

"Shut up!" she hissed. She was about to hit me again when something caught her attention from the corner of her eye. She paused, turning her head toward the window. "There. It'll all be over soon. Jeffrey's coming up the drive now. He'll be with us shortly."

Unbridled worship shone in her eyes as she gazed through the glass. I glanced at Melanie and saw panic welling. She looked like a taut wire about to snap. I laid my free hand across her bound wrists and felt her hands trembling beneath mine. I tried to look confident, but I was scared to death and had been, thus far, completely ineffectual. I wasn't fooling anyone.

Somewhere downstairs, a door closed.

Geneva glided across the room and threw open the door, shouting, "Darling! We're in Trina's room! Hurry up, now. I have a surprise!" She turned to me and said, "He'll be so thrilled you've come. He really does hate you, you know. He thinks you stand between him and Trina." Her gaze wandered to Melanie, and she smiled.

"How could he ever forgive you for killing her?" I wondered aloud.

There was only the most subtle muscular shift around her eyes, so infinitesimal it almost went unnoticed. But I was desperate and alert to anything that might help. Somewhere in my head, something clicked.

"He doesn't know, does he?" I asked.

Her mocking laughter was a shadow of its former self. "Don't be ridiculous. Of course he does. Jeffrey becomes confused, but he knows Trina is gone. For the moment, in his mind, she lives on. She has returned in the form of your lovely Melanie. Eventually, he'll see through her 'disguise,' just as he has with all the others."

I started to say more but realized I didn't want to push her too far. If I wasn't careful, Geneva would snatch the rifle up and put a quick end to me. I would just be another in a long string of victims.

325

The soft hum of the elevator floated in from the hall, and I swear my stomach dropped all the way down to my testicles. The murderous little prick had stood within inches of me, and I hadn't known. *I hadn't known.* As the elevator car came to a stop and the doors whisked open, my blood ran cold, and I realized knowing made all the difference.

He looked wild-eyed and wired when he appeared in the doorway, his wispy blond hair drenched with sweat and standing on end. His breathing was accelerated, and his entire outer layer seemed to glow from the rush of blood flowing just beneath the skin. He wore dark gray sweatpants and a heavy sweatshirt, all heavily stained with rings of perspiration.

Geneva met him at the door and gave him a warm hug and an affectionate kiss that unsettled my stomach. "See darling?" she said, sweeping a hand my way. "Mommy's brought you a present."

Jeffrey's eyes followed her direction and focused on me. The nervous tic was apparently hereditary, as his right eye began to spasm irregularly.

"What are you doing here?" he asked, cocking his head curiously to the side. His tongue darted out and moistened his upper lip in a very lizard-like fashion. Geneva stood behind him, her smirking face visible over his shoulder. She was anxious for the kill, ready for the carnage to begin. She absolutely craved my death.

I had only one chance, and I prayed to God it would work.

"I came because I'm a private investigator," I said. "Somebody killed Trina, and I came to find out who."

His lips quivered and formed a gruesome smile while his eye went into convulsions. "Trina's right beside you."

I shook my head. "Look closer, Jeffrey. She's not Trina. Your mother killed Trina to keep her away from you."

His head jolted as if I had slapped him. "That's absurd! Mother wouldn't do a thing like that."

"Of course I wouldn't," Geneva interjected smoothly, stepping around her son and cupping his face in her hands. "She's right there on the bed,

326

waiting for you. All we have to do is eliminate one obstacle, and he's right here, too. Isn't that—"

"Your mother hated Trina for stealing you from her," I continued, trying to keep my voice steady and even. "She held her down in the bathtub, the one right behind you. She held her down until—"

"*SHUT UP!*" Geneva shrieked, her fists raining a battery of blows against my defenseless face.

"I found her body, Jeffrey," I said sharply. "Trina's body. It's buried by the old gazebo out back. How could I *know* that? How could I—*unh!*" Geneva connected with a solid right, and a sea of stars swam before me.

"Mother?" Jeffrey's voice had taken on a strange, little boy quality, its pitch high and unsure. In the background, I could hear water from the bathtub overflowing onto the tiles.

Geneva's assault abruptly ended, and she turned to face her son, her knotted fists suspended in midair. Some of the rollers had fallen from her head, and her hair stood out in places in wild clumps.

"You know I'd never do anything to hurt you, Jeffrey." Her voice was imploring, sickeningly sweet.

I had experienced firsthand Geneva's deceptive skills, and the woman was a pro. But standing in front of her son, gazing into his empty expression, her words sounded hollow and unconvincing even to me. I could see her shoulders shaking, her open hands frozen and outstretched, hanging in the air.

"Mother?" Jeffrey absorbed the truth like a blow, staggering backward and reaching out to steady himself against the dresser. "You—you *killed* her?"

"No, Jeffrey," said Geneva, finally breaking her stance to reach out for her son, but he shrank back, avoiding her outstretched hands. "He's lying, Jeffrey, he's *lying*. He's trying to—"

"Trina was afraid of you, Mother. She was always afraid of you," said Jeffrey. "Why was she afraid of you?"

"She wasn't afraid of me, she—"

"Is that why it happens, Mother? Is that why I keep seeing Trina everywhere she isn't? Is she a ghost, Mother? Is she haunting me for what you did to her?"

"*Please*, Jeffrey," she implored. "I'm your mother! I love you."

Jeffrey's thin lips pressed into a tight line, then all hell broke loose.

His hands were on Geneva's throat, and he lifted her from the floor as effortlessly as if she were made of smoke. She shrieked like a crow as he swung her to the side, slamming her flat against the wall. Her cry weakened as he applied even more pressure to her neck.

I didn't have much time. I focused all of my attention on Melanie's wrists, using my one free hand to pick frantically at the knot that kept the clothesline together. I was beginning to make progress when I heard a sickening *pop!*, and Melanie's eyes widened in horror.

I turned in time to see Geneva's limp form slide down to the floor, her head bobbing bonelessly on her shoulders. Jeffrey crouched over her like an animal, his arms positioned like a gunfighter, his fingers curled into claws.

He turned toward me, and when I saw the raw fury in his eyes, I couldn't meet them directly. He took a step toward me and stumbled over the bulk of his father, still lying in the middle of the floor. He looked down, and for the first time actually realized what he was seeing.

"Father?"

"She killed him, too," I said. "She—" I was cut off by his icy glare.

"Please, Jeffrey," said Melanie. "You have to let us go. This has to end—"

"*SHUT UP!*" he said, digging into his temples with his knuckles. "I can't think now, I can't—" He looked again at his fallen father, sprawled out on the floor with bloodstains pooling across the back of his shirt. "Everything's falling apart, I-I—"

"We can get you help, Jeffrey," I said. "We—"

"Help? Get me help?" he mimicked. "I don't need help. You're the ones who need help. You're so pathetic with your plebian condescension. Don't you know who I am? I am a Carter! I have more money than you'll ever see in your lifetime! Do you know what that means? *Do you?* It means there *are* no rules. I will never do jail time because there is always someone willing to strike a deal. Do you know how easy it is to do what you want when you've got more money than God? Let me give you an example, Mr. Morrow. Your home security code is 02563."

I couldn't hide my surprise.

"A very nice man by the name of Herbert Turnbull was kind enough to supply me with that information in exchange for enough money to ensure the education of his grandchildren. He had worked for Alarmex for thirty-five years and was implicitly trusted." His smirk was smug and self-satisfied.

I noted his use of the past tense. "Turnbull isn't with Alarmex anymore?"

"He had an unfortunate automobile accident last week. And he was the only one who knew I had purchased that bit of information about you, Mr. Morrow. What a shame," he said, shaking his head. He leaned in so close that I could smell the fetid stench of his armpits. "I have stood over you while you slept, Mr. Morrow. Do you know how easy it would have been to finish you right then and there?"

"W-why didn't you?" I asked, turning my head to avoid his face.

He grabbed my chin and turned it back. "There's no fun that way."

I had a sudden, frightening realization. I wasn't getting out of this. No matter how badly Geneva had wanted me dead, her hatred for me was minor league compared to that of her son. His right eye continued to throb, and beads of perspiration dribbled over his forehead from his scalp. He grinned in anticipation of the mad plan that continued to develop in his head, and I knew that he was going to enjoy killing me in a different way than he had ever enjoyed killing before. For him, this was so much more personal.

He suddenly stood and walked over to where his mother lay. He rifled through the pockets of her bathrobe and stood with the set of keys that fit my handcuffs. After three long strides, he was twisting the key in the lock and releasing the shackles. He pulled me to my feet and landed a solid punch to my gut before I had a chance to get my footing. I fell back against the wall and doubled over just in time to run my face into his swinging fist.

Stars exploded across my field of vision, and my kneecaps turned to gelatin. The sound of Melanie's scream penetrated the fog that was enveloping me, but I could do nothing more than drop clumsily to my hands and knees.

The toe of Jeffrey's running shoe arced toward my face.

Another ferocious burst of fireworks.

Darkness nibbled at the corners of my perception, and I thought I was going to black out. I could still hear Melanie's cries, but they seemed to be coming from far, far away.

I was suddenly on my back, staring up at the ceiling. I had no idea how I'd gotten into this position. Maybe I *had* blacked out for a moment; my head was spinning, and the ceiling was moving—no, *I* was moving. Jeffrey was dragging me across the floor by my wrists. None of my motor senses seemed to be cooperating, and I stared helplessly as I was pulled past Alan Carter's body. My cheek felt hot, throbbing from where the bastard had kicked me.

Melanie's words ran together in my ears, but I knew she was pleading with Jeffrey, begging him not to hurt me.

My head lolled backward as we passed into the bathroom, and for a moment, I thought he had stabbed me. A warm wetness settled around my shoulders, and the farther I was dragged into the room, the lower the wetness spread. It took a second to realize it was only the water from the bathtub, cresting and running over the rim, pooling on the tiles and soaking into the fabric of my shirt.

Suddenly, we stopped, and Jeffrey was standing over me, panting wildly while his eye tick-tick-ticked. In one fluid motion, he gathered the front of my shirt into his clenched fists and hoisted me up and over the edge of the tub, bending me backward so my legs and torso extended out into the room while my head was driven to the bottom of the lukewarm water.

I clamped my lips together and tried to fight the urge to breathe, but I hadn't had enough warning to inhale deeply before going under. My eyes burned, but I kept them open, staring up at him through the water, his image rippling and distorting as I attempted to shake him off, but he wouldn't budge, dammit, he wouldn't budge!

My arms were pinned beneath his, unable to break away from his iron grip. His face was only inches above the surface, staring down through the water with insane delight, watching the panic welling in my bulging eyes. What little oxygen I had managed to retain began to escape in tiny schools of bubbles from the corners of my mouth, and blackness began to close in.

Goddamn it, I was going to die, and then Melanie would, too.

I gave one final, futile sweep with my leg—and connected with Jeffrey's foot.

It wasn't much of a kick, but it was enough to push his foot out from underneath him on the wet tile. He went down hard on his knee, and his grip abruptly loosened on my shirt.

The next bit I can only attribute to a rush of adrenaline or something like it; I don't remember it clearly. I was out of the tub and on top of Jeffrey in a fractured slideshow of snapshots.

His ears clenched in my hands.

His skull against the hard, ceramic tile.

Again and again and again.

There were hands on my shoulders, hands on my arms, so many I couldn't possibly struggle against all of them. I let go of Jeffrey's head, and it fell with a hollow thud into a shallow puddle where the bathwater had turned pink with blood. Part of Jeffrey's ear had torn loose in my hand at some point and now floated in the water beside him.

"It's okay, Dwayne. We can take it from here." Nina Crockett looked at me with eyes both sympathetic and horrorstruck. She patted me on the arm and eased me away from Jeffrey. Brady Garrett squatted beside me, his eyes recording every detail for the morning edition. His swollen, purple nose was half-obscured by crisscrosses of white medical tape. A uniformed officer was freeing Melanie from the tangled rope that had held her in place for so long.

"I ought to kick your ass, you know," muttered Brady.

"How did you find us?" I croaked, my words slurring through swollen and split lips.

"It was really only a hunch," he said, handing me a photo. I saw it was one of the snapshots I had taken while following Alan Carter. From the date, I could see that it was taken the day I had found Tina Barlow's mutilated corpse. Alan was sitting on a park bench in Franklin Park Conservatory, just as he had done on so many occasions. Making small talk to strangers, as he had done on so many occasions. Only this was no stranger sitting beside him. It was Jeffrey.

"You asked me earlier tonight how Alan Carter could have gotten out of that alley before you entered it," continued Brady. "It occurred to me he might have gotten a ride from someone he knew."

"Just like me," said Melanie, easing up behind me and gingerly putting her arms around my shoulders. "I should have never gone with him, Dwayne. I'm sorry."

"Then why did you go?" I asked.

"He came back to apologize for earlier, for blaming his mother's 'death' on you. He showed up minutes after you left. I was so frantic about the way you had left I nearly bowled him over at the door, begging him to take me to the Rail Trail. We were so sure the killer was Brady it never occurred to me—" She shot Brady an apologetic glance before turning back to me. "You were going to kill him, Dwayne. I couldn't let you do that. You would have been exacting revenge, not justice. You're not that kind of man, or at least I don't think you are."

I looked beyond Brady to where Nina squatted over Jeffrey's motionless body laying by the tub. "So, what do you think of me now?"

EPILOGUE

I spent quite some time wondering if I had killed a man.

Jeffrey Carter hovered at death's door for weeks, suffering from multiple contusions and abrasions but most significantly, a fractured skull he had received courtesy of yours truly.

Ultimately, he stabilized and was transferred to the Franklin County Correctional Facility to await trial. His lawyer filed mental incompetence and proceeded to march an entire team of expert psychiatrists through the judge's chambers in a series of heated meetings with the DA's office. It's too soon to know the outcome, but I can't help but remember Jeffrey's words:

"I will never do jail time because there is always someone willing to strike a deal. Do you know how easy it is to do what you want when you've got more money than God?"

Sometimes I awake in the middle of the night, drenched in a cold sweat, those words echoing through my head.

The media devoured the story like the hungry predators they are, filling headlines and newscasts until it seemed I couldn't get away from it. I was hassled and hounded by everyone from Natasha Brickman to Anderson Cooper, but I really felt that if my story had to be told at all, I owed it to Brady Garrett. He has covered much of the action for *The Columbus Dispatch* and his story about me was picked up by the Associated Press. We may never see eye to eye, but I suppose he isn't such a bad guy after all.

Sheila and her baby are on the road to recovery, but my brother still isn't speaking to me. Regardless of the ultimate outcome, Sheila's attack would

334

have never happened had it not been for my involvement in the case. It's hard to argue with Matt's logic since I agree with him. I hope someday he'll get over it. I've never been at odds with my brother, and it's very foreign territory.

The phone calls began shortly after the publicity. Desperate people in dire straits, looking to hire my services to find their missing daughter, follow their suspicious son-in-law, locate their father's missing will—it was overwhelming. Rejecting them was always difficult. Some didn't understand that I couldn't help them without a license. Others understood, and their helpless frustration was contagious. I don't know which was worse. After a while, I let the machine pick up, ashamed to be screening my calls but unable to cope with all of the dejection.

I was surprised when one afternoon, it was Doug Boggs's voice on my machine. It appeared he and his mother had reconsidered my proposition about opening a Columbus office, and everything was suddenly a go. With all of the free publicity I had received, Doug was obviously seeing dollar signs, but who was I to bitch about motive? I was finally going to be able to do this deduction business on my own terms. I might even be able to help some of the people who had been calling, begging for my assistance.

*****

The sun was rising in a clear blue sky when Melanie and I finally left the Carters' that morning. Brady told me I might as well use his car since I still had the keys. The estate was crawling with official activity, FBI agents combing the grounds while the local cops kept curious onlookers at bay. We rolled down the long driveway as ambulances arrived to take away the wounded and the dead. In comfortable silence, we made the journey home.

We made love that morning. What began as a tender examination of each other's scrapes and bruises became a gentle exploration of each other's bodies. We moved together with such ferocity and eagerness, it was nearly overwhelming. I have never felt such an explosive need or desire for anyone else in my entire life.

After we were completely spent, we lay tangled in bed sheets and each other's limbs. Melanie had already drifted off from sheer exhaustion, and I watched the gentle rise and fall of her breasts as she softly purred in her sleep. Her right eye was nothing but swollen purple tissue, and a jagged gash graced her forehead. Her blonde hair stood out wildly, splayed on the pillow like the feathers of a peacock.

She had never looked more beautiful.

THE END

COMING SOON

RETRIBUTION
Dwayne Morrow Mystery #3

CHAPTER ONE

Once again, I was beginning to rethink my career choice.

It's extremely difficult to remain enthusiastic while squatted down amongst piles of moldering garbage in a sleazy, low-income section of Columbus's south side. I lay with my face near the ground, my hands sticky from something I had inadvertently touched, and my features twisted in an involuntary grimace of disgust and discomfort. I dared to glance at my watch. Another half-hour to go.

Shit.

My name is Dwayne Morrow, and I was on my first real assignment since Boggs Investigations had opened its little satellite office on West Broad Street in Columbus, Ohio. Doug Boggs was the owner, a former classmate turned private eye who had until recently confined his professional activities to the southern part of the state, Lymont to be specific. Our hometown of Lymont is one in a series of eroding small towns that bank on the Ohio River, population dwindling as unemployment soars. For the past several years, Doug had managed to keep a tenuous grip on the eye-spy business he had co-founded with his mother despite shrinking revenue, and when I had suggested in the early spring that he branch northward, he had stubbornly refused—or more to the point, his mother had stubbornly refused. Loretta Boggs doesn't much like me; I had to beat the shit out of her son once, and although Doug has since gotten past it, I doubt she ever will. It's fine with me; I don't much like her, either.

I don't want to give the impression Doug and I are best buds or anything. He sees himself as a sort of miniature Arnold Schwarzenegger although the world is more apt to see him as a young Danny DeVito. His frequent stories always include exaggerated retellings of his mundane daily chores, wringing the utmost from an encounter with a cheating spouse who had spotted him lurking in the bushes or a mad dog he had been forced to disable while taking photos for a client. In reality, the cheating spouse had been taking trash out to the alley in his underpants and wasn't likely to do much more than go back into his lover's house after he stumbled across Doug. And the dog? Disabling it, run through the Boggs Vocabulary Translator, meant he had simply stepped beyond the reach of its chain.

It was only after I had helped stop a vicious murderer from continuing his killing spree that I heard from Doug again. He had been reading all of the publicity I had received in the aftermath, and he suddenly wanted to go ahead with a Columbus branch. Was I still interested? Hell, yes, I was interested. Despite the obvious drawbacks to working with someone whom I did not particularly like, the situation was ideal. As originally proposed, Doug's constant presence wouldn't be necessary; he could operate his Lymont office while I tended to the Columbus branch. He could check in as little or as often as he liked.

That's where I made my mistake.

He was checking in entirely *too* often. I had envisioned a scenario in which *I* would be in control of my assignments. Instead, Doug was steady feeding me a list of chores, most of them revolting, and demanding written reports upon completion of each task. If he happened to be in Lymont, he expected the reports to be emailed immediately. This was not at all what I had planned, and I had told him so.

338

And he had told me if I had a problem with it, he would simply fire me and close the office. The cold-blooded bastard had me over a barrel, and as simian as I would like to believe his intellect, he was sharp enough to realize it. Despite my growing recognition as a competent sleuth, I was not yet licensed to practice on my own. For the past ten years, I had operated as a freelance systems consultant, offering discounted prices to corporate customers who were looking to give their computer systems a facelift. The pay was good, and the work was challenging but ultimately, I found it unfulfilling. However, the realities of being a homeowner with a homeowner's bills and responsibilities dictated I do nothing more drastic than cut back a little on my consulting duties, picking up evening hours for Boggs, thus ensuring a steady cash flow. If I were to ever obtain my license, I needed to apprentice with a practicing PI or a security firm, neither of which would have been able to offer me the flexibility in scheduling I required. So, I was stuck with Doug Boggs, and he damn well knew it.

Tonight's challenge was another episode of *Jerry Springer*. An enormous man with large breasts and smelly armpits had hired us to stalk his young wife, a pretty if hard-faced woman in her late twenties, as she went out on one of her frequent girls' nights. She was supposed to be hitting the brewery district with a bunch of the women she worked with at the beauty salon, but he was pretty sure she was boffing a skinny punk with apocalyptic acne scars who lived a block over; by now, I was pretty sure he was right. I had followed them to a club that smacked of *Urban Cowboy* where they did things on the dance floor I believe should have gotten them arrested, then to a Waffle House where they were oblivious to everyone else in the room but each other, then back to his one bedroom house where they had immediately made use of the one bedroom. I was flat on my stomach in the alley that ran behind the house, between the house's rear wall and an enormous pile of moldering garbage. I feared there wouldn't be enough hot water in the free world to rid me of the stench.

Fat Man wanted pictures, and I had a whole roll for him. I took no pleasure in providing documentation of these scurrilous affairs. As private eyes, I felt we were operating like ambulance-chasing lawyers. I didn't understand why Doug was so reluctant to take a bite of something bigger, something—less odiferous. The publicity I had received had already brought several of these higher profile clients calling, but Doug had told them our schedule was currently full. He hadn't lied; it was full of the type of cases I was currently working. I think he enjoyed sending me off on these humiliating excursions.

After what seemed an eternity, the bedroom light suddenly winked off, and a few moments later, I heard the sound of the front door opening, then closing. A moment after that, I heard the familiar *click-click-click* of the adulteress's high heels, fading in the direction of her own house, just a block away. Girls' night was over.

Careful to make as little noise as possible, I began to work my way out of my hiding spot. I was nearly free of the pile of plastic garbage bags when I heard the startled cry of a woman at the far end of the alley. Suddenly, there were running footfalls, one set in the forefront, and I couldn't tell how many following from a distance. I forgot completely about my assignment as I turned away from the unfaithful wife and squinted off into the far end of the alley.

A young woman burst onto the scene, her cheeks puffing in and out rapidly while her legs worked like pistons. Her gait barely stumbled when she spotted me standing in the alleyway, but she recovered quickly and soon was headed directly toward me, her dark hair flapping like raven's wings.

"*Please!*" she gasped, grabbing my arm and pulling me in the direction she had been running. "You have to help me! They're going to kill me!"

Stopping even this long had given her pursuers time to reach the other end of the alley. I could only discern the shapes of two men—one large, one not so much—and they were approaching quickly. Just as I recognized the telltale glint of moonlight on metal, I heard a bullet thud into one of the

340

garbage bags I had been hiding behind. I needed no more coaxing after that. We turned and ran for our lives.

My Optima was parked on the intersecting street, and I guided the woman in that direction, awkwardly fumbling in my pocket for the keys so that I could deactivate the locks with the key fob. I had the keys in the ignition almost as soon as we had slid in and said a silent prayer that my usually dependable wheels wouldn't pick this particular day to break down.

The engine turned and caught just as my rear glass exploded.

I grabbed the woman by the back of her neck and shoved her forward and down, trying like a turtle to pull my own head down into my shoulders at the same time. I snapped the gearshift into drive and cut the wheel blindly to the left, stomping the gas pedal. The car lurched out into the street, clipping the corner of the car parked in front of it, but mercifully not meeting any oncoming traffic; to be stopped now would be a death sentence. I braved a glimpse over the steering wheel to make sure we weren't about to crash into one of the many other cars parked along the curb in this poor residential area. A heard another telltale *thump* from the back end as a bullet tore into the metal of my trunk.

But we were getting away.

I straightened in my seat as we approached an intersection I knew would lead us to the interstate and, thus, population. My hands were twitching on the steering wheel, and I was surprised to find myself giggling a bit.

"Are you all right?" I finally managed, forcing my inappropriate giddiness to subside.

The woman looked at me from within her shroud of dark tresses. Her eyes were startlingly blue, almost frosted in appearance. She was young, no more than nineteen or twenty, and wore blue jeans and an Abercrombie shirt—not exactly the kind of attire you usually come across in the neighborhood from which we had fled. She was trembling more noticeably than I, and for a moment, I thought she might be in shock. But then her eyes seemed to refocus, and she cleared her throat, surprising me with a throaty chuckle of her own.

"Thanks, mister," she said. "You just saved my life."

"I saw that," I said. "You wanna tell me what that was all about?"

When she looked at me again, her lips were pressed together in a tight line. She shrugged her shoulders and said, "Not really."

We rode in uncomfortable silence for a few moments, then I said, "Do you want me to take you to the police?"

"No, thank you."

I arched an eyebrow and glanced pointedly at her. "Those were real bullets back there, you know."

"Yes, I know."

Her words were direct and to the point, each one carefully articulated to be polite but firm. She offered me her sheepish smile again, then returned her attention to somewhere in her lap.

"Look," I persisted. "If you're in some kind of trouble, I might be able to help you. I'm a private detective."

She looked at me curiously and squinched her nose up. "You smell like a vagrant," she said.

"Yeah, a vagrant who saved your life," I reminded her. "As I see it, I have two bullet holes in my car that weren't there before you came running down that alley. The least you can do is tell me what's going on."

She glanced in the rearview and side view mirrors before turning back to me. "I think we've lost them. Why don't you drop me off at that Dairy Mart?" She indicated the red and gold building on the far-right corner.

I looked at her curiously. "This isn't the best neighborhood."

"It's better than the last one. Don't worry. I'll call a friend."

She had the car door halfway open before I had even stopped. She slipped out and quickly disappeared around the side of the building, never once looking back. I sat for a moment, mulling my options. I could follow her around the building and make more of a nuisance of myself, demanding she answer my questions, but considering her earlier obstinance, I figured it would be useless. It was Friday night, and I had a very long day ahead of me on Saturday, one that started much earlier than I considered humane. There was no sense hanging around and waiting for those gunmen to stumble across me, either. I sighed and put my car back into gear.

I headed for home.

RETRIBUTION
Dwayne Morrow Mystery #3

COMING SOON

acknowledgements

I am fortunate to surround myself with smart people who enjoy reading the type of book I write and aren't afraid of bruising my fragile ego. They are my sounding board once I think the job is done, and it rarely ever is…

With that in mind, I want to thank Lynne Hobstetter and Teri Lott for lending their time and talents to make my work better. They have smacked my knuckles when needed to correct grammar, continuity and poor word choice. Sometimes, I am not nearly as funny as I think I am, and they rein me in when needed. Also, a *huge* mea culpa for omitting an Acknowledgements page in *Reunion*—these wonderful ladies did the same heavy lifting for that book, too. I will always value your feedback and suggestions.

I also want to thank my daughter, Nicki Miller, and niece, Regan Scarberry, for again taking my idea for the cover and interpreting it through their own lens. I love that we are in this together.

Last, but definitely not least, I want to thank Traci Steele, wife extraordinaire, for reminding me over and over I can *do* this.

ALSO AVAILABLE

REUNION
Dwayne Morrow Mystery #1

about the author

Darin Miller was born and raised in the southern hills of Ohio and currently resides in Grove City. While he has worked in Information Technology for three decades, he has *not* solved a single, solitary crime to date. He enjoys reading, spending time with his family and spinning up alternate realities, one of which is the world of Dwayne Morrow. He invites you to come inside and enjoy the ride.

Stay current with updates, free downloadable short stories and other special promotions at www.darin-miller.com.

Made in the USA
Coppell, TX
14 December 2021

68701058R00197